D0065632

The Hopefuls

Center Point
Large Print

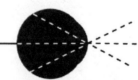

**This Large Print Book carries the
Seal of Approval of N.A.V.H.**

The Hopefuls

Jennifer Close

CENTER POINT LARGE PRINT
THORNDIKE, MAINE

For my brothers,
Chris and Kevin

This Center Point Large Print edition is published in the year 2016 by arrangement with Alfred A. Knopf, an imprint of The Knopf Doubleday Publishing Group, a division of Penguin Random House LLC.

The text of this Large Print edition is unabridged. In other aspects, this book may vary from the original edition. Printed in the United States of America on permanent paper. Set in 16-point Times New Roman type.

ISBN: 978-1-68324-127-0

Library of Congress Cataloging-in-Publication Data

Names: Close, Jennifer, author.
Title: The hopefuls / Jennifer Close.
Description: Center Point Large Print edition. | Thorndike, Maine : Center Point Large Print, 2016.
Identifiers: LCCN 2016028926 | ISBN 9781683241270 (hardcover : alk. paper)
Subjects: LCSH: Married people—Fiction. | Political culture—Fiction. | Washington (D.C.)—Social life and customs—21st century—Fiction. | Large type books. | Political fiction. | Domestic fiction. | GSAFD: Humorous fiction.
Classification: LCC PS3603.L68 H67 2016b | DDC 813/.6—dc23
LC record available at https://lccn.loc.gov/2016028926

Washington, DC 2009

Washington is a city of southern efficiency and northern charm.
—JOHN F. KENNEDY

Chapter 1

This is what people talk about at an Obama campaign reunion:

- How early they joined the campaign
- What they did on the campaign
- Who they slept with on the campaign
- Good hotels
- Bad hotels
- How many Hilton points they have
- How many frequent flier miles they have
- Who worked for Hillary before joining Obama (This was whispered behind the backs of former Hillary staffers like it was a shameful secret. Sort of like herpes.)
- Inside jokes about lost luggage
- How amazing Iowa was (Usually you'd hear someone say something like "Weren't you in Iowa? Oh man, you should've been there. You missed out. It felt like we were changing the world." Then you'd brace yourself for about an hour's worth of Iowa stories.)

We were at a bar near the White House called The Exchange, which had a lot of TVs and smelled like bleach and dirty rags. Matt ordered drinks for us at the bar and then we walked around, stopping every few seconds so he could give someone a handshake or a half hug and say, "Hey man, how've you been?" He was more hyper than usual—being around the campaign people made him jumpy like he'd been chugging Red Bull. All that Hope and Change will do that to a person. Every time he introduced me to someone, he'd put his hand on my back and push me forward a little, saying, "This is Beth, my wife." And when he'd tell me the name of the person I was meeting, he'd always include their job title. "This is Larry, an associate research director at the White House." Each time, I'd say something like "Wow, that's great." I had no idea what any of it meant, but I did my best to look impressed.

Eventually we found ourselves standing in a circle of people listening to this guy, Billy, tell a story about one of the early fund-raising events. He was animated and everyone was hanging on his every word. "So, I was driving the Senator around Minnesota in a rental car," he said. "A Ford Fiesta, I think. This was sometime in 2007. And we hit a pothole and almost lost a tire."

Everyone laughed like this was really funny, so I did too, but it gave me kind of a creepy feeling. Billy was telling this story like it was about potholes or Ford Fiestas, but it wasn't. The real points of the story were:

1. Billy knew Obama when he was a senator and he knew him so well that sometimes he just forgot that he was the president now and still referred to him as the Senator. Such a simple mistake.
2. He joined the campaign so early that there weren't even drivers yet, which means that Billy drove around Minnesota with Obama in shotgun. How crazy is that? How jealous is everyone?
3. And again, just to repeat it, he joined the campaign early. So early. Earlier than everyone else. Before you, definitely. He always knew Obama would be the nominee. Possibly, he was the first person in the world to know.

As everyone laughed at the hilarious Ford Fiesta story, Matt put his hand on my back and I braced myself to be introduced to someone else, but he just leaned down and whispered, "We can go soon, okay?" I nodded and tried to look like I was having fun, like I loved being at this reunion. (Which by the way was a really weird thing to call it—a reunion—because all of these people lived in DC and most of them worked together. If they wanted to reunite, they could do it over lunch or coffee or running into each other in the hallway.) And so, I just shrugged and said to Matt, "Sure, we can go whenever you want."

Matt smiled at me like he knew I was lying, which I appreciated. I was making an effort to be positive about moving to DC, but these people didn't make it easy. Everyone at that happy hour seemed just a little off, in a way I couldn't put my finger on. When I mentioned this to Matt, he said, "It's all people who work in politics. Nature of the beast, I guess."

But as we stood there that night, listening to another story about Iowa, I had a realization. All of the people there reminded me of high school student council members, the ones who fought for pizza lunches and dance themes with great passion. They were all so eager. (And borderline annoying.) Was Matt one of them? Had I never noticed? Had he always been this way or just become one of them when I wasn't paying attention?

I'd been in DC for about a week at that point, and I kept waiting for the newness to wear off, for it to feel less strange. Matt had already been there for months by the time I moved—he'd started working for the Presidential Inaugural Committee right after the election—and he seemed to have no trouble fitting in to this new city. I visited him often while he was working on PIC (the horrible acronym everyone used for the committee, which made me think of fingers in noses), and as I met his work friends and walked around the monuments, I tried to imagine what our life would look like there, tried to see the good parts of DC. But each time I left to return to New York, I was relieved. I'd get off the train at Penn Station, breathe in the smell of urine, popcorn, and dirt, and feel like I was coming home.

After the inauguration, Matt was offered a job in the White House counsel's office and I knew we were really moving to DC. It was what we'd talked about, what we'd planned for. It was the whole reason Matt joined the campaign in the first place. It was too late to back out now.

We found a place just north of Dupont Circle, on a tiny block with five town houses, diagonally across the street from a Hilton. The day we'd gone to look at the apartment, Matt had pointed at the hotel. "Do you know what that is?" he asked.

"What? The hotel?"

"Yeah, that right there. Look at the doorway. Does it look familiar?"

"No."

"Not at all? Just look at it for a minute."

Matt was always doing this, always insisting that I knew things I didn't. Once, when we were on opposite teams during a Trivial Pursuit game with friends, he refused to let me pass on the question "Who once warned, 'Never eat more than you can lift'?" I didn't even have a guess, but Matt wouldn't let it go. "Come on, Beth, you know this," he kept saying, as our friends sat there and I got embarrassed and then mad. "I don't know," I kept insisting. (The answer was Miss Piggy, and to this day, I have no idea why Matt was sure I knew the answer, but it still remains one of the biggest fights we've ever had. We didn't play Trivial Pursuit for years after that.)

Standing in front of the apartment, I didn't have the patience to play Matt's game and guess what was special about the Hilton. "Just tell me," I said.

"It's where Reagan was shot," he said. "It's the Hinckley Hilton. Look, that's where he was coming out of the hotel, and right there is where he got shot. Crazy, right?"

"Crazy," I said. I was tired of walking around and looking at apartments, and knew that my attitude was putting a sourness over the whole afternoon. Matt was just trying to lighten the mood, but it was a little weird to try to cheer me up by showing me the spot of an attempted presidential assassination, wasn't it? (Although I soon found myself pointing it out to everyone who came to visit. When a friend from college who lived in Brooklyn told me that *Sesame Street* was filming on her block, I quickly came back with "From our front door, you can see where Reagan was shot." Take that, Elmo.)

When we signed the lease, the broker took notice of Matt's jacket, a fleece with an Obama-Biden logo embroidered on the chest. These jackets were given to the staff on election night, and you saw people wearing them all over town, like badges of honor.

"Did you work on the campaign?" the broker asked, and Matt nodded.

"It's so great he won," the broker said.

"It really is," Matt agreed.

"I mean, for business it's great," the broker said. "All the real estate agents here are thrilled. We'll be renting so many more places. Republicans don't live in the District, you know, they live in Virginia." He said this like it was a fact everyone knew.

"Isn't that weird?" I said to Matt later.

"Not really." He shrugged. "It's like anything else divided down party lines. Republicans like Fox News and NASCAR and Democrats like MSNBC and Starbucks."

"Simple as that?" I asked, and he said, "Absolutely."

Our new neighborhood was nice—that was my answer to everyone who asked. And then I'd add, "I mean, it's not New York, but it's fine." Dupont Circle was just so different from Manhattan—residential and much quieter; one step closer to the suburbs.

If you walked over to Eighteenth Street, there were a couple of restaurants and a gay bar called Larry's Lounge that advertised "Yappy Hour" on the patio from five to seven, a time when customers could bring their dogs to hang out with them while they got drunk. If you walked five blocks down, there was a stretch of shops and then some more restaurants. Everything looked a little worn, like it was past its prime. Also, we lived just a few houses down from the "original" Ron Hubbard house, which to be honest freaked me out just a little. I wasn't thrilled to have Scientologists as neighbors.

And there were so many trees and so much grass that it was disorienting. Maybe it was just more oxygen than I was used to. After we signed the lease, Matt and I took a walk around the neighborhood. He held my hand and squeezed it. "I think you're really going to love it here," he said.

I hoped he was right, I really did. I reminded myself that I'd once gone to a six-week boot camp class in Central Park, where a man yelled at us as we did push-ups and squats in the grass at 7:00 a.m. If I could convince myself that I liked that, I could do anything.

I spent my first couple of weeks in DC going to as many social gatherings as I could. We said yes to every invitation, asked people to dinner, made plans for almost every night of the week. Matt kept saying, "Once you meet people and get settled, it will feel like home." And I believed him. (Or at least I wanted to.)

So we went to a dinner party where everyone—

I swear to God—went around the table and announced their level of security clearance. As people said "Secret," and "Top Secret," the rest of the guests nodded and murmured. When they got to me, I looked at their expectant faces and then finally said, "Nothing. I don't have clearance for anything." There was a small pause and then the man to my left picked it up and said, "SCI," which apparently stood for sensitive compartmented information, and got the most approving reaction of the night. I just took a bite of my chicken and concentrated on chewing. What a bunch of nerds.

And then one night, we went out with Alan Chu, one of Obama's personal aides who sat just outside the Oval Office all day. Alan was slim and always perfectly dressed, although there was something fussy about his look that suggested he spent twenty minutes picking out his tie and sock combinations in the morning. Alan and his boyfriend suggested we go to La Fourchette, a French restaurant on Eighteenth Street, and I had high hopes for the evening, until it became clear that every one of Alan's stories started with "One time POTUS said" and "POTUS was in a great mood today." I tried to steer the conversation away from work, asking Alan where he was from and where he went to college. Each time, he'd answer me quickly and then resume talking to Matt as if they were the only two there. Alan's boyfriend, Brett, looked just as bored as I felt, and at one point he started playing with the little candle in front of him, tilting it back and forth, letting the wax drip onto the tablecloth.

On top of everything else, the service that night was terrible—there was a private party in the back room and the whole staff (our waiter included) kept rushing back there and ignoring the tables in the main dining room. As the waiters pushed the curtain aside to get back there, we caught a glimpse of Newt Gingrich's round and red smiling face. "It's his birthday," our waiter whispered to us later. He was breathless with excitement. "Welcome to DC," Matt said to me, and I gave a little laugh.

After we left dinner that night, I said to Matt, "When Alan talks about the President, he sounds like an infatuated boyfriend."

"He's not that bad," Matt said.

"Sure," I agreed. "In the same way that stalkers are just passionate."

Trying to make new friends was like dating— meeting so many new people and feeling them out, trying to find common interests and topics of conversation. It was harder than I'd thought it would be. I tried to adjust, tried to remain positive. But the one thing I could never get used to when we were out with these people was the BlackBerries—oh, the BlackBerries that every-one kept close by, right next to their beers or their plates, just in case someone was trying to get ahold of them. If we were with a big group, chimes and dings and bike bells rang out constantly. The table buzzed and beeped, and each time there was a new chirp, everyone reached for their phone, certain that it was theirs, clicked away on the keyboard just to make sure they hadn't missed anything, each of them believing themselves to be more important than the next.

Our unpacking process was slow. No matter how many boxes I got through each day, there were always more, almost like they were multiplying behind my back. Bubble Wrap was strewn everywhere—on the coffee table and the floor and couch. Matt came home one Thursday night, a couple of weeks after we moved in, to find me standing in a circle of boxes, unsure of where to put any of it.

"Hey," I called, as he came up the stairs. I was trapped in the middle of everything and he came over to kiss me hello.

"How's it going?" he asked.

"I don't know how we have so much stuff. We're just going to live out of boxes forever," I said.

"Okay," Matt said. "Fine by me."

"Seriously, this apartment is like twice as big as our last place and I still don't know where to put anything."

"Ugh," Matt said, leaning over to look into one of the boxes, which was filled with the most random of our possessions—Post-it notes, a shower cap, a pair of wooden lovebirds. "Let's just toss it."

"Deal," I said. I stepped over the pile of stuff around me and sat on the couch as he went to the kitchen to get himself a beer.

"How was work?" I asked.

"Good," he said. He sat down on the couch with a sigh and leaned his head back. "I'm so tired."

"Too tired for a trip to the grocery store? I was thinking we could go to the Giant up on Connecticut."

"Why do you want to go all the way up there?"

"We need so much stuff. It's not that far. I can't eat Chipotle again for dinner. The employees are starting to recognize us and it's getting embarrassing."

"I know," Matt said. "The manager seemed genuinely excited to see me last night."

"We basically have no food in the house. I just think the Giant is our best bet."

There were two Safeways within walking distance of our apartment, but they were both disappointing, full of dirty produce and questionable meat. In DC, all of the Safeways had nicknames—the one in Georgetown was the Social Safeway, because apparently it was a good place to find a date, although I never met anyone who actually got picked up there. There was the Stinky Safeway (self-explanatory), the Underground Safeway, the UnSafeway. The two closest to us were the Secret Safeway, because it was tiny and hidden away on a side street, and the Soviet Safeway, because the shelves were always bare. People found these nicknames charming. I found them stupid. When I went to the Soviet Safeway for milk and had to walk away empty-handed because the dairy case was empty, I wasn't amused. I just wanted them to get new management.

"We need a real grocery store," I continued. "One that has actual food on the shelves."

"Do you think you could take the car and go?" Matt asked. He gave me an apologetic look. "I'm so beat."

Matt had started insisting that I drive as soon as I got to DC. "You just have to get used to it again," he kept saying. But I disagreed. After living in New York for seven years, I'd pretty much completely forgotten how to drive. When I went home to Madison, I sometimes dared to take my parents' car a few blocks, gripping the wheel at 10 and 2 and riding the brake the whole time.

Even when I was a teenager, my dad had to beg me to practice driving, taking me to empty parking lots where I coasted along at fifteen miles an hour, slammed on the brake when it was time to turn. Some people love driving, love the feeling of being in control, swerving in and out of lanes; I've always preferred being a passenger.

I'd driven exactly once since I'd been in DC, when we went to brunch in Georgetown. I'd panicked as I tried to parallel-park and a line of cars honked at me like I was purposely holding them up. Matt and I had to switch places so that he could pull the car into the parking spot, which was mortifying. And now here he was, casually suggesting that I "take the car" like he was going to trick me into driving.

"I don't really know where I'm going," I finally said.

"You have the GPS. And you know where you're going."

"I really don't. I have no idea where anything is."

"Beth, it's like riding a bike. I promise. You just need to get back on."

"I think you mean, it's like a horse. The saying is, get back on the horse."

"Yeah, sure, okay. Driving is like that. You need to get back on the horse."

"Well, I hate horses. You know that."

Matt looked at me, like he couldn't decide whether or not to be amused.

"Fine," I said, grabbing the car keys. "I'll go."

I walked out the door, waiting for him to come after me. When he didn't, I said, "Fuck," and went to the car, which was parked in an alley that was home to the biggest rats I've ever seen. Just a few days earlier, one had charged at me and I'd screamed bloody murder. Matt said it sounded like I was being assaulted, and I said that's what it felt like. It was something no one had told me about DC—the rats are bigger there. And bolder. I think the warm weather makes them this way.

I found the store just fine, of course. Deep down, I knew Matt was right about the driving. What did I expect? That he'd drive me wherever I wanted to go, always? Like my own personal chauffeur? As I loaded a case of Diet Coke into my cart, I felt slightly ridiculous for making a big deal out of it.

But then, on the way home I got lost. I missed the turn onto T Street and somehow ended up entering the Dupont traffic circle. The GPS had been telling me to turn around, but as I continued around the circle for the fifth time trying to find the right exit, she couldn't keep up, and just kept saying, "Recalculating." When we'd gotten the GPS, Matt had set it to speak in an Australian accent, which was funny at first but now I couldn't understand the stupid Aussie. "Tell me where to go," I screamed at her. And then, like she would care, I added, "I hate it here."

Leaving our apartment in New York had been harder than I'd expected. It was our home for five years, the first place we'd lived as a married couple, and I was attached to it. It didn't help that my parents had sold the house I'd grown up in just a year earlier, and now lived in an unrecognizable ranch house in a retirement community. Our New York apartment was the only home I had left.

I made a point of telling everyone that we were moving—the man who worked at the wine store around the corner, the workers behind the counter at our bagel place. When I pulled the manager of J. G. Melon aside to say good-bye, Matt looked embarrassed. "What?" I said. "We come here all the time. Don't you think it would be weird if we vanished? If we never came back?"

"People leave New York all the time," Matt said. "I'm sure they're used to it."

"I just want to say good-bye. It's the right thing to do."

The day the movers came, I couldn't stop crying. I cried as they carried out our boxes and furniture, and when I hugged the twitchy doorman, Bob, good-bye. For the whole time we lived there, he'd blushed and said, "Okay, now," whenever I said hi to him or told him to have a good day, and when I wept on his shoulder on moving day, he just about turned purple.

We watched the moving truck pull away, and then we got into our new car, which was loaded with the rest of our things, and started the drive to DC. Matt kept his hand on my leg, sometimes rubbing my shoulder or smoothing my hair to comfort me. But after about an hour, I knew he just wanted me to stop crying. And that night, as we got ready for bed, and I still had tears in my eyes, he was a little impatient.

"Come on, Beth," he said. "I know it's hard, but what did you think? That we were going to live in that apartment forever? For the rest of our lives?"

"Maybe," I said. "I guess I didn't really think about it."

He sighed that night and reached over to put his arm around me. "We're here," he said. "And home is wherever we're together."

It was a nice thought, but I didn't totally believe it.

When I got back from the grocery store, Matt came right down the stairs to meet me at the door. "I thought you'd need help with bags," he said, looking at my empty hands.

"I left it all in the car," I said. And then, feeling stupid, "I got lost."

"Oh, no. Did the Australian fail you?"

"Yes," I said. And then, before I could help myself, "I hate it here."

"I know," he said. "I know."

I hated everything about DC. I hated the weather in the summer, how it was so humid you could barely breathe, how you started sweating as soon as you walked out the door.

I hated the way people asked, "Who do you work for?" as soon as you met them, like that was the only thing that mattered. I hated the shorthand people used to talk about their jobs: I work at Treasury, they'd say. Or at DOD, or For POTUS, or I'm an LA. It was like they didn't have enough time to say the whole thing, like if you didn't know what their acronym meant, you didn't matter anyway. (I also hated how it wasn't long before I used these acronyms, how they so quickly became a part of my vocabulary.)

I hated that the Metro was carpeted, and that it was so far underground—you felt like a mole by the time you got down the escalator—and I hated that you had to swipe your card to get in *and* out of the station. I hated that you couldn't eat or drink on the train, and I especially hated that everyone obeyed the rule, like they were afraid they'd be arrested for sipping a cup of Starbucks on their morning commute.

I hated the helicopters that buzzed overhead, like we were in some sort of war zone. I hated how the motorcades stopped traffic, halted the Metros, and clogged up the streets, usually when you were running late to get somewhere.

I hated how young everyone was, especially on the Hill, how they walked around all doughy and baby faced, wearing suits that their mothers had bought for them, thrilled with the fact that they'd accepted a salary of $23K to work for ten hours a day. I hated that they were all so eager, ready to tell you about their passion—healthcare or Planned Parenthood or clean water—whether you asked or not. I hated the way people dressed, in collared shirts and knee-length skirts, muted suits and sensible ties. I hated that all the women looked like they'd just left an Ann Taylor store (and I hated that most likely, they probably just had). I hated that so many women wore sneakers and socks with their suits while they commuted, as if it were still 1987. I wanted to pull them aside and tell them that there was no need for this, that there were very comfortable ballet flats out there they could wear instead.

I hated the way that everyone wore their ID cards around their necks and tucked into their front suit jacket pockets, so that the only things visible were the lanyards, just so they could let you know that they were very important people who worked at very important places.

I hated how the cabs were always dirty, how they took only cash, and how the drivers never seemed to know where they were going. I hated that you couldn't order takeout past 10:00, unless you wanted pizza from a questionable place. I hated that I had to drive to get decent groceries, that there weren't any good neighborhood stores. I missed our neighborhood bodega. I missed it every day.

• • •

That night, after Matt had made three trips to retrieve the groceries from the car, he unpacked them and made grilled cheese for dinner. He insisted that I stay on the couch, and brought me a glass of wine. "For my little driver," he said. "My master of direction." He sat down next to me and ran his hand over my hair. "It'll get better, Buzz. I promise." When we'd first started dating, I told Matt how my parents used to call me Busy Bee as a child, which he thought was hilarious. He started calling me that as a joke, then it turned into Buzzy Bee, and then Buzzy, and then just Buzz, which sounded more like a nickname for a large, bald man and less like a term of endearment. But it stuck.

"Thank you," I said. "That's why I love you."

I tried not to take Matt's kindness for granted, tried to appreciate it. It wasn't always a given that I'd marry someone like this, especially because I spent most of college dating (and I use that term loosely) a guy named Justin Henry, who once told me about a recent date he'd gone on while I was lying naked in his bed and once walked right by me on the street—just completely ignored me and continued down the sidewalk.

Not long after Matt and I were married, I'd said something about craving Indian food and he'd said, "Let's do it," even though he hated Indian food. When I asked him if he was sure, he'd said,

"Whatever makes you happy." It was so easy for him, so simple. He wanted me to be happy and he'd do anything (even eat naan for dinner) to make it happen. For him, kindness was a reflex, and I envied that. I wanted it to be the same for me, to automatically put his wants first. But most of the time I had to remind myself to reciprocate, the way a socially awkward person struggles to remember appropriate topics of conversation.

That night, I ate my grilled cheese and told Matt all the things I hated about DC. I wanted him to understand how I felt, but he just told me it was impossible to hate that many things. "It's not impossible," I told him. "It's hard. And it takes a lot of energy, but it's not impossible."

Matt looked at me like he wasn't sure what to say. He rubbed my leg. "Do you want some more wine?" he asked, and I nodded. He got up to fill my glass, and I pulled a blanket off the back of the couch and covered myself with it, curled my legs underneath me, suddenly tired.

When he handed me my wine, he leaned down to kiss me. "Maybe," he said, "if you try to hate it here a little less, you eventually will."

"I doubt it," I said.

"But maybe you could try it."

"I could," I said. But I didn't say that I would.

Chapter 2

I met my husband at Dorrian's, a bar on the Upper East Side, right around the corner from the railroad apartment I shared with three friends from college. The bar was infamous for being the place where the Preppy Murderer met his victim before he lured her to Central Park. You'd think any association with murder would make a bar unpopular, but you'd be wrong. Every night, it was crowded with twentysomethings who were new to the city. When "Sweet Caroline" played, the whole place pumped their fists, smacked their palms on the tables, and chanted, "So good, so good, so good."

We met in October 2001, and the amazing part about that night wasn't that we found each other in a big city, or that we wound up at the same bar at the same time—it's that I'd gone out at all. I arrived in New York in July, moved into the tiny apartment that took more than half of my paycheck, and for a couple of months, everything was great. I was an editorial assistant at *Vanity Fair*, for a theatrical and judgy gay man, who loved talking about whatever new diet he was on and how fat and gross everyone else was. (Once he walked by my desk in the morning and wrinkled his face at the bran muffin I was picking apart. "Is that fried chicken?" he asked, before disappearing into his office and letting me explain that it was a muffin, that I wasn't in fact eating fried chicken at 9:30 in the morning.)

But regardless, we were all happy and employed, getting drunk most nights, making under $30K a year (except for our one friend working in finance), and supplementing most things with credit cards that still went to our parents, who insisted we use them for groceries ("You have to eat well!") and the occasional night out ("Enjoy the city!") and of course, some clothes every once in a while ("You work so hard! Treat yourself!").

And then, the fall came. After September 11, we all thought about leaving the city. That morning, we'd made it back to our apartment, crying, although we didn't really know what had happened yet. We went out to Long Island, to stay with my roommate Colleen's parents. Mrs. McEvoy served us strange combinations of food—mashed potatoes and spaghetti, chicken casserole with a side of ham—and kept pouring us whiskey, which none of us normally drank but all accepted gratefully.

The second night there, I decided I was moving back to Wisconsin. I was alone and homesick and scared, and I wanted to be back there so badly my chest hurt. Why would I stay in this city, to make lunch reservations and have my food choices mocked by a forty-year-old editor? The Midwest, I decided, was where I belonged.

Of course, I didn't move. None of us did. Julie, who'd been the only one of us downtown when the attacks happened, kept telling us about the people she saw jump, bringing it up in any conversation, mentioning it out of the blue. When she finally went back to work, she'd come home at the end of the day and put her pajamas on and get right back into bed. We didn't know what to do to help her, and to be honest, we just wanted her to get better and to stop talking about it, to stop reminding us of how horrible it was.

One of our neighbors was missing—a boy we called Yale to his face because of the T-shirt he always wore. We didn't know him well, but he'd come over a couple of times to have a beer late at night, when we'd all bumbled home at the same time. His parents were staying in his apartment, putting posters up around the city with his face on them, and we looked down every time we passed them in the hallway, because it felt like we should apologize for still being there, for how easy it was for our own parents to find us.

The four of us stopped going out. We'd taken to ordering Thai food on the weekends and drinking huge, inexpensive bottles of red wine, until our lips were purple. It felt wrong to go out, disrespectful almost, and so we sat in pajamas

30

and watched movies, eating crabmeat wontons and drinking wine until we could fall asleep.

But that Saturday, I suggested we go to Dorrian's. Maybe it was because our apartment was starting to smell like pad thai noodles all the time, or it was the thought of waking up with a pounding headache and purple-crusted lips. Whatever it was, I begged my roommates to put on clothes, telling them we wouldn't have to go far, that fresh air would do us good. And somehow, they all agreed.

It was loud in the bar, and the four of us stayed close so that we could hear ourselves talk. Colleen and I were sitting on stools and Julie and Courtney were standing behind us. None of us were particularly energetic or cheerful, but I still considered the night a success for getting out of the apartment. I was taking a sip of my beer when Colleen leaned toward me and said, "Dogpants is totally checking you out."

"Who?" I asked. I looked over my shoulder.

"Dogpants. To your right." She sounded hopeful, like this situation might make the night more interesting. "He's not awful," she continued. "I mean, besides those pants."

I looked blatantly at Matt then, who was holding a beer and listening to one of his friends. He was smiling in a way that made me think he knew we were talking about him. He was tall, with wavy brown hair and a handsome face, and he was wearing dark green corduroy pants with small yellow Labs embroidered all over them.

"Jesus," I said. "They might as well be whales." (I still don't know what I meant by this, but Colleen quoted me in the toast she gave at our wedding and everyone laughed.)

Matt finally came up to talk to me, a couple of beers later, and Colleen looked right at him and said, "Hey Dogpants, it took you long enough." She slid off her stool and gestured to it with her hands. "Would you like a seat?"

He blushed a little bit then, and I noticed how friendly his eyes were, how they crinkled at the edges when he smiled, and said, "Thanks, I'd love to sit. These dogs are barking."

Matt was three years older than we were, a lawyer, and he lived alone, all of which made him seem like an adult. He took me out on real dates, to dinners and museums and shows. And also, he was just so nice. He was generous to all of my friends—buying them rounds of drinks, helping to prop up Courtney after she drank too much, buying us late night pizza and bringing it up to our apartment. We were used to college boys who thought it was the height of romance to offer you a can of beer from their refrigerators. If Matt had known what he was being compared to, he might have realized he didn't have to try so hard to impress us.

The night I met him, he was out with his friends from college. "We were all at Harvard together," he told me as he introduced us. "You went to Harvard?" I asked, hoping I'd misheard. All I thought was, I am talking to a guy with dogs on his pants who went to Harvard and there is no way I'm ever going to see him again. But I was wrong.

From the beginning, my friends were invested in my relationship with Matt—overly invested, actually. They weighed in on it just as much as I did. When I got ready to go out with him, they all crowded in my room, suggesting I change my shirt or put on lip gloss.

"I'm in love with your boyfriend," Colleen used to say, and everyone would agree. Before Matt, I'd dated a string of guys who always prompted my friends to say, "He doesn't deserve you." I was the sweet and thoughtful one in relationships, and now it was all turned around. "I think you're going to marry Dogpants," Colleen said one day. "I mean, you will if you're smart." Her words stuck with me, like a warning not to mess this up.

Matt proposed in Central Park a year and a half after we met. We'd just decided to move in together, which felt like the most adult decision I'd ever made, and I'd spent hours talking about it with the girls, squealing at the idea of having to go to the bathroom with Matt in the apartment and wondering what it would be like to share a bed every single night. When he pulled out a ring, I can honestly say that I was surprised—and not in the way that my friends would later be surprised when their boyfriends proposed as the years went on, but all-out shocked because I had no idea that it was coming. We'd never discussed it, not in any serious way, and I was mostly just confused when he knelt on the grass and said, "Beth, will you marry me?"

His hands were shaking a little bit, and I could feel the people around us staring, elbowing each other and whispering that there was a proposal happening. "What?" I asked. I looked at him and he laughed. He seemed more confident then, and he took the ring out of the box and started to put it on my finger. "Will you marry me?" he asked, and I laughed too and said, "Yes, of course." I was twenty-three years old.

My wedding was the first one I'd ever been to. No one could believe this, but it was true. I had no idea what to expect and I let the wedding planner (a woman named Diana who carried around five huge binders with her wherever we went) dictate everything. Whenever I asked Matt his opinion about anything, he just said, "It's up to you." We got married in Madison and had the ceremony at St. Andrews, the church I'd grown up going to, and the reception at the Sheraton downtown. We did every last cheesy wedding tradition out there. We had a groom's cake, I threw my bouquet, we smeared frosting on each other, Matt took a garter off my leg, and my whole wedding party danced into the ballroom as they were announced, as if we were all a part of some music video.

It didn't occur to me until years later to be embarrassed about our wedding. It was only after attending the beautiful, tasteful, grown-up weddings of our friends that I began to see that ours was almost a little tacky. But by then, it was too late.

Before the wedding, Diana mailed a list of "bridesmaid dos and don'ts" to the girls. They included tips such as "Don't drink too much! No one likes a drunk bridesmaid." And "Don't expect to be anywhere close to the center of attention . . . this isn't your day!" And "Don't tan before the wedding! You don't want to risk a burn!" And "Do ask the bride how she's feeling and offer emotional support."

Colleen thought this list was the funniest thing she'd ever seen and kept it for years. At the wedding, Colleen got so drunk she fell and ripped her dress. And my best friend from childhood, Deborah Long, used her maid of honor speech to talk about how she was more than ready for her own boyfriend to propose. And when I walked down the stairs in my wedding dress for the first time, my single aunt Bit gasped and said, "Good God, you're just a baby." Then later, she whispered to me, "If you don't want to go through with this, you don't have to." Diana was probably mortified, but none of these things bothered me. I thought the whole day was perfect.

On the day of the wedding, Matt and I agreed we wouldn't see each other before the ceremony. But we met at a doorway, and stood on opposite sides with the wall between us, reaching around to hand each other our wedding presents. He gave me diamond earrings and I gave him a watch. The photographer took a picture of us, holding hands through the doorway, still hidden from each other. It is one of the most ridiculous pictures I've ever seen.

Years later, Colleen told me that my marriage to Matt was a result of terrorism. When she said this, we were at her apartment, lying on the couch and eating licorice out of a giant plastic container. I stopped mid-bite, squinted my eyes at her, and waited for her to explain.

"You know," she said, and took a bite of her Red Vine, "everyone was afraid they were going to die then. So many people had died that it was all anyone could think about. People were looking for anything that made them happy, and they moved fast, like there wasn't a lot of time left."

I wanted to defend my marriage, tell her that our relationship was strong and good and I would have fallen in love with Matt no matter what was happening in the world. But then I thought about what it had been like that month, how Julie was always in bed and how anytime we turned on the TV we heard about survivors and victims and babies being born who would never know their fathers. I thought about how claustrophobic it was in the apartment, and how from the moment Matt and I met, it felt like we were racing toward some-thing, so eager to get to the finish line.

Every so often, it worried me to think that Colleen was right, that we'd gotten married because we were scared. But then I thought about Matt in those pants covered with little dogs, the way he blushed when Colleen teased him, and I figured there were worse ways to end up with someone.

Chapter 3

A few days after my disastrous trip to the grocery store, we were supposed to go to dinner at Matt's parents' house. This wasn't unusual—we were expected every Sunday—but part of me hoped that just this once we could get out of it, that maybe Matt would agree to cancel.

"I'm sure they'll understand if we tell them we need to unpack," I said that afternoon. "And we have food now. We can make a real dinner."

"I already told them we were coming," Matt said.

"I could even make sloppy joes," I said. It was a little desperate to try to bribe Matt with his favorite meal, but I wanted nothing more than to curl up and have a quiet dinner. For as long as we'd known each other, Sunday nights were a time we spent together, actually cooking instead of ordering takeout, trying out complicated and involved recipes. When *The Sopranos* were on, we religiously made large pasta dishes and ate in front of the TV. Now Sunday nights were no longer ours. When I'd mentioned that we were never going to be able to watch *60 Minutes* again, Matt just said we could DVR it.

"We'll do sloppy joes another night," Matt said.

He reached out and pulled me onto his lap, put his face in my neck until I laughed and said, "Your loss."

It honestly didn't occur to me that moving to DC would mean seeing Matt's family all the time. Sure, I figured we'd see them more. Maybe we'd meet for dinner every few weeks—they lived in Maryland, about forty minutes outside of DC, just far enough away to be truly inconvenient. But looking back, it's clear that I was delusional, that I had underestimated the power of the Kellys.

Matt was one of five children. He had three older brothers and one younger sister. And like most big families, they were loud and secretly thought they were funnier and a little more special than everyone else. When Matt's mom found out I was an only child with no cousins, she'd drawn in a sharp breath and said, "Oh, isn't that too bad," as if I'd just told her that I was an orphan or had cancer. Or maybe an orphan who had cancer. I could tell she pitied me and pitied my parents, that she thought the only family worth having was a large one.

When people complain about their in-laws, I usually just smile and make some sort of sympathetic noise, but I don't offer any details about my own. It's too much to get into, and once I start talking about them, it's hard to stop. I'm sure there are worse mothers-in-law that I could've gotten. I'm sure that's probably true.

Barbara Kelly (called Babs by everyone except her grandchildren, who called her BB) was a tall woman, just a couple inches shy of six feet. Standing next to her, I felt even shorter than I am. ("At least you know he's not marrying you because you remind him of his mom," Bit said to me at the wedding.) She kept her hair in a brown chin-length bob, and no matter the time of day or the weather, it always looked perfect. I never saw one hair out of place, and sometimes I'd stare at her head and try to figure out how she did it. Babs loved tennis and golf and was often in a tennis skirt, even on the days she wasn't playing. She wore a lot of pinks and greens, favored polos, and usually had a sweater tied around her shoulders.

Early on, it was clear that Babs and I wouldn't have a close relationship, and I was fine with that. She didn't seem all that interested in me, or in any of her daughters-in-law for that matter. She referred to us as "the outlaws" and sometimes made us sit at a different table at family dinners. "Kellys over here," she'd say, pointing to the dining room, "and outlaws this way." The first time it happened, I thought it was a joke until I noticed my sisters-in-law heading out to a table on the sunporch and I stood where I was for a moment before finally just following them out there, taking my place at the table of non-Kellys.

· · ·

We were late for dinner, mostly because I spent thirty minutes searching for a dress that I was sure I'd unpacked. Matt helped me look for it, anxiously announcing the time every seven minutes or so, until I finally just pulled another dress out of the closet to wear so that he'd stop acting like a talking alarm clock.

By the time we pulled up, the driveway was full of cars, a telltale sign that we were the last to arrive. I could feel Matt stiffen next to me—he hated being late, even if it was just to his own family's house. "Sorry," I said, reaching over to rub his knee. He relaxed and looked over at me. "No worries," he said, putting his hand on top of mine.

The house where Matt grew up was a large redbrick Tudor with a lawn so green it almost looked fake and rows of white flowering bushes in front. It was such an inviting house, picture perfect, the kind you'd dream about living in one day. And it never failed to amaze me how cheerful and warm it looked from the outside, how different it felt once you went in.

I took a deep breath as we walked in the front door. The two of us almost collided right into Rebecca, who was married to Matt's oldest brother, Patrick. She was standing in the front hall, holding their two-year-old, Jonah, and bouncing him up and down, saying, "Shhh, you're okay. You're okay." Jonah's eyes were bright, but he wasn't crying and he gave us a serious look.

"Hey, buddy," Matt said. He rubbed Jonah's cheek with his finger. "Rough day?" Jonah smiled a little and hid his face in Rebecca's shoulder.

"He fell outside," Rebecca said, leaning her face into Jonah's hair. "The older boys were running around and knocked him down." She sounded accusatory, as if we were responsible for the roughness of the Kelly grandchildren. Then, without saying anything else, she turned away from us, and bounced and shushed Jonah into the living room.

Matt turned to me and raised his eyebrows, and I couldn't help but smile back. Rebecca was a difficult person to like, and even though I tried to defend her since she was an outlaw like me, it wasn't easy.

Apparently, when Patrick had announced he was going to propose to Rebecca, Babs gasped and said, "You're really going to marry that Jewish girl?" Patrick had repeated this to Rebecca (why, I don't know), and she'd despised Babs ever since. You couldn't really blame her, I guess.

Now, Babs went out of her way to show everyone that she was completely fine with a Jewish daughter-in-law. Sometimes when she gave a toast at dinner, she'd say, "Mazel," and raise her glass toward Rebecca. More than once someone burst out laughing, and everyone had to

42

yell "Cheers" and clink glasses loudly to cover it up. It was no surprise that Rebecca often opted out of Sunday dinners, and sent Jonah to the house with Patrick, claiming she had a migraine.

Rebecca also had seasonal affective disorder, which she talked about all the time. It was the third thing she told me about herself when we met. She spent two months a year in Florida, sometimes more. Jonah was an only child (which upset Babs greatly), and Rebecca and Patrick were almost always following him around and trying to get him to eat, as though he was going to starve right there. It wasn't at all unusual to see one of them crawling on their knees after Jonah, holding a banana or a cereal bar out, saying, "Do you want a 'nana? Take a bite of the 'nana. Take a bite. Try a bite. Just one bite." And then they'd shake their heads at each other, like they couldn't believe he wasn't eating. Being around them for more than an hour made you consider never having children, just in case there was a small chance you'd turn into them.

We walked into the kitchen and found Babs talking to the housekeeper, Rosie, about the dinner. Babs never really cooked, just gave instructions, but from the way she talked, you'd think she prepared it all herself. Rosie had worked for the Kellys for more than twenty years, and I often wondered how she managed to listen to Babs talk without screaming.

When Babs saw us, she put her palm up to Rosie in a "stop talking" motion, even though Rosie hadn't been the one talking. "There you are," Babs said. "I was wondering why you were so late. I was beginning to worry."

"Sorry," Matt said, "traffic was bad," at the same time I said, "It was my fault."

"I figured," Babs said, and I had a feeling it was me she was answering. She held my arms and kissed my cheek. "The girls are out back," she said, which meant, leave the kitchen. "There's some wine open on the bar."

I headed over to pour myself a glass of white wine, and watched as Babs pulled Matt toward her. "How's the job?" she was saying. "How's it going? Tell me everything." She made it no secret that Matt was her favorite. His brothers called him the Golden Child or sometimes the Chosen One. At first, I thought this was kind of mean, but then I heard Babs talk for fifteen minutes about how Matt once loaded the dishwasher without her asking, and I totally got it.

"It's just because I'm the youngest," Matt said once.

"You're not the youngest," I said. Meg was the youngest by far—almost ten years younger than Matt.

"You know what I mean," he said, like it wasn't a big deal he'd just disregarded his sister's existence. "The youngest boy."

I carried my wine out to the patio, where Jenny and Nellie (who were married to Matt's brothers, Michael and Will, respectively) were sitting on wicker chairs, drinking their own glasses of wine. Behind them, their husbands were throwing a football around with their boys, and their daughters, Grace and Lily, were sitting cross-legged on the ground a little ways away, braiding friendship bracelets. It was a rule at the Kellys' that none of the kids were allowed to have any screen time, and the girls almost always had a craft with them.

"Aunt Beth, look." Grace held up the bracelet so that I could see. I walked over to them and squatted down.

"Oh, I like that one," I said. "I love the blues and greens and how it's on an angle like that. I used to know how to do that."

Lily put her hand on my arm. She was seven, a year younger than Grace. "Grace can teach you. She's teaching me."

Grace nodded in a businesslike way. "She's doing a good job, too."

"Girls, don't monopolize Beth," Jenny called. "Let her breathe."

"I'll be back," I told the girls, running my hand down Grace's hair.

I adored my nieces. They were probably my favorite members of the whole Kelly family. When I first married Matt, I often felt awkward around everyone, not sure where I belonged. Grace and Lily were a great distraction—if I was holding a baby or chasing around a toddler, it gave me something to do and made me feel useful. They were the greatest buffer anyone could have asked for.

Jenny and Nellie were always grateful to have me take a baby from them—Babs wasn't the kind of grandmother who gave bottles or offered to change diapers—and I was always eager to do it. The first time I went on vacation with all of the Kellys, I shared a room with Grace, who was just a baby. (We weren't married yet, so there was no chance of me sharing a room with Matt.) I still remember the relief of waking up to her little smiling face staring at me, how she offered her spitty hand to me through the bars of the crib, and laughed when I held it in mine. I remember thinking that at least one person in the family really liked me.

"Sorry about that," Nellie said, as I sat down with them. She made a face. "They've been talking about showing you the bracelets all week. Be careful, because I have a feeling I know what you'll be getting for your birthday." She and Jenny laughed and I smiled.

Michael and Will were only a year apart—forty and forty-one—and they were often mistaken for twins. Jenny and Nellie had been friends since high school, and now co-owned a store in Chevy

Chase called Pink Penguin, which sold ribboned headbands, flip-flops adorned with flowers, and painted bobby pins. The store had a monogram machine that they used on everything you could imagine. Until I met them, I didn't own anything with my initials on it, and now I had monogrammed slippers, towels, sweaters, blankets, beach bags, and clutches.

My sisters-in-law were always friendly to me, and made a point of inviting me to lunch or dinner with them, which I appreciated. But I always felt a little bit like the third wheel with them. They'd been friends for over twenty years, lived two blocks away from each other, and had three children each (two boys and one girl), who all went to the same school. Their lives were so intertwined, and no matter how much time I spent with them, I was always on the outside.

"Where's Matt?" Nellie asked. "Did Babs steal him?"

"Yep. He's inside telling her every single thing that happened to him this week. No detail too small to leave out."

They laughed, and I sat back in the chair. The basis of my relationship with Jenny and Nellie was that we all understood how ridiculous our mother-in-law was with her boys. They were the ones who taught me not to be scared of Babs, not to get upset when she said something insulting, and I was forever thankful for that. When Nellie was seven months pregnant, Babs had watched her walk into the house and commented that Nellie was gaining "a great deal of weight" in her legs. Nellie had laughed and said, "No kidding."

The two of them resumed the conversation they'd been having before I got there, and I half listened as Jenny talked. "So, what I was saying is that Emma's mom—remember Emma? She's the one with the bowl cut? Well, her mom, Susie, just wouldn't admit that Emma had a learning disability, when it was so obvious to everyone that she did. Anyway, they finally figured out that she was dyslexic or something, but in the meantime, Emma developed a stutter. Like, a really bad one. I know, the poor thing. Like it could get much worse? Anyway, then she started seeing a speech therapist and then we find out that Susie is having an affair with the therapist. And now she's leaving her husband for him. Do you believe it?"

The two of them laughed and wiggled, but also made sympathetic noises to pretend they cared about Emma. Poor Emma, I thought. Poor little dyslexic Emma. Jenny and Nellie were horrible gossips, and hearing stories like this made me pity the other mothers in the school.

After they'd laughed enough about the speech therapist scandal, Nellie turned to me. "So, how's everything going?"

They'd asked me this same question about

thirty times since I'd moved. I think they could tell that I was unsure about DC, that I missed New York. But they'd grown up there, and I didn't want to insult the city they were from, so each time I just said, "It's going really well!"

We chatted for a while and sipped our wine, watched as Lily and Grace wove the colored thread. The sky had just started to change color when Rebecca stepped outside, still holding Jonah on her hip. Unsmiling, she said, "It's time for dinner. Babs is requesting your presence inside."

In the kitchen, Babs and Matt were still talking and Patrick was taking containers of food out of the diaper bag and getting ready to warm them up for Jonah's dinner. They always brought separate food for Jonah, because he had a dairy allergy, and Rebecca had just told me that they also thought he had a sensitivity to wheat. Babs dismissed these food restrictions as pure nonsense and was always trying to sneak ice cream and yogurt to Jonah. When Patrick would stop her, she'd throw up her hands. "How can his stomach get used to it if he never eats it?" she'd say.

Patrick spooned some vegetables into a bowl and held it up. "Mom, is this bowl okay to go in the microwave?"

"That should be fine," Babs said.

There was a rumor that when Patrick didn't get into Harvard, Will overheard Babs talking about it to her bridge club. "Well, Michael will definitely get in, but we all knew Patrick wasn't going to make it. You know how it is—you always throw the first pancake out."

Part of me hoped this story wasn't true, that it was a lie made up by one of the Kellys, just a joke that had lasted through the years. But another part of me thought there was a good chance Babs actually had ridiculed Patrick in front of all of her friends. When Patrick wasn't around, his siblings referred to him as Pancake, which seemed cruel. Patrick had the same features as his brothers—thin nose, strong cheekbones, blue eyes—but they didn't come together the same way on him, and he was much less handsome. His eyes were just a little large for his face, his nose just a little too sharp, and something about him reminded me of a deer— he was always so jumpy and unsure.

He tried hard to please Babs, but it didn't seem to matter. He could've moved somewhere far away, but he stayed close by and came to Sunday dinners. I always wondered why. If it were me, I would've moved to the other side of the country.

Matt's dad was standing at the end of the kitchen table, and all of the grandchildren were vying for his attention, interrupting each other with news about school and field trips. Charles was a quiet man who worked a lot—all the time, really. Even now that he was officially retired he spent most of his time in the office. But he also adored his grandchildren and tried to attend as many soccer games and gymnastics meets as he could. He never raised his voice and he didn't have to—as soon as he started talking, everyone got quiet. I could never figure out how he and Babs ended up together. Did she marry someone quiet to make up for all the noise she made? Did they balance each other out on a kindness spectrum?

The kitchen was full and noisy then, everyone talking at once. Babs looked at all of us and said, "Okay, now. Don't just stand there like lumps. Go sit down." And because we always did what she said, we walked quickly into the dining room.

The bright side of Sunday dinners was that the food was always really good. I tried to concentrate on that when I was there. This Sunday was roast chicken with lemon and garlic, twice-baked potatoes, and a kale salad.

"Kale?" Meg asked, as it was passed to her. She sniffed. "How trendy of you, Babs."

Meg was twenty-three and still living at home. She'd had two different jobs since graduating from Trinity, and probably could've moved out, but I think she enjoyed the benefits of having Rosie iron her clothes and make her bed each morning. Once, when I said something about how fun it was to live with my friends after graduating, and how I wouldn't have wanted to move back home, she looked up and said, "That's because your parents live in Wisconsin. Gross."

When Matt and I first started dating, I thought I'd become friends with Meg. She was closer to my age than anyone else. But she didn't have much interest in me and, to be honest, was sort of a spoiled brat. Even Babs didn't seem to know what to do with her. Jenny and Nellie had known Meg since she was a baby, so they thought she was adorable, and when she rolled her eyes, or christened something disgusting or revolting, they thought it was a riot. They were always commenting on her clothes (Meg had a wardrobe that would make anyone jealous) and asking her for accessory advice or pressing her about her dating life. Meg found them amusing, and tolerated their questions, sometimes even smiling briefly at them.

Most of the time, Meg was on her phone, which made it difficult to have any sort of conversation with her. Babs, who was firm about her grand-children not having any screen time at the house, seemed to have very little power over Meg and her iPhone—once I watched as Babs tried to take it away from her, and Meg whined like a sick pony or a panicked toddler.

As dinner started, I braced myself. When all

of the Kellys were in one place, the noise was constant, like construction. I never got used to the way the grandchildren raced through rooms, running into people and tripping over carpets (which was probably how poor Jonah was mowed down earlier). And there was so much food—enormous platters of food, so many mouths gobbling things down, so many glasses of water and wine being poured. Each dinner felt like a small fund-raiser. More than once after I married Matt, someone said to me, "That's so nice you finally got yourself a big family," like it was something that I always wanted, like it was something that everyone hoped for.

Really, most of the time I longed for my own house. Since I was an only child, raised by a librarian and a professor, our house was almost always peaceful. In the evenings, no one yelled up the stairs for everyone to come to dinner, or fought over the TV. Usually my parents watched *Wheel of Fortune*, and would sound out the puzzles together. When one of them got it right, the other would say nicely, "Good job" or "Well done."

At the Kellys' Sunday dinners, I could mostly just stay quiet and zone out as I ate and listened to the conversation. But tonight, as soon as everyone was served, Babs turned to me. "So, Beth, have you heard any more about the job?"

I took a sip of water before I answered, "Oh,

no. Not yet." I'd interviewed at a website the week before, for a position that I wasn't even sure I wanted. But of all the résumés I'd sent out, it was the only place that had even bothered to call, which was slightly embarrassing and not something I wanted to share at the dinner table.

"Well, I'm sure you will," Babs said. "You must be going crazy sitting in that apartment all day."

"Oh, it's okay," I said. I took a large bite of kale and willed the conversation to be over. Babs had the ability to make me feel worthless just by tilting her head, and she wasn't the person I wanted to discuss my job options with.

"You know, we could always use another person at the store," Nellie said. She smiled at me across the table, and I tried to smile back. I knew she was just being nice, but the thought of selling monogrammed towels to women like Babs made my stomach hurt.

"It's true. The summer sale is coming up," Jenny said. "Meg, we got a bunch of those makeup bags you liked. Supercute patterns."

I knew Jenny was changing the subject for me, and I appreciated it. I concentrated on my dinner while she continued to talk about makeup bags. Matt turned to Michael and started telling him how everyone was already worrying about the 2012 election. "You wouldn't believe it," he said. "This one's barely over and they're getting ready to do it again." Babs perked up and turned her attention to him, and for the moment, I was free.

When we got in the car that night, I said, "I didn't know you told your mom about my interview."

"Oh, I just mentioned it to her last week. I didn't think you'd mind."

"No, I don't mind. I just didn't want to talk about it in case I don't get it," I said, although that wasn't quite what it was. Babs had never been all that impressed with my career in magazines. I'd never been comfortable talking about it with her because she made it sound like it was a hobby I was trying out. When I'd gotten laid off, she'd just sighed and said, "Well, that's no surprise. Print is dying."

"I'm sure you'll get it," Matt said, giving my hand a quick squeeze. My optimistic husband, always so sure that things would work out.

Colleen had moved to DC a couple of years earlier to cover the Hill as an on-air reporter for Bloomberg. She'd gotten her big break reporting the transit strike for NY1, standing at the edge of the Brooklyn Bridge and doing man-on-the-street interviews with all the pissed-off New Yorkers who had to walk to work that day. When the offer came from Bloomberg, she didn't hesitate. I couldn't believe she'd leave New York and move to a random city. "You don't know anyone there," I said. She just gave me a strange look and said, "This is my dream job." I remember thinking that I wouldn't have taken it, wouldn't have left New York no matter what job was offered to me. But that was the difference between us, I guess.

I'd seen Colleen just once since I'd gotten to DC—she was always busy, had already canceled on me a few times, sending me short texts that she was "treading water" and "swamped with work." But that Wednesday she called to say she was sneaking out of the office early. "Let's get our nails done," she said. "Meet me at that place right by you, Qwest. Do you know it? It's on Eighteenth." I was so happy to have something to break up my afternoon that I wasn't even a little bit annoyed at how bossy she sounded.

When I got to Qwest, Colleen already had her feet soaking in a tub and was tapping away on her BlackBerry. She held up her hand and called my name, then resumed typing, pausing again when I walked over to her to pucker her lips for a cheek kiss.

I slipped off my flip-flops and sat in the chair next to her, smiling at the woman who was filling my tub. "You pick color?" the woman asked, and I handed her a bottle of bright red polish called Jelly Apple. "Oooh, I like that," Colleen said, fully putting her phone down for the first time. "I'll do that one too."

"Who names these things?" I said. "I think I'd be good at that job."

"I'd be great at it," she said. She pressed a button on the arm of her chair and sighed happily as it started massaging her neck.

"Well, I'm the one who needs a job," I said, a little sharper than I intended. She looked over at me and I just shrugged.

"Well, of course you need a job," she said. "Have you heard back from DCLOVE yet?"

I shook my head and answered, "Not yet." Colleen was friendly with one of the founders of DCLOVE and had helped me get the interview there. The website's mission statement said it was "committed to showcasing the unique personality of our nation's capital," and the irony of applying to work at such a place wasn't lost on me.

"Well, I'm sure you will," she said. "But in the meantime, let's figure out who else you should meet. I know someone at National Geographic. That would be a good one. Oh, and I just met someone who works for the Wildlife Fund magazine."

"The Wildlife Fund magazine?"

"Don't be a snob. This isn't New York. You're not going to find a job like *Vanity Fair* here. But you'll find something interesting. What you really need to do at this point is meet as many people as possible to figure out what opportunities are out there. Here, I'm introducing you to this person over e-mail now, okay? You can get lunch and talk."

Colleen was someone who actually enjoyed networking, was great at meeting random people and connecting them to one another. For all of her talk about New York being the best city, DC really was a better fit for her. She loved knowing the important players, loved knowing gossip about them even more. She was also drawn to anything exclusive—the harder it was to join, the more she wanted to be a part of it. When she first moved, she called to tell me she'd been recruited by a group called the Madison DC. She went on to explain the rules of the group, how the member-ship was capped at one hundred women, how you had to be between the ages of twenty-one and thirty, unmarried, successful, and pretty. The whole thing sounded like a club that was dreamt up by a group of thirteen-year-old girls, which is what I told her.

When P. J. Clarke's started a members-only dining room, Colleen had a key card in her possession before most people even knew it existed. At least once a year, she was named to some list, and she'd forward the link to us: DC's 30 Under 30; Rising Stars of DC; DC's Young Power Women. She always pretended like these things were random, that they didn't matter to her, but we all knew better.

I was lost in thought but could feel Colleen staring at me. "What's going on with you?" she finally asked. "You're all doom and gloom."

"No, I'm fine," I said. "I think I just miss New York."

"It's not so bad here, you know. I mean, you have a washer and dryer for Christ's sake. And it's not like you were going to live in New York forever."

"I guess not," I said.

"And everything will work out," she said. "You'll see."

"Yeah," I said. "I know."

It was easier to agree with Colleen than try to explain what I really thought. This move to DC had disrupted things. The truth was, I'd liked being married to a lawyer, liked that Matt's job made sense, that there was a steady future plotted out. It felt like we were ahead of everyone else in the race to become adults. We were married, we owned a home, we were a couple to be envied. I'd always felt so grown up in my life with Matt—at twenty-five, I used to offer to drop off his dry cleaning just so I could say, "Light starch on my husband's shirts, please."

And then, he'd joined the campaign and I'd lost my job. We moved to DC and Matt was making less than half what he did before. I was still unemployed, and we were renting a place with a twenty-year-old refrigerator and water marks on the ceiling. All of a sudden, everything felt uncertain.

"You'll be happier once you find a job," Colleen said.

"I'm sure you're right," I said.

She sat back, looking pleased. "Of course I am," she said.

After our nails were done, we walked back to my apartment—carefully, with our hands held in front of us so that we wouldn't smudge the polish. It was only a couple blocks away, but we were both sweating by the time we got there, thankful for the blast of air-conditioning that hit us as we opened the door.

"How is it so hot out?" I asked. I kicked off my flip-flops.

"This is nothing," Colleen said, removing her own sandals. "It's only June. Just wait until August."

"I can't believe you haven't been here yet," I said. "I'll give you the grand tour." We walked barefoot through the apartment, poking our heads into the kitchen, then went up the stairs to the bedroom.

"This place is nice," Colleen said. "How much are you paying?" She sat down on the bed and leaned back against the pillows, kicking her legs up, which made me smile. Only my college friends would lie down on my bed, uninvited, and ask how much my rent was. There was something refreshing about being around someone who wouldn't hesitate to open my cabinets and help herself to anything in the refrigerator.

We spent the next two hours chatting. Colleen had become obsessed with politics since moving to DC and rarely talked about anything else, except when she was discussing actual people in DC who worked in media or were otherwise important.

The refreshing thing—because honestly I don't know if we would have stayed friends if she only talked about politics—was that Colleen remained a devoted watcher of *The Real Housewives* and *Keeping Up with the Kardashians.* I only tuned in by accident, but she taped them all. She was the only person I knew who seemed genuinely concerned about Kim Kardashian's future. She had just said to me, "I just don't think she's choosing the right guys," when we heard the front door open.

"Hello?" Matt called.

"We're up here," I said.

Matt was already loosening his tie and getting ready to pull it off when he walked into the bedroom, but he stopped when he saw Colleen.

"Oh, well hello," Matt said. "Look who's here."

"Hey, Dogpants," Colleen said. (She still, almost exclusively, called him Dogpants. Once in a while, I heard her call him Matt and it just sounded wrong.)

Normally, Matt would've kissed Colleen on the cheek, but I could tell he was a little uncomfortable that she was lying on our bed, so he just waved from across the room and said, "So, what have you two been up to?"

"Got our nails done, caught up, tried to find Beth a job and convince her this isn't the worst place in America to live. You know, the usual."

Matt laughed. "Oh yeah? Any luck?"

"Yeah," I said. "I'm now fully employed and I love it here."

They both laughed, even though my joke wasn't particularly funny. Matt perched on the bench at the end of our bed, and he and Colleen started talking about how Colleen's husband, Bruce, wanted to take Matt golfing soon. Bruce was seventeen years older than Colleen, which somehow still surprised me. The first time I met him, the four of us went to get drinks at a dark hotel bar that served snacks in white ceramic dishes and had egg whites in most of the cocktails. It was noisy, and Bruce kept leaning forward and cupping his ear toward whoever was talking, which was the same thing my dad did in crowded restaurants.

We all figured they'd break up eventually, that

the age difference would be too much—he had two daughters, who were nine and eleven, and I thought at least that would change Colleen's mind. But they stayed together and got married on Long Island in the church where Colleen grew up. It was by far the strangest wedding I've ever been to. All the girls from college were bridesmaids and Bruce's daughters were junior bridesmaids. We had to walk down the aisle with Bruce's nearly middle-aged friends, who were just as uncomfortable with the situation as we were.

Matt always took on a nonjudgmental attitude when we talked about Colleen and Bruce. He didn't like to gossip or talk behind people's backs, which I know is a good trait, but could be very frustrating, especially when I was dying to dissect a scandalous situation. Sometimes I pressed him, trying to get him to admit that it was a weird coupling. "You can't help who you fall in love with," he said more than once. (Which I've always thought was a ridiculous saying, because of course you can help it—you just don't do it. You remove yourself from the situation.) But at Colleen's wedding, when Bruce danced with Colleen's mom, Matt (who was a little drunk) leaned over and whispered to me, "Well, now, they make a nice couple."

I closed my eyes on the bed and listened to Matt and Colleen talk. She suggested that the four of us get together for dinner that Sunday, and I said without opening my eyes, "We can't. We have to go to the Kellys'."

They continued talking, and I just lay there. I was thinking about something that Colleen had said when we were getting our nails done. She was telling me how smart it was that Matt took this job, what a good move it was for him.

"But what about for me?" I'd said.

"You don't even have a job right now," she'd said. "So what's the difference?"

And just like that, it was like I stopped being part of the equation. Like nothing I did mattered anymore—it was all about Matt now.

At dinner the following Sunday, Babs brought out a picture of Matt in third grade, dressed as Ronald Reagan for Famous Person Day at school. "He brought the house down," she said. I'd heard the story before—how Matt insisted on dressing up as the president, how he gave a speech to the class telling them how he loved Jelly Bellys and got to fly around in his own plane. He handed out little packets of jelly beans and yelled, "Vote for me!"

I glanced at Patrick as Babs told this story. If I'd heard it a dozen times, he'd no doubt heard it hundreds. I wondered if he ever felt like standing up and walking out during a family dinner. Babs said, "That's when I knew! I just knew this little boy would grow up to be a politician, that one day he'd be the one running for office." As Babs kept talking, it occurred to me that she wasn't a good mother. She wasn't a good mother at all.

Of course I had my own issues with her—how she still had a picture of Matt's old girlfriend hanging in the house, or how she always managed to make me feel like my opinion didn't matter— but that wasn't all. Babs never seemed satisfied with her children, she pointed out their weaknesses whenever possible. She was always pushing them to be more successful, to do something fantastic, as if their accomplishments were nothing but a reflection on her.

Why did Matt want to run for office? Because it was something he really wanted to do, or because he knew it would make his mom proud? Was it because she'd whispered in his ear all through his childhood how special he was, how he was meant for something great? Was it because she brought out this stupid picture of him dressed as the president and told the same story over and over again?

I'm sure people would say that my feelings were normal, that of course I thought my parents were better parents than Matt's, simply because they were mine. But I disagree. My parents thought that I was smart and talented—they believed it with all their hearts. They just didn't need me to be the most special person out there.

If I'd stayed in Wisconsin my whole life and become a kindergarten teacher and married another teacher, they would have thought that was great. They would've been proud of me. They would have reacted the same way they did when I brought them to my office at *Vanity Fair*, with wide eyes and smiles. They wanted me to be happy and healthy—wasn't that enough? They weren't selfish people, they didn't want more than their fair share. No, they were practical, and knew that life could be hard sometimes, and thought that if you just wanted a little, if you hoped for a reasonable amount, you might just end up being satisfied.

I may not be right all the time, and maybe I've misjudged people in my life, but I do know this one thing for sure—my own mother would never compare me to a pancake.

Chapter 4

I'd known Matt only a few weeks when he first told me he wanted to run for office. We were lying in his bed on a Sunday afternoon (which is how we spent most of our time those days) and we'd just returned from getting omelets at the diner below his apartment. Our relationship was brand new, and we were so obsessed with each other we couldn't see straight—all we did during that time was have sex and then talk until it was time to have sex again. He was telling me about his job that day, I think, my head on his chest, our hands playing with each other, intertwining our fingers over and over again. I'd never felt this way about another person before, like no matter how close I was to him, no matter how many parts of our bodies were touching, it wasn't enough. I always wanted more of him.

"I like being a lawyer," he said to me. "But my real passion is politics. What I've always wanted to do is run for office one day."

I propped myself up on my elbow and looked at him, feeling giddy. "Really?" I asked. Everything about him was proving to be so different, so much more interesting than anyone I'd ever been with and this was one more thing to add to my list of Amazing Things About Matt. (Of course, to be fair, everything about him delighted me at that point—he could've told me he wanted to be a clown and I would've found it charming.)

"What office?" I asked him.

"It depends. Maybe I'd run for Congress, or a state senate seat, and then who knows? It's something I've always wanted. I just feel like it's what I'm supposed to do."

"That's amazing," I said. "I think you'd be so great at that."

The thing is, as I said that to him, I didn't really think it would ever happen. Even when he told me later that he'd never smoked pot (Never! Not once!) because he didn't want it to be something that could come back to hurt him or that he'd bought the domain names for MatthewKelly.com and MattforMaryland.com, I still didn't fully believe it was something he intended to do.

And it wasn't because I didn't think Matt was smart or talented enough, because I absolutely did. But that same day, I told Matt how I wanted to write novels, big, thick books that swept you away, the kind that made people miss their stop on the subway. And I assumed that our dreams were the same—something fun to imagine, fantasies to pass the time.

I don't mean to be a pessimist—it's just, how often do you hear people say, "I'd love to write" or "I think I'd be happiest teaching high school history"? People say all kinds of things—they want to work in the Peace Corps or write Hallmark cards for a living. It doesn't mean anything. Or that's what I thought, anyway.

Then, in the fall of 2007, Matt started talking about how unfulfilled he was at work, how he'd talked to his friend Kevin, from college, who'd joined the Obama campaign and couldn't stop thinking about it. "I feel like I'm wasting my time at the firm," he said, "when I could be doing something so much more important." Originally,I chalked it up to a bad few months at work—Matt was close to becoming a senior associate and working crazy hours. But then I noticed that he was spending a lot of time looking at Kevin's Facebook page, clicking through the pictures of Obama's events, studying each one closely. He began making phone calls to everyone he knew working in politics, scheduling lunches and drinks with friends, acquaintances, family connections, anyone he thought might be able to help him.

His eagerness reminded me of the way my girlfriends would act at the end of an especially slothful weekend, when we'd eaten cheeseburgers and chips and drunk ourselves silly. We'd all be disgusted with ourselves, swearing to change our ways, scrubbing the apartment, eating salads, and signing up for classes at the gym. That's how Matt acted, his eyes bright and frantic, like he'd just gotten out of prison. "I've wasted so much time," he kept saying. "I should've done this years ago."

A friend of a friend introduced Matt to the New York finance director for Obama's campaign, and he was offered a job. "I told her I'd do anything," he said. "I don't care if I'm answering phones."

"Is that what you're going to be doing?" I asked, trying to keep my voice even.

"Maybe." He shrugged. "She said she'd train me, that I could learn on the job. I got lucky—they really need people. Most of the experienced people are with Hillary and Edwards, but they're willing to let me learn."

"Wow," I said.

"If I really want to run for office," he said, "I need to see how it works. Get some experience. See a campaign like this up close."

Matt's pay cut was pretty severe, but he said he wasn't worried about money, and so I tried not to be either. We'd have to dip into a little of our savings, and his parents had already offered to help out if needed. "They know this is a once in a lifetime opportunity," he said. "I feel so lucky."

"That's great," I said. And I meant it. Of course I did. I wanted him to be happy. What kind of wife would I have been otherwise?

• • •

I don't know what would've happened if Obama had never run, if Matt hadn't joined that specific campaign. Would he have found his way into politics eventually? Maybe. Probably. But maybe not. There was something different about Obama, something almost magical about that campaign. Each day, Matt went to work in a small office with just a few co-workers. Sometimes he called people and asked for money, which he called "dialing for dollars." Sometimes he worked on spreadsheets all day, entering names of the people who were donating or attending an event. He started helping hosts put together fund-raisers, gaining more confidence with each one. I waited for him to complain—even just a little—about the menial parts of his job, but he never did. He was working long hours, going to events at night, and still he was energized, came home talking about his job, telling me every last detail as we lay in bed, pulsing with excitement, filled with hope.

He wasn't the only one, obviously. At that point, it felt like everyone in New York (in the whole country, really) was swept up in this campaign—there was a fervor, a rising, a sense of urgency. We all felt that something big was happening, that a change was just around the corner.

I've never been all that interested in politics. I

vote, of course. I'm informed about the presidential candidates. (Admittedly, much more since meeting Matt.) But when Matt told me about volunteering for Senate campaigns in college and joining the Young Democrats, I couldn't relate. None of my friends in college were political. Sure, Colleen (and a few other girls) dressed up as Monica Lewinsky for Halloween freshman year, wore blue dresses and carried plastic cigars around, but we never had serious conversations about impeachment, or anything else beyond Colleen's acute and often repeated observation about the whole situation, where she'd shake her head and ask, "Wouldn't you just die if your parents knew you gave the president a blow job?"

But in 2008, politics was all we talked about. At bars, we had heated discussions and spent hours imagining the horror if McCain won. My mild-mannered mother called Sarah Palin a dimwit, which was so out of character and shocking that she may as well have called her a cunt. Something had shifted in the country, and Matt was in the middle of it—not just an observer, but a part of this great big movement. At some point over the year, he began referring to the campaign as "We," and it stung whenever he said it, like he was purposely trying to separate himself from me, pointing out that he was a part of something I wasn't.

● ● ●

I got laid off four days before the election—it was Halloween and Matt was already in Chicago. The fund-raising was done in mid-October—there was a lag time between when the money was raised and when it was finally ready to be spent—so Matt didn't have anything else to do in New York and he'd gone to Chicago to help out there. (Which was good, because he would've gone crazy at home.) When I finally reached him that day, to tell him I'd lost my job, he was at campaign headquarters and it was so loud that it sounded like he was at a sporting event. He said everything right and was sympathetic and calming. But still, what I really wanted was for him to be there with me.

"I'm supposed to go out with the girls tonight," I told him. "We were planning to dress up as Starbucks workers. Colleen got the costumes and everything."

"I remember," he said. "You should go out. Have a good night. Have some fun."

"No, don't you get it? I can't dress up as a Starbucks worker on the day I got fired. I'll probably be working there for real in a couple of weeks."

"Beth, that won't happen. I promise."

"Well, I'm not dressing up."

"I think that's fair," Matt said. "I'm sure none

of the other girls will either." But he was wrong. When I showed up at the bar, I was the only one in regular clothes. I spent my night getting drunk with three Starbucks workers and woke up the next morning on the couch, sharing a pillow with a half-eaten piece of pizza.

On election day, I flew to Chicago to be with Matt. Grant Park was swarmed that night—waves of people just kept coming. The weather was unseasonably warm (we didn't even need jackets), which somehow made it all feel a little eerie, a little surreal.

Matt was working at a cocktail party for the major donors, and he snuck me into the tent. I stood with a vodka and soda in a corner and watched everyone around me. I tried to concentrate on what I was experiencing—this is history, I kept thinking, this is important. But I was also feeling slightly sorry for my unemployed self, sipping my drink, wondering what I was going to do next.

When the election was called, all of the donors were rushed out of the tent to a roped-off area right in front of the stage to watch the speech. I was right in front, so close to the next president that it was disconcerting. But I was also aware that Oprah was standing a couple of rows behind me, and part of me wanted to move and wave her forward to take my spot, because it was clearly a huge mistake for me to be closer to the stage than she was.

During the speech, Matt and I both cried—everyone did. "This is it, Beth," Matt said. "This is it." I wanted to ask him what was it, but instead just held his hand. Back in the finance tent, all of the workers started drinking, tossing back vodkas and beer, and hugging, hard, throwing their arms around each other and burying their faces in necks. "We did it, man," Matt said, whenever he hugged anyone. He kept gripping my shoulders and squeezing them like he couldn't contain himself.

Obama came back to the tent to thank the donors for their help, and also took the time to thank all of the workers. He shook Matt's hand and called him by name, which impressed me and made Matt start crying again. "Thank you, sir," he said, about five times.

We went with a huge group of campaign staff to a bar, then another, and then another. I kept waiting for everyone to calm down, but if anything they got more energy as the night went on. Everyone was still screaming and crying and hugging and laughing when we finally left. At some point in the night, Matt turned to me. "I know you're upset about your job," he said. "But maybe this is for the best. Imagine I got a job in the administration—we could move to DC, start a whole new adventure."

I didn't get a chance to answer him because he was swept into a new conversation, a new round of hugs with other campaign people, and I stood there as they celebrated, just slightly off to the side. I had the feeling that you get when you find yourself at home after a day at work, but have no memory of the commute, no real idea how you arrived there.

When we stumbled back to our hotel room sometime in the early morning, I was too drunk and tired to be offended when I heard Matt say as he fell into bed, "This is the best night of my life."

So, yeah, Matt told me about his aspirations right after we met. But my high school boyfriend wanted to be a rapper, and turned out to be an accountant, so I don't think I can be blamed for not taking it all too seriously.

Chapter 5

When Matt asked if I wanted to go to Alan Chu's birthday party, my first instinct was to say no. After a month or so of constant socializing with White House people, I felt like I needed a break. Could I really spend another night at a bar listening as Alan told me how many almonds the President had eaten that day?

"I don't know," I said. "I might not be up for it."

"Are you sure?" Matt asked. "It's just at that bar, Bobby Lew's on Eighteenth. It's really close to us. It'll be fun, I think."

It was Friday night, and Matt was still in his suit and I was wearing the yoga pants I'd had on all day. (No yoga had been done.) I may as well have been in pajamas. I didn't especially feel like celebrating Alan, but I could see that Matt wanted me to go and thought it would be good to put on real clothes for at least a little while. So I agreed, telling myself that if the party was really awful I could just have one drink and be home within the hour.

Bobby Lew's was about as divey as you can get and already fairly crowded. Matt and I made our way to the bar to get a couple of beers and then Matt turned around and surveyed the crowd, which was a new habit of his that sort of disturbed me. It looked like he was searching for the most appealing person to talk to, like he was rating everyone.

"I'm glad you came," Matt said, leaning down to kiss me.

"Me too," I said.

Alan came over to us then, and I said happy birthday to him, and he gave me a look like I was familiar but he couldn't quite place me.

"Is Brett here?" I asked.

Alan blinked several times and then said stiffly, "Brett and I are no longer together."

"Oh, I'm sorry," I said, but really I was happy for Brett. He was free. He'd never again have to listen to Alan talk about the President before they fell asleep at night.

"Let's get you a birthday drink," Matt said to Alan, turning to signal the bartender. I squeezed his arm, thankful for the change of subject, and he winked at me, quickly.

I heard Ashleigh Dillon before I met her. She was standing in the middle of a group of guys, and her voice carried across the bar as she laughed and said, "Y'all are so bad." Even if she hadn't been so loud, I would've noticed her because of how she was dressed—in a belted red and white polka-dot dress with a full skirt. Her blond hair was curled and pinned back on the sides and she was wearing bright red lipstick and heels so high it made my feet ache just to look at them. Her whole look was a little old-fashioned, like she was trying to mimic an old-time movie star.

The guy standing next to her was tall with shaggy brown hair that curled at the ends, like he was in need of a haircut. He was wearing a suit like most of the other guys there (they'd all come right from work), but he'd taken off his tie and shoved it in one of his pockets, and it was hanging out in a careless way like it was going to be on the floor pretty soon. I noticed then that although Ashleigh was standing in the middle of the group, everyone was turned toward the guy with the shaggy hair, like they were orbiting around him. Matt saw me looking over at them, and leaned down to whisper to me, "That's Jimmy Dillon, he works in the White House travel office. He's from Texas. I'll introduce you."

I blushed because I'd been caught staring at Jimmy, who was unquestionably handsome, but Matt didn't seem to think anything of it. He started over toward them and I followed, and when we got close, I saw Jimmy reach down and lightly pat Ashleigh's butt with his hand and then squeeze it. It surprised me so much that I said, "Oh!" and the two of them turned to look at us. I blushed again, like I was the one caught groping in public.

"Jimmy, this is my wife, Beth," Matt said. I had my hand out ready to shake his, when he leaned down to hug me.

"Hey," he said. He smiled like he'd been waiting to meet me all night, and instead of releasing me from the hug, he shifted me to his side and kept his arm around my shoulder. "Kelly," he said to Matt. "This pretty young thing can't really be your wife." He turned to me. "What are you doing with this guy?"

"Jimmy, good Lord, stop molesting the poor girl." Ashleigh hit his arm and shook her head. "You're going to scare her away."

"I'm Ashleigh, Jimmy's wife," she said. And then she leaned forward to hug me too, pushing Jimmy's arm off my shoulder as she did. When she released me, she stood in front of me and squeezed my forearms. "I'm so happy to finally meet you. I just moved here too. Your hubby told me you were finally here, and I said to myself, She sounds like my kind of girl. I need to meet her now."

I glanced over at Matt wondering when this conversation had taken place, but he was leaning over and giving Ashleigh a kiss on her cheek. She puckered her lips and gave him an air kiss in return, then smiled at me.

"I like the manners on this one," she said. "I've never lived anywhere but Texas, and I have to say, the people up north are not what I'm used to."

It was weird to hear Ashleigh say "up north." We were still below the Mason-Dixon Line, a fact that I swear I could feel in the air. DC seemed so southern to me, mostly because it was hot and everyone moved slowly. The first time we went to a deli here, the man behind the counter took so long to assemble the sandwiches, I wanted to jump over the counter and do it myself. DC made me feel so impatient, so fidgety. More than once—when we got annoyed waiting at a restaurant, or speed-walked past a group of people—Matt would say, "Maybe we lived in New York too long."

"Jimmy works across the hall from me," Matt explained. "Ashleigh came in last week to visit and we started talking."

"Correction," Ashleigh said. "Jimmy works across the hall when he's in town, which is almost never." She squeezed my arm. "Girl, I can just tell we're going to be best friends. We're in the same boat—we both moved here kicking and screaming, am I right?" She winked at Jimmy and the four of us laughed.

"Something like that," I said.

Ashleigh corrected me when I said her name. "It's actually 'Ash-lay,' not 'Ash-lee.'" I tried again and she shook her head, although I couldn't hear any difference in how I was saying it. "Don't feel bad, people get it wrong all the time. That's what my mother gets for trying to be all fancy with my name. You can just call me Ash."

Ash was twenty-eight but seemed younger. She was sweet—I hadn't had anyone claim me as a best friend since Deborah Long on the first day of kindergarten, and I was pretty sure that was only because she wanted the Fruit Roll-Up in my lunch. But Ash was almost too sweet. It took me off guard. She was nothing like my other friends—the fact that she kept calling me girl was weird enough. My initial reaction was that we'd have nothing in common, but as the four of us stood there, the conversation flowed easily.

It took me a while to notice that we were talking about regular things. (That is, things other than the campaign and the President.) We talked about the Dillons' place, which wasn't too far from ours, about the neighborhood in between us and which restaurants we'd tried. There was never a lull or a beat of silence when everyone looked around and tried to think of something else to say. Matt and Jimmy left to get us more drinks, and when they got back, Jimmy asked where I was from. When I told him Wisconsin, Ash gasped. "Oh, Wisconsin! I've never been, but I've heard it's lovely." I sort of wondered if she was full of shit—I'd never heard someone talk about Wisconsin in such a way. But she looked completely sincere.

"It's nice," I said. "But maybe I only think that because it's where I'm from."

"Do you miss it?" she asked.

"I do, sometimes. I haven't lived there in a while."

"Is your family still there?" she asked.

"My parents are. I'm an only child."

"So is Jimmy," Ash said, turning to him like this was the most delightful coincidence.

"But it's interesting," Jimmy said, "because it's this one who acts like she was raised an only child." He reached out and cupped Ash's chin. "You should see our bathroom—she has all her potions laid out, taking up the whole counter. I can barely find a place for my toothbrush in there. And she took all the closets in the house for herself, leaving me with just a half of one."

"It's more than half," Ash said. She rolled her eyes at him, but you could tell she was amused.

"Listen," Jimmy said. "Do you guys want to try to sneak out of here and get something to eat? This one will be three sheets to the wind if we don't get her some food soon." As if on cue, Ash teetered a little on her heels.

We all looked across the room at Alan, who was talking intently to another White House staffer that I recognized but didn't know. The guy looked bored, probably because it wasn't really a back-and-forth conversation. Alan just kept talking at him. I felt Matt look over at me, like he was sure I was going to make an excuse for why we couldn't go. But I answered so quickly that I surprised even myself. "That sounds great."

• • •

Jimmy suggested we go to a wine bar on Fourteenth Street called Cork. It wasn't that far away, but Ash insisted we take a cab. "I won't make it one block in these heels," she said.

Cork was crowded, but there was one open table in the corner and we were seated right away. "Thanks, Chloe," Jimmy said to the hostess.

Ash turned to me. "Jimmy knows every hostess in every restaurant on this block. Before I moved here, I'm pretty sure he went out to eat every night."

"I put on fifteen pounds," Jimmy said, and then he smiled at me. "And I also know all the bartenders."

"This looks great," I said, looking at the menu. "We haven't really been over this way."

"To be honest, Fourteenth Street is still a little sketchy," Ash said in a low voice. She put her napkin on her lap. "I don't love walking around here at night."

"It's perfectly safe," Jimmy said. "It's changing quickly. Mark my words, in another year, you won't even recognize this street."

The waitress came over then and Jimmy ordered a bottle of wine and a few of the dishes. "You don't mind, do you?" he asked, although the waitress was already gone. "It's all small plates, so we can share. We can order more, I just wanted to get some food this way, quickly."

"Sounds good to me," Matt said.

Jimmy turned to me. "Beth, did your husband tell you how we met on the campaign?" I shook my head.

"We are not," Ash said, "spending the whole night talking about the campaign. I'll give you five minutes and then we're talking about something else," which made me like her even more.

"What else is there?" Jimmy asked, and Ash just shook her head.

We spent much longer than five minutes talking about the campaign, mostly because Jimmy just kept talking. But he was a great storyteller—funny and irreverent—and we all listened closely, even Ash, who must have heard them all before.

The way Jimmy and Matt met, I learned, was that Matt was helping with a fund-raising dinner in the town house of a donor in New York. He walked in a few hours before it was supposed to start and found Jimmy sleeping on a bench in the front hall.

"I woke up to him shaking me," Jimmy said. "He was so polite. 'Excuse me, sir? Sir? Can I get you something?' He had no idea who I was or he would've been hitting me across the head and yelling at me to get up."

Matt laughed. "For all I knew, you were the son of the host or maybe some drunk donor that showed up early."

"I hadn't slept in two days," Jimmy said. "I was exhausted."

The waitress came then with our bottle of wine and Jimmy tasted it and nodded and shortly after that, our food started arriving. It was funny how Jimmy had taken control of our table and how happy we were to let him—he ordered a few more dishes and none of us suggested anything else.

It was hard to explain what it was about Jimmy that was so appealing. He wasn't the loudest person in the room—he certainly wasn't quiet, but he didn't have that obnoxious slapstick personality that some attention seekers have, when they're desperate to have all the eyes in the room on them. He did talk the most that night, but it didn't feel like he was dominating the conversation, or at least not in a way that was annoying. There was a pull about him, and I remember thinking that first night that he was magnetic, which wasn't a word I'd ever used to describe someone before. When Matt told me later that Jimmy (like him) wanted to run for office someday, I wasn't the least bit surprised. It seemed almost obvious, really.

Jimmy had done advance for the most recent campaign and for Kerry in 2004 and Gore in 2000. "Let me tell you," he said, "you think you know what depressing is, but there's nothing like working on a campaign that ends like that." I didn't know what advance was, and Jimmy explained that he traveled ahead of the President, made sure that everything was set up in the venue, from the lighting to the stage. "Down to the location of the flag," he said. "I'm basically a traveling wedding planner." He said this in a self-deprecating way that I knew was an act, but after months of listening to people brag about their jobs, I found it refreshing.

"Did you always know you wanted to do this?" I asked.

"I fell into it by accident," he said. "I met some advance people right after college, some people my dad knew, and I thought it sounded fun. And once I started, I didn't want to stop. I was supposed to start law school in the fall of '07. I was enrolled at UT, all set to go. My dad told me that enough was enough, that it was time to stop jumping on campaigns and settle into something more serious. But then I did a couple trips that summer for the Obama campaign, and I knew right away this was different. I knew as soon as I met him that I wasn't going to go to law school. My dad was so pissed."

"But now you're working at the White House," Matt said. "He must be pretty happy about that."

Jimmy shrugged, and then said lightly, "Actually, I think he'd rather have me be a lawyer."

I didn't know at the time who Jimmy's dad was,

and you wouldn't have known he was anyone special from the way Jimmy talked about him. Matt told me later that Jimmy's dad was one of the most well-known lawyers in Texas. "Probably the most well known. Famous, really," Matt said. He was also a huge Democratic supporter, and hosted lots of fund-raisers. When Jimmy talked about the advance people his dad knew, it was campaign staff who had been at his house during fund-raisers in 2000.

When we left the restaurant, we were already making plans for the four of us to go out to dinner the next week. Ash took my number and told me she was going to call me the next day. "I mean it," she said. "Don't be surprised when I call you first thing tomorrow. I am in desperate need of some girl time."

Walking home from Fourteenth Street that night, I felt hopeful. It was warm, but not sticky, and there was a nice breeze. It felt good to walk off all the drinks we'd had, and Matt and I were silent for the first few blocks. "I like them," I finally said. And I remember so clearly, how he put his arm around my shoulders, pulled me toward him, and kissed the side of my head. I could feel him smiling as he said, "I'm so glad there's something in this city that you like."

Chapter 6

True to her word, Ash called me the next day, and while I wasn't totally surprised (she had, after all, been insistent that she was going to do just that), I was pleased. After so many awkward encounters with Alan and the rest of the White House crew, it was a relief to feel like someone actually found me to be pleasant company. I'd started to doubt myself. Sometimes I think if Ash hadn't called me, hadn't pursued a friendship, I would've stopped trying to make new DC friends altogether.

The Dillons had a membership to the pool at the Hilton across the street from us, and Ash and I made plans to meet there the following Monday. I couldn't help but smile as I hung up and relayed the conversation to Matt.

"You have a date," he said, laughing just a little. But I could tell he was happy for me, that maybe he'd also been worried I wouldn't make any friends in this city.

"I know. Thank God, right?" And then I started laughing, mostly from relief, I guess.

"Just remember," Matt said, grinning. "Be yourself and don't put out on the first date."

• • •

I was ready early on Monday, and stood on the corner of Florida and T, waiting for Ash, who had texted to tell me she was on her way. It was hot and I could feel sweat sliding down my back as I stood in the sun holding my canvas bag filled with magazines, sunscreen, and a book. I wiped my upper lip, which was already wet with sweat just from standing there. I didn't understand how anyone got used to this humidity, ever.

When I finally saw Ash walking down Florida, I felt suddenly shy and held up my hand in an awkward wave, but she bounced across the street and threw her arms around my neck, giving a little squeal as she did. "I'm so glad you were free," she said. "Isn't this the most perfect day to go to the pool?"

"It is," I said. "Because it's about a hundred and twenty degrees out."

Ash just laughed. "You forget, I grew up in Houston," she said. "This is nothing to me."

We found lounge chairs and unpacked our things, laying out our towels and getting settled. The pool wasn't all that crowded—it was Monday, after all—just a few moms with young children who all seemed to know each other, and a random hotel guest or two.

Ash took a dip in the pool right away, piling her hair on top of her head and only going up to her shoulders. I did the same, and then we repositioned ourselves in the sun, the water evaporating off of our bodies almost immediately. We each took out a magazine and began paging through, chatting a little as we did.

Everything was pleasant, but it was hard for me to completely relax—I'd gone back for a third interview at DCLOVE and had a fourth the next day. It was driving me crazy the way they were dragging this out, and even though I'd been ambivalent about the job in the beginning, I now wanted it badly. (Which sometimes I thought was their whole strategy.) It felt funny to be hanging out by a pool on a day that everyone else was in an office, like it was wrong somehow. I said as much to Ash, and she made a sympathetic noise, but it was clear she didn't share my anxiety about it. She mentioned vaguely that she'd probably start looking for a job soon, but I got the feeling that money wasn't a worry, and when I pressed her as to what sort of job she might be looking for, she didn't really answer, just said that she didn't want to take a job unless it was the right fit and then changed the subject.

When I rambled on a little bit about how many résumés I'd sent out, how I wasn't sure what I'd do if I wasn't hired at DCLOVE, she laughed and waved her hand in front of her, like she thought I was being ridiculous. "Girl, you're too stressed out," she said. "Enjoy this. You'll be fine." Then she waved down an attendant and ordered us two glasses of white wine. "That'll help," she said, lying back in her chair and adjusting her sunglasses.

Our conversation was all over the place, but in a good way. We talked about our husbands and moving to DC, our families, college, *The Bachelor*, and buying swimsuits. But when I mentioned something about Alan's party, Ash snorted. "He is one of the worst human beings I've ever met," she said, and I burst out laughing. "Seriously," she continued. "The first time I met him he told me what the President's favorite snacks were, and what he prefers to eat for lunch. There is something not quite right in that boy's head."

"He makes me feel so stupid," I confessed. "When I told him I'd worked in magazines, he basically just walked away. Like it was so boring he couldn't even bother to come up with a response."

"Oh, don't I know it," she said. "He asked me if I was worried about my brain becoming weak from not working."

"Shut up. He did not."

"He absolutely did," she said, nodding. "I believe his exact words were 'Brains are like muscles.'"

"Ugh. He really is the worst."

"I know. I have no idea why Jimmy bothers with him."

"I thought the same thing about Matt. There's no way he can really like someone like that, right?"

"Stranger things happen," she said. "At least that poor boyfriend of his got away."

I'd already liked Ash, but this conversation confirmed it, made me think that we would be real friends, that I could trust her. "My thoughts exactly," I said.

We had a second glass of wine at the pool and then I went home and fell asleep on the couch in the late afternoon. It was the kind of nap where you wake up and have no idea what time or even what day it is. When I opened my eyes, Matt was sitting next to me watching the news and he gave me an amused look as I startled and sat up, confused.

"I take it your date was a success," he said.

I closed my eyes and tried to gather myself, to wake up a little, and then I stretched my arms over my head and said, "It was. It was a huge success."

The next day at DCLOVE, I met with Ellie, a lifestyle blogger and one of the founding members of the site. Her section was called "Ellie About Town," and as far as I could tell it was basically an online diary of the parties and events she went to. There were a lot of selfies involved.

She'd met me at the elevator, wearing a light blue dress that was tied with pink ribbon bows at the shoulders. Her handshake and greeting were businesslike and short, but as she led me back to her office, she rolled her eyes at the Ping-Pong table that was set up outside. "This place is crazy," she said, but I could tell she got a kick out of it, how informal and funky it all was, that she imagined DCLOVE to be the new Facebook.

"We're sort of a potpourri of information," Ellie told me. Her pitch sounded well rehearsed. "We cover parties and events but also give great restaurant reviews. We want to be the place where people go for news about the town."

"It's really great," I said. "It's entertaining but so informative."

I could tell I'd said the right thing as Ellie nodded, looking pleased. "We recently got a new investor and we want to take this site to the next level." She leaned forward and the bow on her right shoulder came partly undone. "This may have started as a labor of love, but now it's a business. There's a need for a site like ours, a hole in the market that we're filling."

At the end of that meeting, Ellie asked me to write four mock posts for the site. "Use your imagination," she said. On the way out of the office, I passed Miles, who was the first person I'd interviewed with. He was a food blogger who described what he did as "food porn on steroids," which brought unpleasant images to mind. That day, he was wearing a pocket square and colorful striped socks that were peeking out of his suit pants. He was part of a breed of guys in DC who dressed in colorful prints, aggressive plaids and checks, Vineyard Vines as far as the eye could see. Sometimes you'd see them walking down the street in groups, usually in Georgetown, all wearing the same shirt in slightly different shades of pastel. The effect was alarming and a little comical—it reminded me of how the gay men at *Vanity Fair* would dress, only louder. But then again, maybe I wasn't their target audience.

Miles was on the phone, so I just waved and smiled and tried to figure out from his expression if they were going to hire me or not, but his face was unreadable as he waved back at me.

Over the next couple of weeks, Ash and I spent almost every day together. She always had a plan of some sort—to go to a museum or take a walking tour of the monuments. She bought so many Groupons that I began to worry she had an addiction, and she dragged me along for half-price margaritas, a cruise on the Potomac, a tour of Lincoln's cottage. Jimmy was still traveling a ton, but when he was home, the four of us went out in search of the best BBQ places, tried

Ethiopian restaurants (which were a DC specialty) and new Japanese places. "This city is so international," Ash would say, sounding like a guidebook. "We need to take advantage of all it has to offer."

I hadn't expected to make a friend like Ash, someone who I clicked with so completely and quickly. I'd just been hoping for someone I could hang out with, had thought that I was past the point in my life where I'd make a friend who would eat Thai food on my couch with her shoes off, drinking wine and watching a movie while our husbands were at a work party that we didn't want to go to. But from the moment I met her we texted or talked almost every single day, and soon, I couldn't remember not knowing her. I never felt like I had to pretend to be anything else in front of her and got the feeling she felt the same way. At one point, early on in our friend-ship, she convinced me to do a juice cleanse, and we went together to buy all eighteen juices for the next three days. I was starving after the first few hours, unsure how I was going to last the whole time, but I felt like I couldn't give in so easily since it was something we were doing together. Then, at 10:00 p.m. on the first night, she sent me a text that said, *I just ate four pieces of bread,* and I laughed and wrote her back that I was just about to do the same.

· · ·

One of the posts that I did for the website was "DC's Guide for the Homesick New Yorker." I listed the one decent bagel place we'd found, a good deli, and a New York sports bar called the 51st State.

"I love it," Ellie said. "It's so sassy. Exactly what we're looking for here." She liked the other articles I'd written as well, which was a huge relief. I'd worked on them for two days straight, convinced this was my one last shot at a job. Matt found me at my computer at 3:00 a.m., and when he suggested I should get some sleep, I told him I was afraid that if I didn't get this job, I would end up working at the Pink Penguin. He just rubbed my back and went back to bed.

I accepted the job as soon as it was offered to me. Maybe I was supposed to negotiate, or at least pretend to think about it, but I was sure my desperation would give me away if I tried.

The weekend before I started at DCLOVE, I told Matt we should have a party. We were in bed, both reading, although I'd been day-dreaming mostly, my book lying open on my lap. Matt looked up from his issue of *The Atlantic* and raised his eyebrows at me, probably wondering who I was imagining inviting to this party. "A dinner party," I clarified, and he nodded.

"That could be fun," he said. "We can celebrate your new job."

"No, no. No need to celebrate. But I want something to plan. I feel restless."

"Are you nervous about starting there?" Matt turned onto his side to face me.

"Not nervous exactly. More unsure."

I'd gone to one of the pitch meetings at DCLOVE to meet the rest of the staff. Afterward, one of the writers, Maria, asked if I wanted to get coffee. We went to the Starbucks on the corner for iced coffees and I watched as she put eight packets of sugar into her cup.

"The thing to remember," she told me, "is to always come to the meetings with like thirty ideas to pitch. That way, you'll get to write about something you have some sort of interest in. If you don't, they'll start assigning things to you. Last year, I had to write about the pandas at the zoo for months. Months! Just once, I went to a meeting without a list of ideas and I ended up on the panda beat. Panda baby watch, panda birthdays, Panda Cam, pandas getting deported." She shuddered and took a long sip of her coffee. I could hear the sugar crunch between her teeth. "It's the kind of thing that will make you lose all hope in journalism. Sometimes I still have nightmares about Bao Bao."

"So who are you going to invite to this dinner party?" Matt asked that night.

"Maybe just Ash and Jimmy and Colleen and Bruce?"

"That sounds good."

"Is that weird though? Do you think they'll get along?"

"A couple of Texans and a loud Long Island girl with her elderly husband? I think they'll be great friends."

"Very funny," I said. "Beggars can't be choosers."

"You should include that in your invitation," Matt said. "You'll charm the pants right off of them."

"Call me old-fashioned, but I prefer dinner parties where everyone wears pants."

Matt laughed and then turned to me. Put his arms around my waist and rested his chin on my chest. "You are such a liar," he said. "Because I happen to know that you like it best when no one's wearing pants."

"Really?" I asked.

"Really." He kept looking right at me as he took his boxers off, then gave me a little grin before hooking his fingers in the elastic of my pajama shorts and pulling them down.

"I don't know where you'd hear such a thing," I said, as he climbed on top of me.

"Believe me," he said, kissing my neck. "I have it on good authority."

For the dinner, I decided to make Parmesan chicken over arugula with roasted tomatoes. I knew it was a mistake about ten minutes into prepping, when I realized I'd have to cook the chicken right before we were supposed to sit down. I'd spent most of the day cleaning, thinking that the dinner was so simple it would take no time at all. But before my cheese puffs even came out of the oven, the doorbell rang and all four of our guests were standing outside our door, holding bottles of wine.

The kitchen in our apartment was tiny, had almost no counter space, and was walled off from the rest of the downstairs. In our old place, when we had people over, I could chop vegetables in the open kitchen, while taking part in the conversation. Now I was stuck in the back like a servant, poking my head out when people laughed, to ask, "What's so funny?"

Ash and Colleen came into the kitchen to talk to me, but there was nowhere for them to sit, and so they stood awkwardly in the middle of the room and had to keep moving out of the way as I grabbed things from the shelves. Cooking doesn't come easily to me—I had to really concentrate on the recipe, talk out loud to make sure I was measuring correctly, and it was impossible for me to chat at the same time.

"Really, you guys. Go out in the other room," I said. "You don't need to keep me company, I'll be out in a minute." The oven was making the kitchen hot, so in addition to being flustered, I was also starting to get sweaty.

"Oh, we don't mind," Ash said. She leaned against the counter. "We're happy to keep you company."

She was blocking the area where I was planning to bread the chicken cutlets and I had to reach around her to grab my bowl of flour. Colleen was standing right in the middle of the kitchen, slowly turning around to take it all in. "I can't believe they haven't updated this," she said.

I went to place the flour next to the stove, but tripped and spilled a little bit. I could hear Bruce laughing in the other room, loudly, saying something about golf. "Let's just—you know what? Let's go have a drink and some appetizers and I'll come back in a few minutes to get the rest of it done," I said and headed into the living room before they could argue.

Matt turned around, looking grateful to see us coming. "We're going to take a break from the kitchen," I told him.

"That sounds great. Can I help in there?" I shook my head. Matt was always happy to help, but he wasn't any more gifted at cooking than I was. I took a glass of wine and sat on the floor. Colleen squeezed onto the couch next to Bruce, forcing him to shift over a little bit. As he did, he exhaled loudly. He always made a lot of noise—groaning when he moved, slurping when he drank. It's possible they had something to do with his age, all the sounds he made. I tried to be gracious and ignore it, but a lot of the time, I felt like asking, "Everything okay?" when he squeaked and moaned.

Ash plopped herself on the floor next to me and grabbed a cheese puff. I took one too and popped it in my mouth, already filled with regret that I'd decided to have a dinner party.

"So, Jimmy," Colleen said. "What is it that you do?" She leaned forward, as if she couldn't wait to hear his answer, in what we called her Barbara Walters pose.

"I'm the director of the White House travel office," Jimmy said.

"And what does that entail, exactly?" she asked. I could tell that Colleen thought Jimmy was attractive from the way she kept raising her eyebrows. In college, we could always tell she liked a guy when she started resembling Jack Nicholson.

Jimmy answered her question, and she came back with three more. Ash and I swiveled our heads back and forth between them, like we were watching a tennis match. Colleen had come right from work and she was wearing a sleeveless red dress with a split at the neckline. She got her hair blown out each morning, and it was always shiny and smooth. Her makeup was done for the camera and looked a little heavy in real life, but she never wiped any of it off before going out. Either she didn't notice how caked on it looked in regular light or she didn't care. She sat up straight and focused on Jimmy, as if she really were interviewing him. Bruce leaned back on the couch and half closed his eyes. Matt got up to refill drinks, and when he returned, Colleen was asking Jimmy where he saw his career going.

"Give the guy a chance to catch his breath," Matt said lightly, as he handed them both a drink.

"I'm a reporter, Dogpants. I can't help it. And it sounds like an amazing job."

"It does," Matt said. I could tell he was deciding whether or not to say more. "Ask him about riding on Air Force One."

Matt was pretty fascinated with Jimmy's job—and to be honest, with Jimmy himself. He often came home and told me different things that he'd heard about Jimmy from other people—it was the closest Matt ever came to gossiping, although I would never have called it that because there wasn't any ill will behind it. He told me people talked a lot about how surprised they were that Jimmy was hired as the travel director. I thought Jimmy was exaggerating when he'd described his career in advance as accidental, but it turned out he wasn't. "It doesn't sound like he worked all that hard," Matt said to me. "I mean, on the campaigns, sure, he worked hard and did a great job. But in between he kind of just hung out. He had all these chunks of time where he wasn't working at all, and from what I hear, it didn't sound like he was all that concerned about finding a job. I think he really just kept doing it because he thought it was fun."

After the election, Jimmy was offered the travel director job and he'd taken it, but the interesting part was he hadn't been pursuing anything—they went after him. "People just really like him," Matt said. "They wanted him in the office."

I think part of the reason Matt was so interested in Jimmy was that they were so different. Matt was the hardest-working person I knew—he'd had a job from the time he was thirteen and started caddying. He cried when he got a B in sixth-grade science class, worried it would keep him from getting into Harvard. Jimmy was good at what he did, but made no secret of the fact that he didn't especially like to work hard. Matt had wanted to run for office since he was in second grade, and it seemed like Jimmy had just recently looked around and thought, Well, that could be fun. I could almost guarantee that Jimmy hadn't stopped himself from smoking pot (or doing anything else) in college because he was worried about his future political career.

The idea of running for office seemed to be something he just stumbled across and decided to entertain.

Matt was currently a little bored at his job and he liked talking about Jimmy's experiences, which were, without a doubt, more exciting than his own. Matt even enjoyed having Jimmy describe how he packed for trips—he traveled so often that he was basically a professional packer, and he'd shown us one time how fast he could pack for a weeklong trip: laying out his suits and ties in under a minute, rolling his socks with precision, wrapping the hangers on his hanging bag with gaffe tape to keep them from shifting. Matt asked him so many questions about riding on Air Force One that Jimmy swiped a couple of coasters from the plane to give to him. Whenever Matt used them, I could see his eyes turn green.

When Matt was first offered the position of associate counsel, he was thrilled. But it wasn't quite what he expected. The rest of the associate counsels were younger than he was, which I know bothered him. Most of what he did was background checks on prospective hires, and he said in a lot of ways it was just as tedious as when he'd worked at the law firm, that he missed the excitement of the campaign.

"Well, you can't really compare them," I said. "No job will ever live up to the campaign."

"No," he said, sadly, "I guess it won't."

Matt had even begun to think about what he wanted to do next, talking to people about different opportunities. This seemed a little crazy to me, since he'd just started his job, but I didn't know then that this was just part of DC, that everyone was always looking ahead to the next step, peeking around to see what other people were doing, calculating the next move.

Every time I started to get up to go back to the kitchen, Ash would say, "Oh, just stay a few more minutes! We're still filling up on the puffs." Maybe she was trying to be friendly, or maybe she didn't want to be left alone with Colleen, who was still grilling Jimmy. After a while, I didn't even move when I said, "I should start the chicken."

What we learned that night was that Jimmy was from Texas, but also sort of wasn't. "I was born there," he said, when Colleen pressed him. "In Houston. And I lived there until I was about eight and then we moved to a few different places before moving back."

"Where?" Colleen asked.

"Well, we were in New York for a year and then we went to London because my dad opened up a branch of the firm out there. But we always kept the ranch in Johnson City and spent Thanksgiving and Christmas there each year. And then we moved back to Houston when I was in high school and my parents are still there."

"So you went to high school in Houston?"

"No, I went to Choate."

"Jesus Christ." Colleen laughed. "You realize you're basically W, right? You're from Texas, but you're not really from Texas."

"I'm from Texas," Jimmy said. For a second, I saw his eyes flicker with annoyance, but then he smiled. "Once you're born there, that's it. Texas forever."

"How very *Friday Night Lights* of you," Colleen said. She looked at him for a second, but then she decided to drop it and smiled too. "Speaking of which, if you ever run into Tim Riggins, call me immediately."

You shouldn't have a dinner party and not feed your guests for the first three hours. Lesson learned. By the time I went to the kitchen to cook the chicken, I'd lost count of how many drinks I'd had. I stood in front of the stove and closed one eye to concentrate and stop the pan from moving. I wondered if this ever happened to Ina Garten while she was waiting for Jeffrey to come home and decided it definitely did.

We ran out of vodka, so Matt went to the liquor store across the street to get a new bottle. I was a little appalled we'd gone through the whole thing, but Colleen kept saying, "Relax, it's Friday night." Matt came back to find me standing over the stove with one eye closed, and put his arm around my waist and kissed my neck, which is how I knew he was drunk too. I don't have the faintest idea of what dinner tasted like. The last thing I remember is hugging Colleen good-bye, while we told each other how happy we were to be living in the same city again. Bruce was standing by the door, getting impatient, and he said, "Look at you two, you look like a couple of lesbians," which made me realize he was also the kind of person who would get racist after a bottle of wine.

The next morning, I was drinking coffee and feeling out my hangover when Colleen called to talk about the dinner.

"What's Jimmy's deal?" she asked. "He's so on all the time. I kept wanting to tell him to relax."

"I like him," I said.

"No, he's nice. It's just . . . there's something about him, you know? Like his whole, 'I'm a Texan' thing. It feels a little over the top. He said something about a talking coon in a tree last night. Like, okay, we get it. You're super-Texan."

I tried not to laugh. What Jimmy had said was, "She could talk a coon out of a tree," and he'd been referring to Colleen, who was going on and on about all the problems she saw with the healthcare law, talking over anyone who tried to interject.

"And her? Beth, she's so weird. She seems like the kind of person who would be in a crafting group or really into scrapbooking or something like that. When you were in the kitchen, she told me how happy and blessed she was to have met you, and then she said, 'Praise God.'"

"Yeah, she's really religious," I said.

"Normal religious or religious like she's in a cult? I'm guessing the cult."

"Okay, I get your point. You didn't like her, but remember you didn't like me at first either." Colleen and I were freshman-year roommates, but she barely paid any attention to me for the first month of school. She came to school knowing a few people from Long Island, and always had parties and bars to go to (she had a fake ID, I did not) and she never invited me. It wasn't until she threw up in her bed one night, after returning home drunk, and I helped her that she even talked to me. I had to prop her up and change her sheets and she was disobedient and annoying, and I told her she was disgusting. The next morning, I woke up to her eating Cheerios on her bed (Colleen never got hungover), and she smiled at me. "You told me I was like a pig in slop last night," she said. "You were," I told her, and she laughed. "You're funny," she said, and after that we were somehow unexpectedly friends.

On the other end of the phone, Colleen sniffed. "That's not true, I just didn't know you. You barely talked when we first met. And even then, I knew you weren't a total freak."

"I'm just saying, first impressions aren't everything. She's nice. And she's been a good friend to me here."

"Whatever," Colleen said. "I'm telling you, something about them is weird." But then she changed the subject and we talked about another friend of ours from college who'd just broken up with her boyfriend. "I knew he was a creep all along," she said. "Remember when he offered to buy her a Burberry scarf if she lost ten pounds?"

When we finally hung up, I poured myself more coffee and settled back on the couch. I wasn't all that surprised that Colleen didn't like Ash, and I wasn't going to push for the two of them to be friends. We didn't need to keep having them at the same dinner parties. Sometimes friends of friends just plain don't like each other, and there's nothing you can do about it.

Ash refrained from saying much about Colleen for a while, but sometimes she'd bring up Colleen and Bruce and ask me what I thought it was like to have sex with someone so old and wrinkled.

I never told Colleen that she'd guessed right, that a lot of the things she'd said about Ash were pretty close to the truth. Ash was Evangelical, and often referred to the time when she was "saved." Once, I went to church with her because she invited me and we were new friends and it seemed rude to turn her down. Her church was in a theater with a live band and a screen that dropped down for the sermon. There were padded chairs and stadium-style seating, and people sang and clapped and murmured "Amen," and said, "Mmmm-hmmm," loudly, when they agreed with something. As a Catholic, used to kneeling and subdued chanting, I felt wildly uncomfortable with all this, which Ash must have guessed because she never asked me to go to church with her again.

Colleen was right about the crafting too. Ash wasn't a scrapbooker, but she was a stamper, something I didn't know existed before I met her. She had hundreds of stamps, which she kept in a small room in their apartment. She used them on letters, and made her own wrapping paper and cards. After that dinner party, she'd sent a card made on thick white paper, with THANK YOU stamped out, each letter in a different color. There were a bunch of bumblebees on the card, little trails of dots behind them.

Ash and I were friends, but we were also so different. There were things she said that would have bothered me if she was anyone else, hobbies she had that I would normally find ridiculous. She was a grown woman who called her father

Daddy. She was unlike any friend I'd ever had, and sometimes I couldn't believe we got along like we did. There were certain things that we just didn't talk about, because I think we both knew it would bring our differences to the surface, afraid that if we examined things too closely, we'd see that we weren't really meant to be such great friends after all.

But it didn't matter, really. For all the ways that we were different, it was our husbands who brought us together, who made us the same. We had them in common, and they were both chasing after something that neither of us totally understood. Only Ash knew how it felt to be bound to someone like that.

When I opened the envelope with Ash's thank-you note after that dinner party, my first urge was to laugh (which I did later when I showed it to Matt). I pictured Ash carefully picking out colors, biting her bottom lip as she concentrated on stamping out the words. I hung it on the refrigerator, because I didn't know what else to do with it—maybe because it was handmade, or maybe because I felt guilty for making fun of it, I could never bring myself to take it down. It stayed there for the rest of the time we lived in DC.

Washington, DC
2010

If you want a friend in Washington, get a dog.
—HARRY TRUMAN

Chapter 7

Because Jimmy was part of the advance team that staffed Obama, he and Ash spent Christmas and New Year's in Hawaii. They were there for almost three weeks, during which time Ash posted daily pictures on Facebook of her polished toes in the sand, of piña coladas in the middle of the day, of Coronas in front of the ocean. In the meantime, Matt and I spent Christmas in Wisconsin eating lasagna with my parents while we listened to my aunt Bit (who watched a lot of Fox News) go on and on about death panels until my mom insisted that we change the subject.

There had been a brief moment in November when Matt tried to convince me that we should also go to Hawaii, saying that Jimmy thought he could get Matt a spot on the advance team. "The DCOS owes him a favor and they still need someone to do airport." (Matt pronounced this "Dee-kos," and I stared at him for a second, wondering if he was speaking in a different language or if I was having a stroke.)

"The who?" I asked. "The what?"

"The deputy chief of staff. Billy. You've met him, right? That's what everyone calls him. The DCOS."

"Oh, right," I said, like this made any sense to me. "But you don't even do advance."

Matt looked so hopeful as he said, "But I could."

It wasn't that Hawaii didn't sound great (because obviously it did), but I couldn't bear the thought of canceling on my parents, of leaving them to celebrate alone. I already felt guilty enough that we had to alternate holidays with the Kellys—it seemed unfair because there were so many more of them and just the two of my parents. So we went to Wisconsin, which was nice and quiet as it always was. Matt didn't mention Hawaii again (he understood why I couldn't go), but I could tell that when we were sitting around the table talking with my parents about their cat, Snickers, or their bridge club he was thinking about it. My parents read a lot, watched several light mystery shows, and (if it was nice enough) went for daily walks—and so when we were with them, we did all of the same things, which I found sort of relaxing and was pretty sure that Matt found suffocating.

And Ash's pictures kept popping up: a plate of French toast with the ocean in the background and a caption, "Breakfast with a view at the Surfrider!"; a picture of turtles about to be released into the ocean; a tower of sushi at Morimoto. I couldn't mention them to Matt because I was the one who'd insisted we go to Wisconsin. And so I sat and shivered under a blanket in my parents' house and flipped through Ash's beach pictures, each one making me slightly crankier than the last.

We were back to DC for New Year's and went to a party with all of the White House people we always saw—minus Ash and Jimmy, who were still in Hawaii, which made the whole night pretty boring. I figured we could leave right after midnight and I counted down the minutes until then. But as the ball dropped on the TV, Matt kissed me and said, "Happy New Year's to my favorite wife," and I thought how sweet he was, how he'd been in Wisconsin with me when he really wanted to be in Hawaii. So I smiled and stayed at the party with him until 3:00 a.m.

Ash called me the day they finally returned and I almost squealed on the phone when I heard her voice. "I feel like you guys have been gone forever," I said.

"I know it," she said. "It's good to be back."

We made plans to meet for dinner at La Tomate, an Italian place at the top of Dupont, and when we walked into the restaurant, Ash and Jimmy were already there, both so absurdly tan that it made me dizzy to look at them straight on. They stood to greet us, all of us embracing like we'd been apart for years. When we finally sat down, I turned to them and said, "So, clearly you spent some time in the sun. How was it?"

Jimmy got a serious look on his face and said,

"You know, this was a different kind of trip. Normally we're advancing the President for meetings with officials, for speeches, for official visits. But this was advancing him for a vacation—figuring out where he's going to eat dinner and play golf. And usually, we didn't know what he was going to do until the night before. You know, sometimes he'd want to play golf and then would decide at the last second to do a beach day with the family."

"Wow," I said. I was already regretting asking about the trip because Matt was so jealous he was practically shaking.

"I know," Jimmy said. "It was a whole new spin on what we do on regular trips."

"That's crazy," Matt said. "It must have been hard to adjust to that."

"It was," Jimmy said, looking so intense that I wanted to roll my eyes. "I mean, look, don't get me wrong—we were in paradise, so I'm not complaining. It was just a different kind of job to advance the gym for him each morning. Can you believe he works out every single morning on vacation? His discipline is amazing."

"Totally," Matt said, and Ash made a sound of agreement.

"And the Secret Service has a tough job there too," he went on. "Basically everything is an OTR stop." (At this point, Matt turned to me and whispered, "Off the record," so that I could understand the conversation, but Jimmy didn't even pause.) "He walks down the street to get shave ice and people just go crazy. We tell a restaurant about twenty minutes before he's going to get there—the reservation is under a different name—and then they have to get in there and start magging people—you know, checking them with the handheld metal detectors. There's so much work that goes into just one outing."

The two of them started talking about how the team managed to get reservations for so many people at such great restaurants, and then Ash turned to me. "Have you ever had shave ice?" she asked. "It's so delicious."

"It's like a sno-cone, right?" I asked.

"Yes, but so much better," she said.

"I'll have to try it sometime."

"Oh you do! You two have got to go to Hawaii. It really is just the most beautiful place I've ever been."

"So what did you do all day while Jimmy was working?" I asked. It wasn't that I wanted to keep talking about the trip, but I sensed that there was no getting away from it, so I just gave in.

"Oh, sometimes I lounged around the hotel—the press pool stayed there too, so there were other spouses and family around and we all just got to be so friendly with each other. And then sometimes I'd tag along with Jimmy if the first family was doing something fun, like the beach or something. I'd just tuck myself to the side and enjoy it."

"That sounds great," I said.

"You know"—Ash looked thoughtful—"I just really admire Obama so much. He's very real. Do you know what I mean? He was always aware of how hard everyone was working for him, always thanking everyone. And when we would all be on the beach—and I mean, the staff wouldn't be right next to the family, because my goodness, they need their space and privacy— but he'd always walk down to say hi to us, always take the time to ask us how we were enjoying Hawaii."

All I could think when Ash told this story was how annoying it must be for Obama to have to always be on—to make sure he remembered to thank everyone, to take the time to say hi to the families of his staff, when he'd probably rather just sit and relax with his own family on the beach. I mean, yes, he's the President and that's part of the job and he got to spend an amazing time in Hawaii, so it's not like I felt bad for him. Except I kind of did. It must be exhausting to always be that pleasant, to always be watched. I couldn't help but wonder who would want that kind of life, and then I looked over at Jimmy, his eyes gleaming as he talked about the trip, and I had my answer.

The stories went on and on for the rest of the

night: The President made fun of Jimmy's golf shirt! He wore flip-flops the whole time! (This really seemed to excite everyone, but I guess it is rare to say you saw the President's toes.) They went snorkeling at Hanauma Bay! Everyone bought surfboards to take home! Obama gave the shaka sign to locals!

The waiter came over to ask if we wanted anything else and I shook my head no, started to say we were probably just ready for the check, but before I could get the words out, everyone else said dessert sounded great. (So it seemed I was the only one who wanted to end our dinner early.) Ash ordered ice cream and Jimmy and Matt both got tiramisu and I ordered nothing because I thought it would seem weird after I'd already said I didn't want anything.

Jimmy was still talking as the waiter brought over the desserts. "His best friend there is the greatest guy," he said. "I mean all of his friends that came with were great—like a family really. And you can just tell what a solid person he is that he has this amazing group of friends, and that he's had them for years."

I had to look away as Jimmy said this, because it was hard to sit there and listen to Jimmy dissect the President's character, like his opinion was important. The man had won the presidency, for Christ's sake. He didn't need the approval of some random guy in his advance office.

"But this guy, his friend that still lives in Hawaii," Jimmy continued, "he has this amazing place on the North Shore and he threw this luau and invited the whole staff and we just, like, hung out. We played volleyball against the President and his friends, and after I made a great save, he started chanting my name." Jimmy paused to smile here and tried his best to look embarrassed, but didn't even come close.

Ash joined in then, telling me about Michelle's swimsuit and how lovely she was. This maybe bothered me more than anything because it was the one thing that made me jealous. I'd always had the feeling that Michelle and I would've gotten along. I secretly thought of her like a pretend celebrity friend, which may have been a little pathetic, but still—she would definitely like me more than she liked Ash. We had way more in common.

This was the first time we'd hung out with the Dillons when I couldn't wait for the night to end. I could see Matt thinking about how he'd spent Christmas listening to my crazy aunt Bit and popping Benadryl because he was extremely allergic to Snickers, while Jimmy and Ash had been holding hands with Obama and all running into the ocean together to bodysurf as a happy group. (Or at least that's what they were making it sound like.)

"He was so relaxed there," Jimmy said. "Which

was just really great to see." He sighed like he was one of Obama's besties and had been worried deeply about his stress levels.

Finally (finally!) we paid the check and left the restaurant. As soon as Jimmy and Ash jumped in a cab and we were alone on the sidewalk, I said to Matt, "You know, Jimmy makes it sound like they were all just hanging out in Hawaii together, like they were on a group vacation instead of being there to work."

"It did sound pretty fun," Matt said. He looked miserable. We started walking the few blocks back to our apartment, not talking much. I was worried that Jimmy was turning into Alan, that he was soon going to be incapable of having a discussion that didn't revolve around the President. And if that was the case, it was going to be a long winter.

It wasn't a coincidence that right after our dinner with the Dillons, Matt decided his New Year's resolution would be to start looking for a new job. The counsel's office wasn't what he'd thought it would be and he told me he was mostly worried that he wasn't visible enough. "What does that mean?" I asked.

"I just don't think this is setting me up for any sort of run. It feels like I could still be working for the firm in New York, just sitting in a room and doing busywork."

"Well, what do you think you want to do?" I asked. I felt for Matt in these moments. He was so clearly frustrated at how slowly things were moving in his career and I wanted him to succeed—not because I especially cared about it, but because I knew that's what would make him happy.

"I don't really know," he said. "It's not just about my résumé. I mean, part of it is. I just don't feel like I'm getting the right experience. But that's not all. Jimmy meets so many people, he gets face time with the President and the senior staff. Everyone knows him, everyone likes him. When he decides to run for office, he's going to have that support, people to ask for advice to help him out. No one even knows who I am."

"That's not true," I said, but my heart hurt just a little because I could tell he believed what he said.

In February, Snowmageddon (or Snowpocalypse, if you preferred) hit the East Coast. DC was in a panic and you couldn't turn on the news without hearing the weather people screaming about the snow that was coming. I was pretty sure everyone was overreacting (even Obama had publicly mocked DC for its wimpy attitude toward snow after it shut down schools for a light flurry earlier that winter), but I also thought it was better to be safe than sorry, so I went to gather some supplies the day before the storm. Of course, I went to the Soviet Safeway and found that the shelves were empty and people were waiting ten deep at the registers with overflowing carts. I walked up and down the aisles, just to make sure I wasn't missing anything, and finally grabbed the last bag of cheddar Goldfish and a package of Oreos that were haphazardly shoved on a shelf with paper towels and figured we'd have to make do.

"People are really freaking out," I said that night. Everyone had been sent home early from work and school so that they could hunker down and wait for the snow, which was what we were doing too.

"It sounds like it might be really bad," Matt said.

"DC is so weird about snow," I said. "This storm probably won't even happen. All this worry will be for nothing."

But when we woke up the next morning, it wasn't nothing. It was actually a pretty sizable amount of snow and it continued to come down through the weekend. Sunday night, Matt got an e-mail that the government would be closed, and immediately after, I got the same e-mail from DCLOVE. (That was how DC worked—once the government made a call about the weather, everyone followed.)

And it kept snowing all Tuesday and Wednesday, and even I was shocked at how much piled up outside. The whole world was white. "It feels like *The Shining* in here," I said to Matt, and he replied, "That makes me sort of nervous to be housebound with you."

I thought maybe this break would be good for Matt. He'd been so stressed about finding a new job that maybe a few days off would be relaxing, but he just seemed antsy. We were both doing a little bit of work—I covered a snowball fight between Georgetown and GW, and Matt answered some e-mails. But after a few days we were bored of sitting in front of the fire and had gone through everything on our DVR.

Our firewood was running low and our food supply was even more pathetic than usual. On Monday and Tuesday, Matt had gone to get us sandwiches at Dupont Market, which was one of the only places that was open. By Wednesday, I couldn't stomach the thought of another one, so I made tomato soup from a can and threw some Goldfish on top. Matt poked at the little crackers as they floated around. "It's storm food," I told him. He gave me a skeptical look and went back to dunking the Goldfish with his spoon, letting them bob back to the surface.

My phone rang then and I grabbed it, happy for the distraction. It was Ash, calling to invite us over. "I know it's a beast out there," she said. "But I've got chili on the stove and Jimmy's about to start drinking whiskey. Get over here and save me!"

I watched Matt playing with his crackers and answered quickly, "We'll be over soon."

We walked to the Dillons' because there were almost no cabs out and the ones that were around had no idea how to drive in the snow. No one did. Cars crept down the street at fifteen miles an hour, fishtailing until they landed with soft thuds against the huge piles of snow.

None of the sidewalks were shoveled, so we walked in the middle of the street. It felt like we were in a ski town.

"It's kind of pretty," Matt said. We watched a man spin his wheels as he tried to get out of his parking spot.

"In Wisconsin, this would already be plowed."

"In Wisconsin, this is just a dusting."

"Very funny," I said. We put our heads down against the wind and kept walking, listening to our breath and the crunch under our feet.

The Dillons lived in a gated community in Adams Morgan called Beekman Place, which was a development of town houses surrounded by a large stone wall that used to protect a castle. To get inside, you had to stop at a gate out front and have a security guard buzz you in. It didn't feel at all like DC in there; it was more like a tiny secret suburb hidden in the middle of the city.

They'd started renting their town house from a woman in the State Department who was out of the country on assignment. But shortly after they moved in, the woman put it up for sale and they decided to buy it. "We just love it here," Ash said. "It feels safer than the rest of the city." She whispered this last part, as if she didn't want anyone in DC to be insulted that she found parts of the city dangerous.

At first, the Dillons' place looked similar to ours and that of every other thirtysomething couple we knew—Pottery Barn–esque carpeting and furniture, with some random flea market bookshelf and one expensive chair that you got as an investment piece, but didn't really want anyone to sit in. But when you looked closer, you noticed that the Dillons' furniture had a little more heft and their rugs weren't the same mass-produced familiar patterns you saw in other apartments, but were actual Orientals. Ash told me that the furniture had been handed down from both families, but that she'd had to re-cover everything Jimmy's parents gave them. "It's some beautiful furniture," she said. "But good glory does his mother love ugly fabric."

It was always nice to spend time at their place, although when I returned home, our apartment seemed flimsier in comparison. I could almost feel the couch bending when I sat on it.

By the time we got there, I was excited to wait out the blizzard with the Dillons. We'd barely knocked when Ash answered the door wearing dark jeans and a low-cut red blouse with ruffles along the neck. She was barefoot and had on more makeup than I wore on my wedding day. (Ash was never without makeup, which fascinated me. She called it putting on her face and she did it every morning. Even if she was alone in the house, she had mascara and eyeliner on. At night, she'd smear Pond's cold cream all over her face, letting it sit a minute before wiping it off, and the smell always lingered on her.)

I'd worn a long sweater, leggings, and huge rubber boots to make it through the snow. My hair was in a ponytail and I barely had any makeup on. Suddenly, I felt underdressed for Snowmageddon.

"I loved your snowball fight story," Ash said without bothering to say hello. Ash commented on my blog posts more than anyone. Her screen name was sparklycowgirl, and I was always worried that people thought she was some sort of stripper. She was the only person (besides my mom) who read every single thing I wrote for the website. Not even Matt kept up with it all. Her comments on my stories ranged from "Girl, you're so right about this!" to "LOL, I'm dying" to "We need to get drinks here ASAP!" It was so obvious from what she wrote that she was a friend of mine, and I was half afraid Ellie was going to say something to me about it. But I didn't have the heart to tell her to stop.

Ash was holding a drink as she ushered us in the door. As we stamped the snow off our feet, I could hear voices coming from the other room.

"Who's here?" I asked.

"Oh, we just invited a few people. We were going stir crazy."

There were about fifteen people at the Dillons', which made it feel like a full-blown party. Alan Chu was in the corner talking to a guy named Benji, who was the assistant to the President's chief of staff. (Everyone called him Donna, because he had the same job as Donna did on *The West Wing*.) He was a likable twenty-five-year-old, who was petite with dusty blond hair and freckles and looked no older than fifteen. He was always cheerful and had nicknames for everyone—he called Matt "Mr. Kelly," and Jimmy "the Ambassador." He and Alan were the most unlikely friends—they were ten years apart and Benji was adorable while Alan was horrendous—but apparently they honestly enjoyed each other's company. I'd commented on their friendship once, how strange their pairing seemed, and Matt had just shrugged. "Politics makes strange bedfellows," he'd said. "But Benji's not gay," I'd said, and Matt had laughed for about twenty minutes straight.

The two of them were talking to Lissy, the White House receptionist. She was a pretty girl from Arkansas who had a constant smile on her face, which I guessed must be a requirement for the job. Everyone called her ROTUS (short for Receptionist of the United States), and she seemed to be okay with this nickname, but it always made me think of a strange shape of pasta. Lissy's best friend, Cameron, was across the room talking to some guy I didn't know. Cameron was whip-smart and worked in the communications office. She also rarely smiled and scared me just a little bit, so maybe Matt was right about the strange bedfellows.

Billy (the DCOS) was there too, and was standing next to Jimmy at the bar. Jimmy (who loved to make signature cocktails) was mixing up a pitcher of Frostbites. I didn't know what was in them other than peppermint schnapps, but I did know that I felt warm and dizzy after my first one. The snow made everyone feel festive, gave them permission to act a little crazy. "Have another drink," people kept saying. "It's blizzard season."

Ash and Jimmy were great entertainers, happiest when everyone around them was eating and drinking. They were unconcerned with people spilling drinks or recipes turning out perfectly. Unlike me, who felt pressure to have everything in perfect order before a party, they were always inviting people over last minute. Ash's cooking was reminiscent of another time. She fried things in Crisco ("Butter doesn't give it that same oomph," she explained to me) and served dips made with sour cream, mayonnaise, cream cheese, and dried soup mixes. She loved casseroles of any kind, was always using her slow cooker, and was unapologetic about her Jell-O salads and spaghetti pie and snickerdoodles.

That day, they'd set up a chili bar on their dining room table. The chili was in a chafing dish with bowls of toppings all around—cheese, onions, Fritos, oyster crackers, sour cream, chopped tomatoes. Whenever people felt like it, they'd grab a bowl and eat wherever there was room, standing by the fireplace or sitting on the couch. I watched nervously, waiting for someone to spill a hunk of chili on the beautiful rug, which made me feel silly because neither of them seemed to care.

Everyone loved being at the Dillons' house, and truly, their parties were always the most fun. I remember once watching Ash drop a bottle of red wine in the kitchen, everyone standing paralyzed as the wine went everywhere. I would have been mortified—at most people's homes this would be an incident that could ruin the night, but they just looked at each other across the room, and Jimmy started laughing. "I think the little lady might need to be cut off," he said. As they mopped everything up with mountains of paper towels that turned red, Ash said, "Good Lord, it looks like a murder scene in here!" And then the party continued.

● ● ●

Ash and I spent most of the blizzard party sitting on the corner of the couch and chatting. Alan came over once to say hello to us, perching on the arm of the couch. I think he knew that we disliked him and felt he should give a little effort. (Or maybe he felt sorry for us because we were only talking to each other and thought he'd take pity on us.)

"Beth, hello," he said. He was always awkward. Whenever I tried to hug him hello, he stiffened as though I were trying to make out with him, so eventually I just stopped.

"How are you?" I asked.

"Good, good," he said. "Busy, of course. The boss doesn't rest, but you know that! And how are you? What are you up to these days?"

"You mean, like jobwise?" I said, and he nodded. "I'm still at DCLOVE."

Alan tilted his head at me and then said, as though he just remembered, "Oh, that website?"

"That's the one," I said.

"She's their star writer," Ash said, leaning over to pat my leg. "You should be careful, Alan. She may write an exposé on you!"

The two of us laughed, but Alan just looked uncomfortable and scooted away, which made us laugh even more.

Ash had spent the last weekend of January in Puerto Rico with her high school girlfriends for a bachelorette party. "I am telling you, it's nice to just be home," she said. "I'm exhausted from all the sun I've gotten this winter!" That Ash could say these things to me with complete seriousness was maybe the greatest proof—along with the album that held the pictures of her as a debutante at her coming-out party, which I often pulled off the shelf to look at when we were there—that she was a true southern belle.

Matt was in a great mood, and I was happy to see him enjoying himself, laughing loudly and gesturing to Megan, the President's personal aide, about something. I wondered how many Frostbites he'd had—he came over at one point to say hi to me and smelled minty as he leaned down for a kiss. I thought maybe I should get him a glass of water, suggest he slow down, but then I looked around at everyone else, and decided there was no reason to worry. Everyone was getting a little sloppy. In the corner, I could see Benji making out with Lissy, and it was clear that the two of them were so drunk they believed themselves to be invisible. Every so often, someone raised a glass and yelled, "Snowmageddon," and the rest of the party would cheer and raise their own glasses in response, echoing back, "Snowmageddon!" and then drink.

When I was at parties like this, I'd often take a minute and sit back and think, These people all work at the White House. It happened to me a lot during those eight years. And I don't mean that I sat back and was impressed by this. (Although of course it was impressive to work at the White House.) It was more that it was shocking to think that these normal, often overserved, people were important to the country. It was strange to think that they had the same relationship problems everyone else did, beyond weird to watch one of the speechwriters drink fifteen eggnogs at the White House Christmas party and then throw up on the sidewalk outside.

As the night went on, I was aware of people congratulating Jimmy, who was holding court by the bar. (This was another thing I started to notice about Jimmy—how when we were out or at a party, he didn't have to move around the room. He stayed in one place and let people come over to him, which they always did.) At first I thought maybe I'd imagined it, but then I heard Alan say, "This is such a great opportunity for you," and I turned to Ash and asked her what he was talking about.

"Oh, Jimmy got a new job," she said, rolling her eyes and shaking her head like it wasn't even worth talking about. "Still in the White House, just doing some different things." Jimmy's new title was Deputy Director of the White House Office of Political Strategy and Outreach, which Ash told me only after I asked specifically. We'd been talking for hours and she hadn't so much as mentioned it.

"What does that mean?" I asked.

"Who knows?" she answered.

Matt seemed to sober up on our walk home. We weren't the last to leave the party, but we were pretty close. It was just so cold and dark outside, so we kept having one more drink, and I started to think we were going to have to spend the night until finally, a little after 1:00 a.m., we put our coats on and left.

"I can't believe Jimmy got that job," Matt said. "He didn't mention anything about it before tonight."

The air was frigid and damp, and I moved my fingers around in my gloves to try to warm them up. "We haven't seen them much," I said. "Maybe he just didn't get a chance." But from Ash's evasiveness, I had a feeling there was more to it.

"Yeah, but I mean, you think he would've e-mailed me or something. It's a huge job. It's like he was keeping it from me."

"Really?"

"I don't know," he said. "Maybe not."

"Why would he do that?"

"I don't know," Matt said again, but this time he sounded irritated. "I mean, to be honest, it's a job I would've loved. One that I'm probably better suited for than he is. And he knows I'm looking for a new position—I've been asking him for advice. I didn't even know David was leaving or I might have pursued it."

"He probably didn't know that," I said.

"Maybe. Probably not," Matt said, although he didn't sound sure.

We walked the rest of the way home without talking, just watching our breath become little white puffs in the air. It was quiet, like the city was empty or everyone was already asleep. This wasn't the case—later, when DCLOVE did a special post on all of the couples who met during the blizzard, I realized that there must have been parties in every apartment we passed. We weren't the only ones celebrating the snow. But that night, it felt like we were the only people left in DC.

That was the only time Matt acknowledged that he was upset about what happened with Jimmy's job. Maybe he was embarrassed that he'd accused Jimmy of being sneaky or maybe he figured it just wasn't worth it. Whatever it was, from that point on he went out of his way to be enthusiastic about Jimmy's new position.

But at home, when it was just us, he talked more often about needing a new job, almost like it was a dire situation, like he wouldn't survive in the counsel's office much longer. And there were times when Jimmy would tell us about a trip he'd just taken and Matt would stiffen next to me—just for a second—and I had no doubt that he thought he deserved Jimmy's job, that he believed he could do it better.

Matt's jealousy no longer surprised me. I'd figured out that DC was a city that was crammed full of jealousy, that there was, in fact, a hierarchy of jealousy among the people we spent time with. Matt was jealous of Jimmy, who was jealous of Alan, because he got to spend every single minute with the President, got a Christmas present from him, got to walk alongside him in the West Wing. And Alan was jealous of Drew, who was the trip director and also one of Obama's favorite golf partners because he was such a great player. (Rumor had it that Alan played golf once with the President and was so bad that he stopped on the third hole after almost hitting Obama with a ball after a wild swing. He was so ashamed of this that no one ever mocked him, never made one joke about it, which was very telling. This was a group that taunted and made fun of each other with a sibling-like viciousness.) And almost everyone was jealous of Pete, a cranky thirty-something who worked in the speechwriting office, who the President found hilarious and who was always asked to play Hearts with him on Air Force One.

The only person who didn't seem to be jealous of anyone was Drew, who was happy to golf with the President, was friendly to every person he met, helped anyone who asked him to, was always pleasant and kind, and truly just didn't seem to give a shit about any of the rest of it. But he was an anomaly.

It wasn't that I didn't understand it, this jealousy, because I did. It's just that it was hard sometimes to watch a group of grown people act like seventh graders trying to sit next to the coolest kid at the lunch table. Honestly, it just made you feel sad because you always thought people would outgrow this, thought that adulthood would be different. And it wasn't.

All I could do was listen, really, when Matt talked about the kind of job he was looking for, when he told me that he felt like he was wasting time. It started to consume him. "I know you'll find something," I told him almost every day. And he'd look at me like he both was grateful for my support and knew I had no idea what I was talking about.

Everyone returned to work on Friday, and the snow took a while to melt but eventually did, making that lost week feel almost like a dream, like we'd all imagined the three feet of snow that had clobbered the city. I was busy at work, and if I wasn't wildly excited about what I was doing there, I was at least content. The site was expanding quickly, and Ellie put me in charge of several different sections, including one called "Query," where we answered e-mail questions from readers. Some of them were silly, about the best places to get a sandwich around the White House or the best burger on Capitol Hill. And some were about the layout and logistics of the city. Why were there so many goddamn traffic circles? Where was J Street?

It was the J Street question that stuck with me, that I always remembered, because I'd wondered about it too. There is no J Street in DC—the streets skip right from I to K, and there's a rumor that L'Enfant did it on purpose when he designed the city, that he hated John Jay and left out J Street as a big fuck you. Some people say it's because John Jay was having an affair with L'Enfant's wife. Some say it's because John Jay insulted his design. And some people think it's Jefferson that L'Enfant was trying to snub.

"It's just a rumor though," I explained to Matt when I was writing the response for the site. "Most people think it has nothing to do with any drama or jealousy, that maybe it's just because *I* and *J* looked too similar."

Matt tilted his head when I told him this. "Well that makes more sense," he said. "It seems kind of far-fetched to alter the layout of a city just for revenge."

"Really?" I said. "It seems to me that's exactly the kind of thing that would happen in this town."

Chapter 8

The truth about DCLOVE was that it was a little trashy, sort of like the *Us Weekly* of Washington, DC. We did plenty of restaurant reviews and things like that, but what really got Ellie and Miles excited was gossip and party pictures. All you had to say to get a story approved was "Well, no one knows this yet, but—" and Ellie would scream out, "Love it!" before you even finished.

They founded the website in 2009, when the whole world was obsessed with Obama's administration—Gawker couldn't get enough, writing about the hot young speechwriter and how he was maybe dating the twentysomething woman who worked in foreign policy and had also posed in *Maxim*. Even Jimmy was on Gawker a couple of times, once in an "Obama Hotties" roundup that named the most attractive staffers. But by 2010, the world was sort of over it and Gawker went back to writing about socialites and celebrities.

And DCLOVE picked up the slack, was committed to reporting every little bit of gossip in the District. Our most popular section was "Movin' On Up and Movin' On Out," which reported notable hirings, firings, and job jumping. We weren't the only place to do this—Politico

Playbook did it quite well, with snappy anecdotes and fresh language. But the difference between us and Politico was that they were classy about it and we weren't. We always trashed up the announcement with a takedown or a quote. We didn't mind printing anything. For example:

> Regional Communications Director Bobby London is leaving his post at the White House and heading to PepsiCo, where he'll be Director of External Relations. Sources say he beat out co-worker and nemesis Maggie McDonnel, White House Director of Press Advance, for the job, mostly because of his family connections, and not because of any real qualifications. Co-workers say they won't miss his standing desk, which he constructed out of cases of Diet Coke (take note, Pepsi!), or his half-pack-a-day habit, which supposedly left a Pigpen-like cloud of smoke around him. "He judged the rest of us for sitting all day," one officemate said, "but all he did was smoke cigarettes and eat bacon, so really, good luck to him."

When I told people I worked at DCLOVE, especially people at the White House, they often gave me a condescending smile, and would say something like "Oh, I've heard of it," while implying that they would never actually read it. Sometimes I wondered if Matt was embarrassed that his wife worked at a website that put out a monthly list of the "most datable" White House staffers. High-class journalism we were not.

But the thing is, they all read it. And I mean all of them. (Okay, not the President and probably not the other top people at the White House, but everyone else.) When Alan asked what I was up to at the Snowmageddon party, I knew he was just playing dumb, pretending he didn't know exactly where I worked so that I would think he was above reading such trash. But Jimmy told me that after Alan's golf incident with the President, he scoured the site every day, worried we were going to write something about it.

I was happy that Jimmy never pretended that he wasn't interested in DCLOVE—I'm not sure I would've liked him as much if he did. He always talked to me about the things we posted, let me know when everyone in the office was talking about a certain article, and even asked me if we were going to announce his new job in "Movin' On Up and Movin' On Out." He said it in a joking way, but I knew he really wanted it in there. I told him I'd make sure they knew about his new position, and he covered his eyes and said, "Just be kind."

Maybe I should've minded that I worked at a place that wasn't respected, but to be honest, I didn't really care. The website was interesting enough and it paid me more than I'd been making at *Vanity Fair.* Also, I was still a little shaken after getting laid off—I'd worked so hard at the magazine for so many years and then it was just gone. None of that mattered at the end. If jobs could be taken away so easily, maybe it wasn't worth investing so much of yourself into them; maybe working at a semi-trashy website was just fine.

The following week, we posted Jimmy's job announcement on the site:

> Jimmy Dillon, former Director of the White House Travel Office, takes his colorful socks and moves just two doors down the hall today, to start his new post as Deputy Director of the White House Office of Political Strategy, where he'll be the one arranging for important political folks to see the President wherever he visits. He'll also be traveling with POTUS on domestic trips, where he will most likely continue to drink mass amounts of whiskey on Air Force One and occasionally play cards with the Boss. Officemates say they won't miss him

because they'll still be able to hear his Texas twang from 400 feet away. Our source says this is the perfect job for Dillon, who loves hobnobbing with illustrious politicians or, as we call it, being a DC fame whore.

I was happy that someone else was assigned to write the post, not because I felt like it was a conflict of interest (I didn't think the site actually had enough journalistic integrity for that) but because I didn't think I could bring myself to write nasty things about Jimmy, even if they were supposed to be funny.

The day the announcement ran, Ellie stopped by my desk. "Beth, you're friends with Jimmy Dillon, right?" she asked.

"Yeah," I said. "Why? Do you know him?"

"Everyone knows him, don't they?" she asked and then laughed like she'd made a joke. I just gave her a little smile and didn't say anything. "I mean, he gets around," she continued. "A friend of mine worked on the Kerry campaign with him and she said it was hard to find someone on that campaign that he didn't sleep with."

"I doubt that," I said. "He's married, you know," I said. "And they've been together for a long time, definitely during the Kerry campaign."

Ellie tilted her head at me and said, "You've never worked on a campaign, have you?"

I shook my head. "That's what I thought," she said. She sounded triumphant, like she'd just won a debate.

"Anyway," she said, "I was thinking we could interview him for 'Working for the Weekend.'"

"Working for the Weekend" was our section that interviewed one person in the administration each week and highlighted their job, explained what they did each day. It was pretty interesting, actually, and if it hadn't been for the ridiculous name, I would've wanted to write more for it.

"We already did," I said. "We interviewed him when he was in the travel office. I mean, I'm happy to do it again as long as you don't mind having it be sort of a repeat."

"Hmmm," she said. She tilted her head, this time in the other direction. I could tell she was annoyed that she hadn't remembered we'd already profiled him. "I think it's okay. Same person, different job, right?"

"Right," I said. "I'll ask him about it today."

My heart sank a little as she walked away and I realized I'd have to tell Matt we were interviewing Jimmy again. His first profile had been superinteresting. He'd told me about what went into planning an overseas trip for the President, and even though I'd never cared all that much before, I couldn't help but be impressed as he described how thirty staffers would charter one of the "Blue and Whites" (the fleet of planes equipped to transport the President) to the countries that the President would be visiting.

"You mean, like Air Force One?" I asked, and Jimmy laughed.

"It's only Air Force One if the Boss is on board," he said. "Otherwise it's just a regular plane." He paused then and said, "And we take a smaller plane, not the 747s. Just so you don't get the wrong idea about how awesome my job is."

Jimmy told me how when the President went anywhere, a military team took over a whole floor of the hotel, set it up for secure communication. When they were overseas, the advance team had daily calls with the office in DC through video-conferencing, but to make sure it was completely secure, they had to do it in a tent that was constructed in one of the rooms, with white noise or loud music playing outside so no one could hear.

"You're lying," I told him. "You're making that up so that I write about it and look like an idiot." Jimmy was known for pulling pranks, but this time he held up his right hand and put his left on his heart.

"Hand to God," he said. "It's all true."

"It sounds like a spy novel," I told him.

He grinned at me. "That's me. Jimmy Dillon, International Man of Mystery."

That night, Matt picked up Chinese food on his way home and he seemed to be in a great mood as he unpacked the brown bag, taking the lids off the sesame chicken and lo mein, popping a dumpling in his mouth. His tie was loose and he whistled as he went into the kitchen, returning with two plates, silverware, and a beer for each of us. I was pretty sure that most people were appalled at how little we cooked, but Matt never seemed to mind, and whenever I was apologetic about it, he just shrugged and said, "I don't like to cook either, so why would I expect you to?"

He opened my beer and handed it to me, then opened his own and held it up. "Cheers, Buzz," he said, taking a long sip and finally sitting down. "I'm starving," he said. We didn't talk as we piled our plates high with food and took our first bites, but finally Matt put his fork down and picked up his beer.

"So, how was work?" he asked.

I'd been dreading having to tell him about the interview with Jimmy—after he'd read the last one, he'd said, "You should profile me . . . only no one would ever want to read about someone doing background checks for prospective hires." And then he'd tried to laugh, but it was clear he didn't think it was funny.

I decided instead to tell him first about my strange conversation with Ellie, where she implied that Jimmy was having affairs all over town. He listened as I went on and on, his eyebrows wrinkled as he chewed.

"It's not true, right?" I asked when I was done. "I mean, we'd know if it was happening, wouldn't we?"

"DC is full of rumors," Matt said. "You know that." I couldn't tell if he was avoiding my question because he didn't like to gossip or if there was another reason he didn't want to discuss it.

"Yeah, but do you think it's true? Have you ever heard anyone else talk about it?"

"I've heard people joke about some things," he said. "But I have no idea if any of it's true. I've never asked him about it."

"But you must have an opinion. I mean, really, what do you think?"

He sighed. "Does it matter what I think?"

"They're our friends," I said. "It's just weird. What if he really did cheat on Ash or he does it again? Don't you think we have some sort of responsibility to her?"

Matt dunked one of his dumplings into the dish of soy sauce and then chewed thoughtfully for what seemed like a long time before swallowing and saying, "I think no matter what, it's not really any of our business."

I told Matt about the interview later that night, as we were brushing our teeth. He'd had two more beers after dinner and still seemed to be in a cheery mood, so it seemed silly to delay it any longer.

"That'll be good," he said. "His new job is sort of crazy. It'll be an interesting interview."

"Yeah," I said, keeping my voice neutral. "I'm sure it'll be fine. I don't think anyone ever reads that section."

Matt wiped his mouth on a hand towel and then rolled it up and aimed it at my butt, making me jump in the air and laugh as it hit me. "With you writing it, Buzzy," he said, "I'm sure it will win awards."

It took us a while to actually schedule the interview, since Jimmy was now always traveling alongside the President. Finally, almost two months after he started his new job, we found a time to meet for lunch. I made reservations at Old Ebbitt, which was a restaurant right by the White House that was known for being the city's oldest bar and serving good oysters. It was always noisy and crowded, which was part of the reason I picked it, so that it wouldn't feel like people were listening in on our conversation. Plus, Jimmy loved oysters.

I got to the restaurant first and was sitting there daydreaming when he slid into the other side of the booth, startling me.

"Gotcha," he said, laughing.

"God, you scared me," I said, my hand over my heart.

"I waved at you, but you were in a different

world. I'm assuming you were just thinking about how excited you were to have lunch with me?"

I laughed weakly and nodded. "That's it," I said.

I couldn't help but look at Jimmy differently after my conversation with Ellie. I studied him when we were out to dinner with the Dillons, like he was going to do or say something to the waitress that would reveal him as a philanderer, but he was just the same as always. He adored Ash (or seemed to, at least) and was always touching her, always giving her compliments, and I didn't want to believe any of the things Ellie said.

Jimmy waved down the waiter and ordered a DC Brau, and I said I'd have one too, which made him raise his eyebrows at me and say, "Drinking on the job?"

"You are too," I said, but this time I laughed for real.

"We'll take a dozen oysters too," he said, not bothering to ask me if I wanted any. We'd eaten so many dinners with the Dillons at that point that we all knew each other's likes and dislikes.

We talked about random things for a few minutes before I said, "Okay, so tell me. Before you get called away on a presidential emergency. Tell me everything you do as the deputy director of political strategy." I said his title with exaggerated awe.

"Everything?" he asked, raising his eyebrows.

"Everything."

I let Jimmy talk for almost twenty minutes. I had some sort of idea about what he was doing, from things Matt had said to me or conversations we'd had when we were out—I knew he always traveled with the President, that whenever Obama was photographed, you almost always saw Jimmy standing just to the right of him. Sometimes you'd just see half of his face or one arm, but if you looked for him (which I always did) you could find him. It was like a presidential Where's Waldo? game. But I didn't completely understand what his responsibilities were, what it was he actually did.

"So, anytime the President goes anywhere," he started, "he meets with different political people. If he's going to Philly, then Ed Rendell will probably meet him at the airport. Things like that. So, I'm in charge of contacting those people, of figuring out who he should see in each city, and then setting it up. Does that make sense?"

I nodded, and he continued. "And then sometimes it's not politicians, sometimes it's celebrities that are coming to meet him in the photo line or attending an event. So I'm the contact for them, I facilitate that meeting."

"And that's why Scarlett Johansson sends you texts?" I asked. This had happened while we were out to dinner not long ago, and Jimmy had left his phone on the table, so that we could all see when the name Scarlett popped up on his screen.

"Exactly," he said. "That, and because I'm charming company."

"Of course," I said.

Through Matt, I knew that because Jimmy was Jimmy, he befriended almost every celebrity he met, would have drinks with them if they came to DC, offered them private West Wing tours. He showed up on the Instagrams of actresses, as they posed for selfies in front of the Rose Garden. Behind his back, all the people at work made fun of him a little bit, rolled their eyes as he held his phone and pretended to complain that another beautiful actress was texting him, that he'd been out for drinks with Bobby De Niro. But underneath it all was always, I think, a little current of jealousy.

Jimmy was often a ridiculous person, but that didn't stop us from wanting to hang out with him. He'd look at his reflection in the mirror, admire himself, striking dumb poses and saying, "Can you believe I'm this handsome?" When he walked into a party, he'd raise his hands and announce, "Hey-o! I'm here! The wait is over, everyone, Jimmy Dillon has arrived." But to be fair, he also made everyone around him feel good—he was quick with compliments and conversation and (while I never would've said this to anyone because it sounded crazy) he had a nice energy about him.

He created a Wikipedia page for himself,

complete with a head shot and a description of his career that made him sound incredibly successful, almost like he was just days away from running for president himself. His huge ego was made tolerable by his sense of humor, and even when you were rolling your eyes at him or in disbelief about something he said, it was hard to deny that there was something special about him. People wanted to be around him, I think, because it felt like he was going places.

In the meantime, Matt was getting frustrated with his job search, had been in constant contact with the Presidential Personnel Office, met people for drinks a few times a week to talk about different ideas, but still hadn't had a real interview or even figured out exactly what it was he wanted to do. All he knew was that he didn't want to be in the White House counsel's office anymore. And the contrast between his current job and Jimmy's didn't help—he was in an office all day while Jimmy was having drinks with famous people. It was just extra salt to rub in his wound.

"So, you like this job?" I asked Jimmy at the end of our lunch. "You're happy?"

He didn't even sound a little bit jokey as he said, "I feel like it's what I was born to do."

That spring, *The New York Times Magazine* ran a story about all the young staffers working in the administration. The whole point of the article seemed to be, Look, our country is being run by children!

It wasn't breaking news by any means—actually it seemed about a year too late—but still, everyone was buzzing about it. The focus of the article was Benji, mostly because the reporter was a friend of his, was dating his roommate actually. She followed him around for a few days, at work and then at a party he hosted at the house in Logan Circle that he shared with three other young White House staffers. The theme of the party was "America," which wasn't so much a theme as an excuse to make everyone dress up in American-flag-printed clothing. When the article came out, it was mentioned that a group of "higher-ranking" White House staff stopped by the party, and there was a half-page picture of Jimmy, wearing an American flag bandanna around his head, drinking a beer and standing next to Rahm Emanuel.

Jimmy pretended to be embarrassed, but was thrilled with the attention. "I didn't know I'd end up in the *Times* looking like a crazy person," he said to us. But of course he knew that, it had been his whole reason for going. Somehow, he always managed to make it to the spotlight.

"This is exactly the kind of story we should've done," Ellie said in the staff meeting that week. "We can't let the *Times* scoop us like this." I almost burst out laughing at the fact that Ellie could compare DCLOVE to *The New York Times* with a straight face, but I looked down at my notebook and concentrated on doodling.

"We need to be edgier," she went on, "we need to be ahead of the curve." (Sometimes I imagined that Ellie spent her weekends watching marathons of movies that featured unrealistic journalists as characters—*The Devil Wears Prada*, *13 Going on 30*, *The Paper*—and wrote down different ridiculous catchphrases to say at work.)

The takeaway from that meeting was that DCLOVE started running blind items about White House and Hill staffers. I'm not sure why Ellie thought this would bring us closer to *The New York Times*, but I didn't ask any questions. "I'm counting on you to bring us some good stuff," she said to me after it was announced. "Make sure to use all your connections."

Our first blind item at DCLOVE was this:

> Which two White House staffers are secretly dating? One has to schedule herself into her wordy lover's life, and rumor has it they're keeping their relationship on the down low for reasons other than workplace decorum.

"This is mortifying," I said, showing it to Matt. "It's like 'Page Six' and Politico had a baby that's not quite right in the head."

Matt just laughed. "They really think people will get into this, huh?"

"Ellie said she was so excited about the new section she couldn't sleep. She asked us all to pump our most 'in the know' friends for information we could use."

Matt looked nervous for a minute. "You're not going to repeat anything I tell you, are you?"

"No," I said. "I'd never do that. And anyway, you're just not good at gossip. You know that, right?"

"I do," he said. "And that's my burden to live with."

A week or so later, this blind item ran:

> Which talkative southern man is renowned for his amorous ways on campaign trails? No one is off-limits, not a Biden niece or a Gore daughter or even a close and personal friend of the Obamas. The number of campaign staffers that saw the inside of this cowboy's hotel rooms is "too high to count," says our source. "It would be like trying to guess how many jelly beans are in the jar, how many stars are in the sky."

I showed it to Matt that night. "Is this Jimmy?" I asked. Matt read it and laughed. "Jesus," he said. "That is the dumbest thing I've ever read. Can they print this stuff? They're naming real people now."

"I don't know," I said. "Ellie doesn't seem worried about it at all." I noticed he didn't answer my question.

"So is it?" I asked. "Do you think they're talking about Jimmy? Really? It's almost exactly what Ellie said about him before."

Matt looked more serious for a minute. "I don't know," he said. "Like I said, I've heard people joke about things, but, Beth? These are just rumors. That's the whole point of it."

"I know," I said. But it left me unsettled.

On the first truly warm Saturday of spring, we went to have afternoon drinks with Jimmy and Ash at American Ice, an outdoor bar near U Street that Jimmy loved because of its extensive whiskey menu. It was sunny and pleasant and felt great to be day-drinking outside for no real reason.

We'd only been there about an hour when Benji showed up with two of his roommates. "Oh, look who's here," he said loudly. "My favorite old married couple."

He was referring to Matt and Jimmy when he said this and it wasn't the first time I'd heard someone call them that. They were friendly with a large group, but I knew that people saw how tight the two of them were, sometimes felt left out of their friendship. "What are you two up to?" he asked. "Plotting to take over the world?"

"Always," Jimmy said.

Benji turned to me. "Beth, I met your college roommate the other day."

"Colleen?" I asked.

"That's the one. We were in Sidecar and she was there with a girl I used to know who works at Bloomberg now."

"Funny," I said. "How'd you guys put it together?"

"Oh, you know. I told her I worked at the White House and she asked if I knew Matt—or really what she said was 'You must know my friend Dogpants.'" He turned to give a wicked smile to Matt.

"Don't y'all just love that story?" Ash asked him. "It's the cutest New York love story I've ever heard."

Matt sighed and put his arm around me. "I know. Imagine I'd just worn jeans that day. It's possible I wouldn't have ever caught this one's eye."

We all laughed, but what I really felt was a sense of claustrophobia, something that had been happening more and more. It was like the city was getting smaller the longer we were there. It was incestuous, the way everyone knew everything about people. There was no such thing as a secret in this town, and I thought that if any of the rumors about Jimmy were true, it would only be a matter of time before Ash found out—or I found out and had to tell her.

Benji joined our table, leaving his other friends to go inside and get drinks. "So, is Alan on his way here?" I asked, half joking.

"I think he might actually meet us later," Benji said. "And a few other people from work, too."

"Great," I said.

Ever since Matt had made the strange bed-fellows comment about Benji and Alan, I couldn't stop thinking about their friendship. Was it real? Or was it more a marriage of convenience? They each got different things out of it, both benefited from the pairing, and sometimes I wondered if that was the only reason they were friends, if they even liked each other at all.

And I asked myself the same thing about Matt and Jimmy—Jimmy introduced Matt to people, made him more social, more fun. And Matt grounded Jimmy, gave him an air of gravitas. But that wasn't why they were friends, was it? Or at least, it wasn't the only reason. I watched them that day, Jimmy laughing loudly, smacking Matt on the back, my stomach twisting just a little.

A new spinning studio opened on Fourteenth Street and Ellie asked me to review it. The name was (no joke) the United States of Spinning. "It's brand-new," Ellie told me. "Based only in DC."

"I figured," I said.

The walls of the studio were covered with pictures of all the presidents, and everything was red, white, and blue. The spinning shoes were white, the bikes were blue, the walls were red and white striped, the towels were blue with white stars. It made you kind of dizzy to be in there.

When I interviewed the owner, Andy, a fit and handsome man in his early thirties, he told me that while he loved SoulCycle, he felt it lacked personality. "I wanted this studio to reflect DC. This has been my home for twelve years, and it's such a special place."

"It really is," I said. (I wasn't being sarcastic—*special* can mean different things to different people.)

"My husband and I had this idea a few years ago and we knew we had to take the leap. We wanted to combine our love of politics and spinning."

Andy told me that each ride would be dedicated to a different president. "But it will be a surprise," he told me. "You'll have to come to class to see which president we're honoring that day!"

He sounded so excited, and I said, "I can't wait."

Ash came with me for the inaugural ride—I could always count on her to accompany me to random places and events that I was covering for the website. I think she looked at it as a free Groupon.

The ride started with "Proud to Be an American"

blasting through the speakers and ended with a funky version of "Sea to Shining Sea," but fortunately had normal pop music in between, like any regular spin class. Reagan was the President of the Day, and his picture hung up front, so that you had to look at him the whole time, which I found slightly uncomfortable. Andy wore American flag kneesocks and yelled out motivational things to the class. "Let's be grateful," he shouted. "Let's give thanks that we have two legs and two arms to spin, and that we live in the greatest country in the world!" The class cheered and I panted, trying to keep up.

"This is the dorkiest thing I've ever seen," I whispered to Ash as we stretched after class.

"Oh, I don't know. I kind of like it," she said.

As I toweled off and changed out of my spinning shoes, I saw Ash talking to Andy. "I'll be back for sure," I heard her tell him.

It was 7:00 p.m. when we left, but still light outside, and we decided to walk to Sweetgreen to grab salads for dinner.

"Did you know that Andy had Jimmy's job under Bush?" Ash asked me as we walked down the block.

"Really?" I asked. I was more shocked that our gay spinning teacher was a Republican than I was that he'd had the same job as Jimmy. (Although when I thought about the choice of Reagan as the first "honored president," it made more sense.)

"They met during the transition. It's such a small world," Ash said. And there it was again, that claustrophobia, the feeling that you were always being watched. I wondered what Andy knew about Jimmy, if he'd met Matt, what he thought about me. And maybe I was being paranoid; maybe he didn't care enough about any of us to even form an opinion.

Ash sounded amazed that she'd discovered this connection. But the truth was, those coincidences happened all the time. If you played the name game long enough, it always worked. It's why Ellie's blind items did so well. In New York, you could live years without running into someone you knew, but DC was different. It was smaller, everyone worked in the same business. Sometimes it didn't feel like a real city at all.

Ash loved this part of DC. She said it made her feel like she was home, how nice it was to bump into people you knew at the grocery store or walking down the street. I sort of hated it. I hadn't been in a place where everyone was so scrutinized since college. And it started to make me feel tired—how intertwined everything and everyone was, so that it was normal for your boss to gossip about your best friend's husband, for your spinning teacher to know the people you hung out with.

"Not such a small world," I said to Ash that night. "But definitely a small town."

Chapter 9

At the beginning of the summer, Jimmy was asked to play golf with the President at Andrews Air Force Base. I braced myself for this invitation to become a regular thing, for Matt to start obsessing over it, but it only happened one other time. As far as I could tell, there was an unofficial ranking of the staff who played golf, and Jimmy was pretty low on the list. There had to be about ten other people out of town or otherwise occupied for him to even be considered. He tried to downplay it, but you could tell he desperately wanted to move higher up, not just because he kept talking about how much fun he'd had, but because he started going to hit a bucket of balls after work and spending his Saturdays playing eighteen holes.

Right after this, Matt signed us up for lessons at his parents' club and then the four of us started playing together almost every weekend. Jimmy was a pretty good golfer (there was no chance that he'd endanger the President with his aim as Alan had) and Matt wasn't bad either, and the only weird thing about these golf games was the idea that Jimmy was just using us to practice, hoping he'd get good enough to earn a regular invitation to play with Obama.

I'd noticed early on that Matt paid close attention to the things that Jimmy said and did, in the same way that preteen girls mimic the queen bee. Playing golf was just the tip of the iceberg. It was because of Jimmy that Matt got involved in the State Societies, which are basically clubs where people from the same place can get together for events. Jimmy was super-involved in the Texas State Society, always going to a Boots & Spurs happy hour or a breakfast club with a famous Texan as the special guest. He loved going to these meetings. "It's just nice," he said, "to be around people who feel familiar."

The State Societies were a good idea, I guess—it was nice to think that a young homesick assistant on the Hill could go to a happy hour and meet people from home, could form a network in a new city. But still, I was surprised when Matt joined the Maryland chapter. "Why do you need a state society?" I asked him. "You can drive ten minutes north and be in your state. If you want to be around people from Maryland, you can just go there."

Matt laughed. "It's about networking," he said.

"Of course it is," I said. What wasn't about networking in DC? I ignored him when he suggested I look into the Wisconsin chapter. I didn't need to sit around and talk about cheese curds with a bunch of strangers.

• • •

We had dinner with the Dillons every Friday night—it had become a standing date, a tradition. Really, we spent so much time with them that it was almost hard to remember how we'd filled our days before. They were low maintenance, which I came to appreciate more than anything—we could call them last minute to get dinner on a Tuesday, or they'd invite us over Saturday afternoon when Jimmy was cooking a brisket. It was just easy, especially compared to making plans with Colleen and Bruce, where we had to schedule everything weeks in advance and always ended up doing something complicated, like driving to Virginia or watching the Caps play in Bruce's company box.

When we were in New York, the only other couple we'd ever spent a lot of time with was Chrissie and Joe, who'd both gone to college with Matt. We often went out to dinner with them in the city, and once wine tasting for the weekend in North Fork. But our friendship was more out of necessity than anything else—we were one of the only other married couples in Matt's group of friends, so if they wanted to do coupley things, we were their only choice. The three of them had known one another for so long that sometimes hanging out with them felt like a college reunion that I'd ended up at by mistake. Chrissie was one of those girls who always wanted to make sure I knew my place, wanted to remind me that she'd known Matt when he was just eighteen, and she made a point of referencing inside jokes or calling people by their college nicknames, so that I spent much of the conversation one step behind, asking, "Wait, who is Cheeks? And why did Cheeks hate milk shakes?"

Sometimes when the three of them were talking, I dug my fingernails into my thighs, just to have something to do.

But with the Dillons, it was different—I don't know if it was because we all met one another at the same time or if it was just a matter of chemistry, but our foursome could happily split off into any combination. Jimmy was a big fiction reader, and he and I traded books back and forth, e-mailed each other reviews of new novels we wanted to read. Sometimes when we were discussing a book, I'd hear Matt or Ash (neither of whom read much fiction) say to the other in a mocking voice, "Shhh . . . don't interrupt. They're in middle of another book club meeting."

When we were over at their house, Matt (a huge TV snob) would even watch *The Voice* or *The Bachelorette*. "As a joke," he'd say. I thought maybe he was just doing it to be polite or to blend in (since Jimmy was an unapologetic fan of crappy TV), but once I saw Matt lean in close during a rose ceremony.

Matt relaxed around them in a way he couldn't

with any of the other people we'd met. I'd never thought of my husband as an anxious person, but DC had turned him into one. It was like he constantly monitored his behavior, making sure that he was acting appropriately. But around Jimmy, he wasn't worried if he was drinking too much or being too loud (maybe because Jimmy was always drunker and louder) and he was able to actually just enjoy himself.

On the weekends when the Dillons were out of town or we couldn't get together, we felt lost. Sometimes we went out anyway, just the two of us, but it was always a quiet dinner, like we didn't know how to go on a date without Jimmy and Ash there, and sometimes we didn't even bother going out, just put on sweatpants and ordered takeout. If I thought about it too much, the whole thing made me nervous, like maybe we needed the Dillons to be happy.

It was almost like the four of us were all dating each other, like we were one big couple. I tried to explain that to Colleen once and she wrinkled her nose. "How kinky," she said.

"Gross," I'd said. "Not like that. You're such a perv."

The Fourth of July was on a Sunday, which meant that we'd have that Monday off. We were all delighted with the idea of a three-day weekend, and we made plans way in advance—a BBQ at the Dillons' on Friday, Saturday we'd be at Matt's parents' club—golfing in the morning, hanging out by the pool in the afternoon, and dinner in the dining room that evening—Sunday we'd watch fireworks on the South Lawn, and Monday, we'd recover.

We'd spent a lot of time at the Kellys' club that summer, and while Matt and I were in the process of becoming members, we weren't officially in, so we were charging everything to his parents' account. Matt didn't think twice about this, but it made me feel funny. Sometimes we'd see Babs and Charles in the dining room and they'd come over to say hi—Babs thought Jimmy was "a hoot"—and I always felt like we'd been caught stealing from them. Once, I asked Matt about paying his parents back for those dinners, but he just shook his head. "They love when we use the club," he said, like we were doing them a favor.

That weekend, Matt had insisted on an 8:00 a.m. tee time, "to get the most from the day," and we were outside the gate at Beekman Place to pick up the Dillons at 7:15, a little bleary with coffee cups in hand. When we saw them coming toward the car, I got out and climbed in the backseat.

"Beth, stay where you are," Jimmy said, when he saw me. "I'm fine in the back."

"I'm already here," I said, shutting the door behind me.

We often rode like this, and it felt weirdly old-

169

fashioned to have the men up front and the women in the back—something grandparents would do—but Jimmy was tall enough that I always felt bad making him squeeze in the back.

"Not necessary, but thank you, sweetheart," he said as he got in.

Ash placed two large bags between us, one with clothes to change into for dinner and another with a bathing suit and magazines for the pool. "It is hotter than Hades out there," she said, fanning herself. "I'm glad we decided to only play nine, because I'm already dying to get in the pool."

In the front, Matt and Jimmy started immediately discussing the interview that Matt had had the week before for a position as the White House liaison for the Department of Education. When he'd first mentioned the interview to me, I'd told him it sounded great and then paused and said, "Although I have no idea what that means."

He'd laughed, looking happier than I'd seen him in a while, and said, "I doubt anyone really does."

The job would mean that he was the go-between for the DOE and the White House. It wasn't a clear upward move—in fact, everyone that Matt talked to agreed that it was probably lateral. But he was excited at the idea of not being in the office all day, of going to meetings, being a part of different projects. "This could be my chance to get involved in policy," he'd said, and I'd nodded but hadn't asked him to elaborate. He was pretty sure he was going to be offered the job—Jimmy had asked a friend he had in the Personnel Office, who had insinuated that Matt was as good as hired.

I badly wanted Matt to find a job that he liked so that he would be happy and also so we could stop talking about it. His job search had dominated all of our conversations in the past few months, and it was exhausting. I felt a little ashamed as I settled into the backseat that day, because while I probably would've given Jimmy the front anyway, it was just an extra bonus that I didn't have to be up there, listening as Matt listed the pros and cons of the liaison position for the hundredth time.

As we got ready to head out on the course, we noticed that they'd put our clubs on the carts so that my bag was with Jimmy's and Ash's was with Matt's. If this had happened with Bruce and Colleen (or any other couple, really), there would've been an awkward moment where we tried to switch the bags without being rude. But that day, we all just jumped into our carts without thinking about it.

"Are we betting today?" Jimmy asked, looking over at Matt and Ash. "You two want to take us on?" I already knew that I was the worst golfer out of the four of us, so this wasn't a great bet for Jimmy to make.

"Absolutely," Matt said. "Get ready to lose."

"Oh, I'll get ready," Jimmy said. "I'll get ready to crush you." He drove the cart away as fast as it would go, and I saw Ash rolling her eyes at me.

They went ahead of us after the second hole, because we were searching for my ball that had gone sharply left when I wanted it to go straight. When we joined them at the third hole, Matt was bent over and at first I thought he was sick, but as we got closer, I saw that he was laughing helplessly, tears in his eyes.

"Stop," we heard him say to Ash. "Please stop!"

"What's so funny?" Jimmy asked, pulling up next to them.

"I was just telling Matt about Hector the pig and how he attacked Daddy's ankles that one time. Daddy learned the hard way that you should never smack a pig."

This sent Matt off in a new laughing fit, and when he was finally able to sit up, he had to wipe his eyes. "Jesus," he said, trying to catch his breath.

His laughter was contagious, and I couldn't help but join in even though I had no idea what they were talking about.

"Ah, Hector," Jimmy said, turning to me. "The most famous pig in Texas. He was Ash's pet growing up, lived in the house like a dog because Lauren Sybil was too allergic to have a pet with any fur."

"Seriously?" I asked.

"Seriously," Ash said. "He was a great pig until he turned. Daddy was happy to get rid of him, because we didn't eat pork while he lived with us, out of respect, of course. Daddy smacked him when he was just a piglet and years later, Hector got his revenge on him. Pigs have a long memory, you know."

We were all laughing now. Matt looked like he was in pain, like his stomach hurt from the effort, and soon none of us could catch our breath.

"You don't spank a pig," Ash said, shaking her head. She looked completely serious. "You just don't do it."

Ash and Matt beat us handily, and I told Jimmy he should never bet when he was on my team. "Hogwash," he said, winking at me. "The two of them probably cheated."

After we were done golfing, we all went to the locker rooms to change into our suits and claimed four lounge chairs farther back on the deck, away from the children who were running and jumping into the pool over and over again. I'd brought a book with me, but I was happy to just lie in the sun for a while. Matt and Jimmy went to put our order in for lunch at the snack bar—

chicken Caesar salads for me and Ash and burgers for them—and I watched them across the deck, talking to each other and laughing.

"This day is perfect," I said.

"I know," Ash said. "It's amazing. Aren't we just so lucky to be here?" I knew from Ash's tone that she didn't just mean she felt lucky to be near a pool on such a hot day, but that she meant it in a larger sense. Ash often commented on the things she was grateful for—our friendship, our privilege, our place in life. It made me a little uncomfortable the way she said it, like she thought we were being rewarded by God for being good people, instead of it being completely random. Sometimes I wanted to point out that some truly shitty and evil people were filthy rich and led happy lives. But that day, I just said, "We are lucky."

She sighed and closed her eyes to the sun, stretched out like a cat and smiled. "We're blessed," she said.

We didn't eat dinner until almost 8:00 that night, and when we gathered at the table, we were all a little sun drunk and sleepy, our cheeks and foreheads pink and tight. Because I was sure at this point that Ash had no intention of getting a job, I thought I'd misheard her when she announced to the table that she'd just been hired.

"What?" I asked, looking up from the menu.

"I got a job," she said. "I'm a working girl now!"

"Congratulations," Matt said. He held up his glass and clinked it against hers, and then Jimmy and I raised ours and did the same.

"That's great," I finally said. "I didn't even know you were looking." I was trying not to sound too surprised, but Ash had been in DC for over a year now and hadn't talked about working in months. Matt and I sometimes speculated about what she did all day and what her plans were (or I speculated, and Matt listened), but we'd just accepted that she was happy not working and that apparently she didn't have to.

"I wasn't looking exactly," Ash said. "I mean, I had my eyes open in case the right thing came along. And then one of my old sorority sisters contacted me when she started working with this great company, thinking that I'd be a good fit."

"What will you be doing?" Matt asked.

"Well, it's sort of an entrepreneurial opportunity. It's a fun accessories company—their stuff is supercute—and I'm going to be starting as a stylist, hosting and organizing some trunk shows and recruiting new people."

My heart sank as I heard the description. "That sounds great," I said. "What's the name of the company?"

"Stella and Dot," she said, and I nodded. "I've heard of it," I told her.

I'd seen the company name pop up all over

175

Facebook in the past couple of years, mostly from my friends who'd had babies and were looking for part-time jobs. I'd even been invited to some of the trunk shows, which were really just new versions of Tupperware parties. And once I'd been contacted about "joining the team" by this girl Janie Jenkins, who grew up next door to me in Madison and babysat for me as a teenager. "You seem like the perfect fit," she said to me. "I'm working on growing my team and I thought of you immediately. I'm so excited to be a part of the Stella and Dot family."

Janie had been part of a cult for a few months after college, so I politely declined. I wasn't going to be convinced to join anything by a former cult member, thank you very much. (Apparently, the cult was quite peaceful and mostly just focused on organic farming, but I mean, still.)

At worst, this jewelry company seemed like a pyramid scheme and at best it was a reason to drink wine with a group of women and buy costume jewelry that you'd never wear. But if Ash had any idea that this was anything less than a great opportunity, she didn't show it. She was enthusiastic and excited as she talked about it. "It's flexible hours and it just really seems like the perfect thing for me," she said. (What she needed flexible hours for, she didn't say.) She was smiling widely, and in that moment I felt very protective of her.

"It sounds great," I told her, and she immediately asked if I'd host her first party for her.

"Of course," I answered. Because really, what else could I say?

The morning of July 4, Matt got a phone call. It was the person he'd interviewed with at the Presidential Personnel Office, telling him that he'd gotten the liaison job, that he'd be receiving a formal offer on Tuesday.

"Why did they call you today?" I asked.

"He said he knew I was anxious to hear," Matt said. "That he thought it would be nice for me to know so I could enjoy the Fourth. Now I don't have to worry about it, don't have to spend the day thinking about it."

And talking about it, I thought. But I just gave him a huge hug and said, "That's so great." Matt was beaming as he hugged me back and said, "I know."

We got to the South Lawn around 4:00 and set up a large quilt that the Dillons had brought, and it wasn't long before we were surrounded by Matt and Jimmy's co-workers, spreading out their own blankets to claim a spot. The Fourth was a great event at the White House, my favorite event actually—they served wine and beer and cotton candy and popcorn, and kids got their faces painted and ran around with ice cream sandwiches, while everyone posed for selfies in front of the White House.

Ash and I walked around a little bit, then sat and shared a bag of popcorn. Matt and Jimmy stood at the end of the quilt, talking to everyone who walked by. The current White House liaison at DOE came over to say congratulations to Matt (while it was still unofficial, it seemed that everyone knew about his job), and I could hear Matt asking him a few questions. I noticed that Jimmy stood there proudly, truly happy for Matt, smiling like he was the one who'd gotten a new job, which made me feel silly for ever doubting the basis of their friendship.

When it finally started to get dark, Matt and Jimmy sat down on the blanket with us. I could feel Matt's good mood radiating from him, and I leaned back against him as the Killers started to play on a stage to the right of us. I felt all at once lucky to be there and surprised to feel that way. It was possible that Ash was rubbing off on me. There wasn't one thing about the day that I would have changed. It was perfect. The Killers played their final song just as the fireworks started, and Matt leaned forward and whispered into my ear, "You have to admit, this is pretty great."

"Yeah," I said. "It's not bad at all."

Washington, DC 2012

What Washington needs is adult supervision.
—BARACK OBAMA

Chapter 10

The first time I dreamt about Mitt Romney was in June, not long after he'd clinched the nomination. It wasn't a particularly scary dream—he was riding a bike around me in circles, demanding that I help him make spaghetti for dinner—but I woke up with a start and, in the process, woke up Matt too.

"Are you okay?" he said groggily. My right arm had hit the mattress next to him as I shot up.

"Yeah, I think so," I said. My heart was racing and I waited a moment for my mind to wake up before telling him about my dream.

"No more falling asleep to MSNBC," he said, patting my arm, his eyes already closing.

"Deal," I said. He fell back to sleep immediately, but I lay there for a while in the dark, thinking about my dream, shivering at how shiny Mitt's hair had been as he circled around me.

The next morning, Matt was already dressed in his suit and eating cereal at the table when I finally managed to come downstairs, still in my pajamas. I poured myself a cup of coffee and sat across from him while he gave me a sympathetic look.

"Did you get any sleep?" he asked.

"I think an hour or two," I said, yawning, as if

just talking about it made it worse. After the Mitt-on-a-bike dream, I'd tossed and turned, falling asleep to more creepy Romney dreams that were equally bizarre.

"Oh, Buzz," Matt said.

"I know. It's stupid. It's not like I think he's even going to win. It's just—what if he does? Can you imagine?"

"No." Matt's voice sounded certain, but I knew he was worried. We'd spent the whole night before, in fact, discussing what would happen if Obama lost—not just how disappointing it would be, but also how strange. Matt would lose his job (along with everyone else we knew who worked in the administration), DC would empty out, all of our friends would go back to where they were from—Chicago or Texas or Iowa. And maybe the strangest part of all was to think that Matt and I would most likely stay. Maybe we'd move to Maryland right away, live on the same block as Matt's brothers, start playing tennis with Babs. Who knew?

I hadn't expected to feel this way, to be so invested in the election. In some ways, it felt bigger to me than it had four years ago. I was always aware that our life in DC was temporary, that there was an expiration date—but now with all of the election coverage, I had a daily reminder that things might change overnight. Everything seemed so tenuous. We could pretend that this town was ours, but really it was just on loan.

I drank my first cup of coffee quickly and poured a second, holding it in my hands and willing the caffeine to kick in. Matt checked his BlackBerry, knowing without me having to tell him that I wasn't up for conversation just yet, and I watched him from across the table. He always did this thing when he ate breakfast, where he'd put his tie over his shoulder to keep it from getting dirty, like some old-fashioned businessman. It killed me. It must've been something that his father did, a habit he picked up along the way, and there was just something about it that I loved.

He looked up to see me watching him, smiled back, and stood to carry his bowl to the sink. I listened to him rinsing it out and putting it in the dishwasher. When he came out of the kitchen, he flipped his tie back to its proper place and smoothed it down with his palm.

"Look," he finally said. "This is stressful. It's going to be a stressful few months. All we can do is try not to worry about it. And vote, obviously."

"Obviously."

"Are you going to fall asleep at the office?"

"Actually, I might work from home today," I said, meaning that I would be heading back to bed for a couple of hours as soon as he left. I hoped Ellie wouldn't mind much. Or at least that she wouldn't notice.

"That sounds like a good idea," Matt said,

leaning down to kiss me good-bye. "And remember—we'll just stay positive, right? Positive thoughts?"

"Yes. Positive thoughts," I said. And then when the door shut behind him, I said again, to no one, "Positive thoughts."

The next Saturday, Ash insisted that I meet her for brunch. We hadn't gone out with the Dillons on Friday, because Jimmy was traveling, and I figured she just wanted to get together, but when I'd suggested that we cancel (mostly because I was tired from not sleeping all week and kind of just wanted to sit on my couch) she'd whined, "Noooo, I have to see you." And right then I knew what she was going to tell me.

We met at Saint-Ex on Fourteenth Street, and when I got there, she was already at a table outside, waving at me like a little kid and smiling widely. I'd barely sat down before she said, "I'm pregnant," and I tried my best to look both excited and surprised.

"Oh my God," I said, "when did you find out?"

It turned out that Ash was barely pregnant, had basically peed on a stick and then decided to announce it to me. "Are you worried about telling people so early?" I asked.

"Oh, no. I probably won't tell anyone else, but I had to tell you or I was going to burst. You're my best friend! I almost called you right after I took the test, but then I wanted to see your face when I told you in person."

When the waiter came to our table, Ash ordered a club soda with lime and then looked up at him pretending to be embarrassed. "I'm pregnant," she said. I wanted to tell her that it was 1:00 in the afternoon and she didn't have to explain to the waiter why she wasn't drinking, that really he probably didn't even notice. But I just ordered a Bloody Mary for myself and kept smiling.

The next Tuesday, Colleen and I had planned to go for an early evening walk through Rock Creek Park (which was our way of pretending to exercise when really we just wanted to talk), but when she came to my door that night, she looked exhausted and said, "Do you mind if we just order dinner instead?"

"Sure," I said. "Are you okay?"

"Not really. I'm pregnant. And so fucking tired."

She told me they'd been trying for a few months. "I mean, I would've waited another year or two, but time is marching on. For Bruce I mean," she said quickly. "He's already going to be an old dad, but I'd rather people don't think he's the baby's grandpa."

I tried to figure out why I didn't take this news so well. I should've been thrilled, two of my best friends having babies. But I wasn't. I didn't want to talk to them about how they'd tracked their ovulation schedules or how often they had to go to the bathroom. I knew how awful I was being. Maybe it was all the pressure of the election, knowing that so many things might change. Maybe I just wanted things to stay the same for a little while longer. But mostly, I think, sometimes it's just really hard to be happy for other people.

When I talked to Matt about it, he said, "Are you jealous?" He looked hopeful, like I was going to get caught up in some pregnancy pact with Ash and Colleen, decide that we should have a baby immediately.

"No, it's not that. I just—I know what it will be like. This is all they're going to talk about." Matt was silent, and then I said, "Just so you know, I realize how shitty I sound. I can't help it. I'm a bad friend, I guess."

"You're not a bad friend," he said. "But I think maybe you think this is worse than it is."

"I mean, I'm happy for them," I said. "I just wish it wasn't happening right now."

"They're not going to stop being your friends just because they're having babies."

"They won't be able to drink."

"I'm sure you can work around that," he said, all of a sudden speaking slowly, like I was a brain-damaged giraffe.

"You don't get it. It's different for guys."

Matt looked at me, like he was trying to decide

if he should continue this conversation. Lately, there had been a different tone when we talked about babies. It was a subtle shift, but I felt it. Now when Matt showed me pregnancy announcements on Facebook, I felt like he was really saying, What d'ya think? Are you ready? It was stressing me out. I started to blame Facebook and everyone's need to announce their impending babies in creative ways, like they were all involved in some giant Pinterest competition. If I saw one more tiny pumpkin with a date on it, one more Big Brother Promotion sign, one more picture of an actual bun in an oven, I thought I might lose it. Or vomit.

"I'm sure it is different," Matt said. He cleared his throat. "But it's not like we're so far away from having a baby."

"I just feel like we're not ready yet. Don't you?" I sounded desperate for Matt to agree with me.

He shrugged. "I feel ready," he said. "But we both need to get there."

Our conversation was awkward and I could tell that neither of us knew how to make it less so. Shockingly, we'd never talked about any of this, not in any sort of serious way. We were so young when we got married that we didn't have to discuss timing—we had all the time in the world! And now, all of a sudden, we didn't anymore.

"Yeah," I said, trying to make a joke. "It is something we should both be involved in."

Matt attempted a smile. "But we should start thinking about it," he said. And then he was the one trying to make his voice jokey. "It's not like we're spring chickens."

All I could manage was to say, "Ha," like a low-budget laugh track. His comment stayed with me, sat funny in my chest. Even though he was older than I was, it felt like my ovaries were being insulted, like he was trying to shame them into action.

Jimmy was busy that summer, traveling with the President everywhere, which now included campaign stops, and we rarely saw them for Friday dinners. (Most of the administration couldn't take any part in the campaign, because of something called the Hatch Act, but there were exemptions and Jimmy was one of them, which he pretended bothered him but I knew made him feel important.) Sometimes we went out with just Ash, but it felt a little strange, like we had a sister-wife situation going on. This was mostly because Matt insisted on paying for Ash and treating her like she was handicapped instead of just pregnant, pulling out her chair for her and making sure she had enough water. Once, he asked the waiter if the cheese on her salad was pasteurized. "I just wanted to make sure," he said, after the waiter left our table. "Oh, you are the sweetest," Ash said.

Honestly, that night I hated them both just a little.

When Jimmy was in town, we talked only of the campaign. In July, during one of the rare Fridays that he was there, the four of us went to Mintwood Place, a restaurant in between our places that had opened that winter but that we still hadn't tried. I'd been looking forward to it, had been feeling nostalgic for our Friday dinners, but as we sat there and talked about Romney and fund-raising and polls, I got agitated. "Remember when we were the only couples in DC who had real dinner conversation?" I asked. No one answered me, although Ash did make a face like she was annoyed too, but didn't do anything to stop it.

Jimmy was describing a campaign event in Las Vegas when Matt said, "God, sometimes I wish I'd jumped on the campaign."

"You do?" I asked. He didn't seem to realize that this was surprising and also a little hurtful. Did that mean he wished he was in Chicago? Or that he was traveling? Either way, he'd be away from me.

"Absolutely," he said. "All the time."

"You know," Jimmy said. "They always need volunteers on trips. A lot of people are taking vacation days and jumping on. Just to feel like they're doing something."

"Volunteer?" I asked. But no one really

answered me. Matt just turned and said, "Yeah, Hatch. You know."

"It's something to think about," Jimmy said to Matt, who was already nodding in agreement.

There was no doubt in my mind that Matt would arrange to go on a trip. Never mind that he'd be using all of his vacation days and we wouldn't be able to go anywhere, or that he'd never really done advance in the first place. "They know I can figure it out," he said, when I brought it up. "I did enough events in finance to know whatgoes on. Plus, I'll probably just be a P2."

"A what?"

He sighed. "Assistant to the press lead," he said.

"Right," I said.

But the thing was, I didn't totally blame him. We both felt powerless, and despite his promise to stop watching MSNBC at night, that was all we did. I could hear Rachel Maddow in my head, always. Within a week of that dinner, Matt was scheduled on a trip and I was left to watch twenty-four-hour campaign coverage all by myself.

I wish I could say that I got over my initial reaction to Colleen and Ash and was a good friend to them that summer. But I didn't. Even though it was lonely with Matt traveling, I sometimes made up excuses not to see them. It was a pity party of the greatest kind.

Ash had always been a big fan of Facebook. She posted everything—oversharing and updating her status about things no one could possibly care about, like "Just got my butt kicked at Bar Method!" "Time for a pedicure to reward myself!" But her pregnancy posts took it to a whole new level. She made her sonogram her profile picture, gave weekly measurements of the baby, updated everyone on her food cravings and aversions. There were times I'd start to feel bad that I was avoiding her, and then I'd go on Facebook and see "Feeling sick. Threw up three times today. Baby Dillon sure knows how to let her mama know she doesn't like Mexican food." Or "Feeling HUGE! My maternity jeans no longer fit. I'm a whale. ☹"

Was she going to live-tweet her birth? Why did she feel the need to share everything? And of course the comments on her posts were even worse, most of them from her girlfriends she'd grown up with in Texas. "Stop it! You are looking beautiful, Mama!"

When, I wondered, did every pregnant person get together and decide that *Mama* was the appropriate term to use? Why did having a baby turn these people into hillbillies?

Ash had a gender-reveal party, where she and

Jimmy strung up a piñata on their back patio, took turns whacking it until pink knickknacks and candy sprinkled out of it. "It's a girl," she shrieked, and everyone clapped. I always judged Ash for the way she thought God personally looked out for her, but I myself thanked the good Lord above that they scheduled that party on a weekend I was already set to visit my parents in Wisconsin. (But don't worry, she posted the video of the two of them taking a bat to the piñata, just so anyone who couldn't make it was still able to watch.)

I'd sworn never to force Colleen and Ash into a social situation again, but that summer I did just that and suggested that we all go to brunch together. I was slightly worried they wouldn't have much to say to each other, but they quickly bonded over their pregnancies, moaning about finding cute clothes that fit them, listing all of the things they couldn't eat.

As Ash and Colleen talked that day about coffee and lunch meat and sushi, I was reminded of a gluten-free girl who worked with Matt and once asked if she could smell my Bo-shaped cookie at the White House Christmas party. "I miss cookies so much," she said. "Can I take a sniff?" I didn't know what else to do, so I held out the little frosted dog for her and she leaned over and breathed in deeply. When she was done, I put the cookie down on the table. I didn't want it anymore. Her nose had been too close to it and it had lost its appeal.

I knew that girl didn't want to smell my cookie, she just wanted to remind me that she couldn't eat it. So when Colleen said dramatically, "I really miss eating fried eggs," and Ash said, "Oh girl, me too!" I just sipped my coffee and spaced out.

At the end of brunch, Ash and Colleen exchanged phone numbers and made plans to send their registries to each other, so they could make sure they weren't missing anything, and I watched them hug good-bye with the beginning of a headache behind my eyes.

I'd hoped that going on the campaign trips would make Matt happy, that it would settle his restlessness just a little. But it didn't. He returned from these trips tired and cranky, annoyed that he had to go back to the DOE.

He wasn't happy with the White House liaison job, and I tried to be sympathetic, but I started to think that no job was going to live up to what he wanted. The things he complained about sounded childish: "I'm so far away from the White House," he'd say. "I can't walk in there anymore, someone has to meet me at the gate. I have to wear a visitor's badge."

What was I supposed to say to this? I'm sorry that you have to take a cab to the White House now? I'm sorry that you have to wear a different color badge so that everyone knows you're not as important as they are?

I always tried to stay positive. "You said this is good experience," I reminded him. "That working for the DOE would help you if you ran for office. That it could be part of your platform."

"I know," he said. "It's just not what I thought it would be."

"Don't you kind of think everyone feels that way about their job?" I asked.

Matt looked up at me for a moment and then said, "No. I don't."

The last couple of months before the election were brutal. It was like we were all just waiting, killing time, hoping for the best. My insomnia and night terrors got worse, which was sort of embarrassing. Of everyone in DC, I probably cared the least about politics—so why was I plagued with night-mares? Was this what living here did to you? What was wrong with me?

"You're just stressed," Matt said. "So are you," I said, "but you don't wake up screaming. You're not having nightmares about Paul Ryan's widow's peak."

Matt was always willing to talk to me until I calmed down those nights, partly I think because he wasn't sleeping all that well himself. But most of it, I knew, was that he was worried about me and was just being nice. We'd chat into the darkness until my eyes were heavy. Sometimes we came up with fake stories that I could write for DCLOVE. My favorite was "The 10 Biggest Douche Bags to Date in DC."

The night of the widow's peak nightmare, we discussed theme songs of old sitcoms, challenging the other to sing the theme of whatever show we named: *Growing Pains*, *Family Ties*, *The Fresh Prince of Bel-Air*. We were both weirdly talented at this game and we couldn't stop laughing as it just went on and on.

"Can we monetize this somehow?" Matt asked. "This might be our greatest gift."

Finally, we were both stumped at *Mr. Belvedere*, and after twenty minutes of trying to figure it out, we googled it and played the opening credits about five times, singing along after we remembered the words. Eventually we just started watching a full episode on my phone, propping it up between us. "I thought Wesley was the funniest kid ever," Matt said. "I wanted to be him when I was little." His eyes were half closed,
but he was still watching the tiny screen.

"Really?" I said. "You never told me that before."

"We've never talked about *Mr. Belvedere* before."

"True." It was almost 4:00 a.m. by that point,

and I knew we'd both be useless the next day, but I didn't really care. I moved a tiny bit closer, resting my head against his shoulder, my mind quiet for the first time that night.

By October, Matt had used up all of his vacation time and wasn't able to do any more advance trips for the campaign. He'd so badly wanted to help with the second debate, and instead was watching it at home with me.

I'd made popcorn and opened a bottle of red wine. Neither of us was all that hungry, and I thought maybe the popcorn would make the night feel more festive. Ash came over to watch with us, bringing a plate of brownies.

"I baked," she said, holding out the plate to me. "I was so nervous, I couldn't sit still."

"Perfect," I said. "It will round out our well-balanced meal."

Ash set the plate down and unwrapped it, then plucked a brownie off the top of the pile and ate it. She was due in February, and her stomach was already swollen against her clothes; her face was rounder, which had the strange effect of making her look younger. She didn't seem to care about what she ate or how much weight she was gaining—not that she was being a pig, more that she accepted that her body was going to change and wasn't going to obsess about it.

She picked up another brownie and took a bite. "I thought the last election was crazy," she said. "But this feels bigger, somehow. Doesn't it?"

"This election is almost more important," Matt said. "I mean, if he loses, then what? All we worked for is gone. He's basically just Jimmy Carter."

"Jimmy Carter does amazing things," I said. I felt like I should defend that peanut farmer. Poor Jimmy Carter, always brushed to the side. Did no one think about Habitat for Humanity?

"You know what I mean," he said.

The last debate had been less than stellar, and we all felt how much was riding on this, knew that Obama needed to be great. (Or at least that's what every pundit had been saying on repeat for the past week.) The three of us sat down on the couch, and fidgeted as we waited for it to start. Matt looked at his phone, texting his friends and obsessively reading Twitter. "I wish I could have some wine," Ash said softly, and for once I wasn't annoyed at her bringing up her pregnancy restrictions. Wine was the only reason I wasn't jumping out of my skin.

"Jimmy texted that there's going to be a great line about the Navy," Matt said, already texting him back.

"How does he know that?" I asked.

"He sat in on debate prep," Matt said.

"Really?"

"Yeah. How awesome is that?"

I almost pointed out that even if Matt had gone on the trip, he probably wouldn't have been able to be in the room while the President was getting ready, but I knew that wouldn't make him feel better. So, I just said, "Cool."

When the line about the Navy came, we all laughed and clapped. Ash shook her head like she was reacting to a sassy friend and said, "Whooooo!" Matt pumped his fist and screamed, "Fuck, yeah!"

When we settled down a little, Matt's phone dinged with another text from Jimmy and he read it to us. "Yeah, Jimmy said the line was originally supposed to just stop with the aircraft carriers, but during rehearsal POTUS kept going with comparisons and Axe and Plouffe were cracking up," Matt said. His phone dinged again. "Plouffe told him to go for it."

I watched the air go out of Matt, watched his elation disappear as he realized he wasn't the one with the inside knowledge of debate zingers, that he wasn't referring to one of Obama's top aide's as Axe. Matt's change of mood was so slight that Ash didn't notice, but I did. When Romney talked about "binders full of women," Matt did clap his hands a couple of times and say, "That's it, you moron. Keep them coming," but it was more subdued.

Before we went to sleep that night, I kissed Matt and said, "It went well, right? We should be happy."

"Yeah," Matt said. "I know."

Just days before the election, Hurricane Sandy hit the East Coast. Jimmy was out of town and so Ash came to stay with us, because we didn't know how bad it would be. Matt suggested it first (but I would have eventually), and when I agreed, he said, "I mean, I just don't think she should be by herself in her condition."

We were prepared with candles and food and extra batteries, but in DC the storm was just a lot of rain and some strong wind. Our power never even flickered. Ash ended up staying with us for two nights, because Jimmy went to help with the President's visit to the Jersey Shore, which was hit hard.

Ash and I sat by the windows with cups of tea and watched the rain come down. Matt was there, but was on his phone, reading articles about the election while watching coverage on TV. I remember feeling so antsy that day, just waiting, again. Waiting for the storm to get worse, waiting for the power to go out, waiting for it to be over.

The next day, we watched as Obama landed in New Jersey, as he and Chris Christie hugged, which Jimmy had already told us was the plan.

"So smart," Matt muttered. "This could be the thing that pushes Obama over the top, the thing that secures it."

I watched the two men hug, watched it replay a million times, and I couldn't help but think: If a televised hug could affect an election, weren't we all just really screwed?

Matt and I had decided months earlier that we'd go to Chicago for election night. Most of our friends (including Jimmy and Ash) would be there, and it felt like we should be a part of it. We flew in early that afternoon, dropped our bags at the hotel, met a few people for dinner, and then headed to McCormick Place.

I don't remember that much about the actual night—Jimmy arranged to get us into one of the donor rooms, and for most of the time I stood next to Star Jones and drank wine, feeling slightly ashamed that I was wishing for a better celebrity sighting when there was so much more at stake. After the election was called, we were ushered into a roped-off section and stood next to Rahm Emanuel as Obama spoke. It was a blur of cheers and confetti.

But what I do remember perfectly is the next day, when Jimmy took us to campaign head-quarters. "The President is going to stop by," he said, "and you should be there."

That place was like nothing else I'd ever seen.

It was a little bit like a frat house after a party and a little bit like the dorms on the last day of school—everyone was exhausted, hungover, ecstatic about winning, and sad as they started to realize it was all over.

The campaign office was mostly one big open room with desks and tables crowded so close together that you couldn't tell one from the other. There were a few offices around the perimeter, but most people sat in the middle, using whatever they could for a work space. The whole place was dirty and lived in—empty pizza boxes on the floor, Tabasco bottles on desks, containers of Parmesan cheese and open bags of nuts strewn everywhere. It was clear that the staffers had been eating all of their meals in the office, that they'd probably even slept there every once in a while. The air was a little stale, the way it gets when there's too many people crowded in one area for a long time.

Around each work space were different decorations—college flags hanging from the ceiling, state posters hung up with clips, American flags, and more Obama 2012 posters than you could count. Deflated balloons were tied to someone's chair, leftover from a birthday celebration. Whiteboards and chalkboards were still filled with notes and schedules, signs made out of construction paper were taped on the wall, inside jokes and memories, I assumed:

REMEMBER IOWA, WE'RE NOT BINDERS, and DON'T FORGET TO BREATHE.

The office was full of people, but no one was sitting at their desks. There was nothing more to be done. Exercise balls that had been used as chairs rolled around as everyone milled about, hugging each other, sometimes laughing or crying with relief, sometimes doing both at once. All around me, I heard people saying over and over again: Congratulations, we did it, and good-bye.

There was a young staffer who'd died during the campaign—unexpectedly and suddenly—and in the corner was a makeshift shrine to him. It had notes from his friends and co-workers, a bottle of his favorite liquor, and a big sign that said, DO IT FOR ALEX. I was tired that morning (we hadn't slept much the night before), and although I'd never met him, I cried openly as I read the Post-its that people had put up there after he was gone, little random thoughts and notes addressed to him: "I miss you"; "I wish you were here to make binder jokes"; "You would have loved the event today." Most of them were written by his co-workers, but there was also one from the President and another from the First Lady.

I don't know how long I stood there crying, but I do remember Matt coming over and taking my elbow. "Come on," he said quietly, leading me away, probably not wanting the whole office to see his wife weeping.

When the President came, everyone cheered, and I cried some more, but so did everyone else. He talked about how everyone in that room inspired him, how he had so much hope for the world seeing all of these young people who cared so much, how they all made him proud.

Next to me, Matt's eyes filled with tears, and I realized that in the entire time I'd known him, the only two times I'd seen him cry were during the 2008 and 2012 elections.

I think about that day often—it was historic and amazing and I couldn't believe I got to witness it, sure. But it was also the one time I got it, the only time I came close to understanding why Matt did this, why he'd joined the campaign in 2008, why he regretted not doing it again, why he was willing to give up his vacation days to contribute to it this time. Standing there, I could feel it—the energy, the draw, the desire to be part of this great big thing, this movement that was more than any one person, this feeling that you could start to change the world.

Washington, DC
2013

Washington is a very easy city for you to forget where you came from and why you got there in the first place.
—HARRY TRUMAN

Chapter 11

When I tried on my dress for the Inaugural Ball, all Matt could say was "It's really shiny." It was the kind of statement people try to pass off as a compliment: "That's bold." "Your shirt is unusual." "I've never seen a skirt look like that."

"It looks like something Vanna White wore on *Wheel of Fortune*," I said.

"It's not that bad." But a little smile flickered on his lips and I knew he secretly agreed with me.

"Actually," I said, looking at myself in the mirror, "I'm pretty sure she wore this exact dress. What am I going to do? It looked so much better online."

"Why don't you just wear one of the other ones?" Matt said. I'd rented three different dresses from Rent the Runway, one for each of the balls we were going to—the Black Tie and Boots ball on Saturday (as guests of Jimmy and Ash, of course), the official Inaugural Ball on Monday, and the Staff Ball on Tuesday.

"I can't do that!" I said. "We're going to see all the same people at them." Even Ash, who was almost nine months pregnant, had three different maternity gowns to wear. No one was messing around.

Matt just shrugged his shoulders, knowing that anything he suggested wasn't going to calm me down as I stood bedazzled in front of him. After a flurry of text exchanges with Ash, I decided my best bet was to head to Friendship Heights, where there were a million stores and had to be at least one suitable dress. But when I got there, every department store looked like it had been ransacked, like a looting had taken place. Who was I kidding? It was the Saturday before the inauguration and every female in DC was desperate for a gown. I tried on one dress that was a size double zero and got stuck as I attempted to pull it over my head, sweating in the dressing room for almost twenty minutes while I swore silently and prayed it wouldn't rip. There were a few other women there too, circling the store like hyenas, examining the leftover dresses, searching for anything salvageable. Somehow, among the scraps, I found one long black dress that wasn't horrible. I knew I'd never wear it again, but I bought it immediately. It would have to do.

I hadn't gone to any of the balls in 2009—Matt was working that night and I was still in New York anyway and wasn't all that interested. But this year, I was dying to go. I imagined all of us, in gowns and tuxes, sipping champagne and eating cheese while we watched the Obamas dance. It would be sort of like *Downton Abbey*, but with everyone taking selfies the whole time.

After all the excitement and stress of the election, things had been quiet. And while we were thrilled with the outcome, part of me almost missed how purposeful election season had been—all of our energy had been directed at that one thing. Now, without hours of MSNBC to watch and debates to discuss, we had time on our hands. We were lost. The balls were a reason to celebrate again, something to shake us out of our funk.

The Black Tie and Boots ball was crazy—it was less like a ball and more like a gathering of superdrunk Texans. Ash wore a red shiny dress and a cowboy hat and brought along another tiny cowboy hat that she perched on her stomach. Jimmy (of course) wore his cowboy boots. I'd gotten a blow-out that day and asked them to make it "big," thinking that would be festive, but it looked tame compared to everyone else's. At one point, the band played "Deep in the Heart of Texas," and Matt and I got caught in some sort of mosh pit. Our eyes met as we were tossed around by all the rowdy, singing Texans, and I thought for sure it would be the end of us. We had no choice but to join in and wound up drinking whiskey until morning.

The next day, we ignored our hangovers and went to an Iowa reunion party at the Hilton across the street, where I tripped on my heels and fell forward, hitting my head on David Axelrod's back. He was nice about it, but I was mortified and Matt said later, "You just need to watch where you're going," like I was a reckless child.

On Monday, Ash and I got our hair done in the afternoon and then went back to my place to hang out until it was time to get ready. She'd brought her stuff over so that we could get dressed together—we thought it would be more fun that way. "Like prom," she said, and then pointed to her stomach. "Well, not exactly like prom."

We sat on the couch and chatted, sitting upright so we wouldn't ruin our hair. I was already exhausted from the previous two nights and I could feel my eyes closing, and wished I could take a quick nap, but I felt like I couldn't complain in front of Ash, who was going to all the same parties as I was, but carrying an extra person around. She was so pregnant that crowds parted as they saw her stomach coming toward them, which was actually a really helpful way to navigate the parties. "I'm fine," she kept saying. I think she was tired of everyone widening their eyes when they saw her and saying, "Whoa," like they thought she was going to go into labor right then and there. And still, she insisted on wearing heels. Which almost seemed dangerous, but she assured me she could handle it.

Jimmy got dressed at home and then came over,

so we could all ride together, and when Ash and I were done putting on our makeup, we found him and Matt sitting on the couch, each holding a beer and looking bleary.

"How are we doing?" I asked.

"I'm not sure," Matt said. "This is like senior week, only now we're old."

"You ladies look beautiful," Jimmy said, standing up and stretching.

"Beth does, at least," Ash said. "I look like a float in a parade."

"But the most beautiful float I've ever seen," Jimmy said, and Ash stuck her tongue out at him.

Jimmy went out to flag down a cab, which took about twenty minutes. We didn't talk much on the ride there, but I was still excited for the night. In 2009, there had been ten balls that Obama attended, but this year there were just two, and they were both in the Convention Center, on different floors. We were attending the "official" ball, but had gotten good tickets, and Jimmy somehow finagled us passes to a VIP area, where we sat on couches and had access to an open bar. We were in a raised loft that over-looked the room, and we watched as different performers took the stage, laughing and cheering when Alicia Keys sang, "Obama's on Fire."

The ball itself wasn't exactly what I had expected. The Convention Center was huge, and we walked for what felt like miles once we were inside and had checked our coats. There was draping everywhere—to separate the different areas mostly, but also I think to try to make the place look nicer. The whole thing felt like a really big wedding in a warehouse that someone tried to disguise as a ballroom. As we walked to the VIP area, we passed tables of vegetables and dip, and long lines of people waiting for a drink from the bar.

I was afraid we'd all be too tired to enjoy it, but we woke up once we were there and had a few drinks. It helped that it felt like they were pumping oxygen into the cold room, like we were in Vegas. As the night went on, Jimmy was able to get more and more of our friends into our section, and soon it felt like we had our own personal area of the ball. Alan kept fidgeting in his tux, and Benji, with his bow tie already undone, looked so young that he really could have passed for someone going to prom. Lissy and Cameron were there, wearing matching dresses, both from Rent the Runway. "We didn't coordinate before we ordered," Lissy told me with a strained smile, like she was trying her best to find it amusing. "That was our mistake."

Cameron shrugged like she couldn't have cared less. "I've already seen three other women wearing this anyway," she said. I think she was trying to make Lissy feel better, but instead, Lissy's eyes got wide.

"Well, that's just great," she said. "The worst part is, we can't stand next to each other for the whole night." And then she turned and walked away in a huff.

At one point, we started a little dance floor, Jimmy spinning Ash around until she laughed and said she was afraid she might tip over.

When the Obamas came out, we all stood at the edge of the balcony and clapped. The President gave a short speech and then they danced as Jennifer Hudson sang Al Green's "Let's Stay Together."

"They are just the best couple," Ash said, holding her hands to her heart, as if we really were at a wedding of our dear friends who just happened to invite about a million people and some really famous musicians to celebrate with them.

Toward the end of the night, I couldn't find Matt. At first I was worried and then annoyed as everyone started leaving and my feet started throbbing. He'd been gone for over an hour and wasn't answering his phone, but I stood with Ash and Jimmy and just kept calling him again and again.

"No one knows where he went," Jimmy said, but he was sort of slurring and I had the feeling Matt could've walked right in front of him and he wouldn't have noticed.

"We'll wait with you until you find him," Ash said.

"No, that's crazy. You need to get home. I'll be

fine. He couldn't have left without me, right?" I forced a laugh, but it came out sounding kind of angry. "Really, go," I said, giving her a hug. "I don't know how you're still standing."

"All right," she said. "I should get this man home. But text as soon as you find him, okay?"

I promised that I would and, after they left, went to sit on a couch along the wall. Now that Jimmy and Ash (and most of the people we knew) were gone, I felt like an impostor in the VIP section, like someone might come along and kick me out. I sipped my drink, which was mostly melted ice, just to have something to do and sent Matt a string of angry texts: *Where are you?! Call me! WTF?*

After thirty minutes, I'd just decided that I was going to leave when I saw Matt bounding up the stairs to me. His face was flushed and he was smiling.

"Where have you been?" I asked. I was so mad my hands were shaking. "I've been calling and texting you for almost two hours," I said.

"I know," he said. "Sorry. But listen, Beth. Something great just happened."

"You know? Did you hear it ringing? Why didn't you tell me where you were?"

"Just listen," he said. "Billy took me to another area downstairs, a different VIP room."

"Well, great," I said, sarcastically. "I'm so glad you were having fun."

Matt continued talking like he hadn't heard me. "The executive director of the Maryland Democratic Party was there, and he told Billy he wanted to talk to me."

"Why?" I asked, my curiosity overriding my anger for a moment. "Do you know him?"

"I've met him once before."

"So, why did he want to see you?"

"I'm not really sure, but we talked for a long time. He asked about my job and my time on the campaign and then about running for office."

"How did he know about that?"

"I don't exactly keep it a secret," Matt said. "Anyway, he asked a ton of questions and then asked if he could take me for a drink next week. Said he had something he wanted to talk to me about."

"Really? What do you think it is?"

"I don't know," he said. He was so excited and fidgety that he was almost bouncing. "But I think it's something good."

When I got up the next morning, everything hurt—my feet, my hair, my head. I was still cranky about the night before. Matt and I had bickered on the way home, and I mentioned it again as soon as we woke up. I kept insisting that he should've told me he was leaving or at least answered my text. "What did you want me to do?" he asked. "Interrupt the guy and say, 'Sorry, let me just text my wife'?"

"Yes," I said, and he laughed. He was still giddy, so much so that he wasn't bothered at all by my anger. We were working from home that day, which meant that I stayed in bed until noon and wrote a shitty first-person account of attending the ball. We both had bags under our eyes, but Matt didn't seem tired at all. He whistled as he checked his e-mail.

When he said we should be ready to leave by 7:00, I sighed and said, "I'm so sick of going to balls." Matt just stared at me, and I said crossly, "I know that sounded ridiculous."

The Staff Ball was also at the Convention Center, so we took a cab there again. It was just like the night before, except my feet were more swollen. Ash texted me right after we arrived to let me know that they were standing in the coat-check line. This ball was much smaller, contained in one room, but it was still crowded, and maybe I was imagining it, but everyone seemed just as cranky as I was; we all looked a little rumpled, a little warmed over.

When Jimmy realized it wasn't open bar, he said, "Are you fucking kidding? We didn't have to pay for drinks in '09."

Ash rolled her eyes behind him and then whispered to me, "I woke up at three a.m. to find him eating a jumbo slice in bed, so I don't think he needs unlimited whiskey tonight."

Benji had four friends from college staying with him, sleeping on his couch and floor. They'd all come in from out of town for the inauguration and he'd gotten them tickets to all the events. But when we saw him that night, he was alone. "Are your friends here?" I asked him, and he shrugged.

"They're around here somewhere," he said, like he didn't care at all. "Those fuckers were up all night drinking. I didn't sleep."

Lady Gaga's performance cheered everyone up a little bit, but we all left right after Obama spoke. I was so happy as I crawled into bed that night. I felt like I could sleep for a year.

"We survived," Matt said. His voice was hoarse. "What did you think? Was it everything you imagined?"

"It was great," I said, my eyes already closed. "And I'm so glad it's over."

The next week, Matt went to go meet the executive director at a bar in Annapolis. "Call me as soon as you're done," I said. "Before you even start the car." I waited with my phone next to me all night, and finally got a text that said, *Heading home now. All good news! But I'll tell you in person. Love you!*

I was tempted to call him right back, but I was

the one always telling him not to be on his phone while he drove, so I didn't. It felt like forever before I heard his key turn in the lock, and I ran down to meet him at the door, which made him laugh.

"Finally!" I said. "I've been dying here. What happened?"

He kissed me hello and then I followed him up the stairs, waiting right behind him as he took off his jacket and hung it on the banister. He was smiling, looking like he had a good secret and was enjoying making me wait to hear it.

"So you know Dan Cullen? He's the state senator for District Sixteen?" I nodded even though I didn't really know who he was, but the name sounded vaguely familiar and I wanted Matt to keep talking. "Well, it turns out he's thinking of retiring, which means his seat would be open in 2014."

"And?"

"And they wanted to know if I'd consider running for it." Matt looked puffed up at this point—his chest and cheeks big, like he was actually going to burst.

"I can't believe it," I said.

"I know," Matt said. "I mean, it's still over a year away, and nothing's definite. He just wanted to float the idea, to see if I'd be interested. That's all."

But I could see he was already picturing it—

the house in Maryland, the campaign, his dream becoming a reality. In his mind, it was a done deal.

District 16 covered the area where Matt's brothers lived, not too far from where he grew up. It contained parts of Bethesda and Silver Spring, which were a couple of the towns that he always suggested would be nice for us to live in one day. We'd been up there a bunch, of course, to spend time with his family, and it was nice and suburban and still pretty close to DC, which Matt always used as a selling point.

When Matt told Babs the news, I could hear her scream through the phone. It's possible she was even more excited than he was. Probably, she was just thrilled there was a chance Matt would be living even closer to her than he was now. The two of them talked on the phone for over an hour that night. I could only imagine how many more times we'd have to listen to the story of Matt dressing up as Ronald Reagan over the next year, and my heart broke a little in advance for Patrick.

I asked Matt if he was going to tell Jimmy and he told me he already had—which meant he'd called Jimmy from the car, which bothered me although I pretended it didn't so it wouldn't ruin Matt's excitement. It meant that instead of calling me right after his meeting, he'd chosen Jimmy.

And I knew that Jimmy understood more of this stuff, that the two of them talked about it all the time, but still. I was the one he was married to.

Each time Matt discussed the possibility of running, he made sure to say in a serious voice that it was still too early to get really excited, but you could tell he was just saying it as a formality; a superstition so he wouldn't jinx himself.

Matt started sending me links to houses in Maryland, sometimes over ten a day, and I'd click through them and try to picture living there, examining hardwood floors and remodeled kitchens. None of the places were that far from where we were currently living; distance-wise, they were all less than ten miles away. But it felt like so much more, like it was a whole other world.

One Saturday we went to an open house. "Just to get a feel for it," Matt said. "Just to see what the market's like."

I felt like a fraud taking one of the flyers and walking through the house—surely they'd notice that we weren't really looking, that we couldn't possibly be moving to Maryland. But Matt chatted with the agent, shaking her hand on the way out, telling her we'd be in touch. It was a charming brick house on a hilly street with a little cobblestone path that led from the front door down to the sidewalk.

"What'd you think?" Matt asked as we got in the car.

"It was nice," I said. "Expensive."

He looked over at me. "It doesn't sound like you liked it."

"It's not that," I said. "It's just overwhelming. This is all happening so fast."

"I know," Matt said, grinning at me. For a second, I thought he was ignoring the fact that I sounded unhappy about the whole thing, but I think he was actually too excited to notice.

"It's hard to wrap my head around it," I continued. "The whole thing still doesn't seem real."

Matt drove to the end of the block and braked at the stop sign, waited an extra beat to look around at the neighborhood before continuing on. He sounded cheerful, but also a little firm as he said, "But it is, Beth. It is real. This is happening."

And then just a few weeks later, it was over. Matt came home from work looking miserable and told me that Dan Cullen had decided to run again. "He said he felt like he still had more to give," Matt said.

"Matt, that sucks," I said. "He called you himself?"

Matt shook his head. "The director called me. He told me not to get frustrated, that there would be other opportunities."

221

"Well, that's good," I said.

"It's not good. It's bullshit. He told me there would most likely be a seat opening up in the same area in the House of Delegates."

"And you're not interested?"

"No," Matt said. His words were clipped. "Last election, a twenty-three-year-old kid got an open seat. I don't want to waste my time with that."

"Matt, I'm sorry. I know how much you wanted this. But just think how fast this all happened. You'll get another chance to run if you want to."

"It's not that easy," Matt said. He went upstairs to change out of his suit, but didn't come back down like he usually did. Finally, I went to look for him, found him sitting on the bed on top of the covers, slumped and looking at his BlackBerry.

"Hey," I said. "Do you want to order dinner?"

He shrugged. "I'm not really hungry."

"Okay," I said. "Maybe I'll order some sushi. I'll get some extra for you to eat later?"

"Whatever."

I walked over to Matt and kissed the side of his head, then walked downstairs without saying anything else. I was afraid if I stayed in the room too long, if I tried to comfort him any more that he'd figure me out, if he hadn't already. Because when he'd told me the news, my heart broke for him—but right before that, for a split second, I have to admit that I felt relieved.

. . .

Vivienne Rose Dillon was born on February 14, a couple of weeks early, but healthy. Ash posted pictures of the baby just hours after she was born, with lipsticked kisses all over her head and face. The caption read: "Our little Valentine is here!"

"Look at this," I said to Matt, holding it up for him.

"Huh," he said, and then turned back to the TV.

"It's probably not superhealthy to put lipstick on a baby that's like two hours old, right?"

Matt shrugged. We'd been doing this for a few days, since he found out about the senate seat—I tried to bait him into conversation and he replied with as few words as possible. It would take time, I figured, for him to shake this off. And in the meantime, I'd just be cheerful and supportive.

"I told them we'd come see the baby tomorrow," I said. "You should text Jimmy."

"I did."

I tried to think of something else to say, some question to ask him so he'd have to keep talking to me. This version of my husband was hard to handle—usually he was the upbeat one, and I was already exhausted by the level of pep I was trying to maintain. I sat there for a few minutes, but when I couldn't think of anything else to talk about, I got up and left him alone. He didn't really seem to notice.

• • •

The next night, Matt got home as I was in the middle of tying a bow onto a bag of little gifts for Ash. "Hey," I said. "Do you think you'll be ready to leave in like twenty minutes?"

He stared at me with a blank look for a second, and so I said, "For the hospital?"

"Oh right," he said. "I forgot. Do I really need to go?"

My hands were still holding the ribbon, and I stopped tying and stared at him. "Are you kidding?" I asked.

"No," he said.

"We already told them we were coming," I said.

"I'm sure they'll live," he said. "I really don't feel like it. Just tell them I'm busy."

"Matt, they're going to know that's not true. Come on, it will just take an hour."

He sighed like he was being unfairly treated. "Fine," he said. "If it's that big of a deal, I'll go."

We drove the five minutes to GW in silence and I almost regretted insisting that he come. I didn't want Matt to be sulking in the corner and I really didn't want him to announce the reason for his bad mood either—Ash had gone into labor before Matt could tell Jimmy about Dan Cullen's decision, so they didn't know that anything had changed.

"I know you don't feel like doing much," I

224

said as we parked the car. "But I think this will mean a lot to them."

Matt turned off the ignition and said, "Whatever. Let's just get this over with."

But when we arrived at their room, Matt put on a smile. Jimmy was holding the baby in a light pink blanket, and Ash was sitting up in bed, eating chocolate pudding. Her face was a little puffy and her eyes looked tired, but she had makeup on and her hair was curled. "My mom did my hair," she said, when I told her she looked great.

Jimmy put the baby right in my arms, and she was so light it made me nervous. I slowly lowered myself into a chair, and then pulled the blanket back to get a better look at Viv. Her hands were clasped together, like a little worried old lady. Viv had a headband on, with a bow so large it looked like it might harm her. (She was wearing this bow in even her earliest pictures, and I can only imagine that Ash had barely finished pushing her out before leaning over to strap it on her head.)

"We've been telling her all day that her godparents were coming to see her," Ash said.

Jimmy laughed and said, "So that's our way of asking if you'll be Vivienne's godparents."

"Of course," Matt said. "We'd be honored."

Matt and I looked at each other across the room then, and I smiled to thank him for pretending to be in a good mood. Jimmy saw us and said,

"Oh, I know what that look means. I bet someone has baby fever." Matt and I managed to make ourselves laugh, and I hoped we were the only ones who noticed how fake it sounded.

Colleen had her baby just a few days after Ash, a little girl they finally named Bea after a great deal of discussion. "Bruce wants to call her Theresa," Colleen told me when I visited her in the hospital. "Theresa Murphy. It makes her sound like a nun."

I didn't ask Matt to come with when I went to visit Colleen. It didn't seem worth an argument, so I went back to GW myself, right back to the maternity floor where we'd just been. And when I told her that Matt was busy at work, she just said, "Oh, that's fine," as if it hadn't even occurred to her that he would be there.

But it bothered me. I knew Matt was upset, but he'd always been the kind of person to brush off disappointment, knowing somehow that something better would come along. The way he was acting now was different from anything I'd ever seen before and it unsettled me. I didn't say any of this to Colleen, of course. Instead I just cooed over the baby, smiled, and said, "He so wishes he could be here."

Later that week, Matt and I brought dinner to the Dillons. Matt wasn't in a good mood, exactly, but for the most part he'd stopped pouting. He was quiet, but when I told him we were taking dinner over there, he just nodded in agreement. He did say, "That's so midwestern of you," but it didn't sound particularly mean, so I just said, "I know."

I was expecting the Dillons' place to look like a disaster area—bottles and diapers everywhere, but when we arrived it was neat and tidy and Viv was sleeping. They even had a fire going. "Everything looks amazing," I said as I hugged Ash. "You two are superheroes."

"Oh, Celeste came today," Ash said. "She's going to come a few times a week until we get a hold on things."

Celeste was the cleaning lady we both used. We shared so many things with them—vacations, secrets, dinners—that it only seemed right that we shared her too. It was the Dillons who'd found her first and raved about how great she was.

I'd wanted a cleaning lady for a long time, but Matt had resisted, saying it was just the two of us and we could handle our own mess. Babs was always suggesting that Rosie come to our house, saying they were out of town often enough that she didn't have enough to do there.

I tried to decline this offer, but Babs waved me off. "She used to the do the same for the other boys," she said. "But now they all have their own cleaning ladies, naturally." I was uncomfortable with this arrangement for a lot of reasons—was I the only one to see how strange it was to have Rosie "lent" to us, like she belonged to Babs? (The answer to that was yes, because when I brought it up, Matt looked at me like I was crazy. "No one," he said slowly, "thinks anyone owns anyone else.")

It didn't make sense to me that Matt was against hiring a cleaning lady, but completely okay having Rosie do our cleaning. We argued about this, and I felt like I was never going to win. But after the Dillons hired Celeste and kept insisting we should do the same, Matt agreed. "Sounds perfect," he said. "We've been looking for someone for a while."

I almost choked on my soup, but didn't say anything. If Matt's Single-White-Female attitude toward Jimmy was going to get us a cleaning lady, I was happy to keep my mouth shut.

Right after we got to the Dillons' that night, I put the lasagna in the oven and the salad on the table. Ash had insisted that we could bring dinner only if we stayed as well, and when I tried to say that seemed to defeat the purpose of being helpful, she said, "We want to spend time with you two. That's the purpose. You have to stay."

Viv woke up shortly after I put the lasagna in, and Ash took her over to the couch to feed her.

I sat next to her, but Matt and Jimmy stood having a drink in the other room. (Mostly I think, because Matt looked uncomfortable as soon as Ash started unbuttoning her shirt.)

I'd heard Matt tell Jimmy about the senate seat, and heard Jimmy say, "Oh man, that sucks," and then move on to another topic. I couldn't tell if he didn't want to dwell on it for Matt's sake or if he just didn't know how upset Matt really was. Ash and I chatted on the couch about breast-feeding and how sore her nipples were, a conversation that I'm sure Matt was happy to miss. By the time the lasagna was ready, Viv was fed, burped, changed, and already sleeping again. We all stood looking at her for a moment before sitting down. "I mean, all she does is sleep and eat," Jimmy said. "She has it pretty good."

I cut the lasagna and scooped it onto the plates, concentrating so hard on keeping the cheese from dripping onto the table that I missed part of the conversation and only tuned in when I heard Matt say, "Really? Congratulations!"

"Congratulations for what?" I asked.

"Jimmy got a job at Facebook," Ash said.

"I didn't want to curse it," Jimmy said. "So I didn't tell anyone I was interviewing. I just got the offer today."

"Wow," I said. "That's great." I held up my glass and we all clinked. I couldn't bear to look over at Matt as we did this, but I snuck a peek at him as Jimmy started talking. Matt looked somber while Jimmy described his position as policy communications manager. "They have an office in Houston, too," he said. "So eventually we can make that move."

We didn't make any plans before consulting the Dillons and vice versa—there was no party we RSVP'd for, no new restaurant we tried, no vacation we booked without discussing it with them first. We were a team, the four of us. Or so I'd thought. But that night, as Jimmy spoke, I felt something like distrust. It was so similar to what had happened the last time he got a new job that I had a sense of déjà vu as he spoke.

I couldn't tell you what we talked about for the rest of the dinner—we weren't there all that long. Viv woke up again and I insisted on cleaning up, loading the dishes into the dishwasher as quickly as I could. The timing of this couldn't have been worse, Jimmy getting a great new job while Matt was still dealing with his disappointment. And I couldn't stop thinking how strange it was that Matt told Jimmy everything but that it didn't work the other way around.

When we got home, Matt went to the kitchen for a beer. I wanted to ask him if he felt the same way I did, like the Dillons were keeping things from us, but even in my head it sounded paranoid. Maybe it was just that I'd thought our friendship was more than it was. Ash once got drunk and told me that she and Jimmy liked to role-play in the bedroom, that she owned a dirty schoolgirl costume for this very reason. And Jimmy always joked about the first hand job Ash had given him, how awful it was, how he thought she'd permanently harmed him but continued to date her anyway. I'd just assumed that friends who would tell you that much about their lives would tell you everything. But maybe I was wrong. Maybe I'd been wrong about them all along.

But I didn't want to upset Matt any more by talking about it, so I just opened my own beer and the two of us sat on the couch with the TV on, staring straight ahead, but not really watching.

"I wonder if they'll move soon," Matt said finally, and I didn't mean to sound as irritable as I did when I replied, "Who knows what they'll do?"

The next week, Celeste came to our house to clean, and at one point she said, "It's so exciting about Mr. Jimmy's new job."

"It is," I said.

"It will be exciting for him at the Facebook."

I smiled at Celeste, wondering when she'd found out about the job. I imagined Ash telling her about the interview weeks earlier, unable to keep it in. And when Celeste said, "It's going to be very big," as she ran her dustcloth over our shelves, I just nodded and said, "Very big."

• • •

When the Dillons told us that April that they were moving, I cried. Ash did too, and we hugged like we were never going to see each other again. But to be honest, there was a part of me that felt relieved, that thought maybe it would be better for us if we didn't spend so much time with them. They were just so lucky, so charmed. Everything was working out for them, life was unfolding exactly as it should—and most of the time, it seemed like it was all happening without any effort on their part. And when they sat and marveled at Viv and Jimmy talked about his new job, Matt and I would watch them, more aware than ever of what we didn't have. Sometimes when we were around them, I'd feel a sharp sense of betrayal, like they'd left us behind.

But I never said any of this out loud. Instead, we went over to their apartment the night before they left, sat in a circle of lawn chairs (all of their furniture was gone), and drank vodka out of plastic cups. And at the end of the night, when we hugged good-bye, I said, "What are we ever going to do without you here?"

Chapter 12

I sat on the bed and watched Matt pack his suitcase, carefully, as he always did. He was an unusually slow packer, folding a shirt over and over to get it right, rearranging piles to make sure they fit just so. Usually, I teased him about it, sometimes setting a timer to see if he could set a new record. But he had the same look he'd had on his face for over a month now—mouth set in a straight line, eyebrows wrinkled like he'd just heard unpleasant news—and I knew he wasn't in the mood for a joke.

"Are you bringing your running shoes?" I asked.

"Yeah," he said, not looking up.

"Okay. And you think we should leave by ten a.m. tomorrow?" At this, he just nodded. I waited a few seconds and then said, "You know, if you don't want to go we can skip it. Or go later in the week."

Matt looked up, surprised. "I never said I didn't want to go."

"I know. It's just you seem . . ." I tried to find a nice way to say angry or annoyed.

"What?" he asked.

"I don't know, never mind. It was just a suggestion."

"Plus, we can't skip it. My mom would have a heart attack."

"Yeah," I said. "I know."

Matt's parents spent most of the summer at their house in St. Michaels, Maryland, and during the third week of August the entire family joined them. Throughout the summer, Michael's and Will's families went up there other random weekends, and so did Meg, and sometimes even we did too. But Babs was firm on the fact that no matter what, she wanted everyone together for one week. No excuses.

This trip never really felt like a vacation to me, mostly because the Kellys weren't the kind of family who slept in or sat around reading novels in the sun. They took boats out on the water, played badminton or football, organized tennis tournaments and swimming races. They never sat down. It was like spending a week at a weird adult athletic camp with highly competitive campers.

Matt had spent the whole summer focused on Dan Cullen's senate seat, unable to let go of (what he kept calling) his missed chance. He was obsessed with what he should do next and it was almost impossible to have a conversation with him about anything else. Once, he even (God help us) used the word *legacy*. He kept mentioning classmates of his from Harvard (all wildly successful, of course) and comparing himself to them, like everyone he graduated with was going to think he was a failure.

Part of me thought he'd be calmer with the Dillons out of town, but it soon became clear that he missed being able to discuss his career with Jimmy and so I became his default sounding board on all things relating to Matt's Career, and it was wearing on me. It was wearing on us. And I didn't think a solid week with his family would help the situation.

"All done," Matt said, zipping up his suitcase. "What about you?"

"Yep," I said. "All packed and ready to go."

We didn't get on the road until almost 10:30 the next day, which I knew drove Matt crazy. It only took about an hour and a half to get there, but Matt liked to be the first to arrive, because in the Kelly family, even the drive to vacation could become a competition.

"We'll be fine," I said, when we got in the car. "There's no rush to get there." What I meant, of course, was I'm in no rush to get there. I picked up the coffee that Matt had gotten for me and took a sip. He'd added just the right amount of cream, and it tasted perfect. I drank my coffee and stared out the window, knowing that this would be the most peaceful part of my week, trying to savor the quiet.

I never considered myself to be unathletic until I started going to St. Michaels with the Kellys. I played volleyball in junior high and soccer in high school and maybe I wasn't the best on the team, but I certainly wasn't the worst. I was coordinated. I could stand upright and hit a ball. I played shortstop for the *Vanity Fair* softball team, for Christ's sake.

But my first year in St. Michaels, things changed. During a heated volleyball game, Will spiked the ball over the net and it hit me right on the nose. When I opened my eyes, he was watching me through the net with a scrunched-up face. "Everyone, take five," he shouted to everyone who was playing, as if they didn't see the blood that was spilling out of my nose. Will led me inside, sat me down in the kitchen, put a bunch of ice cubes in a baggie, and wrapped them in a towel for me to put on my nose. I'd met Will just a few times before this trip, and I was mortified to have him see me like this.

"It's okay," I kept saying to him. "Really, I don't think it's broken." I had no idea if it was broken or not, but it felt like I needed to reassure him. He was looking at me nervously, like he was afraid I was going to start crying.

"Keep the ice on as long as you can," Will said. Matt had taken his nephews out on a kayak, and Will kept looking at the door hoping that he would show up.

"You can go back out," I said. "I'm okay, I promise."

"Are you sure?" Will asked.

"Yes, I'm totally fine. I'll just sit here with the ice." I wanted desperately for him to leave then, and he finally did after patting me on the shoulder and telling me to "hang in there." I listened to the volleyball game resume outside, and stayed in the kitchen until the bag of ice started to melt and drip down my face.

My nose wasn't broken, but it did swell up and I had two light purple bruises underneath my eyes. There's a group picture from that trip that Babs has hanging in the kitchen, of everyone standing on the dock. Someone must have taken it from a boat on the water, but I don't remember who. (It seems like something they would have had me do, since we weren't engaged yet and Babs didn't like to have non–family members in family pictures.) I always look at the picture when we go to their house—the shot is far away, but you can still see that my nose is lumpy and miscolored.

On the last night of the trip, when Will knew it was okay to joke about my nose (and probably couldn't help himself any longer, because the Kellys needed to make a joke out of everything), he stood up and toasted me. We were all eating crabs, as we always did for the first and last meals of the trip, and Babs had laid out news-papers on the table and put metal buckets in the middle for the shells. Everyone had mallets in their hands, and I was concentrating on my crab, trying to ignore the splashes of butter and pieces of shell that were flying everywhere. (After these dinners, the smell of Old Bay and crab lingered every-where.)

Will stood up and wiped his hands, then hit his mallet lightly against his beer bottle. He cleared his throat. "I'd just like to take a minute to announce that the volleyball MVP award will be going to Beth, who was willing to use any body part to stop the ball. Well done, Beth!" He held up his bottle and chanted, "Hip, hip, hooray!" until everyone joined in.

The whole table clapped and cheered, even Nellie, who'd said, "Oh, Will," in a halfhearted defense of me when he announced my name. I knew that I had to smile, so as not to seem like a bad sport, a killjoy who couldn't take a joke, and so I did even though it made my nose throb. Matt put his arm around my shoulders and pulled me close to him, but he was also laughing. That was the thing about the Kellys, they always thought they were so damn funny.

When everyone quieted down, Babs reached over and patted my arm. "Don't worry about it, dear. Not everyone is an athlete. We all know that."

And I swear to God, with those words I lost any athletic ability I had. It was like the Kellys cursed me. In the vacations that followed in St. Michaels, I fell while running bases, tipped over a canoe, and wiped out on a bike. The harder I tried, the more of a danger I was to myself.

This was never my favorite week of the year, but this time I was really dreading it. Normally in St. Michaels, Matt and I were a team. He watched out for me and brought me Band-Aids when I inevitably hurt myself and started to bleed. We'd go to our room at night and laugh about the things that Babs said to Rebecca, and how drunk Nellie got at dinner. But this year was different. Matt and I were on strange ground—I was at my limit with his career crisis and he was well aware of that. We'd had some snippy exchanges lately, each of us feeling that the other was the one being insensitive. There'd been a few times when I was in the middle of telling a story or talking about work and Matt cut me off to start talking about himself, as if he didn't notice we'd been having a completely different conversation. When I tried to point this out to him, he'd become huffy and told me that it didn't feel like I was supporting him. I was afraid he was losing his mind.

In the car on the way to St. Michaels, Matt said, "Maybe I should start looking in the private sector now, get some experience that way."

"Maybe you should," I said, although I knew he didn't really want my opinion. I was only half paying attention—I'd found it was the best way to get through these long discussions.

"I wanted another year or two in government,

but maybe that's not going to happen. Jimmy said he loves Facebook. That it's the perfect job."

"Did you ever notice that Jimmy loves everything he does?" I asked him. "That he thinks everything is perfect and amazing. Don't you just think that's his approach to it? That he's spinning it that way?"

"I think," Matt said, "that he just keeps getting really fucking lucky." And then we were quiet for the rest of the ride, both of us lost in our own thoughts.

When we pulled up to the house, Grace and Lily were already in their swimsuits and running around the grassy area by the pool, playing some sort of two-person tag and squealing whenever they got close to each other. Meg was in a bikini and sunglasses, lying on her back on a lounge chair, an unopened magazine next to her. She looked like she was sleeping, which she probably was since she'd driven up with Will and Nellie's crew early that morning.

Michael and Will were standing at the end of the dock, each holding a beer, with a large metal bucket at their feet that I knew held ice and more beer. Our nephew Bobby was on the lawn with Jonah, tossing an inflatable ball with him. Bobby was almost twelve and was always very sweet with the younger kids, unlike his brother, Ben, who loved to tease them and who I suspected was a bully at school. Rebecca was on the screened-in porch, wearing her sunglasses and watching Jonah and Bobby like a hawk, like she was just waiting for something bad to happen. She raised her hand at us in greeting, but didn't smile. Matt couldn't get out of the car fast enough, opening the door at the same time he turned the ignition off. "I'm going to say hi to Michael and Will," he said, already walking toward the dock. I stood and watched everyone for a few seconds, and took a deep breath.

The Kellys' place was on a beautiful piece of land, nearly three acres, with one large house and two tiny cottages behind it. There was a pool, and a screened-in porch that overlooked the grass heading down toward the water, and a stone deck on the side of the house with six Adirondack chairs, painted a cheery red, all lined up in a row. There was also an outdoor fireplace, where we gathered most nights after dinner so the kids could roast marshmallows.

Charles and his four brothers had bought the property almost thirty years earlier, and used to bring all their families up at the same time. Now they mostly took turns, although Charles and Babs used it most, not shy about telling everyone that they had invested the most in the place and had the right to do so.

Above the front door, there was a sign that read: THE PANCAKE HOUSE, EST. 1970. The first year I went there, I turned to Matt in disbelief (I'd already heard the Patrick Pancake story by then), and he just smiled and shook his head and told me that Pancake was the surname of the family who'd owned the house before them. "My dad and my uncles got a kick out of it, so they left it up there," he said. The two cottages behind were called Bacon and Eggs, because one was yellow and one was brown and I guess they decided to stick with the breakfast theme. Patrick and Rebecca always stayed in the little brown cottage, and at least ten times during the vacation, one of the Kelly brothers would ask, "Where's Pancake?" and wait for someone to say, "He's in Bacon," so they could all laugh.

Matt and I were always shuffled around to whatever room or cottage was left—we were childless and could stay anywhere. One year, we'd stayed in Eggs, which offered more privacy but meant we had to cross the lawn to get to the bathroom in the morning, so it was a trade-off.

This year, we were in the main house with most everyone else. Babs put us in a bedroom that opened right up onto the lawn with a great view of the water. Patrick, Rebecca, and Jonah were in Bacon (as always), and Eggs would be split evenly between the nieces and nephews, each of them getting three nights there and sleeping on the floor of the living room for the last night. (There had been a fight over how to divide the uneven number of days at Sunday dinner a few weeks earlier, and it had resulted in so much screaming and crying that Babs declared Eggs would stay empty for a night to keep the peace.)

I left the bags in the car, deciding that Matt and I could bring them in later, and went to join Rebecca on the porch. Last year, Jonah had still been young enough that he couldn't really keep up with the other kids. Now he was old enough to play with them and Rebecca seemed out of sorts without him by her side. He was laughing and clearly having fun with Bobby, and she looked like it was torturing her.

"We thought you'd beat us here," Rebecca said as I sat down.

"Believe me, Matt intended to be the first one here. We just had a slow morning."

She nodded. At the end of the dock, Matt was holding a beer and talking to his brothers, waving his hands in an excited way, and I wondered what he could be telling them.

Patrick smiled at me as he came out of Bacon, happy that Rebecca had company, I think. "Everything's unpacked," he said to her. "The air mattress is all set up for Jonah. Hopefully he'll be okay with it."

"Hopefully," Rebecca said. "Otherwise, he'll end up in bed with us."

"Which would be just like home then," Patrick

said to me, but he had a laugh in his voice. He turned back to Rebecca. "Do you need me to do anything else? I was going to go join the guys on the dock, but if you need anything . . ."

"No, I think we're all set," Rebecca said, although you could tell that she wished she had a reason to keep him there.

I didn't blame Rebecca for disliking Babs or not wanting to spend time with the Kellys—it certainly wasn't my favorite thing to do. But then I'd look around at this beautiful vacation house and think, Oh, poor you. Suck it up. Being around Rebecca was a reminder of just how miserable you could make yourself, and I decided then that I would have a good time that week—there is nothing like being around a negative person to make you determined to be positive.

Jenny and Nellie came out of the house then, both wearing Lululemon cropped pants, tank tops, and sneakers. "You made it," Jenny said, leaning down to hug me. "Do you want to come for a walk with us? We're going to power-walk every day. Burn some calories." As she said this, she slapped her right thigh, which was thin and muscular and didn't move.

"I think I'll skip today," I said. "Our bags are still in the car."

"Is Matt already out there with the other boys?" Nellie asked. She shaded her eyes and squinted out at the dock. "God, they act like teenagers here, don't they?" But her voice was full of affection, and I knew she was glad that Will was having fun, even if it meant he'd be drunk by dinner and she'd have to deal with the kids alone.

"Rebecca, what about you? Are you up for a walk?"

"I think I'll sit this one out," she said.

"Good God, is Meg still lying by the pool?" Nellie asked. "She must have gotten wasted last night. As soon as we picked her up, she asked if we could stop at McDonald's, and then she shoved an Egg McMuffin in her face and fell asleep immediately. She reeked of booze. Conor and Lily spent the whole ride putting stickers on her while she slept. They ran out of stickers before she even moved at all." But just like when she talked about Will getting drunk, there was amuse-ment in her voice. All of the Kellys got a kick out of it when someone drank too much. My parents would have been horrified, but even Babs laughed at the story of a drunk Will throwing up on the country club golf course as a teenager.

They walked toward the dock, and Jenny yelled, "We're going for a walk. Are you watching your children?" Michael gave her a thumbs-up and Will held up his beer in response.

It always surprised me how relaxed the Kellys were about their kids on vacation. (Minus Rebecca and Patrick, of course.) The children were allowed to run wild, playing in the woods and swimming as long as an adult was "present," which meant anywhere on the property. And I couldn't believe they were going to let the kids sleep in Eggs by themselves. Weren't they scared that some child predator would come and steal them? Apparently, the Kellys weren't as paranoid as I was.

After Jennie and Nellie left, Rebecca and I chatted about Jonah's school, and she told me about a boy in the class who had been a biter at age three and this year pulled down his pants at least once a week and chased kids around asking them if they wanted a hot dog. "Can you imagine?" she asked. I laughed, which wasn't the response she was looking for. "I think he must have been abused," she said.

"Maybe," I said. "But some little kids are just really weird."

Rebecca gave a low grunt, which was her way of telling me she didn't agree, and then she called out across the grass to where the boys were playing. "Bobby? It's just about time for Jonah to eat." Of course, I thought. When is it not time for Jonah to eat?

Bobby nodded and bent down to pick up Jonah, which was unnecessary and also a little bit of a struggle since Jonah was six and almost too big to be carried by someone Bobby's size. He waddled over to us and set Jonah down.

"Do you want me to get him a snack, Aunt Rebecca?"

"No, that's okay. We have everything in the cottage."

Jonah didn't seem hungry, but this was apparently a mandatory snack time. And it looked like he was used to being interrupted and forced to eat, because he followed behind Rebecca without protesting.

"He's so lucky to have you as a big cousin," I said to Bobby.

"I'm so lucky to have him as a little cousin," he said. His mannerisms and eagerness had an Eddie Haskell vibe to them, and when he talked to Jonah, he did so in a singsong voice that he'd no doubt heard other adults use when talking to little kids. I figured he must be trying to prove that he wasn't little anymore, that he was a grown-up.

Bobby ran off to join the other boys in the woods, and he left so quickly that I suspected he must have really wanted to be with them all along. I stayed on the porch, enjoying the peace and quiet, until Babs and Charles came back with groceries. I walked over to their car to help them carry the bags in. Babs gave me an air kiss and said, "You two finally made it. We thought we'd have to send a search party out for you." And with that, vacation with the Kellys officially started.

I spent the week reading, keeping score during volleyball games, and playing with my nieces and nephews. During a game of Cornhole, I slipped on the grass and banged my elbow, and when I said to Matt, "I figured I'd be safe throwing a beanbag at a hole," he laughed so hard he cried.

At least with more people around, Matt had a bigger audience to discuss his future plans. Babs would (and did) listen to him talk for hours. I wouldn't say that I ignored him, but I did spend a lot of time with the little ones, relieved that none of them wanted to talk about career paths with me.

One morning, while I French-braided Lily's hair (Grace was waiting patiently next to me for her turn), Rebecca set up a station for all the kids to paint rocks. She had googly eyes, pom-poms, and some other accessories that they could glue on, and the girls were wiggly with excitement. Jonah looked less thrilled, and gazed longingly at the older boys playing Marco Polo in the pool.

Rebecca's entire childcare regiment looked like it deserved its own Pinterest board. She had individual containers for Jonah's snacks that he could carry around, kits of rainy day activities, outdoor art projects, scavenger hunts. Anytime she brought out one of her creations, I could feel Jenny and Nellie exchanging a look. Those two liked to act like they were too overwhelmed and busy to pay attention to what their kids were doing, let alone have time to put together crafts. They were constantly congratulating themselves on having three kids by saying, "Once they out-number you, anything can happen." They posted pictures of their kids with paint on their faces, with the caption "Mother of the Year." They thought Rebecca was fussy, that she tried too hard. It wasn't difficult to imagine them in high school, making fun of anyone who put forth effort and showed that she cared. And while they made sure their girls had enough Lilly Pulitzer dresses to choke a horse, they continued to give the impression that motherhood left them too busy to care about any of it.

Rebecca wasn't a big drinker. Compared to the rest of the Kellys, she was usually downright sober. When she showed up at Sunday dinner, she'd have one glass of wine, which she'd sip on throughout the meal. I think it was her way of silently judging the rest of us. If someone tried to pour more in her glass, she'd put her hand over the top, which often led Babs to mutter "Teetotaler" at her, like it was a dirty word.

But on vacation, all bets were off. Maybe it was the close proximity to everyone, or the fact that she knew she was stuck on the Kelly compound, but most days she started drinking white wine in the afternoons and by dinner she was often tipsy.

On the last day of the trip, she and I sat on the patio, each of us relaxing in an Adirondack chair, a bottle of wine between us. The rest of the family was on the lawn playing a huge game of touch football—even Jonah was out there. When Rebecca said she didn't want to play and the numbers became uneven, everyone looked at me and waited for me to bow out, which I did. It was just as well. I didn't need to end up on crutches.

The two teams were huddled separately, shouting funny threats back and forth, pretending to whisper secret plays to each other. They were loud and the kids were laughing. The last game of the trip was always the rowdiest.

"They think they're the fucking Kennedys," Rebecca said, and I coughed on my wine as I laughed. She wasn't looking at me, she was staring at them, and for a second I wasn't sure if she even knew she'd spoken out loud, but then she continued. "Look at them. They think they're so special. Charmed." She paused and squinted like she was trying to figure them out.

"They do," I said, because it felt like I had to say something. I'd always wanted Rebecca to like me, but I didn't want to become her confidante. I wasn't exactly like Jenny and Nellie, but I didn't want to be included in the outcast portion of the family. I was quick to mock the Kellys, but not belonging to their club would be worse than belonging.

Rebecca turned to look at me. "You have it the worst though," she said. She started laughing—hard, and not in a particularly nice way. I gave her a confused smile while I waited for her to continue, and then she said, barely able to catch her breath, "Because if they're the Kennedys, then you're married to John-John."

Chapter 13

A couple of weeks after we got back from St. Michaels, we were sitting on the couch, watching *The Daily Show*, when Matt's phone rang. We glanced at each other, wondering who would be calling, and then Matt looked down at his phone and said, "It's Jimmy." For a second, I thought he wasn't going to answer, but then he swiped the screen and said, "Hey man, what's up?"

He was quiet for a while, only saying, "Really?" or "Okay," and once, "Wow." I kept trying to catch his eye so he could let me know what was going on, but he wouldn't look up. I bent my head in front of him, which was maybe a little obnoxious, and he held up a finger to me, telling me to wait a minute, and then walked upstairs. I muted the TV to listen to the conversation, but Jimmy was doing most of the talking. When Matt finally came downstairs, he looked a little shocked.

"Is everything okay?" I asked.

"Yeah," he said. "Yeah, it's fine." He was speaking slowly, like he was trying to find the right words, and I waited for him to continue. "Jimmy was approached by some people asking if he'd want to run for the Railroad Commission."

"What? What people?"

"Some 'major Democratic stakeholders,'" he said. Apparently, they want someone new in the Democratic field. There's one guy with some sketchy financial stuff and another old guy who's run like three times already."

"That's crazy. Is he going to do it?"

"It sounds like it. I mean, it's kind of a long shot for him to win the general. But it's great experience. And you never know. They want someone young who can bring energy to the party. They also think he can raise a lot of money."

"What's the position again?"

"Railroad commissioner."

"I've never heard of it."

"You're not from Texas," Matt said.

"Neither are you."

"Jimmy's talked about it before. He thought it would be something to aim for in the future. Like years down the road." Matt closed his eyes and leaned his head back on the couch.

"He wants to be in charge of the railroad?" I asked.

"That's not what they do. They deal with gas and oil regulations. It's hard to explain."

"Was he calling just to tell you?" I asked. I was already bracing myself for this to send Matt into a spiral—one more thing Jimmy got that he didn't, one more step forward that he wasn't taking.

"He said he wanted my advice. If he does this,

he's going to have to start fund-raising soon," he said. Then he gave me a wry smile. "He also just wanted to show off, I think."

"The Jimmy Dillon Show has officially started," I said. "He's probably looking in the mirror, smiling at himself and brushing his hair."

Matt made a small "hmmph" sound, but then he laughed and nodded in agreement. "No shit," he said.

Jimmy officially declared that he was running in November, and that same day he asked Matt to help him put together a fund-raiser in DC. "Can he do that?" I asked. "Get money from people outside of Texas?"

"Oh sure," Matt said. "That's part of why they wanted him to run. He has all these DC connections."

They wanted to get the fund-raiser together quickly, to get people excited about the campaign. "We're going to aim for two weeks from today," Matt said. "We think it'll be good for momentum."

Right after that, there'd be another fund-raiser in Houston, hosted by Jimmy's parents. "We'll raise a lot more money at that one, but the DC one will be great to spread the word."

"Sounds like a good plan," I said. I almost didn't notice that Matt referred to Jimmy's campaign as "we."

• • •

I called Ash that night to have her fill me in on everything. "This is bonkers," she said. "It's all happening so fast. Jimmy is running around like a chicken with his head cut off. He doesn't know which end is up." But I could hear the pride in her voice. I told her they should stay with us when they came to town for the fund-raiser, and she accepted right away. "That would be so great," she said. "I've been thinking it would be hard to be stuck in the hotel room with Viv."

I'd made the offer before telling Matt, and I was worried he'd be annoyed, but he just said, "Oh good." It was hard not to notice that he'd been in a better mood since working on the fundraiser, and when I mentioned that to him, he just said, "Yeah, this is exciting," and I kissed him on his temple, which made him smile and say, "Thank you."

For the next couple of weeks, Ash and I texted all the time and called each other at least once a day. A lot of it was just going over the logistics of the trip—they were only coming for one night, but it felt like there was so much to sort out. We'd been in touch since they moved, of course, but it wasn't with the same frequency as when they lived here. It was nice to have a reason to be in contact so often, and as I texted her one night to tell her that the owner of United States of

Spinning was getting a divorce, I realized just how much I'd missed her.

Ash rented a portable crib and high chair from some company that specialized in traveling with infants, and it was all delivered early on the morning they'd arrive. I set up the high chair in the dining room and hauled the crib upstairs to the guest room, then spent the rest of the day cleaning the apartment.

They got there in the afternoon, and when I opened the door, they were standing on the front stoop, each of them holding a bag with two suitcases behind them. There was so much stuff that I almost made a joke about them moving in, but stopped when I saw their strained smiles.

Instead, I leaned down to Viv and unsnapped her from her stroller. As I picked her up, I noticed the little gold balls on her tiny earlobes. "Look at you, Viv," I said. "With your ears pierced already. Such a lady."

"Yeah," Jimmy said. "Ash surprised me with that a couple weeks ago. You should've seen my mom's reaction. She said, and I quote, 'Your baby looks like a gypsy.'"

Ash rolled her eyes. "I don't think we're going to start taking fashion advice from your mother, Jimmy." Then to me, she said, "Doesn't she look sweet?" I just smiled and nodded, afraid that if I spoke, my voice would reveal how much I hated earrings on babies. Viv still didn't have much hair, but she was nevertheless an incredibly cute (if almost bald) baby. She smiled at me, like she knew what I was thinking.

"To be honest, I wasn't thrilled with them either," Jimmy said. "Which is probably why Ash didn't tell me until after there were two holes in our baby's head."

"We just wanted to surprise Daddy, didn't we?" Ash said, leaning down to adjust the bow on Viv's head. "And we also wanted people to stop thinking you were a boy."

"How on earth could anyone think this child was a boy?" Jimmy asked. "She wears pink every day and always has a bow on her head."

We were all still standing in the doorway, but it was like the two of them were so busy bickering they didn't notice. I figured they were nervous about the fund-raiser and tired from traveling with Viv, so I said, "We're so happy you guys are here. Come in, it's getting cold out there."

Matt had run out to pick up posters for the fund-raiser and to swing by the bar to check on the space one last time. I told Jimmy that Matt had been obsessing about the event all week. "He hasn't talked about anything else," I said.

"That makes two of us," Jimmy said.

Viv was quiet in my arms, looking around the apartment with a serious face, like she was trying to figure out where she was. "Do you remember it here?" I asked her. "Do you miss DC?"

"Nah, she's a Texas girl. Isn't that right?" Jimmy leaned in and made a face at the baby, shook his hair back and forth like a wet dog. Viv laughed and smacked her hands on top of his head.

"Jimmy, don't get her all riled up," Ash said.

"Do you guys want lunch or do you just want to rest? What time is Linda coming?" I asked. Linda was the Dillons' old sitter who was coming to watch Viv that night.

"She'll be here around five. I'm going to feed Viv now," Ash said. "And then I can feed her again before Linda comes." She was on her knees, unzipping the bags and rifling through them, taking things out and placing them on the floor around her. "Where did I put that bib?" she asked, looking around the room. They'd been there for less than twenty minutes and already their stuff was everywhere. The apartment had been clean when they walked in and now looked like a disaster.

"I'm going to jump in the shower and change if that's all right with you," Jimmy said. He was already carrying his bags upstairs.

Ash was still sitting on the floor with stuff all around her, and she just watched Jimmy walk up the stairs, then turned to me and said, "He thought we should leave Viv with his parents for the night, but I didn't want to. And now I think he's trying to prove his point by not helping with her at all. Not that he ever does all that much, anyway."

"Well, I'm happy she's here," I said, kissing her cheek. Above us, we heard the shower turn on, and Ash reached into a bag and pulled out a bib. "Found it!" she said, holding her arm up in triumph.

The fund-raiser was in the upstairs of Darlington House, a small bar right off Dupont Circle, just a few blocks from our place. The four of us were there an hour before it started, to make sure everything was set up. "We should get a good turnout," Matt kept saying. We hung signs out front that told people where to go, and a poster with Jimmy's picture on it at the top of the stairs. That took about five minutes, and then there was nothing to do but wait. We all got a drink and sat at a high table and tried to make small talk. Matt was fidgety and it was rubbing off on the rest of us. Ash chewed her straw and kept looking around the room like she was making sure no one had slipped in while we weren't paying attention. Jimmy kept clapping his hands together, like he was going to make an announcement, but then not saying anything. I had butterflies in my stomach even though this night had nothing to do with me. I could only imagine how Jimmy felt.

People started to arrive right at 6:30, and as soon as we heard footsteps on the stairs, Matt said, "Here we go!" The first person to walk in was Benji, and he pretended to look around the room and then said, "I'm looking for the Good Guys Club. Is this the right place?" Jimmy laughed and walked over to him, shaking his hand and pulling him into a hug at the same time. "It is so good to see you, brother," he said.

I'd offered to sit up front and check off the names of the people who had already donated and take money and checks from those who hadn't. As soon as Benji came in, I went over and took my place. The invite suggested a minimum of fifty dollars, but almost everyone was far more generous. Right after Benji, there was a constant flow of guests, and even though I was working as fast as I could, there was a line for most of the night.

Whenever I looked up, it was easy to tell where Jimmy was in the room. Just like the first night I'd met him, there was always a small circle around him. Ash stayed right by his side the whole night, smiling and hugging everyone she saw.

The event was only supposed to last for two hours, but at 8:00, Matt came over and told me that he'd just arranged for us to have the room until 9:30. As long as people were still coming in, he said, he didn't want to miss the chance for donations.

A lot of people stopped by just to donate, have one drink, and shake Jimmy's hand, but plenty more stayed to hang out, and by the end of the night, it was getting a little loud in there. When it was all done, over four hundred people had come through, and I knew Matt was pleased from the way he kept smiling and rocking back on his heels as he looked around.

Toward the end of the night, Alan rushed in looking flustered. "I didn't make a contribution yet," he said, reaching for his wallet. "But I'd like to now." He looked at me as though we'd never met, and I said, "Alan, hi, it's Beth. Matt's wife?" He blinked and finally said, "Oh, hi. Are you working for the campaign?"

"Just helping out," I said, pulling the money from his fingers and placing it in the box.

Benji was not just the first to arrive but also the last to leave, drunk and a little bit sloppy. He stayed with us, swaying as we gathered our things and took down the posters. We all walked out to the sidewalk together and Jimmy asked him if he was going to get a cab home.

"Home?" he asked. "No, there's a party around here that one of my friends is having." He hugged us all good-bye, and then put his two fingers up as he walked away and shouted, "Peace, brother."

"Must be nice to be twenty-eight," Jimmy said.

"Okay, old man," I said, and everyone laughed.

Matt was holding the poster with Jimmy's face on it, and I made the two of them pose around it for a picture, making sure to get the Darlington House in the background. Matt looked straight at the camera and smiled, and Jimmy turned toward the poster and gave himself a thumbs-up.

"Perfect," I said. "That's a keeper."

The four of us walked up Connecticut Ave to another bar, Maddy's, which was still serving food. We crowded into a booth, and I tucked the money box next to me, keeping one hand on top of it. "Do you think someone's going to steal that from you?" Matt asked.

"You never know," I said. "I don't want to be responsible for losing the campaign funds."

We were all a little giddy, overtired and relieved that the night had gone well. "I think that was a pretty good turnout," Matt said, holding up his beer to Jimmy.

"Good?" Jimmy said as they clinked glasses. "Kelly, you outdid yourself."

Jimmy ordered a round of tequila shots, and when Ash and I protested, he said, "I'm the candidate, and if I buy the shots you have to take them." But when he ordered another round, I held up my hand. "Sorry, I know you're the candidate and all, but I have to sit this one out."

"Me too," Ash said. "Since I have a feeling our daughter isn't going to humor us by sleeping in tomorrow."

"Well, Kelly," Jimmy said. "Are you ready to pick up the slack?"

They did the next two shots quickly, both sucking on limes at the end. I could almost feel the alcohol hit Matt as his body relaxed, and he turned to me with a shit-eating grin. "Careful," I said. "Who do you think is going to carry you home?"

He nuzzled his face in my neck and said, "You, Buzzy. You'll carry me home, of course."

We couldn't stop laughing as we ate, and it felt like we were our old selves—not just the four of us together, but me and Matt too. I couldn't remember the last time I'd seen him like this— the success of the fund-raiser combined with the tequila had made him happier than he'd been in months.

After we ate, Ash and I walked back to the apartment and Matt and Jimmy stayed for another drink. "Just one, I promise," Jimmy said, holding up his hand like he was taking an oath.

"That's the biggest lie I've ever heard," I told him, and he grabbed me and pulled me into a hug. "Maybe I have to work on my poker face," he said.

"Oh my God, Jimmy," Ash said, pulling me away from him. "Please don't strangle our host."

I woke up a few hours later when they came in the front door and I held my breath, hoping they wouldn't wake the baby. But no such luck. They were trying to whisper, I think, but they weren't even coming close. I heard a crash from the kitchen and then the sound of Viv's crying. (In the morning, I discovered the Brita pitcher lying on the floor with a bunch of paper towels around it, the cause of all that noise.) When Matt came into our room, he closed the door behind him and stood there for a minute, letting his eyes adjust to the dark, swaying a little. He stripped down to his boxers, leaving his clothes in a pile on the floor, and got into bed.

"Fun night?" I asked, reaching out to touch his head.

"Yes," he said, his eyes already closed. "Jimmy Dillon is fucking crazy."

The next morning, Ash and I took Viv for a walk to get coffee. Jimmy and Matt were still asleep— Matt hadn't even moved when I got out of bed—and we thought we'd be nice and not wake them up. It was chilly, but not freezing, and Ash bundled Viv up in a hat and layers of blankets, so all we could see was her little face peeking out. "I'm sort of jealous of her right now," I said, as we started down the block. "She looks so warm and she gets to be pushed around."

"I know," Ash said. "She's probably tired since Jimmy snored like an animal all night. Once I woke him up, and he told me that I was the one who was snoring."

We walked the three blocks down to Starbucks and sat at a table by the window. "Do you miss it here?" I asked.

"I do," she said. "But it's weird being back. It feels like we never lived here or like it was a dream or something."

"I know exactly what you mean," I said.

We stopped at Bethesda Bagels on the way back, picking up bagels and cream cheese for ourselves, and bacon, egg, and cheese sandwiches for the boys. "Lord knows, Jimmy will need all the help he can get," Ash said. "I have no idea how he's going to get on a plane today."

"I bet they're still sleeping," I said, but when we walked in the door they were sitting on the couch drinking coffee, looking exhausted and rumpled. They stopped talking as we walked in and turned to look at us, making me feel like we'd interrupted them, like they were trying to hide something.

"We brought bagels," I said, holding up the bag and giving Matt a curious look, trying to figure out what was going on. But he wouldn't meet my eyes.

"Oh, thank God," Jimmy said. "You two are a vision."

I set up everything on the dining room table and made another pot of coffee. Ash popped Viv in her high chair with some Cheerios on the tray in front of her, and Viv happily picked them up, holding each one in the air to examine it before placing it in her mouth. "Good job, Vivie," Ash said. "Good job eating your Cheerios!"

"We have to cheer for everything she does so that she doesn't get low self-esteem," Jimmy said, with a smirk. But then he clapped his hands together. "Look at Viv eat her Cheerios. Look at her go!"

"Where did you two end up last night?" I asked.

"Jimmy suggested Russia House," Matt said, looking like just saying the name of the bar made him sick. Russia House was around the corner from us, a dark and musty place with chandeliers and red upholstery. It was a favorite of Russian and Eastern European expats, and people always claimed to see Alex Ovechkin (who played for the Caps) drinking vodka there.

"I'm sure he really had to twist your arm," I said to Matt, and he laughed but didn't meet my eyes.

The Dillons' flight wasn't until late afternoon, but Ash started packing right after we ate, which was a good thing since their stuff was everywhere. We hugged them good-bye and made promises to visit soon, and they hadn't even been out the door a full minute before Matt said, "I know that seemed weird when you walked in this morning, but Jimmy had just asked me to work on his campaign and then you guys came in and I didn't want to talk about it with everyone there."

"Oh, so that's what that was about." I felt relieved to know it wasn't something more scandalous. "It did seem a little strange."

"I know," Matt said. "Anyway, I told him I'd talk to you about it but that it probably wasn't going to happen, that I didn't think we'd be up for it."

"We?" I asked.

"Well, that's the thing. I wouldn't do it without you. I'd have to be in Texas for almost a year and I'd want you with me. And I know that's a lot to ask, which is why I told him it wasn't likely."

"Huh," I said. I wasn't totally surprised. In a way, I'd been expecting it. Jimmy always used to joke about Matt running his campaigns, and ever since he'd asked Matt to put the fund-raiser together, I'd been almost waiting for it.

"Buzz?" Matt asked, and I realized I'd been silent for a while.

"Sorry," I said. "I was just trying to picture us in Texas."

"Really?" he asked.

"I mean, we might as well consider it, right?"

Matt let out a long breath. "Look. It's a lot. I'm not even going to consider it unless you're completely okay with it."

"So what would you be?" I asked. "His campaign manager? His fund-raiser?"

"Both, really," Matt said. "I'd probably be the only paid person on his staff, depending on how much he raises. He's thinking—and I agree— that a small team is best."

"Is it something you really want to do?" I asked.

"I do," he said. "But look—if I don't do it, I'll live. Honest. I don't think Jimmy has a huge chance of winning, but you never know. It would be good experience. And it would be a reason to leave my job now. Which is probably the most appealing part."

"You're not stuck there," I said. "You'll get another job."

"It doesn't feel like it," he said flatly. "But that's not the only thing to consider. Let's think about it for a few days."

But I didn't need a few days. We talked about it all that night, and the next morning I said, "I think you should do it." Matt looked up at me surprised, and I continued. "You'll never get to do something like this again. And it's Jimmy."

"Beth, are you sure? You really have to be sure. We'll be living in Texas for almost a year. And I don't want you to regret quitting your job."

I thought back to the last pitch meeting we'd had, where after every story idea, Ellie had tilted her head and said, "But can you make it sexier?" I looked at Matt, and nodded my head. "I'm sure," I said.

When I think back to why I said I'd go, part of me blames the night we spent with the Dillons after the fund-raiser. We'd had so much fun and Matt had seemed like himself again. He'd seemed happy. And I felt desperate to hold on to that, was willing to do anything to keep him that way. Even move to Texas.

When Matt called Jimmy to tell him he'd take the job, Jimmy let out a whoop and then said, "Wait, hold on." He put the phone on speaker and repeated the news to Ash, who started screaming. "This is going to be the best," she yelled.

"We've got a lot to figure out, obviously," Matt said, "but we'll start working on it right away."

"Hold on," Ash said, "we're going to call you right back."

A minute later, my phone rang with a FaceTime request, and when I answered, Ash and Jimmy were crowded in my screen. I held the phone so Matt could see them, and Ash said, "Look, we've been talking about this. And we really want you guys to come live with us."

"We're asking you to uproot your life," Jimmy said, turning the phone so we saw more of his face. "And we have tons of room. There's no sense in having you pay for a place when you could stay here."

"Wow," I said, and Matt said, "That's so generous of you guys."

I couldn't get a read on Matt's voice and I wanted to turn to him, but I was aware that Jimmy and Ash were watching us. I honestly didn't know how to feel. On the one hand, it would be so easy to move in with them—who wanted to search for an apartment and go through all of that? On the other hand, we'd be living with them, sleeping under the same roof every night.

"How about this?" Ash said. "You move in with us and try it and if you want to get your own place later on, that's great."

"We'll definitely think about it," I said. "That's so nice of you guys."

"It's also nice of your husband to come and help out his poor friend," Jimmy said. He took the phone out of Ash's hand and held it so we saw only his face. "I wouldn't want to do this with anyone else." Then, Jimmy paused and smiled, looked us in the eye like he was already campaigning, and said, "We'll take Texas together."

Sugar Land, TX
2014

Every politician should have been born an orphan and remain a bachelor.

—LADY BIRD JOHNSON

It has been said that politics is the second oldest profession. I have learned that it bears a striking resemblance to the first.

—RONALD REAGAN

Chapter 14

We left for Texas on January 2, and so Babs insisted on having the whole family over for a New Year's Day lunch. Even Meg, who'd been out late with friends the night before, was there, although she spent most of the afternoon lying on the couch, only sitting up once to ask, "So, is your apartment going to be, like, empty?" when she saw Matt giving a spare set of keys to his mom.

"No," Matt said. "It's going to be rented out most of the time and very much full."

This wasn't exactly true, but we'd found a friend of a friend who was moving to DC and looking to rent a furnished apartment for at least a few months, though we hoped he'd stay longer. I was the one who didn't want to get rid of our apartment—it seemed more trouble than it was worth to put everything in storage, and I'd convinced Matt it made more sense to hold on to it, especially if we could rent it out part of the time. "I'm sure we'll be back a few times during the year," I pointed out. "And we'll want a place to stay."

The truth was, getting rid of the apartment seemed final, like we were leaving DC for good. And we weren't. We'd be in Texas for eleven months at the most (less if Jimmy lost the primary) and then we'd return to DC, and surely we'd want to move right back into our place, at least at first. It made me feel calmer to think that we'd still have a home, a place that was ours, even if we weren't living in it.

We got to the Kellys' around one, but it was clear that Rosie had been there for hours. There was chili on the stove and corn bread in the oven and the dining room table was set. In the TV room, college football was on and there was a fire going. Matt and I each accepted a Bloody Mary from Rosie and settled on the couch. Everyone was tired and the noise level was noticeably lower than normal. All of the kids had disappeared to the basement, each holding armfuls of new Christmas toys and games. I chatted with Nellie about the dinner they'd been to the night before, but for the most part everyone just sat and watched football.

Between the fire and the Bloody Mary, I felt like I might just close my eyes and take a nap. But next to me, I could feel Matt fidgeting and checking his watch. He was anxious for this lunch to be over so we could get home and finish packing. We planned to leave by 7:00 the next morning and still had a bunch of things to do, and I knew he was already worried about getting it all done. Matt had been flying back and forth to Houston for the past couple of months and was more than ready to be settled in one place. He'd even tried to get out of the New Year's lunch when Babs first suggested it, which (of course) didn't go over well.

Rosie set crab dip on the table, and Meg practically flipped off the couch to get to it, sitting cross-legged on the floor so she could be within arm's reach.

"Meg, slow down. No one else can get to the dip with you inhaling it," Babs said.

Meg looked up and showed no sign of being offended as she said, "Whatever, I'm starving," then went right back to eating the dip.

As we sat down to eat, I was almost getting a little sentimental about being away from the Kellys for so long. And then Babs turned to me and said, "How will you be spending your time in Texas?" It was almost like it had just occurred to her that I'd be there too.

"Well, I'll be helping with the campaign however I can," I said.

"That should be interesting," she said. "It's not exactly your skill set though."

"No," I said. "Not exactly."

"She's going to take some time to write," Matt said. He'd been bringing this up ever since I agreed to quit my job, and sometimes it seemed that he was more attached to the idea than I was.

"You'll have to find a hobby of some sort to

keep you busy," Babs said, taking a tiny bite of chili.

"Yeah," Jenny said from across the table. She winked quickly at me. "You should start knitting."

After lunch, everyone hugged us good-bye like we were never returning, and Matt kept saying, "You guys, we'll see you really soon." Grace and Lily made a big deal out of presenting a good-bye card that they'd made for us on a large piece of cardboard. On the front, they'd drawn me and Matt with oval limbs, long smiles, and cowboy hats. There was a scrawny-looking horse in the corner and a fat cow by our feet. Matt had a lasso in his hand, and across the bottom they'd written in glittery letters: YEE-HAW!

"I think they're confused about Texas," Jenny whispered to me.

I traced my finger over the chubby cow and said, "Who isn't?"

As we packed the car, Matt started to worry that we should've gotten a U-Haul. "I think we'll be okay," I said, but I wasn't so sure. We were trying to arrange the bags so that we still had a sliver of visibility out the back window and somehow kept making it worse. Most of what we were taking was clothes, but there were some other things I hadn't wanted to leave behind. When I packed the coffeemaker, Matt gave me a look, but didn't stop me. Once we were finally done and everything was in there, the car sagged low to the ground.

"Is that going to be okay?" I asked.

"Sure," Matt said, and then he bent down to look at the tires. "I mean, I really hope so."

We took three days to drive to Houston, even though we could've done it in two. We didn't want to feel rushed and I think Matt assumed (rightly so) that he'd be doing the majority of the driving. I did take over during a quiet stretch in Alabama so that Matt could rest. I was nervous at first, but after a while it felt okay. I didn't dare go over the speed limit and I stayed in the right-hand lane, but I still considered it a success. Matt's eyes were closed and I was sure he was asleep when I heard him laugh lightly beside me and say, "Slow and steady wins the race."

Ash and Jimmy lived in Sugar Land, a city about twenty minutes outside of Houston, which was (as Jimmy always said) considered part of the "greater Houston area." I laughed when I first heard the name, and Matt said, "It gets better. The motto is 'Sugar Land, where life is sweet.' "

I'd seen pictures of the house and Matt had described the neighborhood to me, but it still didn't prepare me for actually driving into their community and seeing all the sprawling lawns and open land. There were manmade ponds all around us, golf courses and pools; we passed a town square that was so artificial-looking it felt like a movie set. And as we pulled into the Dillons' driveway, I turned to Matt and he shook his head. "I told you," he said. "It's huge."

Ash opened the front door before we'd even turned off the car, and started waving like an excited little kid. I'd texted her about a half hour earlier to let her know we were close, and it seemed like she'd been watching out the window for us ever since. "I'm so glad y'all are finally here," she called, running out to our car. She had a sweater on, the sleeves pulled over her hands, but no jacket, and she shivered as I hugged her. "Jimmy just ran to the store, but he'll be back to help you unpack all of that."

She grabbed me by the hand and started pulling me toward the house. "I've got to give you the tour," she said. I turned back to look at Matt, who just shrugged like there was nothing we could do to stop her. He grabbed a couple of bags from the backseat, and Ash looked back and said, "No, no, wait for Jimmy!" but didn't slow down at all.

When we got into the front hall, she finally dropped my hand and turned to face me. "Okay, we'll start here, of course." She clapped her hands together, almost giddy, and I couldn't help but laugh.

"What?" she said, but then she laughed too. "I

know, I'm acting like a complete nut, but I'm just so excited that you're finally here!"

The Dillons' house was grand—that was the first word that popped into my head. The ceilings were high and there was a long curved staircase in front of us. There were five bedrooms, and a guest suite downstairs, and I understood as soon as I stepped inside why they'd insisted that we live there. There was no way they could possibly use all this space; it was almost obscene.

As we walked through each room, Ash talked about the different paint colors she'd chosen, explained in great detail why she'd decided to use wallpaper in the bathrooms. She talked like she couldn't get the words out fast enough, almost like she'd been dying to tell someone all about the house and I was the first person she'd come across.

I recognized some of the furniture as the pieces they'd had in DC, but there were also lots of new things. It didn't surprise me that the whole house was already completely and perfectly decorated, but it was still impressive. I had friends who moved into houses and let rooms sit empty for years, but Ash had every detail taken care of. Every side table had little groupings of tchotchkes, tiny ceramic boxes and silver picture frames arranged just so.

"This is gorgeous," I said. "I can't believe you've done all this already."

"Oh, it wasn't that much," she said, pretending to be modest. "My mom helped a lot. And so did Jimmy's mom, although I didn't ask her to."

We walked out to the back patio, where there was a fire pit and the biggest grill I'd ever seen built into a stone wall. "Jimmy is obsessed with this thing," she told me. "I think it's what finally sold him on the house."

She waited until the end to take me downstairs, where we'd be staying, which made me a little nervous, but once we walked in, I saw there was no reason to worry. Matt had assured me that the area felt completely private, but I'd still wanted to judge it myself. It was basically a little three-room apartment in their basement. (Ash kept calling it a mother-in-law suite, which I thought was hilarious since she'd probably burn the house down before letting Jimmy's mom move in.) There was a sitting area with a flat-screen TV on the wall, a tiny kitchenette, and a bedroom with a master bath attached. Ash and Jimmy's room was two floors up and on the other side of the house, so while I'd been afraid that the four of us would feel like roommates, the size and layout of everything made it more like we were tenants in the same building.

"This is perfect," I said, standing in the middle of the room and turning in a circle.

"I'm so glad," she said and squeezed my upper arm tightly.

While Ash was showing me the house, Jimmy had come home, and he and Matt were carrying all of our bags in from the car and dropping them by the front door. Ash and I came upstairs and met them in the hallway, where Jimmy lifted me into a hug. "Do you believe you guys are here?" he asked. "You're going to love it. I'm going to make Texans out of you two if it's the last thing I do."

We had steak fajitas that night (which Jimmy insisted on cooking on the grill even though it was pretty chilly outside) and Ash made a corn and avocado salad, and as we all sat down, I had a moment of déjà vu—how many times had we eaten dinner together in DC at this very table? I was tired from our drive and had that disoriented feeling that comes from traveling, when you first arrive somewhere and have to remind yourself of where you are. I'm in Texas, I kept thinking, and almost laughed at how absurd it sounded.

"Tonight, we're celebrating," Jimmy said, pouring us each a margarita from a pitcher. "And then tomorrow we can go back to work."

We all clinked glasses. "What are we toasting to?" I asked, and Jimmy gave me a look like I'd just asked the dumbest question in the world.

"Oh, Beth," he said. "To Texas, of course."

When I told Colleen that we were moving to Texas so Matt could run Jimmy's campaign, she'd rolled her eyes and said, "Seriously, Beth?" like we were doing it just to piss her off. I'd explained all the reasons why I'd agreed to go, and her face had softened just a little, and then she'd said, "Well, at least the happy couples can be together again. You'll be like one big dysfunctional polygamist family, all living under the same roof."

"Ha-ha," I said.

"Just don't stay there, okay?"

"Oh my God, never."

Colleen gave me a look. "Never say never. Weird things happen in Texas."

The next morning, I woke up all alone in our room, and even though it wasn't even 8:00 a.m., I had a panicky feeling like I'd overslept. I got dressed quickly and went upstairs to find Ash, Matt, and Jimmy all sitting around the kitchen table drinking coffee. It was clear that they'd already eaten—the remnants of their breakfast were in front of them—and they all turned to look at me as I walked in, making me feel self-conscious.

Viv was in her high chair with a handful of sliced strawberries in front of her, and when she saw me, she held one up in the air proudly, and then shoved it in her mouth. Ash got up to pour me a cup of coffee, and I accepted it and then turned to Matt. "Why didn't you wake me up?" I asked.

"You were really out," he said. "I figured I'd let

you sleep since you didn't have anything to get up for."

This was true, but strangely embarrassing—Ash had to get up with Viv and Matt and Jimmy had work to do, but I had no real reason to get out of bed. No one was relying on me and I didn't have anywhere to be. I could sleep all day if I wanted to. But from that day on, I set the alarm on my phone to make sure I was awake at the same time everyone else was, sometimes racing to the kitchen to be the one to start the coffee, like I had something to prove.

"I made some oatmeal," Ash said, getting up again to get me a bowl even though she'd just sat down.

"I'll get it," I said, following her to the stove, but she swatted me away, spooning some oatmeal into the dish and topping it with cut strawberries.

As I ate, Matt and Jimmy went over their schedule for the week. That afternoon, Jimmy was meeting with a group of small business owners in the area, and Matt was briefing him on things he should cover. "We want to get on their radar," Matt said. "We want them to care about this race." Jimmy nodded and Matt continued to coach him. "Here's the thing we really need to shove down their throats—you're young and you're coming to this position with a whole new perspective."

"Got it," Jimmy said.

"This race isn't something they're paying too much attention to, so we want to give them a reason to get excited, to remember your name."

"That I can do," Jimmy said. He turned to me. "Beth, did you get to see the world-famous Jimmy Dillon campaign office yet?"

I couldn't help but laugh when Jimmy talked about himself in the third person, no matter how often he did it. "I peeked in there yesterday," I said.

"Well, that won't do. Come on, I'll show you where the magic happens."

I wasn't quite finished with my breakfast, but I stood up to follow them anyway. I carried my bowl over to the sink, but Ash intercepted and took it from me. "Don't worry about this," she said. "Go check out the office."

Campaign headquarters was set up in the den on the first floor. "We never used this room anyway," Ash had said when she showed it to me. She'd opened the door briefly and then closed it again so that I'd just caught a glimpse. I had a feeling she hated the clutter in the room—there were two desks in there, facing away from each other and pushed against opposite walls, and all around were signs and stacks of papers, boxes of posters and push cards, the tiny little pieces of cardboard with Jimmy's picture, bio, and platform on them.

"See?" Jimmy said, handing one of the push cards to me. "They're small enough so people can put them in their pockets. And you can only imagine how many people are dying to carry a picture of me around with them."

Matt shook his head behind Jimmy, but he looked amused. There wasn't all that much to see in the office, so after a few minutes I told them I'd let them get to work.

"Wait," Jimmy said. He gave me a large pile of the push cards and winked. "So you can campaign for me."

I took the cards from him. "Of course," I said. "I'll start knocking on doors now." But the thing was, from then on I always had a bunch of his push cards with me. During the campaign we all carried them to hand out at events and lunches and sometimes to random people we met. Once, I gave one to a lady in the grocery store as we chatted in the checkout line. It became such a habit over those ten months that after the election was over, I sometimes found myself reaching for them when I met someone new.

Jimmy's father had footed the bill for a photographer and a messaging and design consultant, which resulted in a two-day photo shoot where Jimmy was captured in ten different outfits and five different locations. Matt was there for the whole thing, and afterward he said to me, "I'm starting to think Jimmy secretly wants to be a model."

The picture that they chose to use on all the promotional materials was a shot of Jimmy standing outside, somewhere in Texas, nothing but open land behind him. He was wearing dress pants and a button-down shirt that was rolled up to his elbows, and his hands were on his hips as he looked straight at the camera, smiling but looking confident. Underneath him was his campaign motto, "Let's Get to Work," which I thought sounded cheesy at first, but grew to like. During those months, I saw this image of Jimmy about four hundred times a day—there were posters and push cards littered all over the house—and after a while when I looked at him in real life, I could almost see the slogan underneath him, beckoning me to get to work.

It also became something Jimmy said often, mostly when Matt was trying to get him to focus. That day, when it became clear that Matt was getting impatient and wanted Jimmy to stop talking to me and start being productive, he stood up straight and said loudly, "Okay, let's get to work!" saluting me as I walked out of the office.

As soon as Matt agreed to run Jimmy's campaign, he thought of little else. He did research on past commissioners, read as much as he could about the oil and gas industry in Texas, like he was cramming for a final. Matt had told me once how much he loved school, how he missed it all the time. "How very Harvard of you," I'd said, rolling my eyes just a little. Because he wasn't talking about the parties or hanging out in the dining hall—no, he missed studying for tests, the satisfaction that came from gathering information and making it his own. And as I watched him run the campaign, this was clear.

Each night, he took stacks of paper to bed with him, highlighting and making notes in the margins. "I feel like there's so much I need to catch up on," he said. Often, I woke up in the morning to find Matt sleeping with papers on top of him, a highlighter still clenched in his hand. Our sheets were soon streaked with neon yellow marks, but he didn't seem to notice.

Matt's approach was to have Jimmy focus on fracking and the environment. (A few months earlier, I'd never even heard Matt say the word *fracking,* and now he probably used it a hundred times a day, like it had always been a part of his vocabulary, like he was an expert on the whole situation.)

"This is our way in," he told me when he first started researching fracking. He sounded excited, almost manic. "The Republicans don't want to touch this. They won't do anything to ruffle the feathers of the oil and gas companies."

If I was being completely honest, I wasn't even exactly sure what fracking was before Matt started talking about it, and I'm not sure Jimmy knew much about it either. I was there when Matt first proposed this strategy to Jimmy, standing in front of him and making his case. "The week that you filed to run was the same week the earthquake hit around Fort Worth," he told him. "These earthquakes aren't right; they aren't normal. The people in these towns are suffering and in danger. They need an advocate, and that can be you."

Jimmy nodded slowly. "I think you're right," he said. And that was all it took to convince him—even I'd asked more questions about it. But Jimmy was content to let Matt run with this, and from that point on he let Matt decide almost every aspect of his campaign. There were times Matt wouldn't even bother to consult Jimmy—he once wrote and sent an e-mail to all of Jimmy's supporters (from Jimmy) emphasizing the need to investigate the harmful effects of wastewater injection wells. It was only after everyone received it that Matt realized he'd forgotten to show it to Jimmy first.

"It just slipped my mind," Matt said. "I'm sorry. We talked about it and I got so caught up in all of it."

"No worries," Jimmy said. "I trust you. This is why I wanted you on the team." I watched Jimmy closely, trying to see if he was upset, but he honestly didn't seem to mind.

I walked by the den one day and heard Matt talking to Jimmy, but it sounded more like a lecture than a conversation. "I think we need to be bold, to propose an end to all fracking in the next ten years," Matt said. "This will reach the people outside of Houston, it will speak right to them. We can get them on our side. Then once we win the primary, we'll push even harder."

I peeked in and saw Jimmy nodding seriously, like a student in a classroom. And this was their dynamic throughout the campaign. It didn't exactly surprise me—this was Matt in his element, absorbing huge loads of information and then dispersing and explaining it to someone in manageable bites. He even did it with me. On Sundays, we'd spend hours with *The New York Times*. I tended to favor the *Book Review* and the style section, and he read just about everything else. But after he'd finish an article, he'd sort of recap it for me—giving me the highlights, answering any questions I had. I figured he liked to talk about the things he'd just read about, that it helped him sort things out in his own head. I don't think he was doing it because he felt like he needed to teach me—although there's no denying that I became a lot more knowledgeable about current events after I met him.

And why wouldn't Jimmy like this arrangement? He agreed with Matt on all the issues he was fighting for. He just let Matt do the research and break it down for him—Matt was like the real-life version of CliffsNotes.

Most of the time, Matt and Jimmy were concerned with raising money. Jimmy's first fund-raising goal (created by Matt) had been to raise $50K by the New Year, which they'd easily done. And while I thought that sounded impressive, Matt told me that compared to the Republican candidates, it was peanuts.

Jimmy had even gone to L.A. for a few days, using all of the connections he'd made while working in the White House. One young actress had a casual cocktail party at her home, invited twenty of her friends to meet Jimmy, listen to his pitch, and give him money. He had a dinner thrown in his honor by a reality TV star, famous only for being pretty and dating athletes. Matt had always thought this woman was an idiot, was annoyed that she was constantly on television, that she got so much attention. "She doesn't do anything," he'd say. But they raised more money at that single event than they had in the prior month. And Matt never said a bad word about her again.

The week I got to Texas, Matt was working on a new fund-raising plan for Jimmy. He told me about it one night before we went to sleep, describing the incentives he had created: If you donated two hundred dollars, you'd be eligible for a raffle to win a private dinner with Jimmy; five hundred dollars got you invited to an intimate evening of drinks with him. And for a thousand dollars or more, you and Jimmy could spend the day at the shooting range together.

"Seriously?" I'd asked.

"Seriously," Matt said. And then like Dorothy before him, he shook his head in wonder and said, "We're not in DC anymore."

Ash and Jimmy lived less than a mile from Jimmy's parents and a fifteen-minute drive from Ash's. Viv was the first grandchild for both families, and they were always stopping by to see her or bring her a present or offer to take her to the park. Every Monday and Wednesday, Ash's mom, Beverly, took care of Viv. She'd come pick her up in the morning and bring her back right before dinner. She always let herself into the house, pausing after opening the door, calling, "Knock, knock!" before walking in. Beverly was like the sixty-year-old version of Ash, and because of this I felt completely comfortable around her. I'd met her a few times when she'd come to visit DC, and she was always pulling me into a hug— just like Ash, she was overly and immediately affectionate. I didn't mind it though. It was nice to rest my head against her soft sweater sets, to breathe in her perfume as she held me against her chest and asked me how I was doing.

Jimmy's mom called often to ask if Viv was available for "a sleepover at Grammy's." She was always pushing the four of us to go out to dinner, trying to find a reason the baby should stay with her. Viv had her own room at Jimmy's parents' house, complete with a brand-new crib, because as Mrs. Dillon told me, "It just made good sense."

"I thought I'd have to hire someone to watch Viv," Ash said, "so I could start to build my Stella and Dot network here, but those women want their hands on their grandbaby so badly we may never have to hire a babysitter again."

Mrs. Dillon (whose first name was Sue Ann, but who never asked me to call her that) was so friendly it was almost frightening. She had a wide lipsticked smile, and she found a way to compliment me whenever she saw me. "Oh, Beth, isn't that an adorable top?" she'd say, or "Isn't that color delicious on you?" I tried to explain to Matt how it was too much, how her compliments in question form seemed almost aggressive (and made me believe that she thought the real answer to all of them was no), but he didn't understand. Mr. and Mrs. Dillon had us over for dinner at least once every couple of weeks, and they both adored Matt. (And he loved Mrs. Dillon's baby back ribs so much that I doubt he would've noticed if she'd called me ugly right to my face.)

Just like Ash's mom, Mrs. Dillon had a key to their house, and she wasn't afraid to use it. "I came home just a week after we moved in to find this in the middle of the table," Ash said, pointing to a large cast-iron Dutch oven. "There wasn't even a note. It was just sitting there, and so we had to call and ask her what it was for. Jimmy thanked her for it—he didn't even think it was weird that she came in while we were gone, and now she does it all the time."

"Did she say what it was for?" I asked. Ash's kitchen was well stocked with beautiful things—I couldn't imagine she didn't have a similar pot somewhere in there.

"Yes. She thought the pot I had wasn't good enough to make chili. And then she said, 'And you know how Jimmy loves his chili.'"

I laughed and made a sympathetic face, and for maybe the first time in my life felt thankful for Babs—whatever things I had to say about her, at least she'd never let herself into our home.

Mr. Dillon wasn't friendly and didn't try to be. He always seemed to be insulting Jimmy, and Ash told me that they'd had the same dynamic since Jimmy was a teenager and a little wild. "It's like he still expects him to get expelled or have a party at the house when they're out of town. He still treats him like an unruly sixteen-year-old." He did seem to take a liking to Matt though, always asking him his thoughts about Jimmy's opponents, listening to his answers carefully. Sometimes at dinner, Matt was the only person Mr. Dillon talked to.

• • •

On Thursday mornings, Ash took Viv to a music class, which was really just a group of babies sitting in a circle and clutching tambourines and shakers as the teacher and parents sang and clapped. Sometimes, Ash got one of the songs stuck in her head and would hum it constantly for days, then shake her head as if she could knock it loose.

When Ash asked if I'd like to come along to the class, I said yes mostly because I couldn't think of a polite way to say no. I'd been there a couple of weeks and I still found myself trailing after her during the days. I just wasn't quite sure what to do with myself—Matt and Jimmy were either in the office, traveling, or out at an event. And Ash was taking care of Viv or doing things around the house or working on Stella and Dot stuff. And then there was me. Sometimes I stuffed envelopes or prepared mailers for the campaign, and a couple of times I opened my computer and stared at a blank Word document, but I still hadn't written anything. I had a feeling Ash invited me to the class because she felt slightly responsible for me.

The class was about a fifteen-minute drive from the house—still in Sugar Land, of course. One of Ash's friends, Charlotte, was enrolled in the class with her daughter, which was why Ash signed up. "But I'm so happy I did," she told me. "I can just tell that Viv loves it."

Sugar Land was originally a sugar plantation, a fact that I found appropriate and creepy. There was a fake sweetness to the place—there were beautiful homes and cute little downtown areas, but it felt so manufactured. Everything was clearly plotted out, had been planned down to the last shrubbery. As Ash drove to the music class, I stared out the window, fascinated by all that we passed. The more time I spent in Sugar Land, the more I understood how strange DC must have seemed to Ash; how she must have felt like she was in another country.

There were ten other babies and toddlers in Viv's class, and she was by far the best dressed. Ash always dressed Viv with a little more care when they were going out, and that day she was in a smocked dress with a monogram on her chest. (Viv was not a baby who wore stained onesies or mismatched socks.)

After thirty minutes of singing and clapping (which had originally sounded like a short time to me, but felt oh so long while I was experiencing it) a few of the moms went to a coffee shop around the corner. I sat and chatted with them as they ordered lattes and fed smooshed-up fingerfuls of muffins to their babies. The strollers were shoved in around the tables, and it was impossible to move without bumping something or someone. Charlotte's daughter reached over and knocked a cup of water across the table, and when I jumped up to grab some napkins, I banged my knee against a stroller, causing the child inside to start screaming. By the time I returned to wipe up the spill, Viv was fussing and Ash was packing up. I handed the wad of napkins to Charlotte and then stood there, feeling like a mother's helper who isn't really old enough to be of any help at all.

At the end of January, Matt hired an intern named Katie, who'd just graduated from TCU that December and was the most serious twenty-two-year-old I'd ever known. She came to the house to meet Matt wearing a pantsuit, her long brown hair pulled back in a low ponytail. Katie was pretty, but wore minimal makeup and no jewelry, and had a very no-nonsense vibe about her. Whenever Katie was around, I could see Ash look at her out of the sides of her eyes, just itching to adorn her, to "fancy her up," as she liked to say. Ash even gifted a necklace to Katie, a long gold chain with blue stones, one of her most popular pieces from the Stella and Dot collection. "I thought it would look great with your eyes," Ash said, and Katie said thank you and put it right into her bag. We never saw it again.

"I graduated a semester early, not the other way around," Katie told me when we first met, although I hadn't asked. "I was just ready to be in the real world. But I loved school. Go, Frogs!"

As she said this, she crooked two fingers at me, like she was making a peace sign but was too lazy to hold it straight. (I learned later this was a hand signal for the TCU Horned Frogs, but at the time had no idea what she was doing and just smiled.)

Katie's family was friends with the Dillons, and she was interested in working in politics, planned to move to DC in the next year or so, and (most important) was happy to work for free, all of which made her a great fit.

"Hopefully we'll be able to pay you as the campaign goes on," Matt told her, but she just waved a hand in the air.

"That would be great, of course," she said. "But I'm not concerned about it. I'm here to learn and I'm happy to help however I can."

That was all Matt needed to hear to make Katie his favorite person in the world. He put her in charge of social media—she started handling the Facebook, Twitter, and Instagram accounts, and also started writing most of the e-mails that were blasted to Jimmy's supporters every few days. I was on this list, and woke up most mornings to a message in my in-box, with subject headings like "We need your help!" Or "Texas, it's time!" At the bottom of each note was a plea for money and a link to the online fund-raising, asking the recipient to give anything he could, even if it was just five dollars. I started to feel fatigued at how often these e-mails arrived, and I can only imagine that everyone else receiving them did too. But the campaign had to keep asking for money, so they kept arriving. A couple of times I donated, if only because I felt like Katie deserved a response for all of her hard work.

When Katie started, Matt told her they'd get another desk in the den for her as soon as possible. "In the meantime," he said, "you can set up in the dining room or use one of our desks if we aren't here."

"That works for me," she said. I saw Ash wince as Katie set up her laptop on the dining room table, banging it down on the wood. Ash rushed over with a place mat to put underneath it. "Here," she said, "this will make you more comfortable."

The next day, a tiny desk and a folding chair arrived at the house and were shoved in the corner of the den. "That was fast," I said to Ash, and she rolled her eyes. "I'm willing to sacrifice quite a lot of things for this campaign," she said. "But I don't see why my dining room table has to be one of them."

I have to say, Jimmy's Instagram got a lot better once Katie joined the campaign—she was always in front of him with her iPhone, capturing the moment that he shook someone's hand or smiled during a speech. One night, when we were all sitting around after dinner, staring at our phones,

I mentioned how good her pictures were. Matt agreed. "She's got a talent for communications," he said. "She's always got the right image to go along with our message."

"Yeah," Jimmy said. "Plus she's great at picking the filters that make me look my best."

Matt and Jimmy spent most weekdays at events around Houston—or at least within a couple of hours of the city—meeting with local groups, stopping by union lunches or DAR teas. On the weekends, they'd travel farther and Ash and I would usually go with them, the four of us (plus Viv) piling into a car and driving to rural areas in East Texas, hitting as many cities as we could in one trip, places I'd never heard of before: Longview, Lufkin, Tyler, and Henderson.

If we were coming back that night, or if it was an incredibly busy trip, Katie would sometimes come along, but mostly if we were staying over-night, she hung back so we didn't have to pay for an extra room. (I'd never seen Matt so thrifty in his life, but he was constantly making sure we were doing things the cheapest way possible, stretching all of the campaign money as far as it would go.)

When Katie wasn't there, I was in charge of the social media, taking as many pictures of Jimmy as I could, sending out tweets, posting on Instagram. The first time I'd done this, Katie had approached me when we returned and not so subtly suggested that I could do a little more. "Make sure to tag all of the places where he is," she said. "We want to get as many eyes on these posts as possible. You can never take too many pictures."

She spoke to me in a tone you'd use to explain hashtags to your grandmother—patiently and with just a touch of condescension and amusement, as if she couldn't believe how little I knew.

Since that day, I'd taken my role as traveling social media person very seriously, once almost tripping Jimmy as I took pictures of him walking into a radio station in Waco.

Ash once told me that Mrs. Dillon loved to talk about when Jimmy was in preschool, how she knew even then there was something special about him. She said every day when she dropped him off, the kids would come running over to greet him. Once, he got there late and all the kids were already sitting cross-legged in the middle of the room, and as Jimmy went over to join them, they all reached their arms up to him, to touch him as he walked by. "Like Jesus," I said, and Ash nodded. "Exactly."

I had a friend who had worked in the Clinton White House who told me that when Bill Clinton walked into the room, the whole place was electric. "He gave people goose bumps just by arriving," she said. "Take my word for it—it's almost like he's magic."

And I'd seen it with Obama—the charm that doesn't feel sleazy, the smiles that seem genuine, the eye contact that makes you believe he's paying attention, that maybe he even remembers you from the last time you met. Each year at the Christmas party, Obama gave a speech and made sure to thank the family members of his staff, telling the spouses that he knew the sacrifices we were making. Now, don't get me wrong—I know he made this same speech at least a dozen times, repeating the lines at all of the Christmas parties they hosted. But still, it felt like he was speaking directly to me, and I cried every time— and it wasn't (just) because of the strong eggnog they served there.

Where do people get the ability to do this? What is it that makes some politicians so attractive? Why did people like Hillary so much more when she cried? Why is it that Obama sings and it's amazing, but Mitt Romney sings and looks like a nightmare you'd have about a wax figure come to life? And why, in God's green earth, could Sarah Palin wink and talk about pigs and somehow make everyone around her forget that she'd basically admitted she didn't read?

I don't know the answers to any of these questions. If I did, I'd be earning millions some- where as a political consultant, teaching awkward people how to be relaxed, making the unlikable appealing.

What I do know is that Jimmy had it—that thing that some politicians have and some don't; that thing that can't be named or explained. I heard him make the same promises to people, over and over, and they still sounded true. He'd shake people's hands and say, "Let's turn Texas blue," and make it seem possible. It was amazing how people turned their bodies toward him as he walked into a room, how his smile made them feel warm. Everyone just wanted to be around him. Even me.

The first time I saw Jimmy talk to a group about fracking, he was unsure and a little shaky. He spoke in vague terms, and it was clear (at least to me) that his grasp of the situation was tentative at best. But just two days later, he sounded more confident, and by the end of the week, it was as if he'd been making speeches about drilling and wells and fracking his entire life.

Sometimes Matt dominated our dinner conversations with new things he'd learned—another town that just discovered water contamination, or a case that the current Railroad Commission had unfairly decided. And I started to notice that Jimmy repeated what Matt told us when he spoke to voters, that he copied whole phrases and stories word for word, even getting outraged at the same parts, acting as if he were the one who'd discovered this information.

"Do you notice," I asked Matt one night, "how Jimmy copies exactly what you say?"

Matt shrugged. "Yeah, but that's kind of the point. I write his speeches. We go over all of his talking points together. That's my job."

"No, I know," I said. I tried to find the right way to explain myself. "It's just funny to see him say exactly the same things you said the night before."

"At least he's not going off script."

"Yeah . . . but, I mean, doesn't it ever bother you? Like you're doing the work and he's cheating off of you?"

Matt looked up at me, considering the question. "That's just how it works. It's the same thing I've always done, to an extent. I'm supporting the candidate."

"You're right," I said. "I don't know why it feels weird."

"It feels weird, because this time it's Jimmy," Matt said. "That's why."

At the end of Jimmy's campaign, there were a million things I was unsure of, and just one thing that was definite: Matt's words sounded better when they came out of Jimmy's mouth. And it wasn't fair, it was just the way it was.

Chapter 15

Ash was different in Texas. For one thing, everyone called her Ashleigh and some people (mostly her family, but a couple of friends too) called her Ashleigh Mae, which sounded ridiculous because it rhymed. Ash-lay Mae—even I couldn't say it without taking on a southern accent.

But it wasn't just that, of course. It was that her personality changed, so that she seemed not quite the same person I'd befriended in DC. I didn't notice it right away, not really. But the more time we spent there, the more I began to see that she acted a little more proper, was a little more done up, a little snobbier. Also her accent was much stronger, almost like she'd been hiding it all those years in DC, and sometimes when I'd hear her call up the stairs, "Vivienne Rose, I hear you fussing and I'm on my way," she sounded like someone I'd never met before.

I began to think of her as Texas Ash, sort of like Malibu Barbie—basically the same, but with a few tweaks and extra accessories.

She took her role in Jimmy's campaign very seriously—her role (as she saw it) being to stand next to him at events, dressed perfectly, smiling at everyone. Not a week went by that she didn't go shopping and come back with bags of new clothes. "I just don't want to keep getting photographed in the same thing over and over," she said, like the paparazzi were following her everywhere, like she was Michelle freaking Obama. And then there was her need to be a super housewife. Ash had always loved entertaining and cooked a lot (or at least more than I did), but now she seemed obsessed with what to make for dinner, insisted on preparing breakfast for us, which I found so strange—couldn't we all just pour ourselves some cereal? Her table was fussier, always set with place mats and cloth napkins, a vase of flowers in the middle. Whenever I tried to help her in the kitchen, she either shooed me out or assigned me a small task—grating cheese or chopping peppers—and then hovered over me to make sure I was doing it right.

A lot of the girls Ash had grown up with lived in Sugar Land too, and even though she always introduced them to me as "my dear friend Ainsley" or "Charlotte, one of my oldest friends in the world," I suspected she didn't actually like any of them all that much.

They called themselves the Dozens, because there were twelve of them, but actually there were thirteen and the last poor girl to join the group, Mary, was always reminded that she ruined it a little bit for everyone when she came along. When I'd meet one of them, Ash would say, "She's a Dozen" or "She's one of the Dozens," like it would mean something to me.

They went on annual trips together and out for "ladies' nights," where they'd inevitably all pose together for a picture, one big group of tiny blond girls, clutching Cosmos and smiling widely for the camera, and sometimes I wondered if the whole point of their friendship was just to post these images, to prove to the world that they had a bunch of pretty friends.

There was an undercurrent of competition with these girls—everything from house size to how many children they had. I wanted to think that Ash was above it all, but once when we were over at her friend Louise's house, she went on and on about Stella and Dot, talking about how thrilled she was that she found success in a career that still let her spend loads of time with Viv. "You know, it's not about the money, obviously. I think working makes me a better mother," she said. "Not to mention how important it is for Viv to see an example of a strong female."

Later, although I was pretty sure I knew the answer, I asked Ash if Louise worked. "Oh no," Ash said, "she's a SAHM."

"A what?" I asked. She'd pronounced it all as one word, and for a minute I thought she was telling me that Louise was part of some strange religion, maybe one that didn't allow women to have jobs outside of the home.

"A stay-at-home mom," Ash clarified. "That's what she does."

In all the years I'd known her, Ash hadn't told me much about these girls. I'd seen a couple pictures of them in their house, and I knew she'd been a bridesmaid in a few of their weddings, but she always just referred to them as her high school friends and didn't elaborate. Now talking about the Dozens was about 90 percent of her total conversation. She updated me on every aspect of their lives, spent at least an hour talking on the phone with a few of them a day, texting constantly, trading information about the others. None of those girls could so much as have an episode of diarrhea without the other twelve knowing about it.

As soon as Ash started talking about one of the Dozens, I could see Jimmy's eyes glaze over. He was polite when he saw them, smiling and kissing them on their cheeks, but I could tell he didn't think much of any of them.

"I don't give a shit about where Kelsey got her furniture recovered," Jimmy said during dinner one night. He wasn't exactly yelling, but his voice was loud and annoyed. "Seriously, Ash. No one fucking cares."

Matt and I glanced at each other and quickly looked back down at our plates. We'd both been pretending to listen to Ash (which was what we did when she talked about her friends), and I could tell he was just as surprised as I was at Jimmy's outburst. Jimmy didn't often get angry, and I don't know that I'd ever heard him talk like that to Ash—they bickered sometimes, sure, but I'd never heard him sound so frustrated at her, so disgusted really.

"All right," Ash said. "I was just telling a story. You don't need to get angry about it."

"That's not a story you were telling," Jimmy said. "I don't know what that was, but it certainly wasn't a story."

"Okay, Jimmy." She gave me a funny look across the table, like she couldn't believe how weird he was being, but I knew what he meant. When Ash talked about those girls there was always an agenda. It was never just a story. We never left an interaction with any of them where Ash didn't immediately start talking shit, telling me about a failing marriage or an accidental pregnancy that resulted in a shotgun wedding, which everyone suspected wasn't accidental at all. All girls—all people really—talk behind their friends' backs. I knew that. And most of the time, I think that's just human nature—people don't mean to be malicious, but it happens out of jealousy or frustration or sometimes genuine concern. Hadn't I spent hours talking to Ash about Colleen's marriage, dissecting each part, trying to understand how she ended up with Bruce?

But this felt different. Before we moved to Texas, I would've described Ash as kind, and now I wasn't so sure. We still had a great time together, just the two of us, but I couldn't quite get over the extra bite in her voice when she gossiped about her friends, as if she were secretly hoping they'd all fail miserably at life.

Matt and I were sharing a small space, but it felt like we were talking less. He was always distracted when we were together, either actually on his phone or computer or sometimes just lost in his head, planning the next event, trying to think of ways to get Jimmy's name out there.

One night, I asked him what he was working on, not because I actually cared all that much, but because we needed something to talk about. The campaign was the one thing that would make him chatty, and it happened again that night. He went on and on, telling me about a nun he'd contacted who was working to educate people about fracking in the Eagle Ford Shale and how she might do a joint event with Jimmy. He got so excited when he talked about these things. Whenever I told him about my day (and granted, I didn't do anything all that interesting most of the time), I could feel his attention wander.

"It's impressive how much you've learned," I told him. "Seriously, it sounds like something you've been passionate about your whole life."

"It's so disturbing, Beth," he said to me. "I just didn't really know much about it before. I don't think a lot of people do, even here. But we have a chance to change that."

I moved closer to him in bed and kissed his shoulder. "Did anyone ever tell you how smart you are?" I asked. "And also, how nice?" I ran my hands over his stomach, letting my fingers brush under the waistband of his boxers. But he just pulled my head toward him for a hug and started reading an e-mail on his phone, wordlessly shutting me down, letting me know that having sex with me was less interesting than a nun and some oil drills. Not exactly what I'd hoped for.

Matt arranged for Jimmy to be gone the weekend of February 14—first at a gumbo festival just outside of Austin on Friday night, and then at four different events in the city on Saturday. When Matt scheduled this, he hadn't realized (I assume) that February 14 was, of course, Viv's first birthday, and so when Ash saw the schedule she had a minor meltdown.

"You can't be gone for her birthday!" she said. She was standing in the office in front of the large whiteboard calendar that hung on the wall and kept track of Jimmy's schedule. She and I had been on our way out to lunch and had stopped in to tell the guys we were going—it was just a coincidence that she looked up at the calendar.

"I'm so sorry, I didn't even think about it," Matt said. He glanced over at Jimmy, who I knew had approved the trip. It was one thing for Matt to forget his goddaughter's first birthday, but Jimmy should've seen this coming.

"It's a weekend trip," Jimmy said. "I just figured we'd all be going." He didn't sound concerned.

"Can't you go down there on Saturday?" Ash asked. She was looking at Matt, who was staring at papers on his desk. "I wanted to have all the grandparents over for dinner on Friday. I figured we wouldn't be able to have a real party for her, but I at least wanted to do that."

"We'll do it when we get back," Jimmy said. "She won't know the difference. She doesn't know what day it is—she doesn't even know where her nose is."

Ash opened her mouth as if she were going to say something more, but then just turned and walked out of the room. I followed her and we went to lunch, where she said to me, "There's no point in fighting it. He's going to get his way anyway."

But that night at dinner, Ash got up when we were just about halfway through, claiming that she had a headache and needed to lie down. A few minutes later, Matt excused himself to go down to the basement to answer some e-mails. He seemed so distracted, so focused on work, that I'm not even sure he noticed the tension at dinner.

"And then there were two," I said to Jimmy, raising my eyebrows at him across the table. He stood up and went to the refrigerator, pulled out two beers, and held one toward me. "Sure," I said. "Why not?"

I got up and started carrying the dishes to the sink and rinsing them off. "You don't have to do that," Jimmy said, carrying his plate over. "Or at least let me help."

"We're not guests anymore," I said. "You can't keep treating us like we are."

"Fair enough," Jimmy said, grinning at me. He sat back down at the table.

"I'd do this more if Ash let me, you know. Last week, she took our dirty towels from Matt's hands as he was going to put them in the wash. She insisted she do them herself."

"Yeah, she's a little anal with everything in the new house," he said.

We didn't talk for a few minutes as I loaded the dishwasher and wiped the counter. Finally, when I sat back down at the table, I said, "It's so quiet."

"Yeah," Jimmy said. "But if you listen closely you can hear the sounds of fracking statistics and angry birthday party planning coming from all around us."

"Don't be mean," I said, but I laughed.

Jimmy grinned and clinked the top of his bottle against mine. "We don't have to tell anyone, but let's just admit that we're the best ones."

• • •

Later that week, I was in the basement on my computer wasting time, which I was becoming an expert at—it was amazing how long I could spend on Twitter and Facebook, going from one random article to the next. I'd just gone down a rabbit hole that involved articles about what the members of the Baby-Sitters Club would be doing as adults, when I heard Jimmy call my name from the top of the stairs. I walked over and looked up.

"I have to make a Costco run to get some stuff for Viv's party," he said. "Want to join?"

"Sure," I said. "Give me two minutes." Ash was at her mom's and Matt and Katie were in the office, but we were pulling out of the driveway before I realized that Jimmy hadn't told Matt where we were going. "He's working on my talking points for the radio interview next week, and all three suggestions I made were shot down quickly. So I figured I'd let him handle it. I mean, what do I know? I'm just the actual candidate."

Jimmy whistled in Costco as he pushed the giant cart through the aisles. He stopped at a display of televisions, and I said, "I thought we were getting stuff for Viv's party."

He sighed. "We are, but Costco is about the experience." He put his arm around my shoulders as if he were a wise man trying to teach me something important, and he kept wheeling the

313

cart along with his free hand. "You need to be open to new things, ready to be so dazzled by a Vitamix blender that you buy it on the spot."

I laughed. "So you're responsible for that blender?"

"They made smoothies in the store and gave samples to everyone. I was hooked."

"Have you used it?" I asked.

"All in good time, Beth." Jimmy stopped to put a large container of cheese puffs into the cart and I asked him if Ash had given him a list, since I was pretty sure she'd sooner die than set out a bowl of cheese puffs for guests. "Not exactly," he said. "It's more of a surprise."

"Right," I said. "How do you think that'll go over?"

Jimmy shrugged. "She can't be more pissed than she is now."

An elderly couple passed us, and Jimmy smiled at them. "How're y'all doing today?" he asked, and they smiled back and said they were doing just fine. I could tell that they thought we were married, that they assumed Jimmy was my husband from the way they looked at us, which of course made sense—we were both wearing wedding rings and shopping at Costco together on a weekday afternoon.

"You should appreciate this," Jimmy said, as the couple moved down the aisle ahead of us. "This is what's so great about Texas. Giant stores with giant carts where you can buy huge bottles of whiskey and a seventy-two-pack of frozen taquitos."

"You know they have Costco everywhere, right? There was one in DC."

"It's not the same," he said. He looked at me out of the corners of his eyes. "So, how's things? You're going home next weekend, right?"

"Yeah, just to see my parents for a couple of days. I haven't been back since Thanksgiving so I thought it would be nice."

"It must be so strange to have two nice parents," Jimmy said, taking a bag of party mix off the shelf and then returning it.

"You have two nice parents," I said.

"Beth, please. You don't have to pretend. We both know my father is a giant dick." My face must have looked shocked, because he laughed and said, "Calm down. I said he *is* a giant dick not *has* a giant dick."

"Good God," I said. The couple who had just moments ago smiled at us like we were adorable turned around with disapproving looks on their faces. "Maybe you can say *dick* louder so the whole store can hear you," I suggested. Jimmy opened his mouth like he was going to scream, and I hit his arm. "Don't. I was kidding." We walked a little farther and I said, "I'm not agreeing with you, but I can see how he's hard on you."

"*Hard* is one word for it. He actually just really doesn't like most people. But he is enamored with your boy-wonder husband."

"They really do seem to get along, don't they?"

"Like gangbusters."

"It's weird. I feel like lately Matt's more excited to spend time with your dad than with anyone else."

Jimmy looked at me seriously for a few seconds, and I thought he was going to say something more about Matt, but he just put his arm back around my shoulders and said, "Come on. Let's get you a giant tub of animal crackers."

Ash was perfectly pleasant on Viv's birthday, but she did dress the baby in a T-shirt that said BIRTHDAY GIRL on the front and told every person we met at the gumbo festival that Viv's first birthday party had been delayed for the campaign. "But we don't mind," she said, smiling and squishing Viv's cheeks. "We just want to show our support for Daddy, don't we, baby girl?"

I talked to Colleen at least a few times a week— she was back at work and called me when she was walking to and from the Metro or out grabbing lunch. We talked about nothing really, which was sort of our specialty. (We'd spent so many hours of our lives in conversation with each other that a disappointing salad she'd ordered from Sweetgreen could give us twenty minutes of discussion material.)

It was weird, but when I spoke to her she felt so far away, farther than she really was. It reminded me of junior year, when we were both studying abroad—she was in London and I was in Cork—and when we'd call each other, it felt like she was living a made-up life, because I didn't know anything or anyone she talked about. "Describe your room to me," I said to her on one of these calls. After living in the same space with her for so long, it didn't seem right that I couldn't picture where she was sleeping at night.

And that's how it felt when I talked to her in Texas—I wanted so badly for her to understand what it was like there, and I'd tell her about the weird towns we'd visit, would describe the Dillons' house, repeat the things that Ash said about her friends.

But I might as well have been telling her a fairy tale, and even though she'd respond by saying, "Wow" or "That's so interesting," I knew she had no idea what I was talking about, that no matter how much I explained, she'd never really understand my life in Texas.

It looked as though Jimmy had a good chance of winning the primary—he was up against an eighty-year-old man who had run for the commission (and lost) three times already. But still, Matt wasn't taking anything for granted. "You never know," he kept saying, like he didn't want to get his own hopes up.

The primary would be the easy part—or at least much easier than the general, but it still wasn't certain. "I can't imagine losing and just having this whole thing be over so quickly," Matt said one night. He was lying in bed and staring at the ceiling, which was a habit he'd picked up since moving to Texas.

"That would be awful," I said, thinking about packing ourselves right back up after basically just getting there.

"I know," Matt said, sounding almost irritated, like he hadn't been the one to bring up the possibility of Jimmy losing in the first place.

"I'm sure he'll win," I said. I doubted this was reassuring, but I felt like I needed to say something.

"I'll feel sure when it's all over," Matt said and continued to stare at the ceiling, like he was waiting for answers.

Katie was taking the lead on planning the watch party for the primary. "It should be somewhere fun," I heard Matt tell her one afternoon. "Not stuffy. Somewhere that reflects how young Jimmy is." As always, Katie took down notes and nodded seriously. I'd seen her smile maybe three times, and that was only when she was first meeting people and forced the corners of her lips upward for a few seconds, because she knew she should. She wasn't joyless—it was more she gave the impression that there was so much to do she couldn't be bothered to waste her time with pleasantries.

Later that same day, Matt and I were sitting outside on the patio, enjoying the unusual seventy-degree late February day. Matt was in a rare relaxed mood—maybe the warm weather had tricked him somehow—and we were talking about his sister, Meg, who'd just announced that she was moving out of their parents' house.

"I can't believe it," Matt said. "It's like the end of times."

"I can't believe she's lived there so long. What would've happened if she just never showed signs of moving out? Wouldn't your mom eventually kick her out? Or gently suggest it?"

"Who knows?" Matt said. "I had visions of her being one of those weird adults that live in their parents' basements forever."

"Like a really well-dressed Boo Radley?"

"Exactly."

I was enjoying this conversation immensely, just so happy that we were talking about anything other than Jimmy and the campaign for a few minutes. Katie came out the back door and cleared her throat, like she thought she was interrupting something and wanted to make her presence known.

"I came up with some options for the watch party," she said, still standing on the edge of the patio. She waited until Matt answered to walk closer and hand him a paper. "It's a list of five different sports bars, some pros and cons about the areas where each is, and some pictures of the interiors. We can bring our own food into all of them, which is great, since I figured you'd want it catered."

Matt flipped through the pages, and they discussed a few of the locations before deciding on one. "That's what I thought you'd pick," she said. "I'll send the owner a note now." She was already typing away on her phone.

"That's great," Matt said. "Thanks so much." We watched Katie walk to her car and waved good-bye as she pulled out of the driveway. I figured that the spell was broken, that we'd stop talking about Meg and go back to discussing contaminated water, but Matt surprisingly still seemed relaxed.

"Don't be jealous, Buzz," Matt said. "But I think I might be in love with that little OCD Texan."

"Oh, I've noticed," I said. "You probably dream about how organized your life would be with her. Your sock drawer would be legendary."

Matt reached over and took my hand. "It would be," he said, smiling and closing his eyes as he aimed his face to the sun. "But don't worry. I'd never leave you for her, no matter how inferior your tweeting skills are."

When the day of the primary finally came, I somehow felt surprised by its arrival. We'd been living at the Dillons' for two months at that point, talking of little else, and still it felt like it had snuck up on us, like maybe we weren't ready. We were all up early that morning, nervous and jittery. Ash made a huge pot of coffee and by 6:30 a.m. was already brewing another one, although it was the last thing we needed. Matt was at the kitchen table, clicking away on his BlackBerry, his leg jumping up and down in rhythm with his typing. I put my hand gently on his knee to calm him down, and he stopped the bouncing for just a couple of minutes before starting up again.

Jimmy wouldn't sit down, kept finding reasons to get up and walk into the other room before racing back to the kitchen like he'd missed something. Ash was ready for the day in a blue cocktail dress, her hair curled and makeup on, and it was only when she went to feed Viv that she realized her mistake.

"I'll do it," I said, taking the yogurt from her. Viv had recently discovered the joy of spitting food at the person who was feeding her, and there was no doubt in my mind that she'd do it today. I'd seen her laugh wickedly after spraying Ash's face with oatmeal—she knew what she was doing. "Oh, thank you," Ash said. "I don't know what I was thinking. I just opened my eyes at four a.m., wide awake, and figured I'd get a jump on the day." "You've been up since four?" I asked her. She nodded. "I didn't have a prayer of falling back asleep. I'll probably be a zombie in an hour."

Viv took a bite of the yogurt, eyeing my pajama pants and T-shirt, sizing me up and then apparently deciding it wouldn't be worth wasting her breakfast on me. She was holding on to an extra spoon, banging it on her tray, telling me (I think) to hurry it up.

Katie knocked on the side door to announce her arrival, before opening it up and letting herself in. She was wearing a button-down shirt and dress pants with heels and carrying a pink bakery box. "I brought some reinforcements," she said.

Matt and Jimmy both reached for the box as soon as it was on the table. I shook my head when Matt first nudged it toward me (my Texas eating habits were quickly becoming frightening), but then I said, "Oh, what the hell?" and took a vanilla glazed. Ash watched me and then did the same and through a mouthful of donut said to me, "We need all the energy we can get today, right?"

The day passed in a blur. Ash and Jimmy went to the polls to vote early in the day with Viv in tow.

Ash had dressed Viv in a shade of blue that complimented her own dress and had (no surprise) strapped a huge bow on her head. Because Viv still had barely any hair, Ash had to rely on the stretchy headbands, which looked uncomfortable, even to me. All morning, Viv kept reaching up to pull off the bow, throwing it to the floor with a defiant look.

Right before we left, Ash was following Viv around, replacing the headband over and over and begging, "Please, baby girl. Please keep it on for Mama."

"Maybe today's not a day for a bow?" I suggested, and Ash looked so close to crying that I quickly said, "Or maybe she just needs a break? Maybe you can put it on when you get there?"

By some miracle, Viv was in a better mood by the time we arrived at the polling place and stayed still as Ash strapped the bow on her head. Jimmy picked up Viv, then he and Ash walked into the building together, holding hands and smiling. Katie stayed in front of them, taking pictures and posting to Instagram without breaking her stride, which was extremely impressive. I wondered how she could work that into her résumé.

When Jimmy and Ash came out, there were a few people outside, and a couple of them clapped. Jimmy smiled like he was embarrassed, but then walked over to the group, shaking hands and saying, "Thanks for coming out to vote, y'all."

• • •

I got to the bar early with Katie, to help her make sure that everything was set up right, although she didn't really need me there. The caterers brought in the food—shrimp, red beans, chicken, and salad—and Katie stood right by them as they arranged everything. "This looks good," she said to me, and I agreed. "Simple but homey."

"It does," I said. "You've done a great job."

But she didn't answer, just went back to typing on her phone. We sat in silence in the empty bar and waited for everyone to arrive, and finally I took out my own phone and examined it closely, as though I had important things to attend to as well.

There were about sixty people at the party, including Jimmy's parents and Ash's family. Ash's sister, Lauren Sybil, was there but her boyfriend was not, and she was drinking white wine at an impressive pace. She worked the room in a circular fashion, coming back to us every twenty minutes or so and saying, "I'm so nervous. Aren't you nervous? I could just die!" The fourth time she looped around, Ash handed Viv to me. "Lauren Sybil, let's get you a glass of water," she said and led her to the bar by her elbow, turning back to give me an exasperated look.

I lowered Viv to the floor, and she gripped my fingers as she took some unsteady steps. She'd been so close to walking for a while now, but as soon as any of us let go of her, she immediately sat down on her bottom like she thought we were trying to trick her.

I wouldn't describe the party as fun, at least not the beginning of it. There was a sense of impatience all around us, everyone trying to distract themselves with other things, but really just killing time until the race was called—like we were all just standing on a subway platform, waiting for a train. I held Viv's hands and walked her around the room for a while, her wide wobbly steps making her look like a little drunk lady, and then Lauren Sybil took her and I went back to where Matt was standing near Jimmy, picked up my drink, and resumed marking time.

We found out that Jimmy won when *The Texas Tribune* tweeted the news at him. Jimmy got a ding and looked down at his phone, which was in his right hand. "Holy shit," he said. He held it out to Matt, like he didn't trust himself. "Does this say what I think it does?"

Matt looked down at the phone and then broke into a huge smile. "You did it," he said. "Congrats, buddy."

The people right around us were starting to catch on to the news, and Jimmy put his fingers in his mouth and whistled, quieting down the room. "Everyone," he said, "I'm so thrilled to announce that *The Texas Tribune* has just called the race for me!"

The room broke into cheers then, loud whooping and clapping. Ash came running across the bar and flung herself into Jimmy's arms, in a way that was slightly over the top and made me understand why she'd been so good in pageants. "Oh, baby, I'm so proud of you," she said, putting her hands on either side of his face. Jimmy kissed her and then spoke to the room again.

"I want to thank each and every one of you. I couldn't have done it without you—I really couldn't—and your support means everything to me. So thank you!" Jimmy raised his glass, and everyone cheered again.

On the other side of the room, Lauren Sybil was still holding Viv and swaying to the music with her like they were dancing, but she kept leaning a little too far to each side and I was keeping an eye on her, hoping she wasn't about to tumble over. I was relieved when Ash's mom finally leaned across and took Viv right out of her hands.

Matt had been accepting congratulations from the people around him, and finally he was free and I was able to give him a kiss. "Congratulations," I said. "I'm really proud of you."

"Thanks, Buzzy," he said, looking not as happy as I would've imagined.

"Are you okay?"

"Yeah, definitely. I'm thrilled. Just already thinking about the next race. If Jimmy could really win, it would be groundbreaking."

"Maybe you should try to take tonight off," I said. "Just enjoy this."

He nodded, but his face remained serious. Jimmy came over then and lifted Matt off the ground in a bear hug. "Kelly," he said, "this is fucking amazing. Have I told you that you're a genius?"

"It was all you, man," Matt said, which I knew he didn't believe, but it was nice to see him being generous. Ash came over to join us, and we stood in a circle, just the four of us, shoulder to shoulder. We were only there for a minute or so—shortly after, Jimmy's phone started ringing with congratulations and he was calling supporters to thank them. But for a moment, he was focused on us and I remember feeling lucky, like we were being singled out as special.

The bartender was setting down rows of shots on the bar, and Jimmy turned and grabbed four of them in one quick movement, handing one to each of us. We clinked them together and held them there for a second, all four glasses touching.

"Are we toasting to Texas again?" I asked.

"No," Jimmy said. "To us."

"To us," we repeated, all tipping our heads back and drinking down our shots in one single swallow.

Chapter 16

The morning after the primary, Matt woke up early—even earlier than he normally did. But when I felt him get out of bed around 6:00, I assumed he was just going to the bathroom and fell right back to sleep. It wasn't until a few hours later (when I finally got up myself) that I realized he'd never come back. We'd been out late the night before and there'd been more celebrating (and more shots), and my first thought was that he must be feeling sick, but when I peeked in the bathroom it was empty. I zipped a sweatshirt on over my pajamas and went upstairs, where I found Ash and Matt sitting at the table with coffee. Matt had his computer in front of him and was typing away, and Ash was resting her head in her hands.

"Hey, guys," I said. Ash murmured something back to me that sounded like "Good morning," and Matt just nodded.

I poured myself a cup of coffee and sat down at the table with them. Matt was still typing away, and I reached over to rub his shoulder. "Why were you up so early?" I asked.

"I couldn't sleep," he said. "I had all these ideas and things I wanted to start getting done. I couldn't lie there anymore."

"My mom called to say they were bringing Viv

back," Ash said. "Otherwise, I'd still be in bed myself."

Ash's parents had taken Viv to their house the night before, so that Ash could stay out and celebrate, and she'd done just that. Now she looked like she was regretting it—and also like she might get sick at any moment.

"I thought maybe you guys would take the day off," I said to Matt, and he looked so serious as he answered. "We can't afford to waste a day," he said. "We can't afford to waste a minute."

Jimmy slept until almost noon, and when he woke up, Ash and I were in the TV room, each lying on a couch while Viv played on the floor. What I really wanted to do was to go back to bed, but it seemed unfair (and downright mean) to leave Ash by herself, so I stayed.

When Jimmy finally appeared in the doorway, he was shirtless, wearing an old pair of sweat-pants, and his hair was sticking straight up off his head. It was also possible he was still a little drunk. "Holy Moses," he said, leaning against the doorframe. "I really did a number on myself last night."

Viv made a little squealing noise and then said, "Hi! Hi hi!"

"Hi, baby girl," Jimmy said, looking down at her and waving. Then Viv looked at him and said, "Uh-oh," which she said about fifty times a day, but Jimmy laughed and said, "Yep, uh-oh is right."

"Good Lord, Jimmy. You didn't want to make yourself decent?" Ash closed her eyes like she was annoyed, but really I think she was just tired.

"It's just Beth," Jimmy said, grinning at me. He flopped himself down on the couch where Ash's feet were, making her rearrange herself so her legs were in his lap.

"Oh, Jimmy, you stink!" Ash said, covering her nose. "You smell like you just took a bath in whiskey."

"Who's to say I didn't?" Jimmy asked.

We all turned as Matt came into the room then and stood in front of us. "I thought I heard you," he said, looking at Jimmy. "How does it feel to wake up as the Democratic nominee?"

"It feels great," Jimmy said. "I mean, I feel like a pile of shit, but the rest of it feels great."

"I have some things we should go over," Matt said. "I came to see if I could get lunch for everyone."

"Oh my goodness, you're a savior," Ash said. "Please bring French fries. Anything with French fries on the side."

"Is that okay with everyone?" Matt asked, and Jimmy and I nodded. "Great, I'll be back in a few."

We were all quiet as he left the room and we listened to him start the car and pull out of the driveway. Finally Jimmy said, "How on earth is he not as wrecked as the rest of us?" I just shrugged and said, "I have absolutely no idea."

Over cheeseburgers and fries, Matt talked about how now was the time to focus on money. The Republicans were headed to a runoff election, so Jimmy's opponent wouldn't be decided until the end of May. Matt felt that the next three months were crucial, that Jimmy needed to use this time to try to get ahead. Jimmy had mostly relied on his parents' network up to this point, and could probably count on them for some more money, but Matt emphasized that he needed to reach further, to find new people to donate. The rest of us chewed as he spoke. "We really need to ramp up our fund-raising," he said. "This is push time."

"Isn't that what you have been doing?" I asked, and Matt gave me a look.

"I think we need to get you on the phone," Matt said. "Calling people, telling them about yourself, asking for donations."

Jimmy still looked so tired, like he wasn't even sure what day it was, and I felt like he would've agreed to anything at that point just to end the conversation. He nodded at Matt and said, "Whatever you say, boss."

The very next morning, Matt set up Jimmy in the office with a list of contacts and gave him a pep talk about fund-raising. "You can do this," Matt said. "You'll be great. Just remember—this is about money. If we want to compete in any real way, we need to raise money."

Matt sounded so energized that I half expected him to start jumping around, like a coach trying to psyche his team up before a big game.

For about a week, Jimmy did as Matt said and spent hours calling people and asking for their money, saying the same thing over and over again. And then one day, he started to complain. "I don't come across well on the phone," Jimmy said. "I'm better in front of people. I need to get out there."

"You also need money," Matt said.

"So set up some fund-raisers where I can meet people face to face. I'm going crazy spending all this time on the phone."

To Jimmy, Matt said, "Look, I know this is frustrating. But it's hard to raise money for a down-ballot race—you know that. We just need to keep plugging away at it. I promise I'll think of some ways to get you out there." And then later, to me, he said, "Who does he think is going to come to these fund-raisers? He thinks we have hundreds of people ready to come to a black-tie dinner and drop thousands of dollars? Most people don't even know his name. I don't know who he thinks he is."

This was the first disagreement that Matt and Jimmy had during the campaign. (Or at least the first serious one, that wasn't about what time to leave for a trip or what radio station to listen to in the car.) And it never got resolved—they continued to argue about how much time Jimmy should spend on the phone, every day, both of them repeating themselves, the conversation going in circles. Their fights were so predictable—like a rerun you've seen a million times before, except it wasn't the least bit funny. And I started to notice how it changed things, how it made the air around us unpleasant, always.

When he wasn't trying to raise money, Jimmy was traveling to south Texas to talk to people suffering from air pollution and to north Texas to talk about earthquakes. The traveling wasn't just happening on the weekends now, it was all the time. "We need to reach as many people as we can," Matt said. "We want them to feel heard."

Ash and I went on these trips, for moral support and to help out, and Viv came along so Jimmy could hold her and look like a family man. We traveled so many places in the eight months before the election that I often woke up not knowing where we were. We were always packing and unpacking, taking the clothes out of our bags just to wash them and put them right back in. Every day was another city, sometimes two. Just when I was sure that I'd seen all of Texas, Matt would announce a new place we'd be going to—Azle, Reno, Arlington, Denton. There were times we drove four hours for a two-hour event and came back that same day.

Because Viv's car seat was in the second row, I usually sat in the way back by myself. But I didn't mind. It was sort of peaceful there, and I usually just stared out the window and let my mind wander, watching all of Texas go right past me.

At the end of May, Candace Elroy won the Republican nomination for railroad commissioner, narrowly beating out the Tea Party candidate in the runoff. Elroy had spent the past twenty years as a consultant for the oil industry, and they were willing to give her gobs of money to get her onto the Railroad Commission. When we found out she won, Matt closed his eyes and said softly, "Fuck," which was somehow more disturbing than if he'd screamed or hit something.

Right away, she started out-fund-raising Jimmy, almost to a laughable degree, and while it was probably impossible to even think about catching up with her, Matt was determined to try. One day, after reading about a fund-raiser she'd held, Matt looked like he was going to cry. "Strangers are giving her money without her even having to ask for it," he said, and I imagined Candace Elroy walking down the street while random people threw cash at her.

Matt was haunted by Candace Elroy. He thought

about her more than he thought about anything or anyone else, all day, every day. Once, I swore he said her name while he was sleeping.

Most of it was about the money—Elroy had enough to hire a large staff. She had a scheduler, a campaign manager, a fund-raiser, a speechwriter. For Jimmy, Matt was all of those things put together, and his only help came from Katie and from other volunteers. He was outnumbered. Each time Elroy hired new people, Matt pored over their bios—they all had years of experience in their fields. After she hired the speechwriter, Matt looked defeated. He closed his eyes and shook his head. "I can't compete with that," he said. "I don't know how to do any of this shit. I'm just making it up as I go. Fund-raising is the only thing I really had experience in, and that was for a presidential election. It's not the same at all. The rest of this? Managing a whole campaign? Writing speeches and press releases? I have no idea what I'm doing."

"That's not true," I said. "You're a great writer. You've done an amazing job so far. Just because you've never done these things before doesn't mean you're not good at them."

"That's exactly what it means," he said. That was the only time he ever admitted exactly how this campaign made him feel. He was failing just by waking up each day, running a race with his legs tied together, no chance of catching up.

Candace Elroy also had a private plane at her disposal, borrowed from her father's company, a fact that was always mentioned at least once during one of our long car rides. One day, when we'd spent over ten hours driving, I said, "I bet she has one of those really small planes. The kind that are super scary to fly in because it seems like they could fall right out of the sky. We wouldn't want to be in a plane like that anyway."

Everyone in the car, even Jimmy, who was driving, just turned to look at me, and then turned back without saying a word.

I felt horrible for Matt. I really did. He was struggling and there was nothing I could do to make it better. I tried to be supportive, to talk to him about how hard this must be, to reassure him that he was doing all he could, but often it felt like I was making things worse. Once, I said, "It must be so frustrating to put everything into a race and still be losing." He turned to me, like I was stupid for thinking such a thing, and said, "It's not like this is a surprise. We always knew this would happen."

He was so angry that he couldn't even remember what he was angry about. He shut down in a way I'd never seen before, acting like a sullen teenager, not looking at me when I'd talk to him, grunting in response. Often, I'd say something to him and he'd pretend not to hear me, hoping that I'd go away if he ignored me long enough. I didn't know how to deal with this, so mostly I'd just stand there and say, "Matt," over and over, until he'd looked up from whatever he was doing, already annoyed by my presence, and finally answer me. "What?"

Ten years earlier, Matt and I had gone to South Africa for our honeymoon. He'd been dying to go to Cape Town and thought a safari would be amazing. I agreed, because I didn't really care where we went—our honeymoon, I assumed, would be amazing no matter where we were.

The flight to Cape Town was over twenty hours and I barely slept. Still wired from our wedding weekend, I sat awake on the dark plane while Matt snored beside me. We'd both taken Ambien, but it didn't work for me—I'd woken up after only about thirty minutes, feeling nauseous and disoriented. When we landed, I was so exhausted that I had trouble walking through the airport. Everything was so loud and bright and I kept tripping over my feet.

"I'm so tired I can't see straight," I said to Matt.

"I told you to sleep on the plane," he said, like staying awake was a poor choice that I'd made. I walked behind him trying not to fall, stepping where he stepped, keeping my eyes on his feet.

That night, I crawled into bed, took another Ambien, and closed my eyes, hungry for rest. But three hours later, I sat up in the dark room, my heart racing, my mouth dry. I looked over at Matt and for a few minutes didn't recognize him, had no idea who was lying next to me. Finally, my mind cleared and I remembered: That is my husband, I'm on my honeymoon. And then I tried (unsuccessfully) to go back to sleep.

We were in South Africa for fifteen nights, and I spent most of them staring into the darkness and wanting to cry, because more than anything, jet lag is lonely. During the days, I'd nod off at lunch, beg Matt to go back to the room in the afternoons for a nap. Once, I laid my head down on the table in a restaurant like a child, not caring what anyone around me thought.

"Maybe I have a resistance to Ambien," I told Matt.

"I don't think that's the problem," he said.

It was the worst during the safari. At night, the noises around us made me shiver, and the days made me feel like I was losing my mind. I'd look at the animals—so large, so beautiful, so frightening—and I'd tell myself to pay attention, to appreciate that I was seeing a lion, an elephant, a goddamn hippopotamus. But I was so tired that my eyes pulsed, light danced in my peripheral vision, and all of it felt unreal, like watching a nature documentary on PBS.

Matt wasn't very sympathetic toward me. If anything, he was irritated that my insomnia was interfering with our trip. "You need to get on schedule," he'd say, not bothering to hide his impatience. And soon, it wasn't just at night that I didn't recognize him. I'd look at him through my foggy eyes as we walked around in a foreign country and think, I don't know you at all. I married a stranger.

After we were back in New York and sleeping again, I didn't tell anyone about my jet lag or the thoughts I'd had about Matt. It didn't seem normal, so when people asked about the trip, I just said, "It was amazing. A once in a lifetime experience." And after enough time had passed, I almost believed it.

But that year in Texas, it started happening again, and there were times that Matt seemed unfamiliar to me, when even his voice wasn't his own. I remember once staring at him across the room, an expression on his face that I'd never seen before, his eyes blank and unreadable, and my chest got so tight I could barely breathe, because I didn't recognize him at all.

One morning, we drove four hours to Arlington, Texas, to visit a woman named Angela Kinsey, who'd just been diagnosed with cancer, most likely the result of exposure to the chemicals from the nearby drilling. Angela arranged for a few other women from the neighborhood to join her, so they could share their experiences with Jimmy, tell him about all the health problems they were facing.

We dropped Ash and Viv off at the hotel—it didn't seem right to bring a healthy, squealing sixteen-month-old along while these women talked about the nosebleeds and headaches that their own children were having—and I went along, supposedly to get pictures, but I knew as soon as we stepped into the house that I wouldn't even bother taking my phone out. (How crass would it be to snap a photo of Angela crying as she told Jimmy she didn't know who would care for her children while she started chemo? I didn't care if Katie got mad at me. Some things weren't meant to be photographed.)

The house was small and dark, even though it was sunny outside. For a brief moment, the darkness was a relief from the heat, but then almost immediately, the air began to feel stuffy. There was an overpowering mothball smell inside and I figured I'd get used to it, but it seemed to get stronger the longer we were there.

Angela took us into the living room, where a few women were already sitting on a flimsy-looking floral couch. Jimmy sat at one end and I found a seat on a rocking chair in the corner, while Matt sat on an orange recliner.

By this point, Jimmy's spiel was so polished— he was fluid when he spoke, sure of his words. He was great in front of crowds, could get up in front of fifty people and capture their attention. "These failed policies are hurting us," he'd say. "I want to be an advocate for all Texans, an advocate for you. We've had enough with the insiders, who are only concerned with protecting the oil and gas industries. You deserve someone to protect you. They accuse me of being an outsider, and you know what I say to that?" Here Jimmy would smile and pause and wait for a couple of laughs. "I say, You're right! I say, Being an outsider is what makes me so qualified for this job. I'm not in bed with oil and gas—I'm just a Texan interested in looking out for other Texans."

But where Jimmy was his best was in small, unscripted moments. No other time on the campaign showed this more than the afternoon we spent at Angela Kinsey's house. It was amazing to watch him there, looking like he belonged among all of these women. He sat on that floral couch in that mothball house and talked to them like it was something he did every day. His body was relaxed as he accepted tea from Angela. He didn't shift as the couch sagged underneath him. I wondered if these women knew that Jimmy had grown up in a mansion, that he'd gone to boarding school, that his whole life was unrecognizable compared to theirs. Maybe they did know and it didn't matter. Maybe all they cared about was that he was there now.

He sat forward as one of Angela's neighbors told him about her son's asthma. "You must feel like you're living in a nightmare," he said to her. "You don't deserve this, none of you do. These health problems aren't a coincidence and everyone knows it. We need to do something— and I really do believe that something can be done. People might be turning a blind eye to you, pretending that this isn't happening, that you don't exist, because it's easier for them. But this is happening. I'm here and I'm a witness to it. I want to be the one to help you, to make sure you're heard."

Jimmy's voice was soft as he spoke. There was nothing forced about his response to them. And even though his words could have come off as dramatic, they didn't. He sounded empathetic and determined, and each woman nodded at him whenever he said something.

I didn't doubt that Jimmy was just as invested in this issue as Matt was—you couldn't sit in these homes and listen to people describe the different ways they were being poisoned and not care about it.

Matt was the one who'd found Angela Kinsey and arranged the meeting with her, and he'd spent the car ride there talking about the safety measures that should've been taken to protect the neighborhood. But once we got into the house, you would've never guessed how much Matt wanted to be an advocate for these people. He looked awkward as he held a cup of coffee on the orange chair. He wasn't the one running for office, sure, and you could say that he was trying to stay out of the way and let Jimmy shine. Maybe that was part of it. But every once in a while, Matt chimed in, and the women would listen politely, but you could almost see their eyes glaze over, just waiting for Jimmy to start talking again.

Winning the primary had given Jimmy more confidence—not that he'd really been lacking it before. But you could see now that he had a little more swagger as he walked into a room, a little more pride in his voice as he introduced himself as the Democratic nominee.

There was a fair amount of media attention on Jimmy, mostly because everyone was paying extra attention to all the Democrats running in Texas that year, hoping that an organization called Battleground Texas really could turn Texas blue. And while Jimmy's race wasn't nearly as high profile as some of the others and he wasn't as well known, journalists liked the fact that he'd worked for Obama and was young and handsome. He made for a good story.

Houston Style Magazine did the biggest profile of him, complete with a spread of pictures showing him speaking to a group of farmers, shaking a supporter's hand, and also at home in the backyard, throwing a laughing Viv up in the air with Ash smiling beside him.

When the issue came out, the magazine sent over a bunch of copies and we each took one, flipping through the pages and reading silently. For whatever reason, I looked up to see Jimmy staring at the pictures, and saw as he nodded just a little bit, smiled, and then said quietly to himself, "Well, look at this."

At the beginning of the summer, Rachel Maddow highlighted the Railroad Commission race, profiling Candace Elroy and her oil and gas connections, and then discussing a situation in Weatherford, Texas, where there was so much methane in the well water that people could light it on fire. The current Railroad Commission had closed the case, declaring that it didn't have anything to do with the oil and gas production.

The end of the segment showed a picture of Jimmy—the one of him standing outside—and we all screamed when it came on the screen. Rachel Maddow went on to say that no one in Texas thought Jimmy had a chance to win—he was a Democrat after all—but that maybe, since things had gotten so bad, maybe because water was actually catching on fire, Texans needed to pay attention and rethink things.

The segment was less than four minutes, but still one of the most exciting parts of the campaign. Jimmy seemed to ignore the fact that Rachel Maddow had announced that he was almost definitely going to lose, and was ecstatic about the coverage. Maybe he was already at peace with the outcome of the election, maybe he knew all along what was going to happen. Or maybe he was just so happy to be on national television that he didn't really care.

Whenever Jimmy mentioned any good press or told us about a new interview request, Matt would almost immediately counter with a negative story he'd read about him, or remind everyone how much of an advantage Candace Elroy had. I don't know if he was conscious of this or if it was just a reflex, but after it happened a few times, Jimmy started calling him Debbie Downer—I can still remember the first time it happened, how Matt's face got hard and Jimmy laughed in a way that didn't sound particularly friendly.

I didn't want to think that Matt was trying to bring Jimmy down in these moments—maybe he was, but I told myself it wasn't out of spite. I hoped Matt just wanted to pull Jimmy back to reality, to remind him that there was still a lot of work to be done. Matt was someone who was always genuinely happy for his friends' good news, who believed that there was always enough to go around—but maybe he only thought that when he was getting the most.

After the *Rachel Maddow* segment, while the rest of us were still buzzing from the thrill of seeing Jimmy on national news, Matt said, "Too bad we're the only people in Texas watching MSNBC."

Throughout the campaign, Ash was still booking jewelry parties. (Or trunk shows, as she called them.) Right after I'd gotten to Texas, I'd gone along with her to one of these parties that was hosted by one of the Dozens. There was nothing memorable about it, except that when we got back, Ash said, "Don't worry, I won't drag you along to all of these! I don't want you to feel obligated. They can be such a bore."

I was relieved when she said this, since I actually did find the parties a little boring. But after meeting all of her friends and seeing the dynamic between them, I began to get a little paranoid that she was embarrassed by me. I told myself that even if this were true, it wasn't the worst thing in the world. After all, it hadn't always been my favorite thing to introduce her to new people when we were living in DC. I remember once when she came to a happy hour with all of my work friends, how I'd winced when she kept telling stories that started, "My daddy said . . ."

Ash and I had figured out how to keep our friendship separate, or at least I thought that's what we were doing, until one day in June, when she invited me to a jewelry party that her friend Charlotte was hosting. "She specifically asked for you to come," Ash said. "Don't feel obligated, but I'd love it if you did."

"Of course," I said. What other choice did I have? Was I going to tell her I was busy, that I had to sit in the basement that night and couldn't be disturbed?

"Great," she said. "It will be tons of fun."

I told Colleen about the party, how I was strangely nervous about going. I'd told her all about these girls, so she wasn't surprised by my hesitation.

"I just don't know why they'd invite me. It's not like we really hit it off," I said.

"Oh my God, do you think they're going to Carrie you?" Colleen asked.

"To what?"

"Carrie you. You know, dump pig's blood on you, humiliate you, all of that."

"Oh my God. You're crazy. They're not that bad."

"Yeah," Colleen said. "They sound great."

The night of the party, Ash came down to the basement as I was getting ready. "Can I do your makeup?" she said. "I'm in the mood to play around."

She'd never asked to do my makeup before—as close as we were, this felt weird, but I agreed and sat with my eyes closed while she swept brushes across my face and updated me on everything that was happening with her friends, which meant telling me who was trying to get pregnant and who was having money problems. I mostly just said "Mmm-hmm" as she chatted. When I finally looked in the mirror, I had smoky eyes and dark lips. "You look so great," she said, nodding her approval, and I made myself smile and say thank you.

The party was fine. Everyone was friendly, at least to my face, and we all drank wine and bought some jewelry. I was different from these girls, and thank God for that, but they weren't so bad. Honestly, I'm not sure they even thought about me enough to judge me. But the whole time I watched Ash make her presentation, there was part of me that wondered what she really thought of me, if she wished I wore more makeup, was a little more ladylike, and most of all, if she talked about me the same way she talked about all of the Dozens. I couldn't shake the feeling the whole night, and I was happy when it was finally over.

Matt looked up as I came down to the basement after the party. "Whoa," he said when he saw my makeup. "Ash did it," I told him. I didn't feel like elaborating any more about it, and went to the bathroom to get ready for bed. It took me much longer than normal to wash my face, and I realized why Ash needed to use cold cream every night—it was like stripping paint.

When a friendship ends, people don't always give it the same amount of thought that they do relationships. With an ex-boyfriend, there are discussions of bad timing or different expectations. But most of the time, friendships end in a different way—slowly, and without declaration. Usually people don't really notice until a friend has been gone for a while and then they just say they grew apart, or their lives became too different. But as I brushed my teeth that night, I wondered if people ever blamed the end of friendships on geographical differences, the divides that come from being born in different areas, culture clash.

I was exhausted as I climbed into bed. Matt was under the covers, but sitting up with his laptop open, typing away at something. "Did you have fun?" he asked. I lay down and closed my eyes. "Something like that," I said.

A few weeks later, Jimmy and I were on our own for dinner—Ash was doing another jewelry party at a friend of her mom's and Mr. Dillon had invited Matt out to a steak house. I thought it was weird that the two of them were going out to dinner without Jimmy and said as much to Matt, but he just shrugged like it hadn't occurred to him.

"He said he wanted to talk about my career and where I see it going. I think he has some ideas for me."

"He's sort of an asshole," I said. "Don't you think?"

"Not really," Matt said.

"We've been here for six months and he's never taken Jimmy out to dinner. Don't you think it's sort of rude for him to take you?"

"He's so well connected, Beth. He likes me and wants to help." There was a tiny bit of pleading in Matt's voice, like he was asking me not to push the issue any further, and he looked grateful when I just kissed him good-bye and told him to have fun.

I wandered upstairs a few minutes later and found Jimmy on the patio having a beer. "Hey," I said, poking my head out the door. "What are you up to?"

"Not much. It's just you and me for dinner tonight, you know."

"I know. I figured we'd head to Torchy's?" Torchy's was Jimmy's favorite taco place, and he was thrilled that I loved it as much as he did. The only thing they served was tacos—breakfast tacos, fish tacos, fried avocado tacos. My favorite was one called the Dirty Sanchez, and it said a lot about how delicious it was that I was willing to overlook the embarrassment I felt when I ordered it.

Ash thought Torchy's was gross and Matt just

350

didn't see the appeal. "They're okay," he said once. "Kind of like Chipotle, I guess." I was appalled at this comparison, shocked that he couldn't appreciate how great this place was. "It's my favorite thing about Houston," I said, and Matt just shrugged. Now whenever Jimmy and I found ourselves alone for a meal, we drove to stuff our faces with a bunch of tacos.

"I was thinking something different tonight," Jimmy said.

"Probably for the best," I said, sitting on the bottom of the lounge chair next to him. "I'm starting to blame Torchy's for my rapid weight gain."

"Oh stop," Jimmy said.

"It's true. Even if I wanted to, I couldn't live here. Texas is making me fat."

"Beth, that body of yours has never looked better, so let's cut the self-deprecation crap."

"Ha-ha," I said. Jimmy gave out compliments to everyone so frequently, I usually didn't even notice. But the things he said to me were normally a little milder, more of the "you look nice" variety. I was pretty sure he'd never mentioned my body before in any capacity, and I was trying not to show that it had flustered me.

"I was thinking," he said, "since Matt's off having steak and Ash is peddling her wares, that we should take ourselves somewhere nice tonight."

"Sounds good to me."

"Great. Let's leave at eight."

We ended up going to a diner-type place, and I was relieved that this was Jimmy's version of "nice" and that we weren't headed to a fancy dinner somewhere. The restaurant had an over-the-top fifties theme with jukeboxes and vinyl booths. "I know it's a little much," Jimmy said, "but the burgers here are really good."

We each ordered a cheeseburger, fries, and a beer, which wasn't any healthier than Torchy's, and I almost made a comment about it but didn't want to call attention to the conversation we'd had earlier, like I was fishing for compliments.

A couple walked by our booth, and I saw the girl do a double take when she spotted Jimmy. She backed up and waited for him to notice her before saying, "Jimmy, hi!" She kept looking over at me, quickly, like she was trying to be sneaky. Jimmy took a sip of his beer and said, "Hey, Alexis. How's it going," but made no move to introduce us. Finally she put out her hand to me and said, "Hi, I'm Alexis."

"Beth," I said.

Jimmy smiled as we shook hands, and I could tell he hadn't introduced us on purpose. "You haven't met Beth yet?" he asked her. "She's Ash's best friend from DC and the wife of my campaign manager."

"No, we've never met," Alexis said. She looked slightly disappointed that I wasn't some secret girlfriend, but she managed to shake my hand and then turned to the guy standing next to her. "This is my husband, Fletcher." Fletcher gave us a small nod and stood off to the side, making it clear he had no interest in joining our conversation. Alexis stood at our table awkwardly for a few more seconds and then said good-bye.

After they walked away, I looked at Jimmy, who had an amused expression on his face. "What was that about?" I asked him.

"She was in Ash's class in high school," he said. "She's the worst."

I laughed and looked past him to make sure Alexis was out of earshot. "Really," he went on. "She's even worse than the coven that Ash is always with now. She would have loved nothing more than to be able to report to the whole town that I was eating dinner with an unidentified attractive woman."

"Really?" I asked.

"Really. She's nothing but awful. In high school, she once fed so much beer to someone's pet bird at a party that it died."

"Oh, God," I said.

"I know. She had all the makings of a serial killer. Poor Fletcher better watch his back."

The waitress brought our food over then, and we didn't talk as we arranged the onions and tomatoes on our burgers, poured just the right amount of ketchup on them. I'd just taken a huge bite when Jimmy said, "So the question is, do you think my dad will legally adopt Matt as his son by the time dinner's over?"

I laughed because I knew that's what he wanted me to do and then managed to swallow and ask, "What do you think they talk about all the time anyway?"

"You know, how smart they both are, stuff like that."

"Ha," I said. And then because I felt like I couldn't ignore it, "I'm sorry if it's weird for you, them going out to dinner. I feel like I'd be annoyed if I were you."

Jimmy shrugged. "Nah," he said and then laughed a little bit. "It's fine. Plus, I'd much rather eat dinner with you than with my dad."

I thought then how happy I was that Jimmy was still himself, that while Matt and Ash were morphing into weird personalities, Jimmy stayed the same. Ridiculous sometimes, sure. Self-centered, maybe. But that's who he'd always been and I felt the most relaxed when he was around.

I put my cheeseburger down on my plate, wiped my hands on my napkin. "You know," I said, "I bet we had more fun than anyone tonight." And Jimmy looked up with a serious expression before winking and saying, "Obviously," then shoving the last large bite of his burger into his mouth.

• • •

Later that week, Matt and I watched Viv while Jimmy and Ash went to a birthday dinner for her friend Ainsley. All of the Dozens were attending with their husbands, and Ash had reminded Jimmy of the dinner no fewer than twenty times. We were sitting on the floor with Viv in the TV room when they came to say they were leaving, both dressed up.

"Have a good night," I said, and Jimmy said, "Oh, I'm sure we won't."

Ash decided to pretend he was joking and she swatted him on the arm. "Very funny, Jimmy."

After they left, Viv wrinkled her brow and cried a little, but she recovered quickly and soon seemed delighted that she had our undivided attention. It felt a little odd to be alone with Matt—since we'd moved to Texas, it had rarely been just the two of us. But I tried to ignore any weirdness and be happy that we were spending the night together now, even if it was just because we were babysitting.

Viv had a koala bear that she was very attached to (Ash sometimes worried that her obsession with it wasn't normal) and she kept handing it to Matt and then taking it back, shoving its arms and legs into her mouth.

"Koala is going to need a bath soon," I said to her, and she smiled and whipped him on the ground.

"Are you mad at Koala?" Matt asked, and Viv looked up at him as if she were considering the question. "Maybe you're just bored with him. You probably want another baby to play with. You should ask your aunt Beth to help you out. Maybe she will. You just have to ask her." Matt said all of this in a singsong voice while looking at Viv, but it was clear he was waiting for me to respond.

I didn't say anything at first, just stared at Matt. It felt like this was coming out of nowhere—we hadn't talked about having a baby in months, not in any serious way. In fact, we hadn't even mentioned it casually, and I couldn't tell if Matt was joking now. Finally, I just said, "Funny, funny."

"I'm not trying to be funny," Matt said. He was looking at me strangely then, and I had the feeling that he wanted to start a fight, to make the night unpleasant.

"You seriously want to have a baby in Texas?" I asked.

"Sure," he said. "Why not? We wouldn't be in Texas when the baby was born anyway."

"Why not?" I asked. "Why not?" was his reason for wanting to have a baby?

"Yeah, why not?"

"Right. So, let's say I got pregnant right now. Then I'd be back in DC looking for a job while I was visibly pregnant? That timing doesn't seem great."

I was aware then that Viv was watching us, and while I knew she didn't understand what we were saying, I still felt strangely guilty having this conversation in front of her.

"I don't think the timing is ever completely right," Matt said. There was a challenge in his voice.

"Maybe not," I said. "But this timing seems completely wrong." I didn't say what I was really thinking—which was that I couldn't imagine having a baby with someone who was so angry all the time. That he barely talked to me lately, that he didn't seem like himself and the thought of negotiating the complications of a child while he was like this seemed impossible, or at the very least, the thing that would end us.

Also, a tiny part of me thought that maybe he wanted a baby because it was something that Jimmy had, that it would be a way to even the score between them. But I just stayed quiet, because it seemed that telling him any of this would most certainly lead to a fight. And finally he sighed as though I were deeply disappointing him and said, "You know, you can't keep making excuses forever."

Chapter 17

Did you see this?" Matt asked, pointing to his computer. We were all in the kitchen eating breakfast and Matt's laptop was in front of him, but I didn't know if he was talking to me or Jimmy or all of us.

"See what?" I finally said.

"*The Dallas Morning News* reported that Candace Elroy raised ten times what we did last quarter. And half of the money came from donations from oil and gas companies. This is so fucked up."

"I'm so sick of this shit," Jimmy said. He was pouring himself a cup of coffee and my heart jumped for a second, thinking he was talking about Matt's constant delivery of bad news. But then he went on, "How can people not see how corrupt this is?"

"I thought we made a rule about these things at breakfast," Ash said, lightly tapping the top of Matt's laptop. He gave her an apologetic look as he closed the computer and placed it on an empty chair. A couple weeks earlier, Matt had sat at the breakfast table and read us an article about Jimmy that picked apart his career, claiming he had no experience with anything remotely related to oil and gas, that his résumé was fluffy and light, that he was trading on being Obama's aide. We all stared at Matt as he read out loud, and I kept thinking he'd stop eventually, especially when it started to get nasty. But he just kept going. The article had appeared on some conservative blog, but Matt said it got a lot of traffic, that plenty of people would read it. After he read the last line, "A Democrat hasn't been elected to the Railroad Commission in two decades," he finally looked up and realized that he'd just ruined everyone's day, all before 8:00 a.m. It was after that that Ash started insisting everyone (meaning Matt) keep the computers off the table while we ate.

That morning, even after the computer was gone, Matt kept muttering about Candace Elroy. "We need everyone to stop reporting on how little we're raising. It's taking away from the real issues of the race." No one responded to him—we knew he wasn't looking for an answer, just thinking out loud.

"What's on the schedule for today?" Ash said in a cheerful voice, a little louder than normal. She was toasting a loaf of sourdough bread and carrying it over to us, four thick pieces at a time. She'd already set out butter and fancy strawberry jam, and a bowl of hard-boiled eggs sat in the center of the table. When I got up to help her carry things, she'd put her hands on my shoulders and said, "Don't you dare," which even with her friendly southern accent, sounded a little bit like a threat.

"We're leaving for Odessa today," Matt said.

"Oh, right. That's today?" Ash set down the last four pieces of toast and then finally sat down herself and picked up her coffee. "I almost forgot."

"How could you forget?" Jimmy asked. "We've been talking about it all week."

My eyes met Ash's across the table just for a second, and then we both looked away, waiting to see if this would escalate. Both of us let out a breath when Jimmy changed the subject, knowing that our breakfast—for that day at least—would be argument free.

The Odessa trip was a point of contention—Jimmy thought it was too far to go for such a small event (a round-table discussion with oil field workers), but Matt insisted it was important and argued with him until he gave in. The plan was to leave Tuesday morning and drive eight hours to Odessa, where they would spend the night and have the round table first thing in the morning, then drive to San Antonio for a fundraising dinner and return home late Wednesday. All of the campaign trips involved a lot of driving, but this was pretty extreme with the quick turnaround.

I'd woken up at 4:00 that morning and found Matt sitting on the couch outside our bedroom, his laptop balanced on his knees. "What are you doing?" I'd asked, half asleep.

"I'm trying to get the points for the water conservation plan down. We need to get it on the website, make sure Jimmy starts working it into his talks."

"It's four in the morning."

"I know."

"You should get some sleep," I said, "if you're going to drive tomorrow."

"I will. I just need to get this done." Matt looked up at me then and I could see how tired he was. Part of me wanted to hug him, to make him come to bed. I knew that his recent irritability and bad moods were made worse by the fact that he wasn't getting nearly enough sleep. But there was another part of me that didn't want to bother because I knew how it would play out—I'd try to convince him to come to bed and he'd tell me he had too much work to do and would eventually get annoyed and huffy with me. It seemed like no matter what I did or said lately, it wasn't the right thing.

"Okay, then," I finally said. "Good night."

Matt and Jimmy were out the door by 10:00, and Ash and I just looked at each after they drove away. "It's so calm in here," I said.

"I know," she said. "Thank God."

It was a relief to have Matt out of the house, to

know that he wouldn't be back that night. Which only made me worry that it wasn't normal to feel that way, wasn't right to only be able to relax when your husband wasn't around.

Ash and I wandered back to the kitchen and sat at the round table. It was sunny and cheerful in there—like everywhere else in the house, there was thought put into every detail. But this room was by far my favorite, with its ruffly curtains and distressed table. I had a feeling that I'd never be able to create a similar space in a home of my own. Decorating skill, it seemed, was one more thing that I was lacking.

We discussed our plans for the day—Ash didn't have to work and so we were free to do whatever we wanted. We were debating taking a walk to the park and having lunch there when I felt Ash hesitate and then she said, "I'm sure this is all normal campaign stuff, and maybe I'm just being sensitive, but I hate the way they're acting with each other. It's nasty."

She'd clearly been thinking about mentioning something for a while—I could tell by the way it just spilled out, like she wanted to say it before she changed her mind. It was strange that we'd never discussed what was happening between Matt and Jimmy. We'd exchanged glances and a couple of comments, but never really acknowledged how bad it had gotten. Their arguments colored everyone else's moods, cast a shadow over the house. If they were on good terms, everyone could be happy. If not, we all had to be on guard.

"I know," I said to her. "It's almost like they can't help it. Like they can't stop the fighting now that it's started." I was aware of how we both kept saying "they," like neither of us wanted to assign blame to the other's husband.

Ash was about to say something else, had her mouth open and ready, and then we heard Viv cry from upstairs and she sighed. "Duty calls," she said, getting to her feet.

We ended up walking to the park, Ash pushing Viv in the stroller, Viv's legs kicking out in front of her. It was a beautiful day—hot of course, but it still felt great to be outside. We stopped to get sandwiches on the way, and once Viv was set up in the sand, we unwrapped them and started eating. Every minute or so, Ash had to get up to stop Viv from putting sand in her mouth, or to take a stick out of her hand and replace it with a plastic shovel. I'd finished my entire lunch before Ash had even gotten through half of hers, and so I moved to sit next to Viv, trying to entertain her so Ash could eat.

It was interesting to be able to observe Ash as a mom so closely. What struck me nearly every day was how almost all of Viv's care fell to her. She had help from all the family around, of course, which was more than most people got. But on a day-to-day basis, Jimmy didn't do much to take care of Viv. Maybe it had always been that way—we hadn't lived with them when she was first born, so how would we know? Or maybe it had changed once the campaign started. Either way, I was pretty sure there was no going back now. Jimmy would hold Viv or carry her to the kitchen, but he unapologetically handed her off to Ash when she needed to eat or get a diaper changed.

It was so personal, what Matt and I were witnessing, a twenty-four-hour view of the Dillons' parenting. And it seemed extreme to me, although I couldn't say how unusual it was since I'd never lived with anyone else who was raising a child. But when we were on the road, Ash never ate a meal uninterrupted. She'd try to take a few bites while feeding and entertaining Viv, but more often than not she just abandoned her plate altogether, while Jimmy sat back, relaxed and taking it for granted that he had both hands free. I wondered sometimes, watching this, if Ash knew what she'd signed up for.

Ash finished her sandwich quickly and carried our trash over to the garbage can. She walked back toward us and held out her hands to Viv, pulled her up to standing. "Do you want to go on the swings?" she asked, already leading Viv over there. I watched as they walked away, as

Ash freed one hand to wave to another mom-and-daughter duo. "Hey, y'all," she said, "isn't this a perfect day for the park?"

Most nights, Ash put Viv down around 7:00, before we all ate dinner. Lately, I'd go upstairs with her and sit on the floor while she changed Viv into her pajamas and read her a story. It wasn't like we needed any more time to talk or that she even wanted me there, it was just that I didn't want to be left downstairs alone with Matt and Jimmy.

But with them gone, I stayed downstairs to watch TV as Ash put Viv to bed, and it felt so freeing—like the first time my parents left me alone when they went out. I poured us each a glass of wine, and when Ash came down, she said, "Oh, that is just what I need."

Neither of us was all that hungry, so Ash just set out cheese and crackers to snack on. Ash chewed on a piece of cheese thoughtfully and then said, "I wonder what the boys are up to."

We hadn't heard from them since they arrived. Matt had just sent one text that said, *Made it to Odessa.* I'd written back to ask how the drive went, but he hadn't responded. I checked my phone once more, just to be sure, like I could've missed something when my phone had been no more than six inches away from me all day.

"They probably just got dinner and went to bed," I said.

"Do you think they're getting along?" Ash asked.

"Maybe," I said. "Maybe being alone will be good for them. Maybe they'll be able to talk some things out." I doubted this was true, but we were both skirting around what was so obvious—that Matt thought Jimmy was being a prima donna and Jimmy thought Matt was jealous.

"Maybe," Ash said, although I could tell she didn't believe it any more than I did.

"It's making Matt so irritable though," I said. "The campaign, I mean. Like he's just mad all the time. Even at me."

This was the most I'd disclosed about what was going on between me and Matt. It was embarrassing, but I figured she was seeing it all anyway and was the only one who could really understand the complications of our situation.

"That must be hard," she said, giving me an exaggerated look of sympathy. She'd snapped back to her Texas Ash voice, the one she used when she talked to the Dozens.

"Yeah, I'm sure it's just stress," I said, hoping we could drop it.

"I'm sure it is," she said, and again her voice had a syrupy sweet tone to it that made me want to slap her. Why was she acting like this? Like everything in her life was so perfect? I'd wanted to tell her so much, how weird things were with Matt, how we barely talked anymore, how we hadn't had sex in weeks, how I'd been shut down so many times when I tried to initiate it that I felt humiliated.

But now I couldn't confide in her. Six months ago, I could have told her everything. But in that moment, I didn't trust her. She'd probably run to the Dozens and tell them all about her poor friend Beth, who was having marital problems. I didn't say anything else, and then she reached over and touched my arm and said in a voice so dramatic it was almost funny, "Don't worry, I know you two will work it out."

Matt and Jimmy returned late the next night, and I was already in bed but still awake and reading when Matt came in, tossed his bag in the corner of the room, and closed the door behind him.

"That was the most annoying twenty-four hours of my life," he said. He wasn't bothering to whisper.

"Why?" I asked, putting my book down.

"The round table was fine. Jimmy did well, although he spent the first twenty minutes shooting the shit with everyone instead of talking about safety concerns. He kept straying from the talking points, but eventually he got there. But then we got to the dinner tonight and we'd been in the car for hours at that point and I'm trying to give him some feedback, some constructive criticism, and he acts like I'm out of line. Like I'm insulting him just for fun."

"So what happened?" I asked. I wasn't happy that they'd fought during the trip, but for once it felt like Matt was confiding in me, like he was finally seeing that we were on the same team. I didn't want to encourage what was happening between him and Jimmy, but I did want him to keep talking to me.

"Nothing happened, really. We got to the dinner and he got pretty drunk right away, which meant that I was going to have to drive the whole way back, which is fine, I guess, but whatever. And then he started talking to this woman, just one on one in a weird way, like no one else was there. Every time I tried to introduce him to someone new, he basically ignored me. Not to mention that he didn't care how it looked that he was hitting on this woman in front of the whole room."

"He was hitting on her?" I asked.

"I mean, yeah. I don't know. You know him."

"Who was she?"

"One of the donors. She sought him out, but he didn't back away. I think he was trying to piss me off."

"Was it bad?"

"It wasn't great," Matt said. But then he seemed to snap out of it and changed his tone. "It wasn't a big deal, really."

"It sounds weird," I said, hoping he'd say more. Matt climbed into bed, leaned back and rubbed his eyes. "It was just a long night. I'm so tired."

It was funny, for all of the things that Matt would say behind Jimmy's back, he never discussed the way Jimmy acted around attractive women, how it sometimes seemed just shy of inappropriate. Matt had always dismissed all the rumors about Jimmy as just that—rumors. But lately, I wondered if he knew something more, if he was just protecting Jimmy the way you protect your candidate.

"What was the woman's name?" I asked, but next to me, Matt was already asleep.

When I think back to our time in Texas, it doesn't seem possible that we actually lived in the Dillons' basement for nearly a year, that we ate almost every meal with them like we were part of some strange commune. There were days that seemed so long, so open—I didn't have a job or a baby, we were staying in someone else's home, and while I was helping with the campaign, it didn't even come close to taking all of my free time. Some afternoons, I did nothing but read, finishing whole books in a day. But somehow, it didn't feel like the time passed slowly, just the opposite really—it seemed like we were moving into the basement one day and out the next.

During those months, it felt like I was floating,

in suspended time. When my birthday came that year, I felt truly shocked to have turned a year older. Everyone around me had a real purpose—sometimes more than one—and while I could mock Ash's jewelry business (when I was feeling hateful), there was no denying that she was successful, that she enjoyed it. And so most of the time when I watched her pack up her samples and get ready to go to a party, it was jealousy that I felt.

There was a lot of fighting that happened in that house, a lot of anxious and tense moments, and days when it felt like we were just marking time until the next argument. But still, when I think about that year, what I remember most is one night that the four of us sat outside on the back patio, first eating dinner and then staying there to split a bottle of wine. Our plates were still on the table, but none of us were in any hurry to clean up. Viv was asleep upstairs and I remember being nervous that our laughter was going to wake her up.

Things hadn't yet turned sour between Matt and Jimmy, and we were all talking about an event we'd been to that day, where an older man had cornered Jimmy to talk about railroads for almost an hour, while Jimmy tried to explain (unsuccessfully) that the Railroad Commission didn't have anything to do with actual railroads. Matt kept impersonating Jimmy during this conversation, and we couldn't stop laughing.

"I think he was a retired Amtrak driver," Jimmy said. "No joke. He was very concerned about our rail system."

"Let's have one more," Matt said, picking up the empty bottle of wine. "You know, in honor of the railroad."

"We should clean this up," Ash said, but she didn't move.

"Nope, Jimmy and I will get it," Matt said, standing up and piling plates on top of each other. "And we'll be back with more wine."

We watched as the two of them filled their arms with dishes to carry into the kitchen. As Jimmy held the door open for Matt, the two of them laughed at something he'd said. We couldn't hear what it was.

"Look at those husbands of ours," Ash said to me. "How did we ever get so lucky?"

Jimmy was invited to speak at the Texas Democratic State Convention at the end of June, which was a big deal—a much bigger deal than I realized when we first heard about it. "This is huge," Matt said. And then again with more emphasis, just in case we missed it, "Huge."

Before the convention, I'd never seen Jimmy get nervous. He could be jumpy before events, but that was mostly just adrenaline and he always calmed down as soon as he started talking. But this was different—from the moment he first found out about the convention, he was terrified. Anytime someone mentioned it, he got a look on his face like he might be sick. He'd be speaking to over seven thousand people—by far the largest crowd he'd ever been in front of—and he'd be alongside much bigger, more well-known Texas Democrats.

He and Matt worked on the speech every night. It contained a lot of the same talking points that he'd used while campaigning, but they'd made it more personal, a little more theatrical. Leading up to the convention, Matt and Jimmy read the speech out loud over and over, tweaking each word, rehearsing it a thousand different ways. On the car ride to Dallas, Jimmy practiced while Matt drove, jumping in every once in a while with a suggestion, and by the time we arrived, I was pretty sure I could've recited the whole thing from memory.

Matt and Jimmy left the hotel early in the day to go to the convention center for a walk-through, and when they returned Ash and I were just sitting down to have lunch at the hotel restaurant. Viv had stayed behind with Ash's mom, and Ash was clearly excited about having a free day, and was on her phone trying to find a place we could get manicures when we were done eating.

I could tell something was wrong as soon as Matt and Jimmy walked into the restaurant. They sat down with us, and immediately Matt said, "There was a little miscommunication," as if he were a PR person trying to smooth over a mishap. "I couldn't practice my speech," Jimmy said. "That was the miscommunication."

It turned out that all of the walk-through time was allotted to the more important speakers. Jimmy had been counting on practicing with the teleprompter while reading his speech, getting a feel for the microphone, but all he got to do was walk on the stage and walk right off again.

"I don't know how this happened," Matt said. He sounded apologetic.

"It doesn't really matter now, does it?" And then Jimmy looked pale as he said, "I've never used a teleprompter before."

"I'm sure you'll be fine," Matt said, and Jimmy just shook his head and said, "God, I hope so."

Jimmy's speech was (by all accounts) great. He was completely natural and engaging, timed all of his jokes just right, and didn't rush through any of it. There was no sign that he was uncomfortable with the teleprompter. It was as though he'd done this a million times before. As Jimmy finished up, I heard Matt let out a long breath that he may have been holding the whole time. "That was good," he said to me, sounding relieved. "Really good, right?"

Everyone congratulated Jimmy that night,

compliments coming from all around. I heard one man say to him, "You're going places, kid," like he was an old-timey politician. On the car ride home, Jimmy repeated all the things people had said to him, even though we'd already heard most of them. He was driving, staring at the road as he talked about all the amazing praise he'd gotten. "Someone said it reminded them of Obama's red state, blue state speech," he said. "Do you believe that?" He laughed like it was a crazy thing to say, but you could tell that he was thrilled by it, that part of him thought it was true.

Just a few days after the convention, we all headed to Luling, Texas, to attend the Watermelon Thump—a festival dedicated to all things watermelon. Anytime this event was mentioned, I couldn't help but laugh at how ridiculous it sounded. I was strangely excited for it, because when else would we ever go to such a thing?

Matt was in a horrible mood after the convention and showed no signs that he'd snap out of it anytime soon. As we packed for Luling, I said in a voice of forced cheer, "Come on, don't tell me you're not excited for the Thump?" I could hear how fake I sounded, like I was talking to a grumpy child. Matt just grunted in response, not looking up from folding his clothes. He couldn't even pretend to smile, and I had a horrible thought—if he wasn't even a little amused by the idea of the Thump, then things were even worse than I'd realized.

The quality of our hotel rooms varied, but they were never what you'd consider nice. The most we could hope for was that they were clean. But the hotel in Luling was by far the worst one we'd stayed in. It was dark and creepy, and there was a musty smell in the room. Everything seemed damp—the sheets, the rug, the towels—and I found myself not wanting to touch anything.

We'd left Sugar Land superearly in the morning and driven right to the Thump, had spent the day doing watermelon-related activities—melon judging, melon eating, and seed spitting contests. We'd been on our feet for hours, standing in the sun, and I'd been looking forward to a long shower. But as soon as I saw the bathroom, I didn't even want to take my shoes off. I washed up at the sink as much as I could, using a washcloth to wipe under my armpits and all around, thinking that this was a low point. As dirty as I felt, I couldn't bring myself to get in the tub.

I met Ash in the hallway before we headed to dinner, and she muttered to me, "We're going to end up with bedbugs."

"Don't even think it," I said. She was holding Viv on her hip, a diaper bag over her shoulder. "Here, let me take the bag."

"Thanks," she said, wiggling her arm to let it loose. "Jimmy jumped right in the shower, didn't even offer to let me get in there first. Not that I wanted to step foot in there."

"I felt the same way," I told her. "Matt's in there now. How can they not be bothered by this?"

"I honestly don't know. I just wiped down the baby with wipes, which she didn't appreciate, and then used them on myself. I feel downright disgusting."

"I know," I said. "Come on, let's wait for them outside. It has to be cleaner than in here."

We walked down the stairs and out front where there was a bench in the shade for us to sit on. The highway was just past a sidewalk and another grassy patch. "At least we have a lovely view," I said, but Ash didn't smile, just set Viv down and handed her a pink car from the diaper bag. Viv smiled and said, "Mama, car!" in a happy voice and then threw the pink, plastic car so that it landed on the dirty grass behind us. Ash and I just sat there and looked at it, neither of us making a move to retrieve it.

We drove to a nearby pizzeria for dinner, some place that Matt had found. None of us really cared where we ate, as long as we didn't have to wait to be seated. We were led to a table that hadn't been wiped down, but the hostess just dropped our menus in front of us and walked away. I tried to get someone's attention, but everyone kept walking by like they didn't see us. Viv was refusing to sit in the high chair, saying, "No!" over and over again, and then screaming so loudly, I was sure she was going to pop a blood vessel. Ash finally wrangled her in there, and Viv arched her back and howled, making it as hard as possible for Ash to buckle her in. When she realized she couldn't get out, she slapped her hand out and hit Ash in the face, then continued to wail, her face now purple.

"Thanks for the help," Ash said to Jimmy, who was studying the menu. Ash never said things like this, but Jimmy didn't seem bothered.

"Should we take her outside?" he asked, by which he meant that Ash should take her outside.

"You mean, so we can fight her back into the high chair again in ten minutes?" Ash said. "No, but thank you for the offer." Jimmy rolled his eyes and went back to the menu.

I didn't blame Ash for getting angry—to be honest, I had no idea how she was managing Viv at these campaign events without losing her mind. We were in the car for such long stretches of time and now that Viv was mobile, she was bored and fidgety when she was strapped in anywhere too long. I also didn't blame Viv for the fit she was throwing now. In a way, I was almost jealous. It probably felt good to let it all out.

We ordered two pizzas and a round of beers as

soon as the waitress came over, and Ash put some puffs on Viv's tray, which she normally loved but this time she looked at them, slapped her hand down, and screamed, "Cookie!" while aiming her face up to the ceiling.

"Give her your phone," Jimmy said to Ash. "Jesus, before we get kicked out."

"We can't do that every time she cries. It's not good for her," Ash said, but then she immediately dug into her bag and pulled out her phone. A few seconds later, Elmo was playing and Viv was quiet—or at least quieter. She was still crying, but it soon slowed to sniffling and finally stopped.

We ate the pizza quickly. It wasn't very good, doughy and flavorless, but we each shoved a couple of slices in our mouths. We asked for the check when our food arrived, so we could get out of there as soon as we were done. Ash cut up a piece of pizza for Viv, who maybe ate one bite before pushing the rest off her tray and saying, "No!"

"Come on, baby girl, just try it," Ash said. Viv kept saying, "No!" and finally Jimmy said, "Just leave her be."

Ash glared at him and said, "So she can go to sleep and wake up in the middle of the night crying because she didn't eat? And then I can get up with her and spend tomorrow exhausted?"

What disturbed me the most about what was

happening between Ash and Jimmy was that they were acting like we weren't even there. We'd spent enough time together as couples that we'd been witness to each other's arguments. But this was different. It was like they didn't even notice that anyone else was around, too far gone to remember that they weren't alone.

Matt was pretty quiet during dinner, almost like he wasn't aware of the fighting at the table. I made a halfhearted attempt to talk about the melon that had won the contest that day—it was so big it seemed almost pornographic—but no one joined in and we finished our meal in silence.

Back at the hotel, Matt sat on the bed and read e-mails on his phone. "Don't you want to take the comforter off the bed first?" I asked, and he looked at me and shrugged, moving just slightly so I could pull it off and throw it on the floor. "Comforters are the dirtiest parts of hotels," I said.

"Actually, I think it's the remote controls," he said without looking up.

I turned on the TV and watched for a few minutes, then finally looked over at Matt. "That was some dinner, huh?"

"Yeah," Matt said, still not taking his eyes off his phone.

"Matt," I said. He finally looked at me. "I hate when you ignore me."

"I'm not ignoring you. I'm just—I'm busy. It's all bad news we're getting. It's not looking good."

"Okay," I said. "I get that. But I also think you should at least talk to me for five minutes a day. It shouldn't be so much to ask. You can't just shut me out."

"I know that," he said. He sighed and looked at me, and I had this weird feeling that he was going to set a timer for five minutes so that he could go back to work after he suffered through a conversation with me. I felt irritation rise in my throat, and I should've just dropped it, should've gone to bed. We were both tired and annoyed—but we'd been tired and annoyed for months now. So instead I said, "I felt bad for Ash tonight. Jimmy just really doesn't help much with Viv."

"I think he's doing the best he can."

"Yeah, but I mean, it's still impossible. She's taking Viv to all these events for him."

"She knew what it would be like," Matt said.

"Did she?"

"Yeah, I think she did. Campaigns aren't easy."

"Well, that's sort of an understatement. Look what it's doing to them." What I really meant was, Look what it's doing to us.

"What do you want me to say?" Matt asked. "This is part of it—it's exhausting for the family too."

"I guess I didn't realize just how exhausting it

would be," I said. We were getting snippier with each thing we said, and I knew we were teetering on a fight.

"What's that supposed to mean?" Matt asked.

"Just that this"—I moved my arms around, gesturing at our room—"is disgusting. And you're in a bad mood most of the time." I saw Matt glance down at his phone and I wanted to say something to get his attention, to make him look at me. "Sometimes I just wonder why we did this. Why anyone would want to do this."

"It's hard, Beth. But this experience hasn't changed my mind. I still intend to run for office one day. I still want that."

"What if I don't want to do it anymore?" I asked. And right then a look passed over his face, and I felt it—that if it came down to it, if he had to choose between me and running for office, he wouldn't choose me.

Matt's eyes narrowed. "I knew you were happy when I didn't get the chance to run for that senate seat."

"That's not true," I said.

"You can honestly tell me that you would've been happy about it? That you wanted it to happen?"

I didn't say anything, and then Matt said, "I knew it. You know, I would never ask you to choose between me and your career."

"You *have* asked me," I said.

Matt snorted. "What? DCLOVE? It didn't take much to convince you to leave that place. You didn't really care about it. And you didn't even have a job anymore when we left New York."

"If I'd have known how miserable you'd be here, I never would've agreed to this."

"We can't all be delightful all the time," Matt said in a snotty voice. We were loud, almost screaming, and I thought for a second that the Dillons could definitely hear us, but then I was too angry to care.

"Look," I said. "I know that this has been hard for you. I'm sure you're a little jealous of Jimmy and I know that—"

"You think I'm jealous?" Matt had an incredulous look on his face, like this was the craziest idea, and I almost laughed.

"Maybe *jealous* is the wrong word," I said. But there was no backtracking.

"I don't want to run for the Railroad Commission," he said.

"No, I know. That's not what I meant."

"That's what you said." He turned away from me. "If you think this is about jealousy, then maybe you don't know me at all."

"Matt, come on."

"Come on? Look, just because you don't understand this, just because you don't know what it's like to have a job that you care about, don't blame me. If you had anything like this—if you cared about writing, if you were passionate about *anything,* maybe you'd get it. But you're not."

I was silent for a full minute. Was this what Matt really thought of me? I shouldn't have felt totally surprised—didn't I sometimes think this very thing?—but it was strange and awful to hear my husband say what I feared about myself.

"I'm sorry you didn't get to run for office first," I said, my voice making it clear that I was anything but. "I'm sorry you're so jealous of Jimmy that you're about to burst. But don't you dare take it out on me." I was so angry that my hands were shaking. We'd fought in the past, of course we had, but it had never felt like this, like things would be different after, like what we were saying couldn't ever be taken back.

Matt stood up and walked right out the door without turning around. I didn't call or text him that night. I assumed that he got another shitty room in this shitty hotel, but we never talked about it. I lay down, still fully dressed, and pulled the sheets over me. I slept fitfully that night—it felt like I woke up every five minutes or so, just long enough each time to remember that my husband wasn't there.

Chapter 18

In July, we went back to DC for a couple of days. Babs suggested it and I was adamant that we go. There was no way we were going to make it to St. Michaels in August, and I thought maybe seeing his family would cheer Matt up, or snap him back to normal, or do something, anything. His parents had talked about coming to see us in Texas, but Matt flat-out told them not to, said that we didn't have any time to spend with them. The fact that I was now pushing to go see the Kellys should've been a red flag for everyone. But I was desperate.

Matt and I were on civil terms, but just barely. After the fight in Luling, we'd ridden home without talking to each other, which was surprisingly easy to do with two other adults and one baby in the car. Ash and Jimmy were still mad at each other too, so our car ride was like one big bizarre game of telephone: Each person could talk to anyone in the car except their spouse. Once, Ash slipped and asked Jimmy to turn down the radio, and then she sat back in her seat, put her sunglasses on, and frowned out the window. No doubt upset with herself for losing the game.

That night, back at the house, I said to Matt, "I'm sorry we fought," which wasn't the same thing as actually apologizing. He looked at me and said, "I'm sorry we fought too," and then we both stood there, waiting for the other one to say something more. Neither of us did. There were moments when I thought about bringing it up, trying to resolve things—and then I'd remember what he said to me, how much his words stung, and I didn't think there was anything that would make it better.

So, the fight wasn't really over, it was just that neither of us saw the point in discussing it anymore. Which, when you thought about it, was so much worse.

The afternoon before we left, Ash and I were out back with Viv, who was toddling around in the grass, and Ash turned to me and said, "How are things going with Matt? I've been worried about you."

She looked at me with such pity, like she couldn't imagine how I was dealing with my horrible marriage. I wanted to ask her if she was delusional, if she remembered all the fights she'd had lately with Jimmy. They'd been on strange terms since Luling, talking mostly through the baby, trading veiled insults all day. I'm sure it made her feel better to tell herself that Matt and I were much worse off than they were. At that moment, I wanted badly not to be living in her house, wished that I was far away from her. The trip to DC was well timed.

"Things are fine," I finally said. "I'm not worried about anything."

Matt and I landed at Reagan on Sunday afternoon and went right to our apartment, which had been vacated the week before by our renter. Matt walked all over the apartment, examining our furniture and the walls, almost like he was hoping to find something that was damaged so he'd have a reason to be angry. But it all looked fine. Babs had sent Rosie over a few days earlier, so it was shiny and clean and smelled like Murphy's Oil Soap. "It's good to be back, isn't it?" I said. "I missed this place."

"Mmm," Matt said, which could have meant yes or no or I don't give a fuck.

I didn't ask him to clarify.

Babs had (obviously) arranged for everyone to come over for Sunday dinner, and I was actually looking forward to it. Part of it was that I didn't like being alone with Matt—when it was just the two of us, it was impossible to ignore that something was wrong—and I thought it would be nice to have the distraction of his family.

Our car was in Texas, so we took an Uber to the Kellys', and I hoped that since Matt didn't have to worry about driving, he'd be able to relax and have a few beers. He spent the car ride looking down at his BlackBerry, which I'd started to think was just a convenient excuse to ignore me. When we pulled up, Babs opened the door before we even had a chance to get out of the car. "They're here!" she yelled over her shoulder and into the house, not taking her eyes off Matt. She hadn't seen him in six months, which was the longest they'd ever been apart, and it looked like she wanted to run right over to him, but she managed to wait until we got to the door before folding him into her arms. "You look tired," she said to him, and he pulled away from her. "I'm fine," he said. She frowned, looking first at him and then at me. "And you look like you've lost weight. Are you taking care of yourself?"

"He's been working so hard," I said.

"Well of course he has," Babs said and put her hand on Matt's back as she led him into the house.

For once, I was grateful for the noise that the Kellys made. It was hard to think about anything amid the chaos. My nieces ran toward me, shrieking and jumping into my arms, being overdramatic and silly as they took turns hugging me. Jenny and Nellie grabbed me and took me out to the patio. "We already got you a glass of wine," Nellie told me. Rebecca greeted me with a smile, sat outside with us for an unprecedented fifteen minutes before going to check on Jonah. "We really missed you," she said before she got up, putting her hand on my forearm. It was the most affectionate she'd ever been with me. Even Meg hugged me before returning into the house to resume texting.

Jenny and Nellie chatted, and I kept an eye on Matt, waiting to see if he'd smile or relax or at least look less miserable. I did see him smiling when he talked to Babs, but even from across the lawn, I could tell it was a weak smile, an obligatory one.

For whatever reason, we were there for over two hours before we sat down to dinner—maybe Babs thought everyone would want extra time to visit or maybe something had gone wrong in the kitchen. (Although I don't think that was the case, because Babs didn't seem annoyed, which she would've been if Rosie had messed something up.)

A little before 7:00, most people had gone inside, but Matt and I were still sitting on the patio. "Are you okay?" I said. I asked him this question all the time during those months—when he was quiet, when he was mad, when he seemed spaced out. It probably made him angrier that I kept asking, but honestly, I couldn't help it.

"Yeah," he said. "I'm just tired. I'd like to eat at some point. This is taking forever."

"Your mom said it was almost ready," I told him, and he nodded.

Our nephews Bobby and Conor were on the lawn, still playing with a kickball, getting goofy and kicking it high in the air, twirling to make themselves dizzy before trying to catch it. They stumbled close to where we were sitting, and Matt said, "Watch it, guys," but they barely paid attention to him. He didn't normally discipline them, but we were the only adults in the backyard at the moment, so maybe he felt like he had to say something. Still, it was unusual.

On the next kick, the ball sailed to our table and knocked a few almost-empty drinks over, one of them landing right in Matt's lap.

"Jesus Christ, you guys. I said to watch it." Matt's voice was so sharp that even I was taken aback, and the two boys stood there, frozen.

"Matt, take it easy," I said quietly, but he just pointed to his pants and said, "Look at this. I'm a fucking mess."

"Sorry, Uncle Matt," the boys said together. They sounded so somber, and I waited for Matt to tell them it was fine, but he just made a big show of wiping himself off with a napkin, before saying, "Fuck," and then standing up and walking inside.

"Is he mad?" Bobby asked me. His eyes were wide. Normally, they would've laughed at Matt's swearing, but they just stood and stared at me. Bobby and Conor weren't strangers to getting in trouble—they were rough boys, mischievous— but I don't think they'd ever heard Matt yell, and they'd certainly never had him yell at them.

"He's just in a bad mood," I told them. "Don't worry about it. Really, it's okay, I know it was an accident. But maybe let's cool it with the game, okay?" The boys nodded and abandoned the ball on the grass, then ran inside themselves.

Right before we sat down to eat, Jenny came up next to me at the bar as I poured myself a glass of wine.

"Is everything okay?" she asked, her voice low. "The boys said Matt yelled at them."

I turned to face her and shook my head, then shifted my eyes to the side so they wouldn't meet hers. "Sorry about that," I said. "He's been in the worst mood lately. Anything sets him off."

"Oh, don't worry about that," she said. "I'm sure the boys deserved whatever they got. I just meant, is everything okay with him? With you guys?"

"Yeah, he's just—" I started to tell her it was fine, but got choked up and she put her arm around me. The rest of the Kellys were in the dining room, and I prayed that no one could hear us. "He's so frustrated with the campaign," I finally got out. "It's not going well and he's doing everything he can, but it doesn't really matter."

"Listen," she said. "This is just how men deal with their shit. Remember when Michael lost all that money in the investment with Chester?" I nodded, even though I had only a faint memory of a deal gone bad years earlier, had never gotten the whole story. "Well, he was a nightmare for months. Once he smashed a plate on the floor when one of the kids left it in the sink. Men don't know how to work through things without being total dicks. They just can't stand feeling like failures."

"I don't know what else to do," I said.

"Just wait it out," Jenny said. "He's wound so tight right now, he can't even see straight. But he'll get through it."

"What if he doesn't?"

"He will," she said, firmly, and I understood that she wasn't going to explore any other possibility with me. But then she gave me a little squeeze. "Just hang in there. Eventually things will right themselves."

On our ride home, I tried to tell Matt that the boys were hurt by the way he'd yelled at them. "I mean, too bad," he said. "They can't just do whatever they want. I know they were just playing, but they were bugging the crap out of me."

I wanted to tell him that six months earlier, he wouldn't have yelled like that. He would've laughed at the spilled drink, maybe jokingly chased after the boys. He'd always had endless amounts of patience with his nieces and nephews, found their rowdiness amusing. But he was already looking at his BlackBerry, so I dropped it.

That night, I lay awake with Matt sleeping next to me and wondered if this was just a phase, like Jenny said, or if it was something more. What if Matt's sunny personality, his happy nature that I'd fallen in love with, had just been conditional? What if he was only pleasant and kind when everything was working out for him, when good things were easily coming his way? This past year had turned him into a miserable person. So what was going to happen now?

The next night, I went to meet Colleen for dinner, and Matt met Benji and Alan and a couple other guys for a few drinks. "Maybe we'll meet up with you later," I said, and Matt shrugged like he didn't really care. "Sure, maybe," he said.

I went to Colleen's place first so that I could see Bea before we went out. Bea was already bathed and in pajamas when I got there, smiling at me from Colleen's arms. I reached for her, not sure she would come to me, but she did, diving right into my arms.

"She's so cute," I said.

"I know," Colleen said, matter of fact. "She's a really pretty baby."

I was biting back a smile at this when Bruce came into the room. He took Bea from my arms and kissed my cheek hello.

"It's nice to see you," he said. Colleen was already throwing keys in her purse, ready to go.

"You too," I said. I squeezed Bea's leg. "And you too."

Colleen kissed Bruce good-bye. And then he said, "You girls have fun," which made him sound like he was our dad.

We went out for sushi, because that's what we always did. It was our tradition. Colleen had been the one to introduce me to sushi in college, acting like it was unbelievable I'd never eaten it before. "Seriously?" she kept saying. "You've seriously never had sushi before? That's so funny." But she sounded more condescending than amused.

I was the first person Colleen ever met from the Midwest, and she liked to let me know how much more worldly she was, like I grew up on a farm. Once, when I'd reminded her that Madison was a city, and a really nice one at that, she'd smiled and said, "Sure, but a city in Wisconsin," like that explained everything.

We went to Raku, which was just a few blocks from my apartment. It felt weird to be back. Weird, but nice. The waitress came over, and Colleen ordered for us, which was another habit we'd gotten into, but I didn't mind. She knew what I liked.

"I think I've been in Texas too long," I told her.

"We drive everywhere, basically. It's so nice to be able to walk to a restaurant."

"So what's new?" she asked. "Tell me everything."

I hadn't decided if I was going to tell Colleen what was going on with Matt—I didn't know that I'd really feel like discussing it all night. But once she asked, I started talking and couldn't stop. I told her how angry he was, how much we'd been fighting. I described everything that had happened in Luling, and how cold things were between us now.

"Whoa," she said when I was finished. "Why did you wait so long to tell me this?"

"It wasn't something I wanted to get into on the phone," I said. "Plus, I still don't even know what this is. I don't know what's going on. The other day, Matt told me he felt like I wasn't supporting him. Honestly. The only thing I do is support him. I'm in Texas supporting him. I moved to DC to support him. He's crazy."

Colleen nodded. "Well," she said. "He probably meant you weren't supporting what he really wants to do. Since you told him you didn't want him to ever run for office. I can't imagine he took that well."

"That's not exactly what I said. And anyway, it's not even happening right now. There's no plan in place. I was just talking, just saying what I thought in the moment."

"Sure," she said slowly. "But would you want him to do it? If something did come up right now?"

"I don't know," I said. "Not really, no." We both took sips of our wine, and I took a breath. "I mean, really, I don't know. But he was so upset that I even questioned it, that maybe I wasn't completely on board with the idea. He said that when he married me, he thought I'd be behind him on this."

"Jesus," Colleen said. "It sounds like he's having a midlife crisis."

"I know. And the thing is, maybe I don't want him to run for office. But is that the end of the world? He made it sound like he only married me because he thought I'd always go along with what he wanted."

Colleen shrugged. "Maybe that *is* what he thought."

"Well, that's really fucked up."

"Not really. I mean, every person expects something from the other one when they get married."

"What do you mean?"

"I mean, everyone has their own reasons for getting married. Look at me and Bruce—he liked me because I was young and thought I was fun and I liked that he was more serious than the guys our age, that he was established. Marriage is a contract, same as anything."

"That's so depressing," I said.

"Not really. It's just realistic. I mean, marrying Matt because you liked that he was passionate and kind isn't the same as a porn star marrying a ninety-five-year-old man because he's rich."

"Well, thank God for that."

"And I mean, look at your favorite couple, Jimmy and Ash. Don't you think he married her because she's pretty and from Texas and looks great standing next to him while he makes speeches? And she married him because she gets to live in a big house and have luncheons."

"Colleen," I said. She held up her hands like she was surrendering.

"It's just something to think about." She waited a beat before she said, "Maybe you guys should see someone."

"Like a marriage counselor?"

"Yeah. I can give you the name of ours."

"You guys went to see someone?"

"Beth, grow up. Of course we did. I married a guy who's almost twenty years older than me. We've had some shit to work out."

Colleen rarely acknowledged the age difference between her and Bruce—she usually just pretended it didn't exist, and it surprised me to hear her say it so plainly.

"I'll think about it," I said.

"It's not so bad going to see someone," she said. "It's like this dinner, sort of, but without the wine."

· · ·

I texted Matt when we were done with dinner, but he didn't answer, so I walked back to the apartment. We were returning to Texas in the morning, and I wished that we didn't have to, that we could just stay here and slip back into our lives the way they were when we left.

Matt was home when I let myself in, watching TV with the lights off. "Hey," I said. "I texted you. I thought maybe you'd still be out."

"Nope. Everyone had to head home."

"Oh," I said. "Did you have fun?"

He shrugged. "Same old, same old," he said, staring at the screen the whole time.

Here's the thing I didn't notice until it was gone: Matt stopped finding me funny. I'd always been able to make him laugh. I was my goofiest around him, my weirdest self. I'd hold up a banana and make it dance and talk, or I'd smooth one of his unruly eyebrows and say, "This guy is just really excited today." And he'd throw his head back and laugh—really laugh from deep down in his stomach. Sometimes he'd shake his head at me and tell me I was weird, but it didn't matter, because I knew he thought I was hilarious. Even in his worst moods, I could get him to smile.

I don't know when it stopped, but I do remember once that summer in Texas, when he was sitting on the couch with his laptop in front of him, probably reading about a new oil well or cyberstalking Candace Elroy's campaign team. I'd just gone for a run, and still had my headphones on, listening to music. He didn't say hi when I walked in, didn't even lift his head. There was some obnoxious Taylor Swift song playing, so I unplugged the headphones and turned the music up, started dancing in a crazy way, slapping the air in front of me like it was the ass of an imaginary person, waiting for him to look up and laugh. I knew he could see me out of the corner of his eye, but he didn't acknowledge me so I just kept dancing. Finally, he looked at me straight on and asked without smiling, "What are you doing?" and I stopped mid-slap and said, "Nothing."

Chapter 19

The last push of the campaign felt more like a death march. We were still traveling all the time and hoping for the best (whatever that meant), but the bad news kept rolling in. The Farm Bureau decided not to endorse either candidate, to stay out of the race altogether, which was a huge blow for Jimmy—he'd been courting them for months and their support would've prompted a lot of people to vote for him. The media interest slowed all through September and then basically stopped. No one cares about a David and Goliath story unless David has a shot in hell of winning. And then in early October, *The Dallas Morning News* (who'd endorsed Jimmy in the primary), endorsed Candace Elroy. This wasn't a surprise, but it felt like the nail in the coffin. After Matt read the piece, he slammed his fist down on the table and said, "Fuck!" making all of us around him jump. The op-ed said that Jimmy was eager and that they admired his intentions, but that Elroy had more experience and a measured approach to fracking regulations. "A measured approach," Jimmy said. "Which means not changing anything."

"Exactly," Matt said. And then we all just sat there, not talking, because what could we say to make it better? Each day, it felt like a little more air was let out of the campaign. It was October and there was still a month left, thirty days until it could be put to rest. By the time it was over, we'd have nothing left.

Later that day, Matt said to me, "Well, that's that." He sounded so defeated, like he wanted to pack it in, call it quits and head back to DC immediately. But you can't just abandon a campaign because you think you're going to lose—there were still so many events to attend, so many trips to take. "You really think it's over?" I asked, and he sounded so certain as he said, "It would take a miracle for him to win."

After Luling, Matt had stopped asking me to help as much with the campaign. I still did some stuff, of course, because it was impossible to live in the same house as campaign headquarters and be completely uninvolved. But where he used to ask me to pick something up at an office supply store or coordinate volunteers, he now asked Katie. I don't know if this was his way of punishing me or if he figured I didn't want anything to do with it, or if he was just trying to avoid fighting. I was still going on all of the trips, but when we were at the house I felt like I'd been cut out of the loop.

Ash had stepped back from the campaign too— just a little bit, but I noticed. She booked more parties than she had all year, and was gone a few evenings a week. She didn't attend any of the in-town events, and she started dropping Viv off at her parents' house almost every morning. Ash would return with Viv in the early evening, giving the impression that she'd been working, but never saying where she was. I couldn't imagine her sitting in a Starbucks on her laptop all day, and sometimes I think she just stayed at her parents' place or maybe just drove around. Honestly, I think she just wanted to be out of the house, and really, who could blame her?

The upshot of all these changes was that we no longer ate breakfast together, and when we were together for dinner, we usually had takeout in front of the TV. We still saw each other plenty, with all the trips we were taking, but things were different. It was clear that if given the choice, we had no desire to be anywhere near each other.

I woke up one morning to find I was the only one in the house. Even with our new disjointed life, this was strange. I'd stopped setting my alarm, no longer caring how late I slept. (Not that it mattered much anymore.) But I realized that morning that Matt hadn't bothered to say good-bye to me—surely I would've woken up if he had, I wasn't that heavy a sleeper—and it made my stomach knot up, his indifference feeling worse, somehow, than an all-out fight.

The kitchen was empty as I made a pot of coffee

and ate a banana. I peeked in the campaign office, just to be sure, but no one was there. Ash, I assumed, had taken Viv to her mom's and wouldn't be back all day. I could've texted Matt to see where he was, but because he hadn't bothered to say good-bye or even leave me a note, I didn't want to.

It was a little creepy being in that big house all alone, and I decided to take a book out to the patio. It was sunny and warm as I stretched out to read on the lounge chair, a glass of iced tea beside me. We'd been traveling so much that it felt nice to relax, and when I finally checked the time, I was surprised to see that two hours had passed.

I began to wonder when everyone would be back and also started to get annoyed at Matt for not bothering to be in touch when I was stranded at the house, stuck in Sugar Land—he'd taken our car and must have known I'd be alone there. The more time that went by, the angrier I got, and I was just worked up enough to give him a call, when Jimmy drove up. He was alone in the car, and held his hand up in greeting, but didn't smile.

"Hey," I called, as he walked over to me. "I was starting to think no one was ever coming home."

"We had that minister breakfast," Jimmy said, lying down on the lounge chair next to me and closing his eyes.

"Right," I said. The event sounded vaguely familiar. "So clearly, it was a ton of fun."

Jimmy smiled, but his eyes were still closed. "It was fine. I just didn't sleep much last night."

"Where's Matt?"

"We drove separately. He said he had some stuff to do after." He opened his eyes and looked over at me. "What are you up to? What are you reading?" I held up the book's cover for him and he nodded. "I read the review," he said. "It sounded good."

"I'll give it to you when I'm done."

"I'm not allowed to read anything that's not about fracking. I can't be wasting my time—my campaign manager said so. At least for another month."

"Yeah, well, I'm sure Matt would think this was a waste of my time, too."

"Oh yeah? What does he think you should be doing?"

"Writing, I guess. I think he had this idea that I'd write a novel while we were here. Or at least try to. That I'd do something worthwhile."

"You should write," Jimmy said. "You're talented."

I laughed. "The only things you've read of mine are the things I wrote for DCLOVE. Did you see a lot of talent in the 'Ten Best Places to Meet a Man in DC' article?"

"I certainly did," Jimmy said, giving me a half smile. "But also, Matt's always talking about how great your writing is."

"Really?" I asked. It was weird to hear something nice that Matt said about me secondhand. It had been so long since I'd felt like his compliments were free of ulterior motives. He'd always told me he thought my fiction was great, but since we'd moved to DC it felt like he encouraged me to write because it seemed more serious; that it would be less embarrassing for me to spend my days writing blind items about presidential aides if I was also working on a novel.

"Also," Jimmy said, "I googled you and read one of your short stories that was published on a website." He had his face toward the sun and his eyes were closed again, which I was happy about because I could feel my cheeks get warm as he told me this.

"You did?" I asked. It wasn't that I couldn't imagine Jimmy taking enough of an interest in me to google my name—or maybe it was—but it surprised me that he'd never mentioned it before, like he was keeping it a secret.

"But that's not how I know you're a good writer," he said. He opened his eyes then and turned on his side to face me. I was on my back on the chair next to him and our positioning felt strangely intimate, like we were lying in bed together. "It's because you're so observant," he continued. "You're always watching people and you notice these little things about them—what makes them tick, what they really want, what they're afraid of. You can sum anyone up in two lines. Most people are too busy worrying about themselves, but you're always paying attention to everything around you."

"Thanks," I said. My voice didn't sound like my own and I hoped Jimmy couldn't hear it. I was flattered that he'd bothered to notice this about me, but our whole conversation was a little odd, a little different from the way we normally talked to each other, though I couldn't exactly pinpoint why. I was happy when Jimmy broke the silence and said, "How about we go to Torchy's and stuff ourselves?"

"Sounds perfect," I said. And by the time we were eating tacos, things were completely normal between us, back to the way they always were.

But that night, as I stared at the back of Matt's head while he slept, I thought about Jimmy's words and how nice it was to have someone say something kind to me; how nice to have someone think about me at all.

When Ash and I were together, we talked only of surface things: logistical parts of campaign trips, new clothes, reality TV. She must have noticed this, the tentativeness between us. I felt angry with her, but didn't know why, exactly. One night, we passed each other in the hallway and she said, "Oh, I saved *Parenthood* for you on the DVR."

"You watched it?" I asked.

"Yeah," she said. "It was a sad one." Since I'd been in Texas, it had been one of the shows we religiously watched together (Matt and Jimmy both refused), and this felt like a slight. But I just said, "Thank you," and left it at that.

It seemed to me that Ash was stepping back from our friendship, that she was the one setting new boundaries, putting distance between us.

But also, there was one week I'd barely talked to her, when I almost couldn't bring myself to meet her eyes. I'd had a dream about Jimmy, one where he climbed on top of me, his body heavy. It was just a dream, but it had felt so real as I woke up pulsing with pleasure, surprised to see he wasn't there, disappointed, really, to see that Matt was.

So sure, maybe that was part of it too.

The last week in October, Jimmy's schedule was completely packed. He and Matt had planned a full swing through Galveston County, Austin, Waco, and San Antonio; five days and four nights of travel, with multiple events in each city. After that, Jimmy would stay in Houston, do a few local appearances, and ride out the end of his campaign, waiting for Election Day.

When this trip arrived, I couldn't remember how or why we'd all agreed to it. It must have seemed like a good idea at the time, but it certainly didn't now. The night before we were supposed to leave, Ash whispered to me that she didn't want to go. "I'm flat-out exhausted," she said. She was folding Viv's tiny clothes as she talked. "But I can't say no—if I tell Jimmy I don't want to go, he'll take it personally, like I don't believe he has a chance." She paused and folded a little pink T-shirt that said DADDY'S LITTLE TEXAN on the front, ran her fingers over the sparkly cowboy hat. "But the thing is, it *is* over. He doesn't have a chance. So why are we still pretending?"

She sounded angry as she whispered this last part, and her eyes filled with tears. This was the most substantial conversation we'd had in a while and I put my hand on her back to comfort her. "Hey, it's okay," I said. "Of course you're tired. This has been hard on you."

"I know it," she said, gulping in some air. "We're all just so run down, aren't we?"

"Yes," I said. "This schedule would make anyone lose it."

It was true, how all the crappy food and sleep deprivation had affected us, and I wondered if that was the reason for our disharmony. Was it possible that we were just too tired to get along, too run down to be decent to each other?

Ash told me that she planned to leave Viv with her mom while we were gone. "I don't want to be away from her for so many days, but it's too much. I'll lose my mind."

"That sounds like a good idea," I said, rubbing her back again. I had a moment of feeling hopeful, of believing there was a chance we could go back to normal when this was all done. But then she straightened up and wiped her eyes.

"It'll be fine," she said. And there was a sharpness to her voice, like she thought I'd tricked her into being honest, like I'd made her cry. She pulled a tiny pair of Viv's pants tight as she folded them, stretching the material as far as it would go to make a crisp crease. "I just need to get everything organized for this week and it will be fine."

The next morning, Matt and I carried our bags to the front hall and walked in on Jimmy and Ash having a fight. They were standing about two feet apart, glaring at each other, and Ash's arms were folded across her chest. They weren't talking, but it was clear they were mad. Ash's mom was also standing there, just to the side of them, looking like she wanted to slip right back out the front door. When she saw us, she gave us an awkward little wave, but Ash and Jimmy didn't even glance our way, and we paused for a moment, unsure what to do.

"Jimmy," Ash said, breaking the silence. "I'm not going to pack up all of her gear and drag this poor child clear across Texas just so you can get a photo op with her. She needs stability."

"She has stability," Jimmy said.

"She doesn't. She doesn't get her naps at the right time when we travel, she doesn't eat as well, she's cranky and out of sorts for days when we get back."

"She's a baby. She'll adjust."

"Exactly. She's a baby," Ash said. They stared at each other for a few seconds without talking and I wondered if this was the time to sneak out, but we just stayed frozen where we were.

"You can't just make these decisions without me," Jimmy said, and I realized that Ash had never told him she wasn't planning to take Viv, that he hadn't known until Beverly showed up at the house.

"I can't make these decisions without you? Why not? I do everything else without you. Do you know how hard it is to care for a baby out of a hotel room? No, you don't, because I do it all."

"You're her mother," Jimmy said. "Isn't that your job?"

Ash turned then and walked up the stairs and Beverly followed quickly behind. Jimmy still hadn't acknowledged us—honestly, it was like he didn't see us—and he stood there, shaking his head. Finally, he said softly, "Jesus fucking Christ," and went up the stairs after them.

I couldn't believe what I'd just seen, the way that Jimmy talked to Ash in front of Beverly. I was also shocked that Ash hadn't told Jimmy about her plans to leave Viv at home. While I knew the two of them weren't exactly communicating in a great way these days, there was no chance it was an accident. She must've known he'd argue, that it would be easier to wait until the last second to deal with it.

We were still standing in the doorway, our bags at our feet, and Matt was looking down at his BlackBerry. I knew he was purposely not meeting my eyes, that he could feel me staring at him but was pretending he didn't notice, and I felt anger rise in my throat. "Matt," I said, sharply.

"What?" he asked, giving me a blank expression. It might have seemed like it wasn't such a big deal, Matt's refusal to look at me, but it was. We used to be a couple who could have whole conversations without speaking—just one look could've conveyed how we both felt about witnessing this fight, how uncomfortable it would make our trip. And now Matt was ignoring me, finding one more way to shut me out.

"You're ridiculous," I said, placing my bag by the door and walking out of the room.

"What?" he said, having the gall to sound surprised. "What did I do?"

By the time the four of us got in the car, no one was talking. I never got the full story of how the Viv situation was resolved, but Beverly left with her and we resumed getting ready for the trip. Jimmy loaded our bags as the rest of us did last-minute things, grabbed bottles of water and phone chargers, went to the bathroom one more time.

As we pulled out of the driveway, everyone was silent. Jimmy was driving, Matt sat shotgun, and Ash and I were in the second row. I wished that Viv were there, just so I'd have a reason to sit in the way back, to be as far away from everyone as possible. Ash wasn't mad at me—or at least I didn't think she was—but both of us were ignoring each other; she was looking at her phone and I stared out the window, imagining what would happen if I just jumped out of the car and ran back to the house. Would they even try to stop me? Would anyone be surprised?

We pulled onto the expressway, and I closed my eyes and said a makeshift prayer, asking whoever was listening to please let us make it through this week unscathed; or at least, no worse off than we were now.

It was Jimmy who spoke first, about an hour into the drive, when he asked if anyone was hungry and wanted to stop at Chick-fil-A. "I could eat," Matt said, and Ash and I echoed him. Jimmy pulled off the expressway and went right to the drive-thru window. Usually, we only ate in the car if we were trying to get somewhere quickly, but I guess he knew we weren't interested in sitting around a table and staring at each other. Jimmy placed the order and pulled up to the pickup window. None of us spoke as we waited. Once we got our order, Matt took charge and handed everyone their food, parceling out fries and milk shakes and chicken sandwiches.

The lunch put everyone in a better mood, like we were cranky toddlers who needed to be fed. Things seemed more normal as we ate—Matt started to go over the schedule with Jimmy, telling him about the potluck we'd be at that night, reminding him who would be there. Ash turned to me and started showing me pictures from Facebook on her phone. Some girl she'd disliked in college had gotten married the weekend before, and Ash was busy judging the wedding. "Do you believe her dress?" she asked, flicking her finger across the screen to show me the pictures, acting like we hadn't just been sitting in silence for the past two hours.

But this moment of peace didn't last: At the potluck in Galveston that night, Ash fawned over a baby and said to the mother, "Mine's at home and I miss her so much I could burst." Jimmy stood to the side smiling and said, "Then you shouldn't have left her there." In Austin, I mentioned something about going to the Salt Lick for lunch one day, and Matt said irritably, "This isn't a vacation," to which I replied, "No kidding."

All of the events went smoothly, despite the friction between us. There a subdued air around Jimmy, and while he still smiled and laughed, he was quieter and a little more serious. When he shook people's hands, he'd just say, "Don't forget to vote," not bothering anymore to talk about turning Texas blue.

Our last stop was San Antonio, and we arrived just a few hours before the event. Ash and Jimmy dropped us off at the hotel and went shopping to get Jimmy a new button-down, since over the course of our trip, he'd spilled barbecue sauce on one shirt and gotten mustard on another at a picnic. "Sweet Lord, Jimmy," Ash said. "You're worse than Viv." You could tell she was trying to make a joke out of it, but it came out sounding unfriendly.

Matt went down to the lobby to work, because he couldn't get a good Wi-Fi signal in our room. I was reading, but had the television on mute, which was something I'd started doing after spending so much time alone in hotel rooms. It made me feel less lonely. My brain felt cloudy from not sleeping well all week, and I kept getting to the end of a page only to realize that I had no idea what I'd just read. Finally, I gave up and turned the sound back up on the TV, watching a rerun of *Friends* that I'd seen a hundred times before.

When Matt returned about an hour later, he was carrying a sandwich and a large Coke. "Hey," he said as he sat down at the little table in our room. I watched him in disbelief as he unwrapped his food and started to eat.

"You got lunch?" I asked. He turned to me while chewing, as if confused by such an obvious question, and nodded. And then I continued, "And you didn't think to ask if I wanted anything?"

He swallowed, and a guilty look flashed across his face. "Sorry," he said. "I didn't think about it."

Maybe it's ridiculous how much this upset me, considering all of the other fights we'd had, but immediately I felt tears come to my eyes. This situation perfectly summed up what was happening with me and Matt—how rarely he thought about me, how little I mattered.

"You didn't think of it?" I asked. "You knew I was in the hotel room, knew that I hadn't eaten lunch, and it didn't even cross your mind to send me a text and see if I wanted anything?"

"I'm sorry," he said. "I can run and get you a sandwich. It's right across the street."

"That's not the point."

"Then what is the point?"

"It's just—" My voice caught here and I took a deep breath to keep from crying. "It's like you don't even think about me anymore. It's thought-less. It's worse than if you did it on purpose."

"Beth, come on. It's not a big deal. It just slipped my mind. Don't you think you're overreacting?"

"No," I said. "I don't." I did start crying then,

hard, and while Matt didn't get up and try to comfort me, he did at least stop eating his sandwich.

The event that night was a small cocktail party in the home of one of Jimmy's supporters. It was a nice get-together, and I got some good pictures of Jimmy chatting with the guests, looking handsome and put together in his new shirt. At the end, he gave a short speech, thanked everyone for coming, and reminded them to vote. "Not that you would forget," he said, laughing. "I think this crowd knows how important it is. But let's spread the word, let's get people out there."

Everyone clapped in a polite and respectful way, and I could see the effort in Jimmy's smile, saw his shoulders collapse when a well-meaning guest said, "You gave it a great run. You should be proud of that," like he'd already lost.

Matt had apologized to me several times that afternoon, and finally I'd just told him it was okay, because he really did look sorry and it wasn't like we were going to solve anything by arguing that night. We still needed to get through the next week.

Jimmy looked relieved when we got in the car, happy that he didn't have to talk to strangers anymore. He sighed and loosened his tie, looked like he could breathe easier as we drove away. "Should we get dinner?" he asked. "We can go to the Applebee's connected to our hotel. You know, really treat ourselves."

"I think you secretly love Applebee's," I said, and then Matt must have been in a generous mood because he laughed and said, "You are always pushing it on us."

"America's best kept secret," Jimmy said, grinning. "Let's do it."

As the four of us sat and had dinner at Applebee's, something surprising happened—we were pleasant to each other, almost kind. "Do you believe this is our last trip?" Matt asked, and Jimmy clapped him on the back. "It's been a good ride," he said. We must have all been feeling nostalgic (and had just enough to drink) because we started talking about the funniest moments from the campaign. Ash talked about the trip when Viv got the stomach flu, threw up on her so many times that she was forced to stop at Target to buy new clothes.

"It wasn't that bad," Jimmy said, laughing. "I mean, you got new clothes out of it, right?"

"Yes," she said. "All from Target. I also got a sweatshirt at Ross." And this sent us into another fit of laughter, the idea of Ash in a discount clothing store too funny to even imagine.

I could see then how we'd remember the campaign in years to come, how we'd airbrush out all the shitty parts, the nasty things we said to each other, the rifts that were formed. You can imagine anything to be fun in retrospect—look at all those people who long for high school.

When the waitress came to take our plates away, Jimmy suggested we go sit at the bar for one more drink, and we agreed. Ash and I ran up to our rooms to get sweaters, because we were chilled from the air-conditioning blasting in the restaurant. We couldn't have been gone more than five minutes—Matt and Jimmy hadn't even left our table yet to go to the bar—but I knew as soon as we walked back in that things had turned.

Matt's back was rigid and his hands were in fists on the table. He and Jimmy weren't yelling—they weren't even talking—but it was clear that something had pissed him off. I knew Ash noticed the same thing, because both of us walked slowly to the table, knowing the fun was gone from the night. We should've left then, just turned and walked right back out of the restaurant. But instead we both sat down, glanced at each other, and waited.

For as long as we'd known him, Jimmy had always called women (even strangers) by generic nicknames—honey, sweetheart, babe, kiddo. When he first decided to run, Matt suggested that he stop this, told him it could come off sleazy to call a supporter darling. But Jimmy refused. "I'm from Texas," he said. "That's how we talk." It was just one of the many things they'd disagreed

417

about. That night, as I sat down, I saw something flash in Jimmy's eyes, and he greeted me by saying, "Hey babe." I knew immediately that he was only doing it to piss off Matt, that it was his own little way of saying, "Fuck off."

Matt looked down at his drink and closed his eyes, like he was too mad to even look at anyone. "Can I ask you something?" he finally said to Jimmy. "Why do you bother hiring people to give you advice if you're just going to ignore it?"

"I don't ignore it all the time," Jimmy said. He leaned back and tipped his glass up, let the ice fall in his mouth, took his time crunching it between his back teeth. "I only ignore it when it's shit advice."

"Fuck you," Matt said. He stood up, pushing his chair back, making it screech along the floor. There were only a few other people in the Applebee's, but they were all staring at us. Matt considered saying something more and then changed his mind and walked out, not looking back at me once. If he had, if he'd even glanced at me, I would've scrambled after him, talked to him about what a jackass Jimmy was being. But this was one more way he was going to ignore me, one more time he'd shut me out, and as I watched him walk away, I felt my chest burn with anger.

Jimmy turned to look at me and Ash then, shrugged his shoulders as if to say, What can you do? Ash pushed her chair back the same way

Matt had just done and stood up and leaned close to Jimmy. "When are you going to realize you're acting like a world class a-hole?"

"An a-hole?" Jimmy smirked at her. "Watch your language! Someone here might hear you."

And then Ash turned and walked out of the restaurant, leaving me and Jimmy alone at the table. What were the people around us thinking? We were at an Applebee's in Texas that I'd (God willing) never go to again, and still I was humiliated at the scene we'd caused.

"What the fuck was that?" Jimmy asked, laughing loudly, and it was only then that I noticed how drunk he was. He'd been drinking faster than the rest of us at dinner, ordering whiskey on the rocks, but until that moment I hadn't really noticed. His movements were slow and his voice was thick and he didn't seem particularly upset about getting yelled at by Matt and Ash. He turned to me, calmly. "So, should we go to the bar?"

"Sure," I said. I wasn't in any hurry to get back to Matt, and it wasn't like he was going to notice or care.

"Might as well, right? Since those two couldn't handle it."

The bar was at the front of the restaurant, and except for one very large man at the other end, we were the only ones there. Jimmy motioned to the bartender and ordered another whiskey, and I got a vodka soda. His arm brushed up against mine and the feeling of skin on skin gave me goose bumps. "Cold?" he asked, looking down, and I nodded and finally pulled on the sweater that I'd gotten from the room.

When the bartender brought us our drinks, Jimmy and I clinked them together, out of habit, obviously, since there was nothing about our night worth celebrating. I drank my vodka quickly, wanting something to make me feel less awful. Jimmy watched as I finished it, laughed, and then said approvingly, "Nice," as he raised his hand to the bartender to bring me another one.

"You know," he said, once I had my new drink. "Your husband thinks he's smarter than me." He was staring at the bar, and for a second I thought he was embarrassed, but then he looked up and I saw that he was angry—angry in a way I'd never seen him before—and it was disorienting. Even when he and Matt were fighting, he could crack a joke a minute later, lighten things up. It always seemed like nothing bothered him for too long. Now his eyes looked dark.

"He doesn't think that," I said, knowing that I didn't sound convincing. "He just gets like that sometimes, you know that. He's a know-it-all. He doesn't even realize he's doing it."

"The reason it pisses me off so much," Jimmy continued as if I hadn't spoken, "is because it's true. He is smarter than me. I mean, he went to

Harvard, after all." Jimmy made his voice high and snotty sounding when he said "Harvard," then loudly crunched an ice cube between his teeth. "And he knows he's smarter, and he knows that I know it, too.

"He thinks it should be reversed, that I should be the one working for his campaign, that I don't deserve to run for office. Of course, he probably wouldn't hire me anyway."

"I'm sure he doesn't think that," I said.

"Of course he does, Beth. Of course he does."

"Is Ash okay?" I asked. "She seemed so angry."

"She's fine. We had a fight earlier and she's still mad. She just needs to calm the fuck down."

"What was the fight about?"

Jimmy sighed. "She told me that the campaign was interfering with her career. Her *career*. Like selling that shit jewelry is going to get her somewhere."

"She's been really successful," I said, trying to be diplomatic, and Jimmy snorted.

"Whatever," he said, dismissing the idea that Ash deserved any credit.

"Also, I'm sure she's just tired." I felt a compulsive need to defend Ash. "The campaign's been hard on her."

"You know what?" Jimmy said. "I don't really care if it's been hard on her. It's my name on the ballot. I'm the one that's going to lose—not Matt, not Ash. Me. That's all people are going to remember. My name and how I failed."

"I don't think anyone thinks about it like that," I said, putting my hand on his forearm. "I promise."

We were quiet for a minute, and Jimmy raised his hand to order more drinks. I felt the vodka hit me then, my stomach full of liquid, my head fuzzy, and I wondered if the bartender would refuse to serve us, if we'd end this night by getting cut off at the Applebee's bar, which would be a new low. But he brought fresh drinks right over to us, and I noticed that the fat man at the end of the bar had his eyes closed like he was taking a nap, so maybe Jimmy and I weren't the drunkest customers of the night.

"Matt's been a real dick lately, hasn't he?" Jimmy said, turning to me. "I think that might be partly my fault. It's probably sucked for you."

"It's not your fault," I said. "It's just how he's acting." Jimmy didn't respond, and then I said, "It's like he doesn't even really like me anymore. And he wants to have a baby, apparently." I was bumbling, but I regretted the words as soon as they were out of my mouth, feeling like I'd betrayed Matt somehow.

Jimmy just nodded, but didn't look surprised, and I wondered if he and Matt had ever discussed this. "And you don't?" he asked, his tone neutral.

"No, I do," I said. "I've always wanted to. It's just now doesn't seem like the right time, you know? How can we have a baby if he doesn't even want to talk to me? It's like borrowing trouble or whatever." I could hear how drunk I sounded.

"Yeah, I get that," Jimmy said. "And I mean, you should be sure, because it's hard. It changes things."

"Yeah," I said. "I'm not scared of things changing, not like that. I'm just—I don't know what I'm trying to say."

"I get it," he said, which couldn't have possibly been true because I was making little to no sense. "You know, since we've had Viv, Ash never touches me, never wants me to touch her. Ever. And I don't mean to sound like some crazy husband, but I mean, never. If we're in public, she'll pretend. But by ourselves? Nothing."

"Well," I said, feeling clumsy. "I'm sure that's normal, right? Just like an adjustment period? I'm sure it is. I mean, I don't know personally, but I think that happens to a lot of people."

"You know that Viv is a year and a half old, right?" Jimmy asked.

"I do," I said. The bartender brought over two more drinks then, without us even asking. Jimmy and I had shared more intimate information in the past ten minutes than in all the time we'd known each other. We'd never talked like this—if we ever bad-mouthed our spouses it was always in the winking and joking manner of happy couples who are free to complain about dishes in the sink and unmade beds because they're so clearly in love. But because we'd gone this far, I said, "I mean, it really feels sometimes like Matt can't stand me. Like he doesn't care about me at all. He never thinks about me. I'm an afterthought, always." I took a deep breath. "Sometimes I feel like we aren't going to make it, I really do."

The words sounded too dramatic, but there was no taking them back, so I just stopped talking.

"I know what you mean," Jimmy said. "I really do."

"No, you don't," I said.

"I do. And you know what, Beth?" He put his hand on my arm, and I turned to look at him. "You deserve someone who thinks about you. All the time. You're so amazing. You deserve the best."

We kept looking at each other, past the point where it felt comfortable. And somewhere in my head, I was aware that his hand was still on my arm. That was the only part of us that was touching, but we kept staring into each other's eyes, and it felt like more, like we were doing something inappropriate, crossing a line. Jimmy reached up and brushed my hair off my shoulder, and finally I broke my eyes away from him, stared up at the TV in the corner of the bar.

"Beth," Jimmy said, but I couldn't look at him. For some reason, I felt like I was going to start crying. "Beth, look at me." I shook my head and rubbed one of my eyes and then felt Jimmy's hand on top of my head, in a gesture that was almost brotherly, like he was about to ruffle my hair or give me a noogie. I did look at him then, and he took a deep breath. "You're going to be fine," he said. "We're all going to be fine."

It was hard to keep him in focus; everything around me was rocking back and forth. "We should go," I said, sliding off the barstool. "We're drunk." As I stood, I knew there was a good chance I was going to be sick and just hoped I'd make it back to the room before it happened.

"Are you okay?" he asked, and I nodded.

"Good," he said.

We walked back to our rooms, which were right next to each other, and Jimmy laughed as I closed one eye to concentrate on sliding the card into the lock. "You got that?" he asked in a stage whisper, and I gave him a thumbs-up before going inside.

I did get sick that night, violently so, and I cursed myself as I knelt on the bathroom tile—for how stupid I'd been, for how much I'd had to drink, for how much I'd said. But when I finally brushed my teeth and climbed into bed, empty and wrung out, I thought of Jimmy's eyes on mine, the way he'd brushed my hair away, and even with my stomach still turning, I smiled into the darkness.

The next morning when we got to the car, Jimmy was leaning against it, wearing sunglasses and holding a tray with four cups of coffee in it. "Here, man," he said, handing one to Matt. "This one's yours. Black."

"Thanks," Matt said and nodded at him. It appeared this exchange was going to be a satisfactory apology for both of them.

Jimmy took out another cup and gave it to me. "One coffee with cream, for you," he said, pushing his sunglasses on top of his head and winking. Jimmy always winked, just like he always called waitresses sweetheart. This was nothing new, but as I took my cup of coffee from him, my stomach flipped.

Ash came out of the hotel then and Jimmy held out a cup of coffee in her direction, which she accepted wordlessly before getting in the car. I settled in the backseat next to her and put my seat belt on. Matt began to drive, and I drank my coffee, willing my headache to go away. A few minutes later, my phone beeped with a text from Jimmy, who was sitting directly in front of me: *Chin up, ok?* I felt my stomach flip again, told myself it was just from all the vodka I'd had the night before, although I knew better.

We were pretty quiet on the ride home, but not in the same way as we'd started the trip. There was a resigned sense in the car, the way it feels when you know something is over and you're just waiting for the end to come.

Chapter 20

Back in Houston, the last few days before the election crawled by. Friday was Halloween, so after Jimmy stopped by a community center and a church group in the morning, he and Matt returned home so he could take Viv trick-or-treating. Ash had decided months earlier that Viv should be a pumpkin for Halloween. ("Because she's our little pumpkin," she explained, as if they were the only people in America who referred to their baby as pumpkin.) Beverly made the costume herself, and it was a beautiful one—a soft round pumpkin body with a jack-o'-lantern face on the front. Viv wore green striped tights and sparkly green shoes and (of course) a headband that had a leaf attached to it.

Ash got her dressed upstairs, then had us all wait in the front hall as she brought her down. Both sets of grandparents were there, and we all stood at the bottom of the stairs, clapping as Ash presented her. Viv laughed at the attention and then started clapping for herself. We all agreed that she made an exceptionally cute pumpkin.

Jimmy and Ash posed with her in front of the house, and I took pictures of the three of them smiling and looking adorable, which were immediately posted to Facebook. (What you couldn't see from the picture was the fight they'd had right before, when Ash asked Jimmy to put on a different shirt so they could better color-coordinate and he said, "What is this, a fucking catalog shoot?" before stomping up the stairs to change.)

Sugar Land went all out for Halloween—there were costume parades and haunted houses in the town square. Families decorated with huge cobwebs and spiders on their lawns, ghosts hanging from trees, scarecrows propped up by front doors. By 3:30, the sidewalks were flooded with groups of tiny costumed children. Matt and I stayed at the house to hand out candy while Jimmy, Ash, and the grandparents took Viv trick-or-treating. (She only made it to about five houses before she was ready to call it quits.)

Later, we all ate the chili that Mrs. Dillon had brought over and drank pumpkin beer and ate left-over miniature Milky Ways. We were acting chipper, maybe for the benefit of the grandparents, but the evening had a strained feeling to it. I got into bed early that night, before 9:00. I wasn't all that tired, but I was ready for the day to be over, impatient for morning to come so we could be one day closer to putting this all behind us. If we could just get through the next week as planned, I felt that things would be okay. But it took me a while to fall asleep that night, possibly because my mind was busy, thinking, Hurry, hurry.

• • •

On Saturday, we went to a Rock the Vote rally and I handed out push cards as fast as I could—I'd noticed there were still boxes of them in the den and I figured the fewer that were left, the less depressing it would be. (I noticed that Matt and Ash were both handing out their own push cards at an impressive speed, which made me think they had the same thought I did.)

Candace Elroy wasn't at this event—the Republicans were always invited but rarely participated—so Jimmy was one of only three Democratic candidates who spoke. As he came up to the stage, I took note of how handsome he looked. He'd always been handsome, of course. This wasn't anything new. And it's not like I'd never thought about it before—it was, after all, the very first thing I'd noticed about him when we met. But my awareness of it now felt different. It wasn't just a fact that I knew about him—like that he was tall or from Texas—it was something I was conscious of all the time, in a way that seemed stupid and dangerous. When we got out of the car that day, he'd brushed by me and my whole body had buzzed. As we walked into the event, he said, "Are you ready for this?" and I said, "As ready as I'll ever be," and then he held up his hand for a high five, and when I awkwardly slapped his palm, I felt my cheeks get warm.

Katie stood next to me while Jimmy spoke.

She was as serious and diligent as ever and had plans to move to DC in January. Matt had already hooked her up with a few people there, and I knew without a doubt that she'd find a job easily, that she'd be successful. She was so certain of what she wanted to do, and I felt something like jealousy that day as she smoothed her ponytail and clapped at Jimmy's words. When he was done, she turned to me out of the blue and said with complete seriousness, "You should be proud of how you handled the social media. Not everyone your age can navigate it so well."

That night, we picked up pizza on the way home and ate an early dinner in front of the television, balancing plates on our laps. We were all quieter those last few days—there was no more fighting or at least none that I saw. Matt wasn't quite so forceful with his opinions, and Jimmy didn't push back as much. The two of them were acting like a couple who are getting divorced but still have to live in the same house after the decision's been made—there was nothing left to fight for so they may as well be civil.

The TV was on MSNBC, but as soon as we sat down, Jimmy said, "Does anyone mind if I put on the Texas game?" We all shook our heads no, and I was happy as the noise of football filled the room, sick of listening to the news.

Ash took tiny bites of her slice and then got up

and walked her plate to the kitchen. I sat a few minutes longer, staring at the game, pretending to be interested, but I didn't care about either team and it wasn't particularly close anyway. I got up to take my own plate to the kitchen, grabbing Jimmy's and Matt's as well, both of them saying "Thanks" while keeping their eyes glued to the TV.

In the kitchen, Ash was on her laptop at the table but looked up as I walked in. "Everyone's done?" she asked, and I said, "Yeah."

I rinsed the plates and put them in the dishwasher, then turned to face her and said, "What are you up to?" It wasn't that I was really interested, but it felt rude to leave without saying anything else.

She sighed. "I'm trying to get some things on the calendar for the winter months. You have to book so early for the holiday season. People just get so busy, but they're also in the mood to buy things."

"True," I said. "I can't believe it's November."

She shook her head. "I know it. And then the time between Thanksgiving and Christmas goes like that." She snapped her fingers.

"Always," I said. This conversation was one I would've had with my mailman, which was depressing, and I wanted it to be over, for us to stop saying these generic things to each other.

"You're leaving so soon," she said.

"I know."

"Do you know what you'll do when you get back?"

"No clue. I thought I'd have a great idea while I was here, but no such luck." I didn't realize this was true until I said it out loud, that some part of me was hoping I'd figure out what I wanted to do with my career while I was in Texas. But I didn't. Almost a whole year had passed and not one thing had changed—I still felt as ambivalent as ever.

"Well, I'm sure you could always go back to DCLOVE," she said, and then laughed at the face I made. "Or you could come work with me. You could corner the jewelry market in DC."

My answer was completely sincere. "I'm not sure I'd be any good at it," I said. "I don't have your charm."

When we'd returned from the last trip, Matt had suggested that he and I move to a hotel on the Sunday before the election and stay there until it was over. "To give Jimmy and Ash some space," he said, which was sort of a ridiculous idea since we'd been living in their house for the past ten months. Why would we give them space now? I knew the real reason was that he didn't want to be there after Jimmy lost, that he thought it would be easier if we could go somewhere else that night.

But I agreed to the hotel because I also thought space would be good, just for different reasons. I didn't want to be in the same house as Jimmy—as hard as I tried, I couldn't stop wondering what would've happened if we'd stayed longer at the bar that night; kept imagining him kissing me, hard, his hands all over me.

It was normal, I told myself, to have thoughts like these. Once, I almost googled it, to reassure myself that adulterous daydreams were common and harmless. (Surely Oprah had done a show on the topic at some point.) But then I imagined Matt using my computer, finding my search history, and decided against it. Which was maybe proof that I was guilty of something.

So I told Matt that I agreed, that I thought the hotel was a good idea.

We each took just a small bag to the hotel, leaving most of our clothes at the Dillons'. We'd need to pack it all soon enough. Matt had already started boxing up some things, eager to get ready so we could leave as quickly as possible.

I thought it would feel weird to stay in a hotel, but we'd stayed in so many the past year that when we got to the Holiday Inn Express, it felt a little like home, which was equal parts reassuring and depressing.

Jimmy's parents were hosting a small get-together for family and friends the night of the election, but Mrs. Dillon insisted that the four of us come over on Monday night as well. "You all deserve a home-cooked meal," she'd said, rubbing Jimmy's back. I could see how much she wanted to do something—anything—to make Jimmy feel better.

Matt and I drove to their house from our hotel and arrived before Jimmy and Ash. As Mr. Dillon opened the door, Matt handed him a bottle of wine that we'd stopped to pick up at Whole Foods. "For you, sir," he said, and I couldn't help but notice what a kiss ass he sounded like. He'd insisted on buying a fifty-dollar bottle of wine, which seemed too much, but when I said something about it, he said, "The Dillons always serve really nice wine," making me feel like I'd suggested getting them a box of Franzia.

The four of us sat down in the living room and made small talk, which mostly meant that Matt talked to Mr. Dillon while I sat stiffly on the couch. (At Jimmy's parents' house, I always had the feeling that I was going to get in trouble for something or be yelled at for having poor manners, like I was a friend they didn't approve of.)

Almost twenty minutes went by, at which point Mrs. Dillon said, "I don't know where they could be. I'm starting to get worried." But just as the words left her mouth, we heard the front door open and Jimmy call out, "Hello?"

Mrs. Dillon got up to give him a hug as he

walked into the room, looked behind him, and then said, "Where's Ashleigh?"

"She's not going to make it. She was at her mom's this afternoon and Viv got a fever, so she gave her some Tylenol and put her down. She's still sleeping, so we thought it was best to just let her be."

"Well, that's a shame," Mrs. Dillon said. She pursed her lips, but made no further comment.

Once Jimmy got there, we sat down for dinner right away, and everyone ate quickly, mostly because no one was talking much so we had a lot more time to concentrate on chewing. Once, I said to Mrs. Dillon, "This roast is delicious," and she answered by saying, "Aren't you sweet?" (Another question I was pretty sure she thought the answer to was no.)

After the plates were cleared, Mr. Dillon asked if anyone was interested in a glass of port, and Matt said, "That sounds great," which was the exact opposite of how I felt. I wanted to say our good-byes so we could get out of there, and it looked like Jimmy felt the same way, but we all followed Mr. Dillon back to the living room and accepted the tiny glasses that he poured. I hate port, but I took it anyway, just wanting to get on with it.

For the most part, just like at dinner, Mr. Dillon and Matt were the only ones talking. They were dissecting the other races taking place on Tuesday, picking apart the campaigns and making predictions. I snuck a look at Jimmy, who seemed tired, and sipped my port, which made me feel warm. When Mr. Dillon picked up the bottle to pour us each another glass, I said, "Oh, I shouldn't. We should probably be going. It's getting late and I still need to stop by Jimmy and Ash's to get a dress for tomorrow—I forgot to pack one before we went to the hotel."

I could feel Matt's displeasure with my announcement. I'm sure he thought it was rude of me to end the night, but I didn't care. And when I looked over at him, he said, "We'll just stay a little longer."

Jimmy put his glass down on the table and said, "You know what? I should call it a night. Beth, I'll go back with you to the house if you want. Matt can pick you up when he's done."

"Perfect," Matt said.

Jimmy and I said our good-byes, and if I felt strange about being alone with him or thought that it was a bad idea, it was too late to do anything about it. Changing my mind then would've seemed weird, so I followed him outside. It was only when the door shut behind us that I realized his car wasn't there.

"You walked?" I asked. Even though Jimmy and Ash lived so close to his parents, they always drove. It was the Texas way.

Jimmy shrugged, looking a little sheepish. "The

other night I had a little too much to drink and drove home." I started to say something and he held up his hand. "I know, I know. You don't have to tell me. I already know. It was stupid and I shouldn't have done it. Believe me, I feel like an asshole."

"Okay," I said.

"Anyway, tonight I figured there was a chance I'd want to get stinking drunk to deal with my dad, so once Ash wasn't coming I figured walking was the best bet."

"Is Viv okay?"

"Yeah, she's fine. She really does have a fever," he said, answering the question I hadn't asked but was thinking. "I mean, I'm sure Ash was thrilled to have an excuse not to come, but the fever part was true."

We walked down the sidewalk and then turned left at the pond, wound our way back to the house. I would never get over the weirdness of Sugar Land, how appealing and repulsive it was, with its large and beautiful homes, its pretty but artificial terrain. We didn't talk for a few minutes, just walked silently past a pond, and then Jimmy said, "So, how's things?"

I gave a short laugh. "Things are fine," I said.

"Really?" He turned his head to look at me, and I shrugged. I knew what he was asking, I just wasn't sure how to answer. Was he hoping I'd tell him that Matt and I were even more miserable than last week? Or that things were better?

"No, not really," I finally said. "Nothing's worse, I guess. I think it's just going to take time."

Jimmy nodded and said, "That makes sense."

The house was dark when we got there, and Jimmy turned on the lights as we walked through each room. "Is Ash staying at her parents' tonight?" I asked, and Jimmy said, like he didn't care one way or the other, "I don't know."

We walked through the kitchen, where Jimmy stopped at the refrigerator. "Want a beer?" he asked, and I said, "Sure, why not?" He grabbed two and opened one before handing it to me. It was one of the leftover pumpkin beers from Halloween and it was a little too sweet, but I took a long drink anyway.

I cleared my throat, trying to think of some-thing to talk about, and then finally said, "I should get my stuff." And as I headed toward the basement, Jimmy walked with me like it was a normal thing to do, followed me down the stairs and sat on the couch outside the bedroom as I went in to grab the dress I was planning to wear the next night. When I returned, Jimmy was reclining on the couch with his feet resting on the coffee table. I draped my dress over the back of a chair and then sat on the other side of the couch, picked up my beer, and took a sip.

In all the months we'd lived at the Dillons', they almost never came to the basement—I could count the number of times Ash had been down there on one hand, and that was only after I'd called upstairs for her to come and give me an opinion on what I was wearing. And I was pretty sure Jimmy hadn't stepped foot in there once. They did this on purpose, I'm sure, trying to give us privacy to make it feel like it was our own space. And they'd done such a good job that I'd almost forgotten this basement belonged to them. Jimmy seemed out of place in it.

"What time does everything start tomorrow?" I asked, at the same time that Jimmy said, "You must be ready to get out of here." We looked at each other, both smiled just a little, and then I answered, "Maybe. It feels sad now that it's all ending, doesn't it?"

"You have no idea how sad," Jimmy said, and I felt like an idiot.

"I'm sorry," I said. "Of course, I didn't mean—" But Jimmy held up his hand.

"It's okay," he said. "I know what you meant."

"How are you feeling? I mean, I guess that's sort of an obvious question." I felt like I was tripping over my words.

"Not that obvious. Do you know that no one's asked me that? Not Ash or my parents. No one."

"I'm sure they just don't want you to have to

talk about how disappointed you are. They already know."

"Yeah," Jimmy said. "It just sucks though, you know? That's really all it comes down to." He set his beer on the table and put his head in his hands and the first thing I thought was, Oh God, please don't cry. But I didn't see his shoulders moving and his breathing sounded normal.

"Hey," I said, getting up and moving next to him, putting my hand on his back. "It's okay."

He looked up then, and I was aware of how loudly my heart was beating. I hoped he couldn't see it. My mouth felt dry as I said, "It won't seem so bad with a little distance."

"I know," Jimmy said. My hand was still on his back, and he put his hand on my leg. "You should listen to your own advice sometime."

It had been over ten years since I'd been in this particular type of situation, and I was surprised at how familiar it still felt—those seconds when you're with a guy and know something is about to happen, when both of you feel the possibility, the electricity between you; but you also know it's still early enough to get out of it, that one of you could shift or look away and let the moment pass, leaving you to wonder later if you'd made up the whole thing in your head. Our eyes met and I told myself this was a bad idea, that I should stand up or walk out, or just do *something*.

And then, a split second later, we moved toward each other. He had his hands on my hips and lifted me on top of him in one quick movement, and then we were kissing, quickly and with an urgency I hadn't felt in a long time. He moved one hand to cup the back of my head, and before I realized what was happening, his other hand was under my dress, pushing my underwear to the side, not bothering to take it off before putting his fingers inside me. I pressed back against him, moaned as he said, "You're so wet," in a way that felt like a compliment, like it was something I could control.

I could feel him hard underneath me, and he started to unbuckle his jeans, which brought me back to reality for a second and I said, "Wait," and then he pulled my mouth back toward him and we were kissing again. It was only when he said my name, when I heard him say, "Beth," in a hoarse voice, that things became clear and I pulled away, sat up sharply, looked at him straight on. It was then that we both heard footsteps above us, and I stood up quickly, realizing as I did that Jimmy's fingers had still been inside me.

I would like to think we would've stopped then anyway—that whatever crazy spell I was under would've broken, that we would've returned to our senses. That's what I tell myself, that anyone can lose her mind for a few minutes. But the truth is, I don't know for sure.

As Matt walked into the room, I was standing next to the couch, where Jimmy was still sitting. There was nothing inappropriate about it—we weren't in any sort of compromising position—but we were flustered and rumpled and our faces must have given us away, because Matt looked back and forth between us a few times, slowly, and then he said, "What the fuck?"

"Matt—" I started, but he gave me such an angry look that I stopped. I glanced over at Jimmy and could see through his pants that he was still hard and wondered if Matt noticed.

"What the fuck is happening here?" he said.

"Nothing," I said.

"Nothing," Jimmy echoed. "Kelly, it's nothing."

Matt lunged at him so quickly that I barely realized he'd moved before he was across the room, grabbing Jimmy by the collar, pulling him up off the couch, and pushing him against the wall.

"What the fuck is going on here?"

"Nothing. Look, I was upset and Beth was comforting me and we were a little too close for a second, but that's all."

"Don't fucking talk to me about my wife," Matt said. Never in my life had I heard him use the word *fuck* so often in such a short span of time. It was so frequent that it was almost ridiculous, like a teenager who's just learned to swear and is trying to sound tough. It sounded wrong coming out of his mouth—he was too proper for that. But each time he said it, everything around me sharpened into focus, like I was waking up from a dream.

"Matt, really," I said. "It was nothing."

"Nothing?" he asked, looking at me and then turning back to Jimmy. "Were you about to fuck my wife?" He pushed him against the wall again. I'd never seen Matt get in a fight, never seen him get physical with anyone. It wasn't his style. He was too practical, too levelheaded to act like this.

Even with my heart beating fast and my cheeks burning, knowing I'd just acted in a horrible and stupid way, the scene in front of me was so dramatic, so over the top that I almost laughed. It was absurd. This wasn't real—things like this didn't happen to people like us. This was an episode of *Jerry Springer*, not real life. Certainly not my real life.

Jimmy wasn't fighting back at all, was just letting Matt push him against the wall, and this seemed more an admission of guilt than anything. Because really, if we hadn't been doing anything wrong, surely he'd be defending himself.

"No," Jimmy said. "I wasn't. Nothing was going to happen."

"Fuck you," Matt said, and then Jimmy actually did react, shoved Matt in the chest once with both hands.

"Go ahead and punch me," Jimmy said. "I know you want to. You've wanted to for a long time now, so here's your chance. Do it."

Matt shook his head. "You're such a piece of shit," he said. "You know that?" And then he turned to me and said, "Let's go."

It occurred to me that Matt was so angry (on top of having had two glasses of port and drinks at dinner) that he shouldn't be driving, but I didn't say anything about it. We climbed into the car—I'd somehow remembered to grab my dress, and I held it in my lap, squeezing the material in my fists. "Matt," I said. "I'm so sorry. You have to believe me that it was nothing. Jimmy was upset, and—"

"Did you fuck him?" Matt asked. Again, with the word *fuck*. I felt the urge to laugh, which has always happened to me in inappropriate circumstances (I let out a giggle at my own grandmother's funeral), but fortunately, it went away.

"No," I said, trying to make it sound as if that were the most ridiculous thing he could've suggested. "We kissed for a second, but it was nothing. Nothing." Without really meaning to, I left out the details of Jimmy's hand under my dress, of his fingers inside of me, like I'd already forgotten it had happened. I couldn't tell him that—it was too confusing, would make the whole thing seem much worse.

"Nothing?" Matt said. He looked over at me.

"Nothing," I said. "We just got mixed up."

"You got mixed up?" I wondered if Matt was going to just keep repeating everything I said.

"Yes," I said. "It was stupid." And then I started to cry, big heaving sobs, bent over in the seat, not able to catch my breath. It occurred to me that now I was being overdramatic, acting like I'd been wronged, crying like I could make Matt feel sorry for me. But I couldn't stop. "I'm sorry," I said, trying to catch my breath. "I love you, Matt. It was just a stupid mistake, that's all."

Then I buried my head in my hands and he let me cry, not saying anything, and eventually I noticed that the car had stopped moving. "Beth," he said, not in a mean way, exactly, but also with no trace of kindness. "Beth, stop. We're here."

We talked that night until we had nothing left to say. I just kept apologizing and crying, thinking at some point my tears would run out, but they didn't. I told him how I'd hugged Jimmy when he was upset, how it led to a confusion of body parts—that's actually what I said: a confusion of body parts. Honestly, it seemed as good an explanation as anything else.

Matt sat in the desk chair and I was on the bed as we talked, my knees pulled up to my chest. "It was just a kiss," I said over and over. "Just for a second."

It felt a little like a business meeting, the way we were positioned across from each other. I don't know how long we stayed there. Hours, I think.

"Has this been going on for a while?" Matt asked.

"No," I said. "This was the only time. Just this one thing. One kiss, that's all."

I was aware of what I was leaving out, of how I edited the story. But even if I'd wanted to tell him everything—which I didn't—I wouldn't have known how to phrase it. (Was there any term more disgusting than *getting fingered?* I hadn't heard anyone say it since high school, since Kelly Klinger told me in homeroom that's what her boyfriend had done to her the night before, and I felt as confused now as I did then about what had actually occurred.) I also somehow knew that Jimmy would never tell anyone that detail, that I could get away with this one omission. So, no, I would never fully explain, but I would apologize over and over until Matt believed me.

When we were winding down, Matt asked, "Do you like him?" This was the only time he showed any emotion during this conversation, his voice catching on the word *like,* making him sound young.

"No," I said. "It's not—I don't want anything with Jimmy. I think I've felt lonely lately, like you're ignoring me or like you don't care. And I know that's not an excuse. It's just—it's what's been going on."

Matt nodded in a businesslike way. "Were you trying to get back at me?"

I shook my head at the same time I said, "No. I wasn't. I know this might not make sense but it was just an accident. A mistake."

Matt didn't say anything then, just looked at me, and I rested my head on my knees and continued to cry.

When we'd first started dating, Matt couldn't stand to see me cry. Any argument we had would be over as soon as there were tears—he'd comfort me, apologize, do anything to get me to stop. Over the years, it had less of an effect on him, and now he seemed completely immune.

I heard a noise then and looked up from my knees to see Matt standing up. "Are you leaving?" I asked.

"I need to take a walk," he said.

"Matt," I said, a new sob in my voice. "I'm so sorry. I really am. I love you, you know that."

He nodded again. "Okay," he said. He walked out the door casually, as if he were just going down to the lobby to get something.

When he left, I cried some more, and then after a while I began to feel bored by my own tears, and they slowed and then finally stopped. I could feel a headache behind my eyes and reached for the remote, turned on the TV to drown out my thoughts. I was still on top of the covers, fully dressed, but I was too tired to bother changing. I fell asleep and woke up after a fitful dream to find that the TV was still on and Matt was just returning to the room. "Hey," I said, as he climbed into bed, and he said, "Hi," before turning off the light and lying down so that his back was facing me.

The next time I opened my eyes, it was 7:00 a.m. and Matt was getting dressed. I sat up and said, "Hi."

"Hi," he said back, looking in the mirror as he knotted his tie.

"Are you okay?" I asked.

"Yeah," he said. "I'm just ready for this to be over." I sat up and pulled the covers off, and he looked at me. "You don't have to get up. Stay here and sleep. Just be ready to go around five."

That was the time we'd have to leave for the election party at the Dillons', and I was surprised that he still wanted me to go, but I just nodded and said, "Sure."

I spent most of the day in the hotel room, imagining what Matt and Jimmy were saying to each other, if they were saying anything at all. What was Ash doing? She hadn't called to yell at me, but that didn't mean she didn't know. I left once to get a salad, but found it impossible to eat and only managed to choke down a couple of bites of lettuce before abandoning it. My stomach twisted and I thought I might get sick.

By the time Matt came back to get me, I'd been dressed and ready to go for almost three hours. He didn't bother to come up to the room, just texted that he was downstairs. As I walked out the door, I tried to think if I'd ever dreaded anything as much as I was dreading this party and decided that the answer was definitely no. I would've given anything to stay at the hotel, even if it meant I'd have only my paranoid thoughts to keep me company. I didn't know why Matt even wanted me to go—maybe he thought it would look bad if I didn't, maybe he wanted me to feel uncomfortable and embarrassed, to pay for what I'd done.

When I got in the car, Matt was typing on his BlackBerry and didn't say anything for a minute. Then he put it down and said, "Ready to go?" and pulled away before I answered. On the way, I asked him about the day, and he answered me in a tone that was both polite and removed, like I was a reporter that he didn't particularly care for, but knew he couldn't ignore. I hesitated, and then asked him if Jimmy told Ash what had happened—I didn't want to, but I felt like I had to know before we got to the party so I could be prepared.

"I don't know," he said, evenly.

"You didn't ask?" I said.

"We didn't talk about it," Matt said. It seemed unbelievable to me that they'd spent the whole day together and never once acknowledged what had happened, but Matt's jaw was firm and his answer didn't leave any room for further discussion, so I dropped it.

As we pulled into the driveway, I said, "Matt, I'm so sorry."

He turned off the ignition and let out a long sigh. "I know," he said.

The actual party wasn't quite as bad as I'd feared, mostly because by the time we arrived, there were already about twenty people there, which made it crowded enough so I felt like I could sort of blend in. When we walked inside, Jimmy was in the corner by the fireplace, talking to one of his father's friends who had donated quite a bit to the campaign. "I should go check in," Matt said, before walking away and leaving me alone by the door.

One of the caterers came up to me with a tray of white wine, and I took a glass, just to have something to do with my hands. Through the doorway, I saw Ash in the other room, standing alone and looking at her phone. I'd already decided that I was going to say something to her right away, to apologize. To wait any longer would just make it worse.

She smiled as I walked over, and before I could change my mind, I said, "Ash, I just wanted to explain about last night."

She waved her hand in the air, like the whole

thing was a silly misunderstanding. "Oh, you don't have to," she said. "Jimmy already did and it's fine." She lowered her voice. "I guess we can't be too surprised they had a fight before this was all done, right? It was coming for a while, I guess. But still . . . it all seems so childish."

"I know," I said, unsure of how to continue. Was it possible that Jimmy had only told her that he and Matt had fought and left out the reason behind it? I had assumed that he'd tell her something, even if it was just a watered-down version of events. But now I wasn't sure she knew any of it.

"I think we're all a little loony after this, don't you?" she said.

"Yeah," I said. "But still, I'm sorry for what happened."

I could've been referring to the fight between Matt and Jimmy, could've been apologizing for Matt's behavior, if that's all she knew about. But something told me it wasn't, because she smiled then and it looked a little tight as she said, "Really. It's fine."

It's funny how unimportant election night actually felt. This was what we'd been working toward all those months, it was why we'd driven all over Texas and gone into the homes of strangers, attended church picnics and potlucks. But that night, there was no more adrenaline, no more

451

excitement. We just waited for an answer we already knew was coming. In some ways it felt like the most insignificant part of the whole campaign.

The call came pretty early, around 8:00 p.m. The television was on in one of the rooms, the sound turned low, but we all noticed when they called the race. It didn't feel especially sad—it was more exhaustion and relief, like the whole room exhaled at once. I'd spent most of the night standing next to Matt while he talked to different guests, not really participating in any of the con-versations, just observing. When they called the race, I put a hand on his back, but he didn't give any indication that he felt it.

Jimmy gave a short speech to thank everyone— his supporters, his parents, and finally Ash and Viv. "I know this wasn't easy for you, and I appreciate all of the sacrifices you made. You two are the best." He looked over at Ash, sounding absolutely sincere as he said, "I'm a lucky guy."

After Jimmy spoke, people started leaving pretty quickly. I was scared we'd be left alone with just the Dillon family, something I didn't think I'd be able to handle, and I was relieved when Matt started saying good-bye to people so we could make our exit.

Before we left, I thanked Mrs. Dillon and said good-bye. She gave me an air kiss and then held one of my hands in hers and said, "Do you know how much you'll be missed around here?"

I refrained from saying, "Not one fucking tiny bit," and instead just smiled and squeezed her hand.

Once we were in the car, Matt drove a couple of blocks without talking. The feeling between us was so strange—not anger or avoidance, more like he was too preoccupied to notice I was there.

"I can't believe it's over," I said, just to fill the silence.

"I know," Matt said.

"Do you think you still want to leave Friday?" I asked. This had been our tentative plan, but we'd left things up in the air. Now I figured we both wanted to get out of Texas as quickly as possible.

"Beth," Matt said. He cleared his throat and didn't take his eyes off the road. "I think you should go home tomorrow."

"You want to leave tomorrow?"

"No, I think you should go home. I looked online and put a flight on hold for you for tomorrow night." Matt sounded so calm as he spoke that it took me a second to understand what he was saying. "I don't think we should drive home together," he continued. "You go and I'll take the car. I want to take some time."

"Some time away from me?" I asked. My voice sounded panicked, and I felt blindsided although I probably shouldn't have. What did I think? That we'd forget what had happened and have a nice drive home together?

"Some time," he said. "A week or two. Maybe more."

"When will you come home? Will you let me know?"

"I don't know," he said. "I'm not trying to be mean. I'm really not." He almost looked like he felt sorry for me. "I'll be in touch."

"Can I text you?" I asked, and he shook his head. I swallowed hard. "Are you sure about this? You don't want to talk about it?"

"No," he said. "I don't."

I nodded into the darkness, feeling like a child being punished, being sent home after behaving badly. I'd been an idiot to think this wouldn't happen—hadn't we already been on shaky ground? Wasn't that why this had happened in the first place? Of course he might leave me, of course this could break us. I thought about arguing, about fighting to stay, but it felt like I'd lost that right for the time being, so I just said, "Okay."

Chapter 21

My flight landed at Reagan late on Wednesday, and after waiting at baggage claim and then again in the cab line, it was almost midnight by the time I got home. All the lights were off as we pulled up and the streets were empty, and as the cab drove away, I felt a surge of fear—it was creepy standing there alone in front of my dark apartment, like something or someone could be lurking inside, just waiting for me. I didn't want to go in, but what choice did I have? And after I unlocked the door and turned on the lights, I almost laughed at how childish I was being. Why was I bothering to invent something to worry about when I already had plenty? No need to borrow trouble, my mom would've said. (Although I still triple-locked the door behind me.)

We hadn't been back to the apartment since July, and even though Babs was sending Rosie over every couple of weeks, it felt stuffy and dusty. I carried my bags to the first floor and left them there as I continued to the bedroom. The bed was made, but when I pulled back the duvet, I saw that the sheets had been stripped and not replaced. I stood there for a minute, trying to decide if I should get a clean set, then decided it wasn't worth the trouble, took off my clothes, and climbed onto the bare mattress, pulling the duvet over me. I turned on the TV, thinking I'd be up all night, but lying there I was so tired I was almost dizzy.

Normally, whenever I traveled anywhere, Matt would say, "Let me know when you get there." It didn't matter what time it was or what else was going on—he always wanted to know that I'd made it safely. But that day, when I'd left the hotel, he'd just said, "Take care."

I plugged the phone in right next to me so I could hear it, just in case. I kept thinking that habit would take over, that he'd check in to make sure I was okay. But my phone was quiet all night.

When we were in college and horribly hungover, Colleen used to look at the clock and say, "By two o'clock we'll feel better. We just have to make it until then." There were times it was hard to believe her, when it seemed like my headache would never go away, felt like my body was permanently damaged. But it always helped, just a little, to have something to aim for, to have some hope.

I found myself doing this while waiting for Matt to come home. In one week, he'll be back. In one month, things will be better. And then, before I could stop myself, I'd think, In one year,

I'll be divorced, and my chest would get so tight I'd lose my breath. I felt sick all the time.

For two days, I stayed inside the apartment, checking my phone obsessively and leaving only when I absolutely had to. I let my thoughts run wild: What if Matt never came home? What if Rosie came over to clean and found me there? How long could I survive on takeout? Was I heading toward a Grey Gardens–like future?

I called my parents to let them know I was back in DC, said that Matt was finishing up things in Texas but would be home soon. I kept the conversation short, making it sound like I was superbusy, like there was a ton to catch up on.

"What an adventure you two had," my mom said.

"I know," I told her. "We really did."

On Saturday morning, my phone rang and I grabbed it, hoping it was Matt and feeling my stomach drop when I saw it was Jimmy. My first instinct was to drop it on the table, like it was contaminated, but then I picked it right back up again. I couldn't ignore it, because then I'd spend all day wondering why he was calling. I answered, hating how unsure my voice sounded as I said, "Hello?"

"Hey, Beth, it's Jimmy."

"Hi," I said. I thought how strange it was that people still felt they had to identify themselves on the phone, when we always knew who was calling before we picked up.

"I was just on my way to the store and I thought I'd call to see how you are."

"I'm okay," I said. And then as a reflex more than anything else, "How are you?"

"Not so bad."

"Really?"

"Yeah, really," he answered with a laugh in his voice.

"Okay," I said. "I just—"

"What?"

"I don't know. I'm actually not okay, you know? I'm not good at all. I feel awful about what happened."

Jimmy was silent for a while, and I wondered if he was surprised or annoyed that I'd brought it up. Did he really think we were going to have a phone call and not talk about it? "Me too," he finally said, but he didn't sound remorseful at all. "But look, things happen. We were both upset. It's been a crazy year."

"I guess," I said, and right then I knew that this wasn't the first time Jimmy had had to make a call like this, that the rumors about him were true. I knew it in a way I hadn't before, knew because of the way he said "Things happen" so calmly.

"Don't beat yourself up about it," he said. "That's what I really called to say." He sounded a little impatient then, like he wanted me to stop being so dramatic. It was a sensation familiar from college—a guy making me feel like I was making a bigger deal out of something than was necessary, who thought I should just (and oh, how I hated this word) relax.

I didn't say anything for a few seconds while I debated pushing further, making him admit that I—that we—deserved to beat ourselves up a little. But what was the point?

"Did Matt pack our stuff?" I finally asked, changing the subject and giving him what he wanted.

"Oh yeah, he couldn't get out of here fast enough. He left on Thursday."

"Thursday?" I asked. This meant that Matt could be in DC soon, could possibly be home tonight. Although I was pretty sure he wouldn't be coming back so soon—or at least, not to the apartment.

"You didn't know?" Jimmy asked.

"No. I haven't talked to him since I left."

Jimmy let out a low whistle. "That's tough," he said. "But listen, you two will work it out. Like I said, things happen."

I envied how casual he sounded and I hated it too, because I knew he wasn't faking it. How easy it must be to go through life being Jimmy Dillon, to always be so sure that things would work out for you, that your messes would be cleaned up.

"How's Ash?" I asked.

"She's good," he said. "Staying busy."

It was ridiculous for me to think there was any chance that Ash didn't know what was going on—the way I'd left Texas, suddenly and without saying good-bye, was absurd. Surely, if she didn't think I had anything to be blamed for, she would've called me by now. And thinking of Ash being disappointed in the type of friend I'd turned out to be—to tell you the truth, it felt worse than anything.

"Thanks for calling," I finally said.

"Sure thing," he said, as breezily as if we'd been discussing dinner plans.

I called Colleen as soon as I hung up with Jimmy. She'd texted me a few times in the past week, asking when we'd be back, and (not knowing how to respond) I'd ignored her. When I told her I was home, she sounded thrilled, started talking about when we could get together, but I interrupted her and said, "I have to talk to you. Now. Are you free?"

"Now?" she asked. She must have heard the neediness in my voice, because she told me to hold on and I heard a muffled conversation take place as she covered the phone. When she came back, she said. "Okay, Bruce can watch Bea. Do you want to meet somewhere?"

"Can you come here?" I asked. I felt slightly

ridiculous that I was being so cryptic, but I couldn't imagine getting into the details over the phone, and I was thankful when Colleen told me she'd be right over.

As soon as I answered the door, I started crying, but Colleen didn't say anything, just walked in and closed the door behind her. I must have looked pathetic, sniffling in my sweatpants and T-shirt. Colleen put her hand on my back and led me up the stairs gently, like I was elderly or maybe just plain crazy.

She must have wondered what was going on—if someone had died or there was another sort of emergency, I would've just told her on the phone. But I think she guessed that it had to do with me and Matt because she sat and patiently waited for me to start talking.

"I did something horrible," I said. Colleen tilted her head at me, like she thought I might be kidding, but then I continued, telling the whole story, all of it coming out in one big mess of words.

When I was done, she leaned back on the couch and looked at the ceiling and then the floor and then the ceiling again. She blew a gust of air up at her bangs, making them flutter, and finally said, "Well, Jesus, Beth. That is not what I thought you were going to say."

"I know," I said, and then surprisingly let out a laugh. "I know, right?" It was shocking how much better it felt to have someone else know what I'd done, like confession. Already, I felt the release of telling her, knowing that she'd talk it through with me.

"How did it happen?" she asked, but she wasn't judging me. She sounded genuinely interested, like she needed all the details before she could understand it.

"I don't even know," I said. And I really didn't, which might have been the worst part. Was I looking for attention? Trying to get back at Matt? Was I bored? Was it a moment of weakness? I'd been attracted to Jimmy, I couldn't deny that. But I certainly wasn't in love with him, didn't picture us running away together. The phone call with him that afternoon, his casual dismissal of things, had reminded me of his worst traits.

"You don't know?" Colleen asked.

"No," I said, and let out a little sob. "Maybe I'm a sociopath."

Colleen rolled her eyes. "All right. Let's not get carried away," she said. And part of me agreed with her, but another part of me wondered how I could so easily betray so many people—not just my husband, but also one of my best friends.

"This isn't me," I said, although wasn't that everyone's first reaction when they cheated? No one ever stood up and owned it, declared that cheating was just a part of their personality.

"I know," Colleen said.

"I feel like a horrible person. No really, listen. Who does this kind of thing? What if I keep doing things like this?"

"Yeah, I wouldn't worry about that. I mean, I don't think you're about to start trying to seduce Bruce." She couldn't help but smile after she said this, and then she looked serious again. "Beth, people make mistakes, you know."

"Not like this," I said.

Colleen looked at me as if she was unsure of how to continue. "Do you have feelings for him?" she finally asked, and I shook my head forcefully.

"No," I said. "It was just a mistake."

She nodded and then perked up, as if just remembering something, and pulled a bottle of wine out of her bag. "I brought reinforcements," she said. I stayed on the couch as she opened the bottle, poured us each a glass, swirling it around before tasting it.

"I don't know how things got to this point," I said. Colleen sat back down and refilled my glass, which I'd already drained.

"Well, it's not like things sounded good the last time we talked." She said this almost gently, like she was telling me something I didn't know. I had a childish desire to correct her, although I don't know why. She was right.

"I know," I said. "I just kept thinking things would get better if I waited it out. And then I made it worse."

"So, Dogpants is still going through his mid-whatever crisis?" she asked. I just nodded. "Well, I mean, look. Couples go through this all the time. I don't think it's as weird as you think it is."

"Maybe. That doesn't mean Matt's going to forgive me, though."

"Maybe not," she said.

"I just—I know I fucked up. But, Colleen, he was awful too. He really was. And I'm not saying that's an excuse, but it's true."

"I know. I don't think you're trying to make excuses."

"He didn't even care if I was there or not. It was like I didn't exist. Like he couldn't even be bothered to talk to me. I moved to Texas for him, for his job, and he just didn't even give a shit." I got angry as I started telling her this, felt the wine warming me up.

"Well that sounds shitty."

"It was. It was completely shitty. He was mean. It was like he was a different person or something. And I was so mad, but it didn't matter. I'm still mad." I got louder with each word.

"Good. You should be mad, Beth. Get mad."

And then I felt my anger crumble and I was near tears again. "I don't want to get divorced," I said, sniffling.

"No one's talking about that right now."

"What would I even do?"

"I don't know," she said. Part of me appreciated

her honesty and part of me just really wanted her to lie and tell me it would all be fine. "I don't really see you eat-pray-loving your way through this. No offense."

I assumed the "no offense" meant, no offense that you're not brave enough to travel alone, no offense that you're such a baby you'd never go to Bali. But I couldn't have cared less that Colleen thought I was an emotional wimp, so I didn't even bother responding.

"Did you eat yet?" she asked, and I shook my head. I think my wild swing of emotions in a three-minute span—from apologetic to angry to pathetic—had alerted her that the wine was hitting me quickly.

She took charge then, and I was happy to let her. I watched from the couch as she ordered dinner and got more wine and called home to tell Bruce that she'd be staying over.

"You don't have to do that," I said. "What about Bea?" I tried to sound convincing, but I wanted her to stay, badly, and I was happy when she just shook her head in a businesslike way.

"It's fine," she said. "Plus, I think you could use the company."

Later that night, after making me drink a glass of water and take two Advil, Colleen got into bed with me. I was drunk—incredibly so—and tired and grateful that she was there. We talked into the darkness, like we had for so many years, the pauses in our conversation getting longer as we each neared sleep. The last thing I remember her saying was "It's not the end of the world, Beth."

"How do you know?" I asked. My eyes were already closed, and I'd been half in a dream just seconds before.

I heard her sigh. "I just do," she said.

The next morning I woke up, remembering in some fuzzy part of my still-sleeping brain that something was wrong. And then it all came rushing back to me. Colleen was already gone, the covers on that side of the bed pulled up and a note left on Matt's bedside table that said, "B—Had to run. Didn't want to wake you. Call me later." I rolled onto my side and closed my eyes, but it was no use. There was no chance of falling back asleep now.

The rest of the week crawled by so slowly that I considered ripping out my hair just to have something to do. Colleen stopped by after work a couple of times, and on Thursday, she insisted I come over for dinner. "You can't just sit inside all day," she said, wrinkling her nose like the apartment smelled. So I went to her house, and sat at the kitchen table nodding every so often as she and Bruce carried on a conversation. I assumed she'd told Bruce the whole story, because when he saw me, he kissed my cheek and then pulled me against him for an awkward embrace, my face smooshed against his shoulder. "It's good to see you, Beth," he said, finally ending the hug but still holding on to my arms. And honestly, I couldn't even muster up the energy to feel embarrassed.

I spent most of the time lying on my back and obsessing over what had happened, going over each step in my mind. I was paralyzed. It felt like I should do something, but I didn't know where to start. Should I look for a job? Contact Ellie to see if there was anything for me at DCLOVE? If Matt and I broke up, would I even stay in DC? My mind was an endless loop of questions, none of which I had the answers for.

Sunday night came and went with no word from Matt. I wondered if he was staying at his parents' house, if he was back in DC, or if he'd gone somewhere random to think things through.

"I could be dead for all he knows," I said to Colleen that night. "He hasn't even bothered to text me. Someone could've kidnapped me or I could be in the hospital."

"So call him," Colleen said. "He's your husband. You have a say in this, too. You deserve to know where he is."

"How can he really not care enough to check in just once?" I asked. Anger flared in my chest. This was the longest we'd been out of contact since we first started dating all those years ago.

Colleen looked at me, then said again, slowly, "Call him."

"I can't," I said.

She shook her head at me, frustrated. "You're always letting things happen to you," she said. "You just wait to react. Do something."

I just looked at her, not knowing how to respond. She was right, of course. But I didn't know how to change that about myself—didn't know if it was even possible.

I couldn't sleep that night, imagining Matt had gone to Sunday dinner at his parents' house, that he was telling everyone what happened, turning them all against me, acting like he'd done nothing wrong. Would he do that? I didn't think so, but at this point, nothing would surprise me. To leave me like this, to care so little that he wouldn't call, or even bother to send a text—that I never could've imagined.

I began to think he was never going to bother coming home, that he was just going to Irish-good-bye out of our marriage. Which, on top of everything else, would be awkward to explain.

As I tossed and turned, I kept trying to picture my life without Matt. It felt impossible. If we split up, no one would ever call me Buzz again. And while there were so many more important things to worry about, it was that thought that made me the saddest.

• • •

But then the next morning, he texted: *I'll be home tomorrow night. We'll talk then?* The question mark made his text seem almost friendly, made me feel hopeful despite myself. I had a million things to say, but I just wrote, *Sure. I'll be here.* And he answered, *See you around 7.*

The next night, I sat on the couch and waited. My heart jumped when I heard the lock, and I stood at the top of the stairs, watching Matt come in. He looked serious and tired. My heart was beating so fast that I thought I might pass out and considered for a minute if this would make him feel more sympathetic toward me.

"Hey," he said, looking up at me.

"Hi," I said. I didn't know how to greet him and I could tell he felt the same. Even when we were mad at each other, we hugged and kissed hello—maybe out of habit, but also because we belonged to each other. Now I wasn't sure that was still true.

He sat on one end of the couch and I sat on the other, my hands in my lap. My heart was still beating so hard that I could hear it and wondered if he could too. I waited for him to start talking, and finally he took a deep breath and said, "I've spent these past two weeks thinking about this, trying to figure out what we should do. I'd be lying if I said I wasn't angry. But I want us to get past this."

"You do?" He wasn't done talking, but I couldn't stop myself from asking the question. I was sure he heard the relief in my voice.

He sounded solemn as he said, "I do. We've put too much into this to just throw it away. We made a commitment to each other. I think we can make this better. If you're willing to." It was such a Matt thing to say—to bring up commitment and work—that I almost smiled. He looked so serious sitting there, my thoughtful husband. It was an expression I recognized from so many times we'd talked about our future or world issues. I'd missed this version of Matt; it felt like forever since I'd seen him.

"I want that too," I said. Our whole conversation felt so formal, like we were negotiating a contract instead of talking about our relationship. Matt looked like he was going to say something else, but I spoke first. "Matt, I want to try to explain. I've been going over everything again and again. And I'm sorry for what happened, for what I did. I will always be sorry about that. But I've also been thinking about us. About how bad things got."

"I know," Matt said.

"I don't know what happened. I've tried to go back and figure out where it was that things started to feel off. You seemed so angry—at me, at the situation. At everything."

"I was," he said. He didn't meet my eyes at first, like he was embarrassed.

"It felt like you didn't even like me anymore," I said, my voice wobbling.

"Beth." He looked up at me like he felt sorry for me, and I felt tears come to my eyes.

I held up my hand, wanting to get out what I had to say. "You weren't talking to me. I felt so shut out. I knew you were upset, but you wouldn't tell me about it. I'm not saying this as an excuse, I'm not. But I need you to know what it felt like. Like it didn't even matter that I was there, like you wouldn't have cared if I left."

"That's not true," Matt said, but his voice was soft. "It's not. I'm sorry if that's how it felt."

"And then you left me. You left me here. Didn't even call once. I didn't know if you were ever coming back. You *left* me." My voice sounded angry for the first time in our conversation, and Matt looked surprised.

He closed his eyes. "I know. I can't explain it. I just needed to think. I just needed space to think."

"This wasn't—it wasn't about Jimmy. I don't know if that makes it worse or not. I think I was just confused and sad and it just happened. But I've never done anything like that before. I promise. You have to believe me about that."

He raised his head and looked right at me. "I believe you."

"Okay, good," I said.

"I know things were bad, Beth. I don't know why, exactly. It was happening and I couldn't stop it. I don't know why I was acting that way. I don't want to be like this. I really don't." Matt had tears in his eyes, but he blinked them back. It was such a simple thing to say, but maybe that's why I believed him. I got up and sat closer to him on the couch, reaching out and taking his hand.

The conversation had gone better than I'd hoped, but I tried not to get ahead of myself. I knew Matt was still angry—I could feel that he was hesitant as I held his hand and knew that wouldn't go away for a while. And I was still angry too, if I was being honest. But he wasn't going to leave, he wasn't going to use this thing that I'd done as an excuse to end things. And I wasn't going to ask him where he'd been for almost two weeks, wasn't going to demand that information. I'm sure Colleen would've said that I let Matt make a decision and then reacted to it—and maybe I did, but I didn't really care. It was what I wanted too, and it didn't matter to me how we got there.

"I want things to get better," I said. "And I know it will take a while, but I think—" My voice broke here and I waited a second to continue. "I think we can do that."

Matt squeezed my hand and then took his away and put it in his lap in a way that felt slightly unfriendly. But then his voice was soft and agreeable as he said, "Me too."

That night we were polite to each other as we got ready for bed, standing next to each other at the sink while we brushed our teeth, taking turns spitting and rinsing like we were new room-mates who didn't know each other very well. We'd been apart for two weeks, but it felt like much longer. Our good-night kiss was dry and chaste, and as I pulled the covers over me I wondered how long this was going to last. Maybe we'd have to live like a prudish Amish couple for a while; maybe that was our price to pay. I guess it wasn't the worst thing in the world, but it certainly wasn't great.

But then the next morning, I felt Matt reach over for me, pulling me toward him, surprising me because he hadn't in so long. I was half awake as he tugged my pajamas off, and I stayed underneath him, both of our movements sleepy and slow. When we were done, we lay on our backs, our limbs just barely touching. Neither of us spoke, but it felt like we'd started to erase something, and it seemed like it was enough for now as Matt rested his hand on my stomach and said, "Morning, Buzz."

Washington, DC

★ ★ ★ ★ ★ ★ ★ ★ ★ ★ ★

Washington isn't a city, it's an abstraction.
—DYLAN THOMAS

Chapter 22

Here's what I still hate about DC: the way that nothing is permanent, the feeling that everything and everyone you know, could (and does) wash away every four or eight years. All of these important people, so ingrained in the city—you can't imagine that this place could exist without them. But one day they're gone and everything keeps moving just the same.

Who can get their footing in a place like this? It feels like quicksand to me.

Once Matt was back, we moved quickly. He took a job (with the help of Mr. Dillon's connections) as deputy political director at the DNC, and that same week we started looking at houses in Maryland and made an offer on one. A few weeks later, I was hired to edit a monthly newsletter at an adult literacy nonprofit. It paid less than I'd made at DCLOVE, but I didn't have to write blind items about White House love affairs and golf games, which was a good trade-off.

I'm sure a therapist would've gotten a kick out of analyzing us, the way we raced ahead, like if we changed enough things in our life, everything would be fine. Sometimes I worried about it too, but mostly we were too busy for me to second-guess everything, which maybe was the whole point.

The house we bought was in Silver Spring, on a street with well-kept lawns and brightly painted mailboxes. I thought maybe it would feel lonely out there, but in the end it was like any move—the surroundings seem strange until they don't and one day the unfamiliar becomes normal.

Our neighborhood was full of young couples, most of them with kids but a few without. The day we moved in, our neighbor Ginny and her husband, Bob, brought over a welcome basket—a real-life welcome basket, full of jam, cookies, and gift certificates to the local pizza place. "We're such a social block," she told us. "You'll love it here." Ginny was the president of the neighbor-hood social committee, a title she said with so much pride, she could've been announcing that she was President of the United States. "It's a lot of work," she said. "But it's worth it."

Within a week, I was invited to join a book club and a Bunco group—a game I'd never played that was apparently all the rage in suburban Maryland. These people didn't joke around about their Bunco.

Ginny was telling the truth about our neighbor-hood—there were BBQs and block parties and group outings to Nats games. There was always something going on and there were nights we turned down invitations just to get a little break, so we could be alone, closing our blinds so we wouldn't offend anyone.

There were a few times that I'd be in someone's backyard, talking about the quality of our public schools or getting a recommendation for a housepainter, and across the lawn, Matt would be discussing the Redskins and flooded basements while someone cooked cheeseburgers on the grill, and I wanted to laugh at the absurdity of it, how ordinary and boring it all was.

But those moments were few and far between. They honestly were. Mostly, I enjoyed myself at these gatherings. I liked all of our neighbors—they were funny and kind and welcoming, and I knew we'd never get to know them really well, that we'd always keep a little distance. We wouldn't have friends like the Dillons again, another couple so entangled in our lives, and that was okay. It was probably the way it was supposed to be.

Sunday nights still belonged to the Kellys, and we showed up there every week without fail. Babs was still herself, but I didn't feel her scrutiny as much—it's possible I was just used to it or maybe it wasn't as intense as before. Either way, I didn't dread the dinners the way I once had. And at least once a week, I met up with Jenny and Nellie, sometimes for lunch or dinner, but mostly to go for walks together; just a bunch of outlaws power-walking through the suburbs of Maryland.

We saw Bruce and Colleen more than we had before, had them over for dinner often, the four of us sitting on the patio and watching Bea run around in the backyard. And maybe it's because I'm older or less judgmental, but I see good things about them as a couple that I didn't before—the way Bruce listens to Colleen's long stories, how nicely she repeats things to him when he can't hear. So much of what I used to think was ridiculous about them, now seems right. They balance each other out.

During our first year in Maryland, I felt Matt coming back to me, little by little. It happened in small ways—how he'd touch my hair as I sat nearby, when he'd bring me coffee in bed. Once, as he leaned down to hug me from behind, I drew in a sharp breath to keep from crying. Because it was only when he was back that I realized how much he had been gone.

We see the Dillons sometimes, not alone, but when they're in town we run into them at parties, and everything is perfectly pleasant, almost normal really. Maybe we know we can't avoid each other and the best option is to act friendly. Maybe enough time has passed. Maybe we remember the good parts of our friendship. Or maybe we're all really good at pretending.

They sent us a beautiful gift when our son,

John, was born—a blue quilt with his name and birth date embroidered in the corner. I called Ash to thank her, but she didn't answer, so I left a message. She responded with a text, which was fine with me. Texting (didn't you know?) is the best way to keep in touch with people you don't really want to talk to.

I do feel guilty that we're Viv's godparents, and I make sure to send presents on her birthday and Christmas and whenever else I think to. I'm sure this will slow down over time, that over the years I'll send fewer things and then eventually stop. I can imagine that when she talks about us, she'll say, "They were friends of my parents a long time ago, but we never see them now." She'll probably look at the pictures of the four of us and try to figure out why these random people were chosen to be her spiritual guides. I'm sure Ash will water down the relationship in her retelling. "We spent so much time with them in DC," she'll say. "Matt ran your dad's first campaign in Texas." But as Viv's friends have their godparents show up at graduations with presents and envelopes full of money, I doubt she'll care about any of that. She'll just understand that she got pretty screwed in the godparent department.

The Dillons still send a Christmas card each year, one long letter that's signed from Viv and written in her voice. It gives updates on Ash and

Jimmy and recaps the year with some pretty priceless lines: "With all the jewelry she's selling (and it's a lot!), my mom says I'm still the most precious jewel of all." "And, Praise be to God! It's finally time to celebrate Jesus' birthday!" It goes without saying that the card is decorated and designed by Ash, a Santa stamped on the outside of the envelope, a baby Jesus at the end of the letter.

I always want so badly to read this card out loud to Matt, since no one else could fully appreciate how ridiculous it really is, but I never bring it to his attention, afraid that mentioning the Dillons when I don't need to will bring up bad memories. So I just leave it on top of the pile and pray that he sees it.

For the most part, I don't miss the Dillons—not exactly, anyway. But there are times when Ash is the only person I want to talk to, when there's something that only she would understand. Last week, we were at our block party and I watched Matt talking to our neighbors. He seemed a little too smiley, a little too friendly, like he was trying to win these people over, like he was campaigning. (We didn't choose this district by accident. The real campaign will be along soon, I know.) And I was dying to call Ash and tell her about it, describe what it was like to watch Matt performing for them, auditioning in the middle of his real life. But I didn't, obviously. I just turned and asked Ginny a question about Bunco and then nodded and smiled as she talked for the next twenty minutes.

Of all that I hate about DC, there are things I've learned to love, or at least to appreciate. There are fall days in October that are so beautiful they take your breath away. The sky is blue and the sun is strong and the air is finally the tiniest bit crisp. Most of the East Coast is already bundled up in their winter coats, but we get to appreciate the last of the sunshine, to hold on to it a little while longer.

And then there's the way that people come here, earnest and full of dreams, believing that they can make a difference. That's the thing about DC—people are always leaving but that makes space for the new transplants, the crowds that keep flooding in, full of energy and wonder.

You can see it on their faces as they walk down the street. You can spot the new people from the way they smile at the monuments, how they stare at the White House as they pass outside the gates, feeling thrilled and thinking, *I'm here, I've made it.* That's what I see, mostly, when I walk around now, which is for the best, because it's not easy to stay annoyed in the face of so much optimism. It's hard to ignore that much hope.

Acknowledgments

I owe so much to my editor, Jenny Jackson, and my agent, Julie Barer. Both offered encouragement, wise notes, and patience with each draft of this book, and I'm honored to have such brilliant women on my team.

I am (as always) incredibly grateful for the support and kindness of my family. Thank you to my wonderful parents, Pat and Jack Close; my brothers, Chris and Kevin Close; Susan Close; the adorable Ava and John Henry Close; and Scott and Carol Hartz.

Many people were gracious enough to share their stories and experiences of working on campaigns and in the administration with me. Thanks to Peter Newell, Kenny Thompson, Casey Breitenbeck, and Bobby Schmuck for putting up with my strange questions and helping me figure out the right career paths for my characters. And while I'm at it, thanks to all of the great people from Obama-world who have adopted me into the group—you are all so much nicer (and much less annoying) than the characters in my book.

I am indebted to Steve Brown, who took time from his busy schedule to explain everything I needed to know about the Railroad Commission and Texas Politics.

Moriah Cleveland is an amazing writer-friend, and I'm so appreciative to her for always being my first reader and offering edits and e-mails to help me along the way.

No place feels like home until you find true girlfriends. Thank you to all of the Muttons— Amy Cogan, Chrissie Graham, Emily Hines, Megan Hughes, Theresa Lepow, Stephanie Schott, and (DC transplant) Mary Colleen Bragiel for helping to change my mind about this place. In the DC game of highs and lows, the time I got to spend with all of you was my high. My low is obviously that everyone keeps moving away. Come back, please!

I wrote much of this book while thinking of Brandon Lepow, which is part of the reason that Jimmy shares Brandon's hometown, job at Facebook, love of colorful socks, and incredible charm. If I ever really tried to model a character after Brandon, no one would believe that one person could be so kind, generous, and funny. DC was lucky to have you and better because you were here. You are so missed, my friend.

It is a privilege to work with the talented and lovely team at Knopf and Vintage. Many thanks to Sonny Mehta, Paul Bogaards, Ruth Liebman, Nicholas Latimer, Chris Gillespie, Julie Kurland, Emma Dries, Helen Tobin, Brittany Morrongiello, Danielle Plafsky, Andrea Robinson, and Alex Houston. I'm especially grateful to Kelly Blair, who worked tirelessly to design this perfect and beautiful cover.

Wrigley Close-Hartz is the best office mate I could ask for and having him curled up under my desk while I write makes my days so much better.

Finally, a huge thank-you to Tim Hartz, who always offers love, support, and calming words when I need them the most. I couldn't have written this book without you answering every question that I shouted downstairs, responding to midday texts about my characters, offering ideas and anecdotes, and reading passages for immediate feedback. I'm so happy that you're my husband.

A Note About the Author

Jennifer Close is the best-selling author of *Girls in White Dresses* and *The Smart One*. Born and raised on the North Shore of Chicago, she is a graduate of Boston College and received her MFA in fiction writing from The New School in 2005. She worked in New York in magazines for many years. She now lives in Washington, DC, and teaches creative writing at George Washington University.

Center Point Large Print
600 Brooks Road / PO Box 1
Thorndike, ME 04986-0001 USA

(207) 568-3717

US & Canada:
1 800 929-9108
www.centerpointlargeprint.com